2

Atsushi Okada

NYANKEES

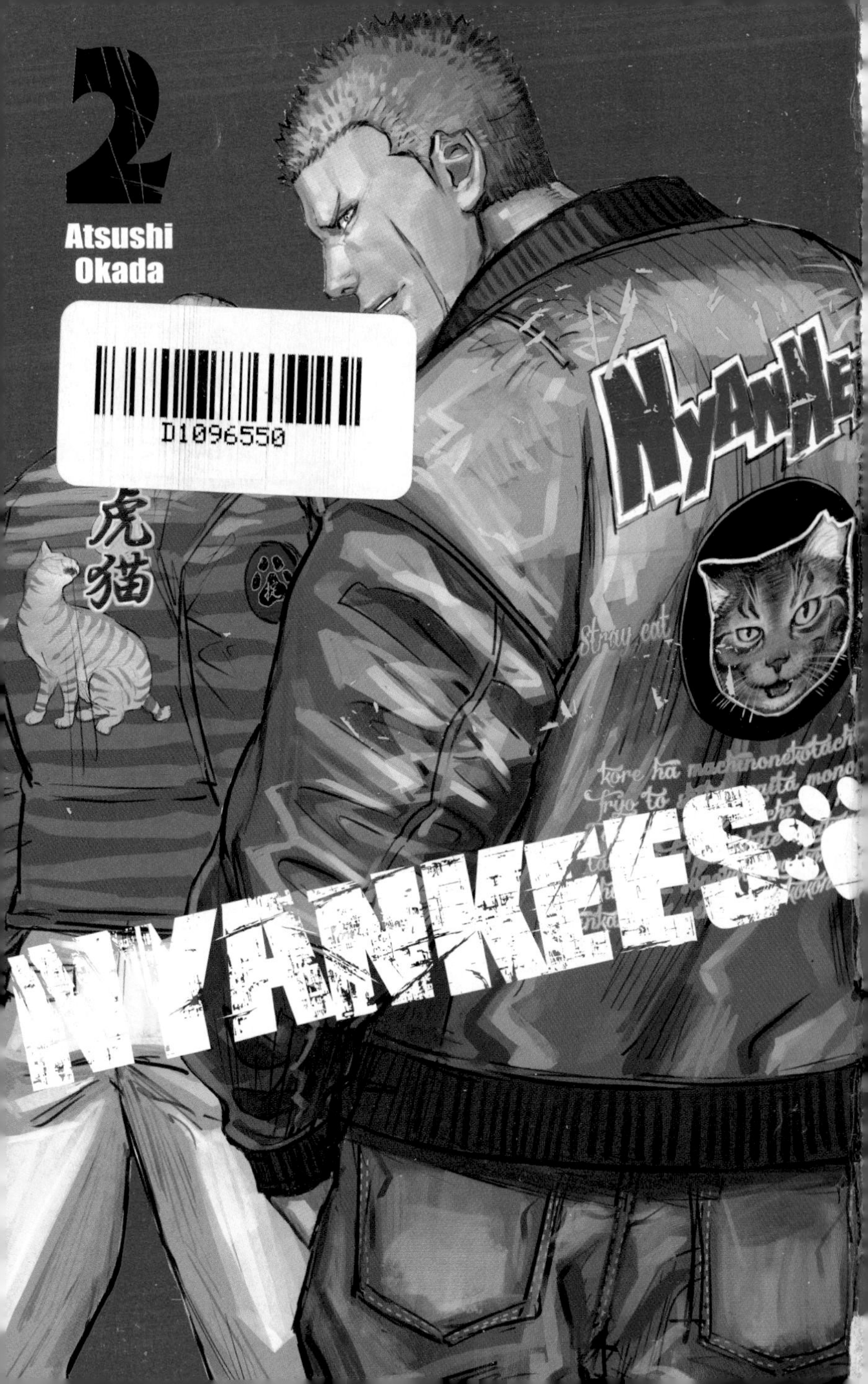
虎猫
stray cat

C O N T E N T S

CHAPTER 7
THE STRONGEST MOLLY

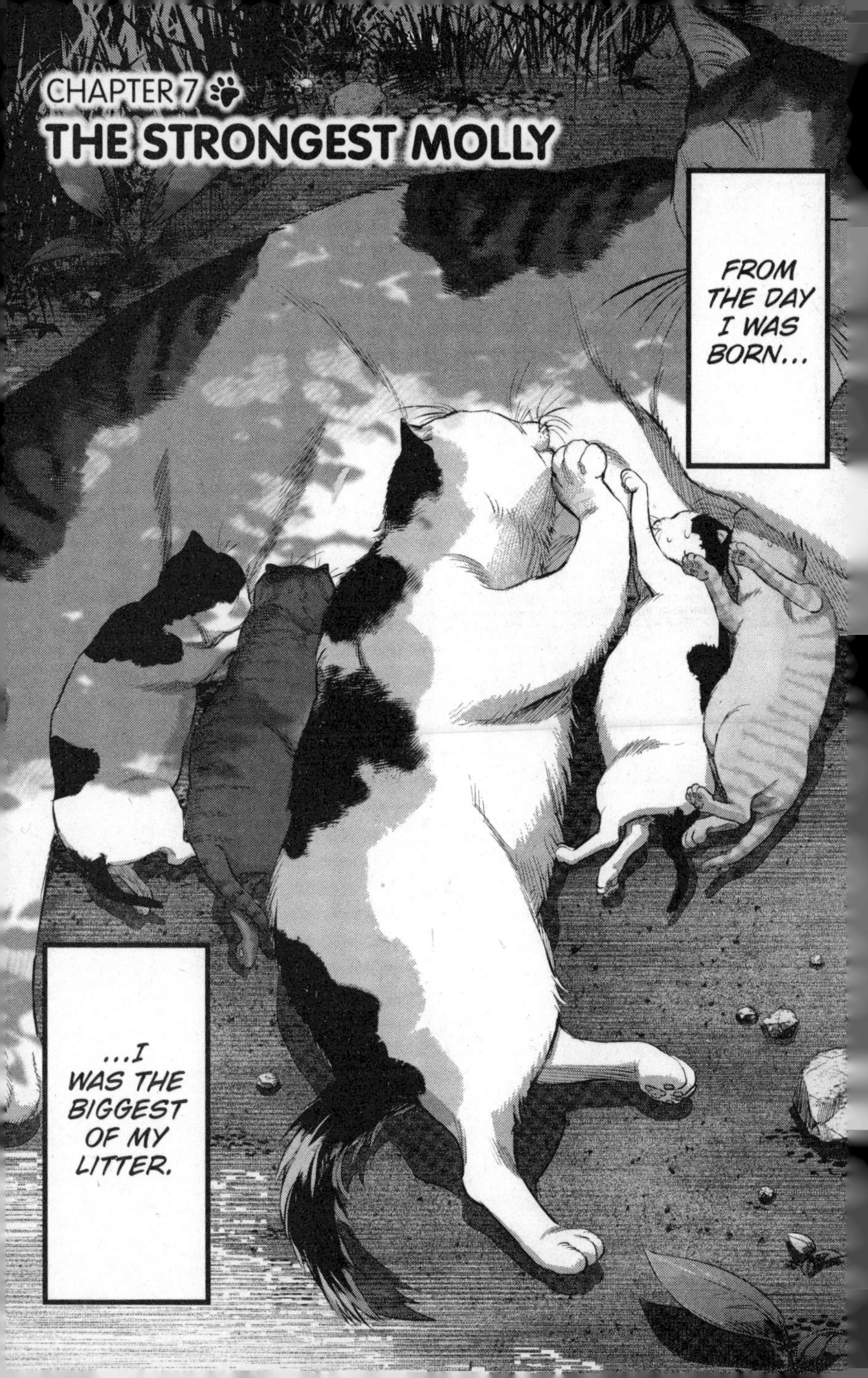
FROM THE DAY I WAS BORN...
...I WAS THE BIGGEST OF MY LITTER.

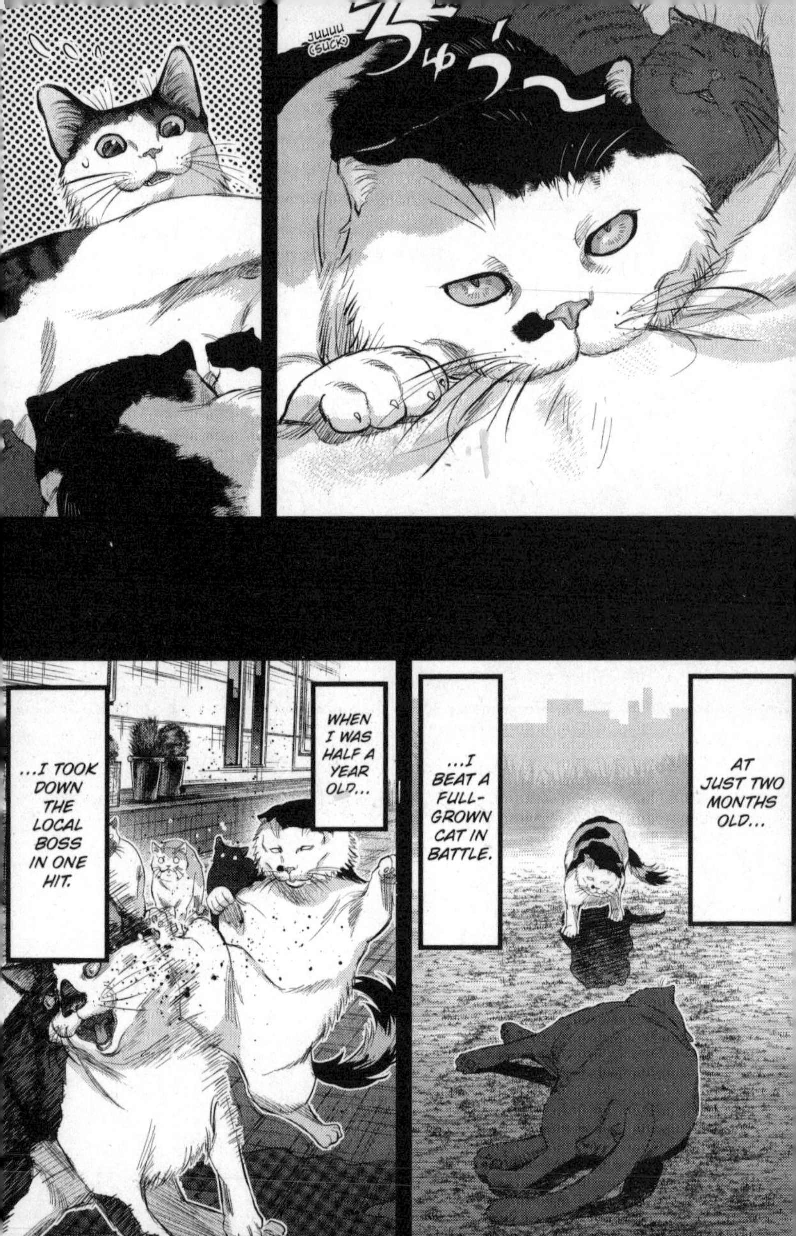
JUUUU (SUCK)
AT JUST TWO MONTHS OLD...
...I BEAT A FULL-GROWN CAT IN BATTLE.
WHEN I WAS HALF A YEAR OLD...
...I TOOK DOWN THE LOCAL BOSS IN ONE HIT.

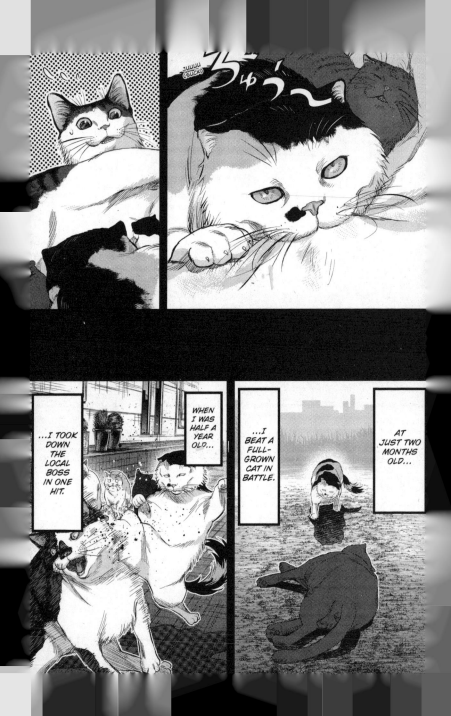

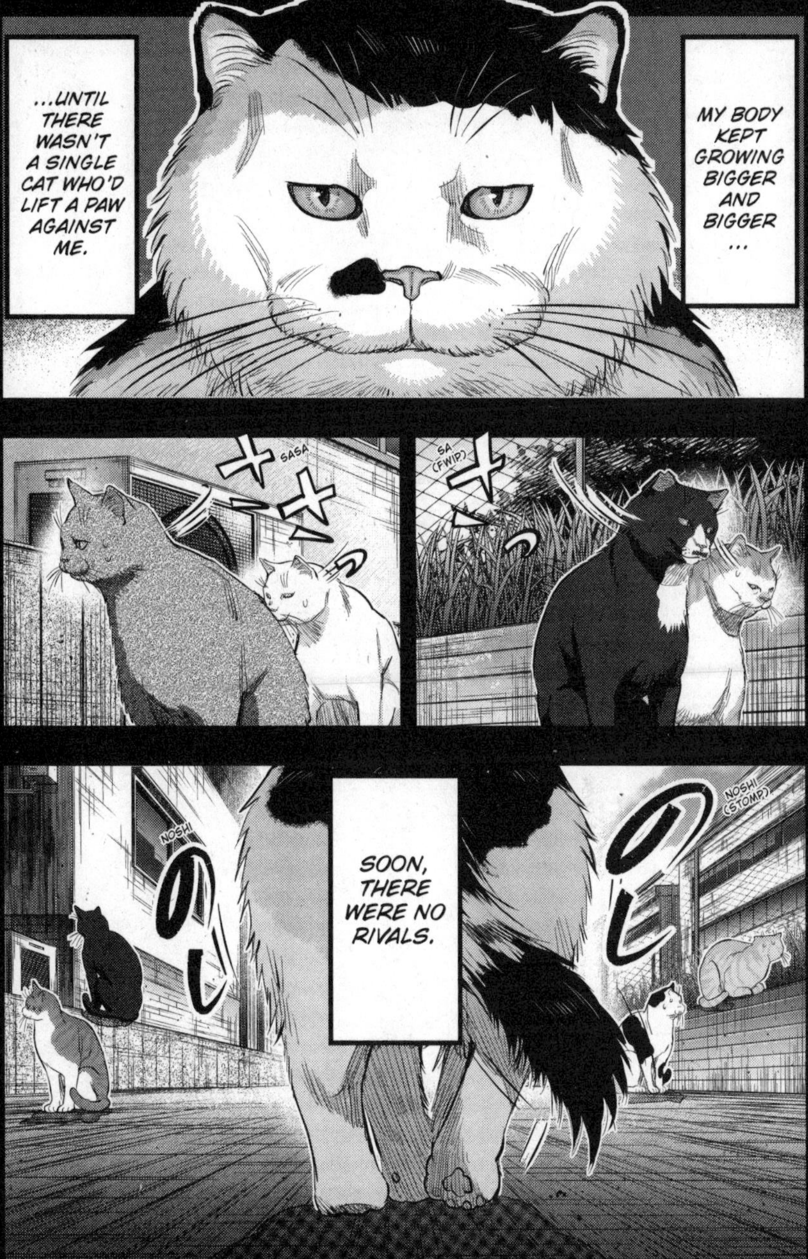
MY BODY KEPT GROWING BIGGER AND BIGGER ...
...UNTIL THERE WASN'T A SINGLE CAT WHO'D LIFT A PAW AGAINST ME.
SA (FWIP)
SASA
NOSHI (STOMP)
SOON, THERE WERE NO RIVALS.
NOSHI

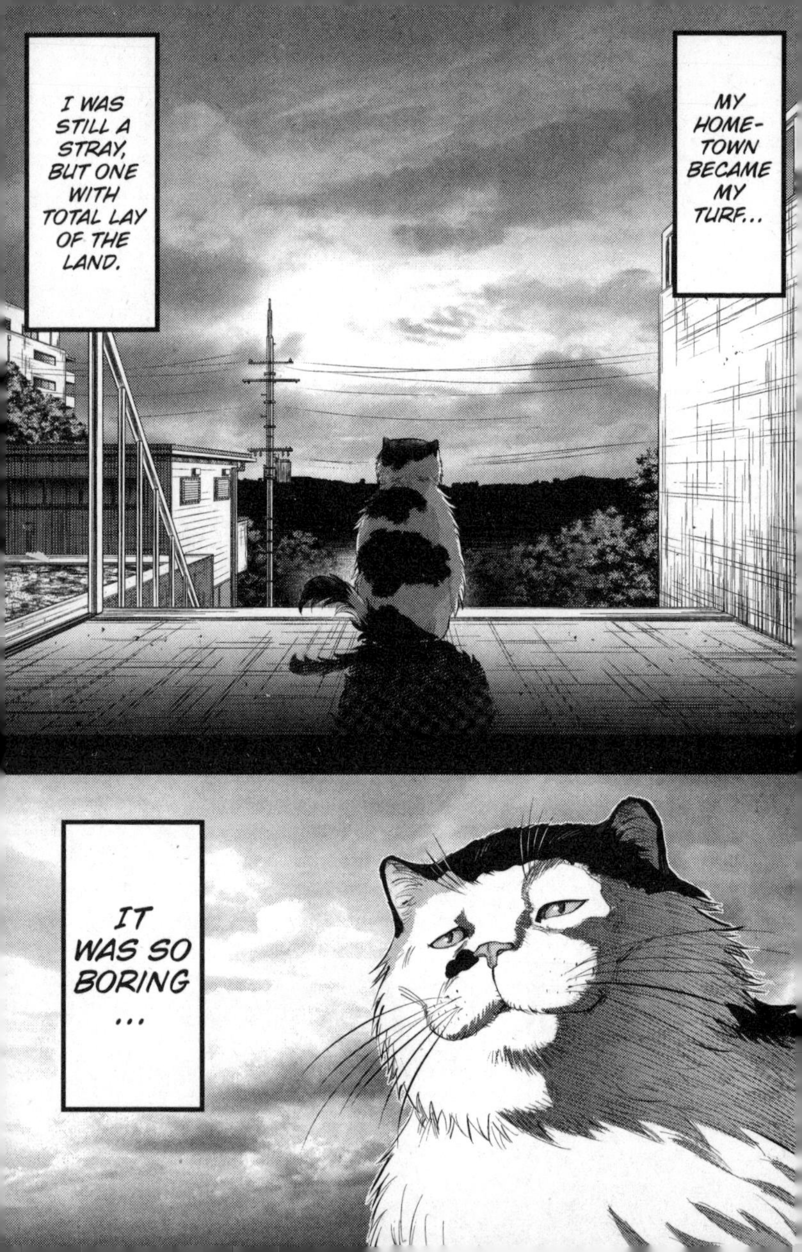
MY HOME-TOWN BECAME MY TURF...
I WAS STILL A STRAY, BUT ONE WITH TOTAL LAY OF THE LAND.
IT WAS SO BORING...

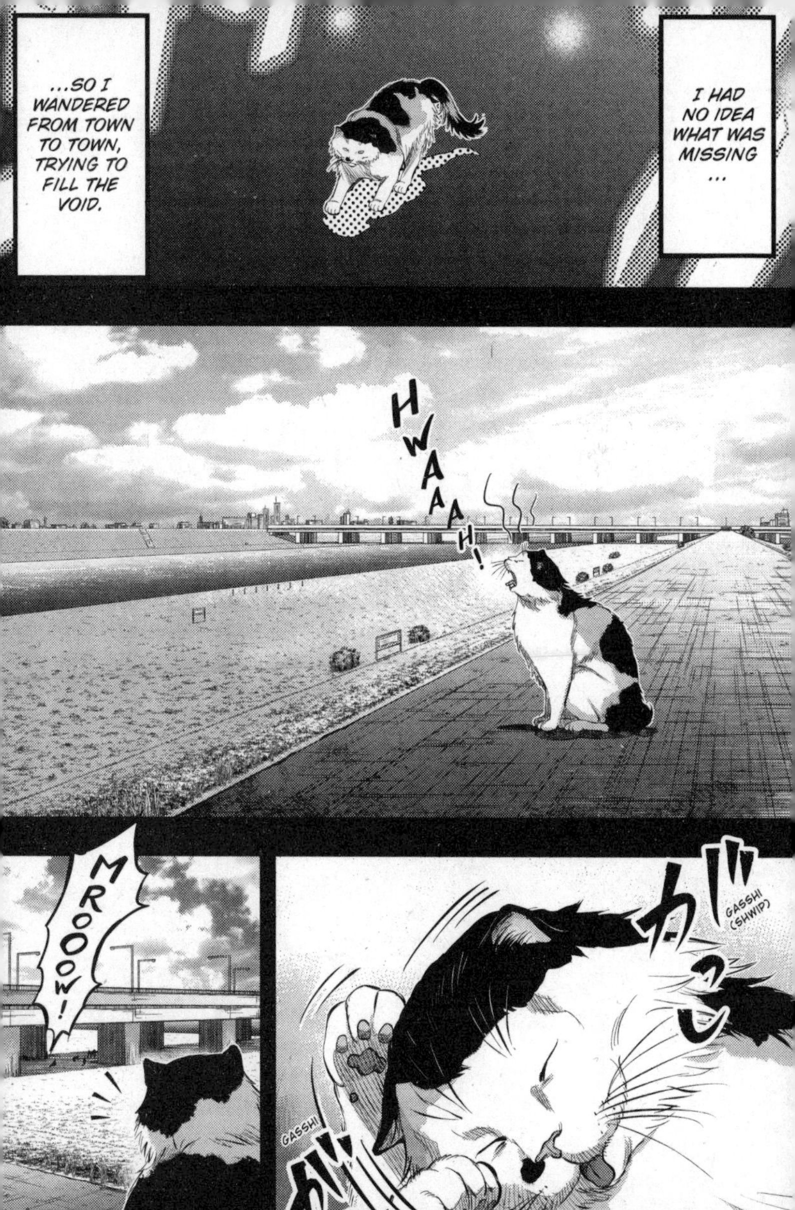
I HAD NO IDEA WHAT WAS MISSING ...
...SO I WANDERED FROM TOWN TO TOWN, TRYING TO FILL THE VOID.
HWAAAH!
GASSHI (SHWIP)
GASSHI
MROOOW!

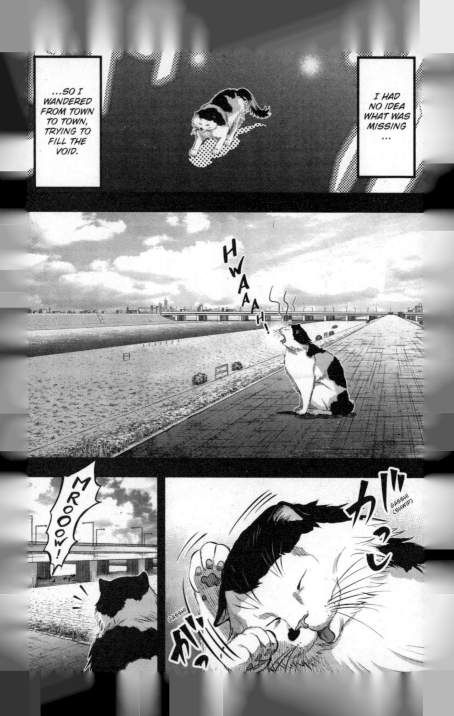

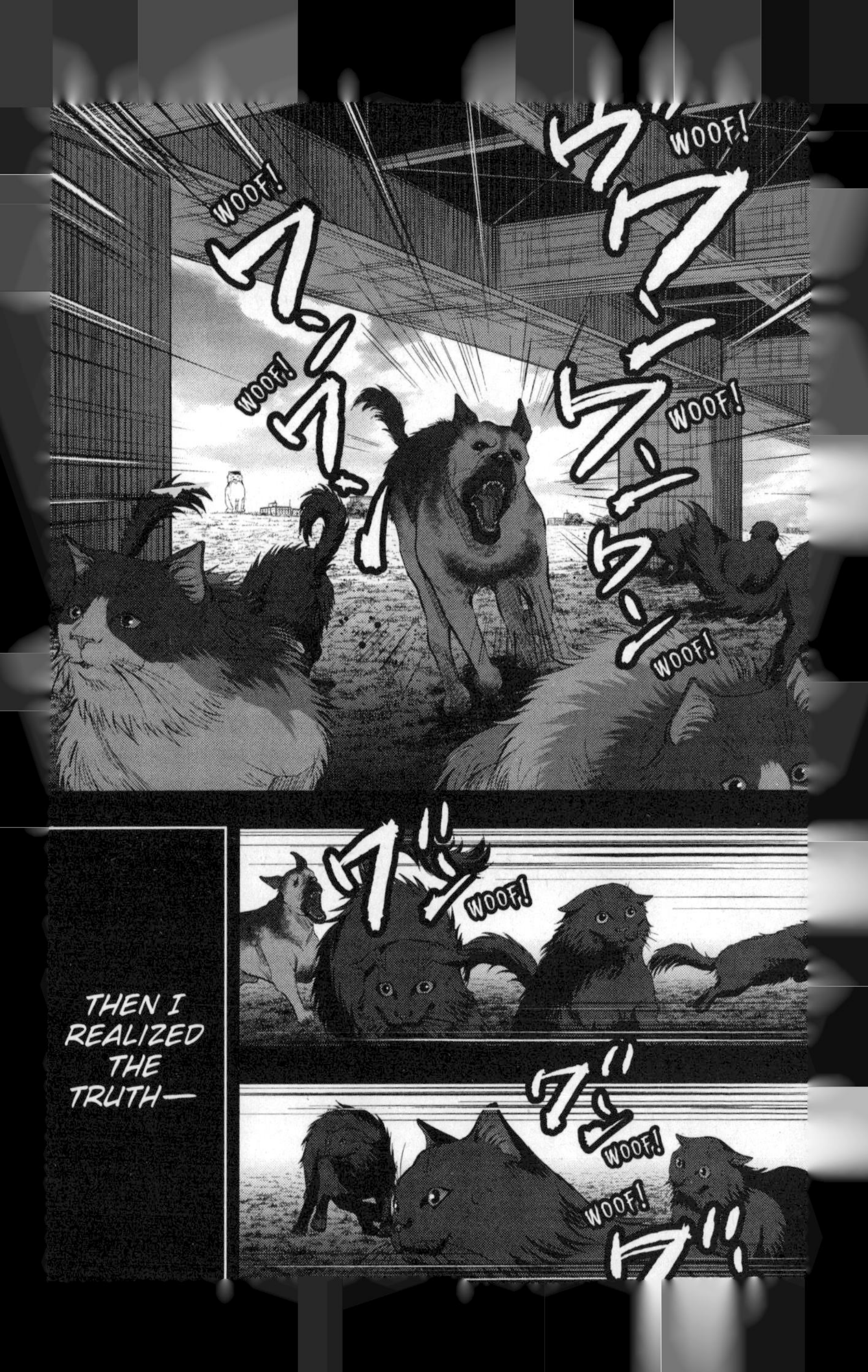
WOOF!
WOOF!
WOOF!
WOOF!
WOOF!
WOOF!
WOOF!
WOOF!
THEN I REALIZED THE TRUTH—

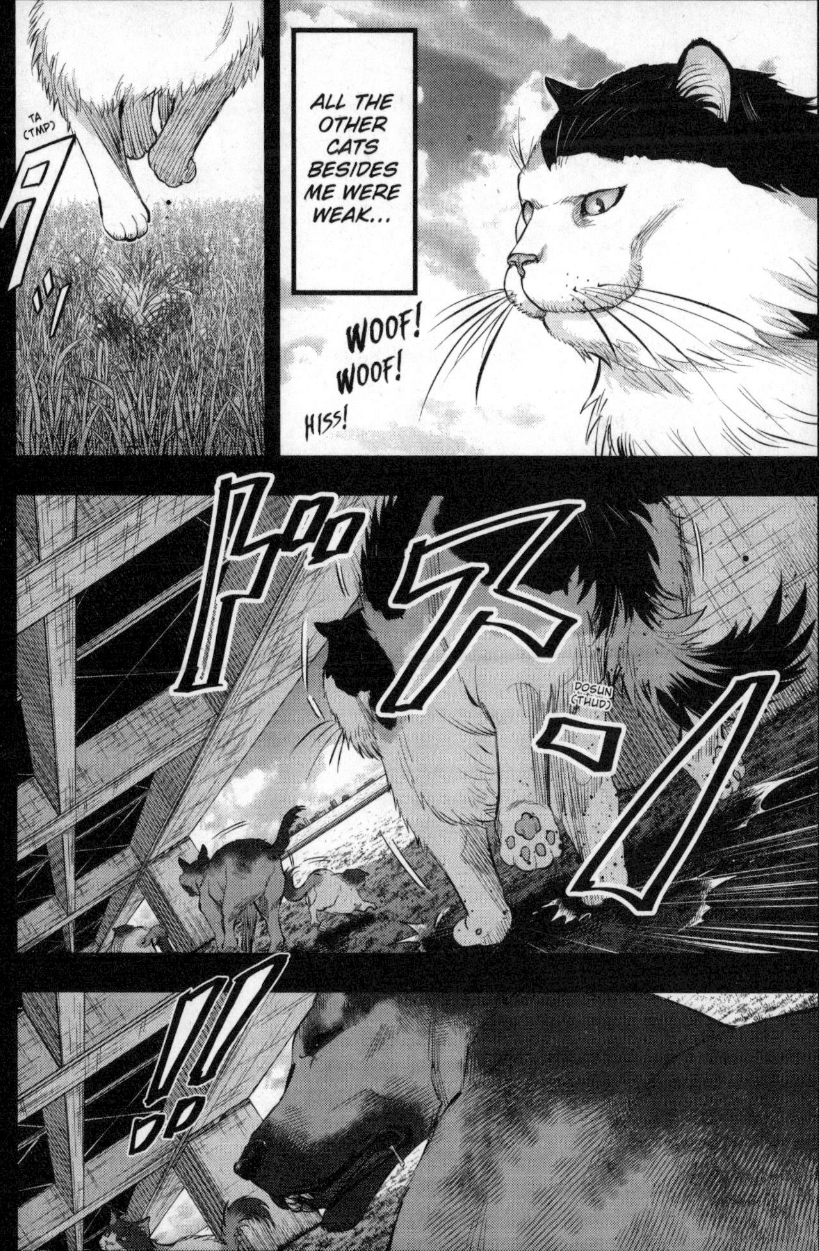
ALL THE OTHER CATS BESIDES ME WERE WEAK...
WOOF!
WOOF!
HISS!
TA (TMP)
DOSUN (THUD)

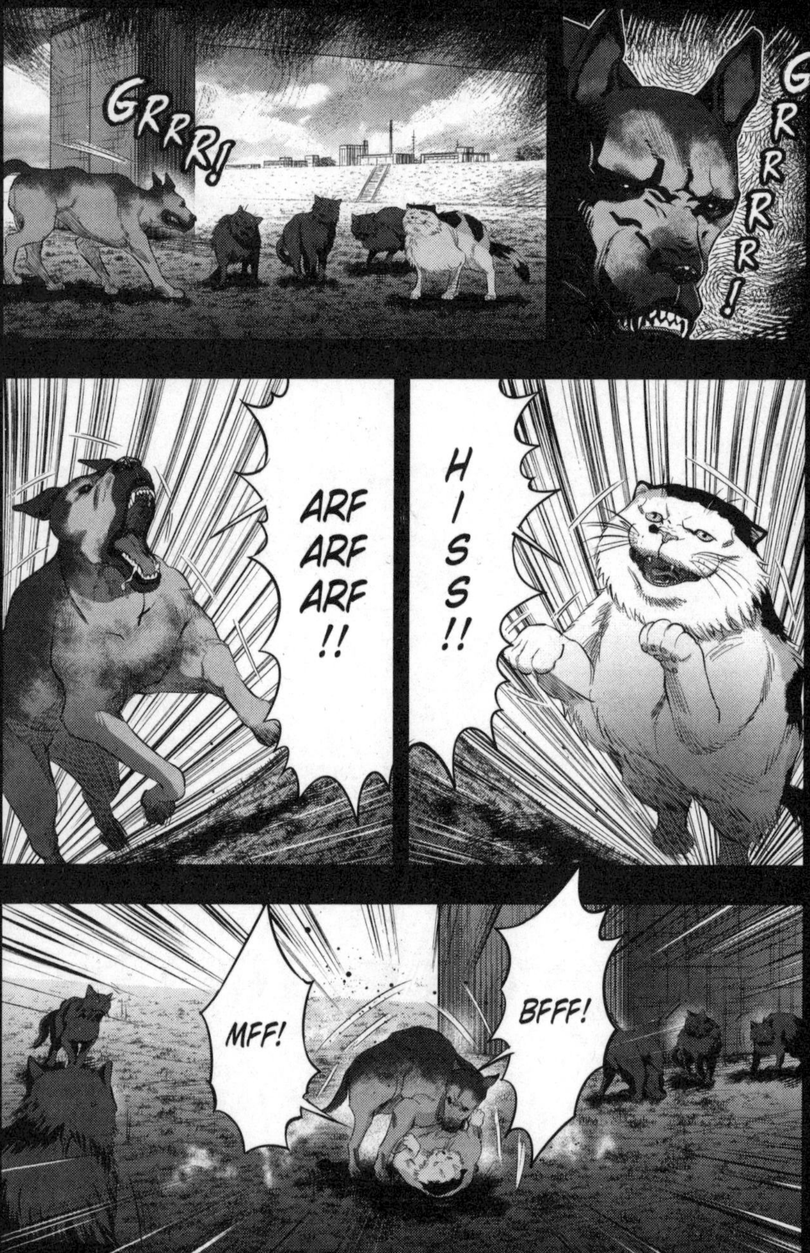
GRRRR!
GRRR!
HISS!!
ARF
ARF
ARF
!!
BFFF!
MFF!

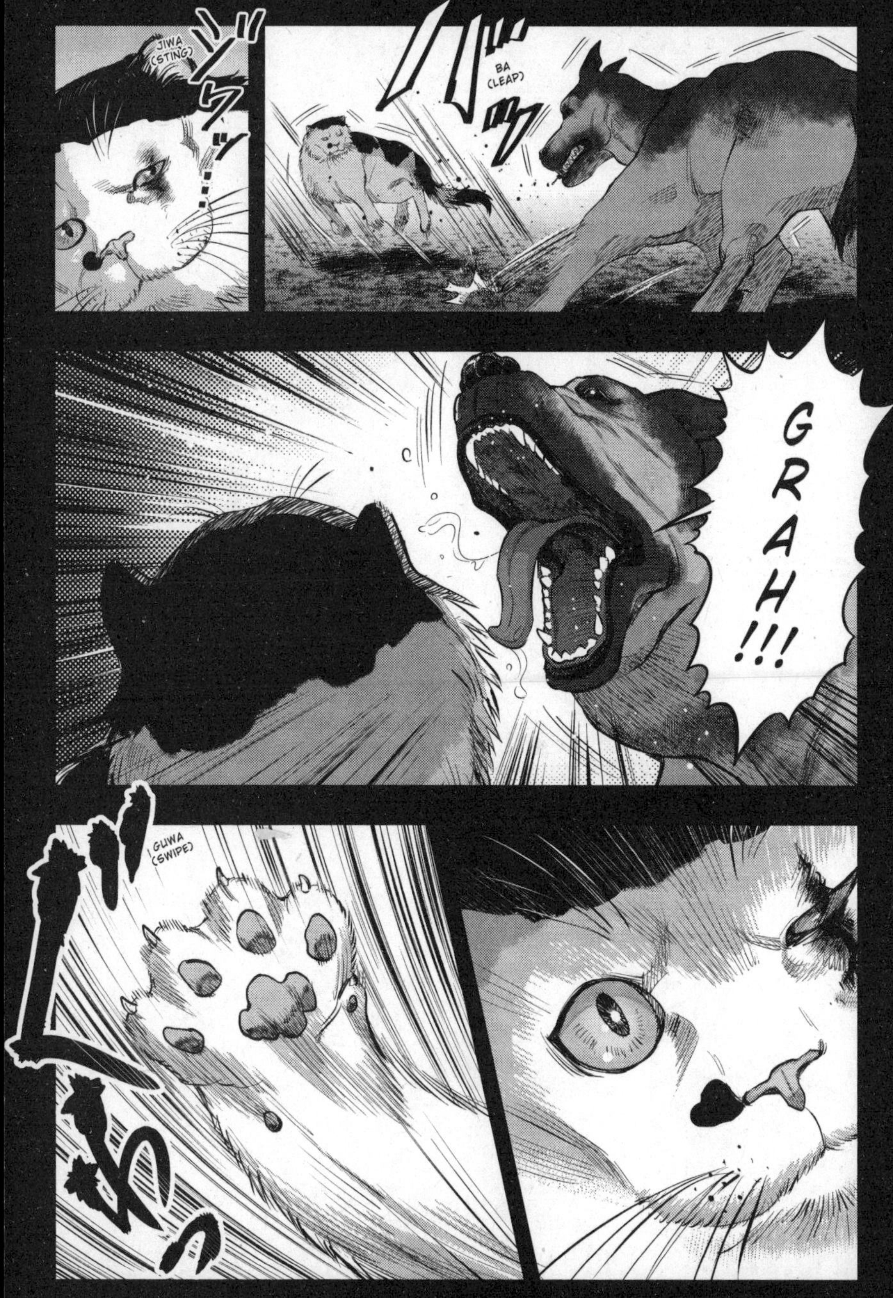
BA
(LEAP)
JIWA
(STING)
GRAH!!!
GUWA
(SWIPE)

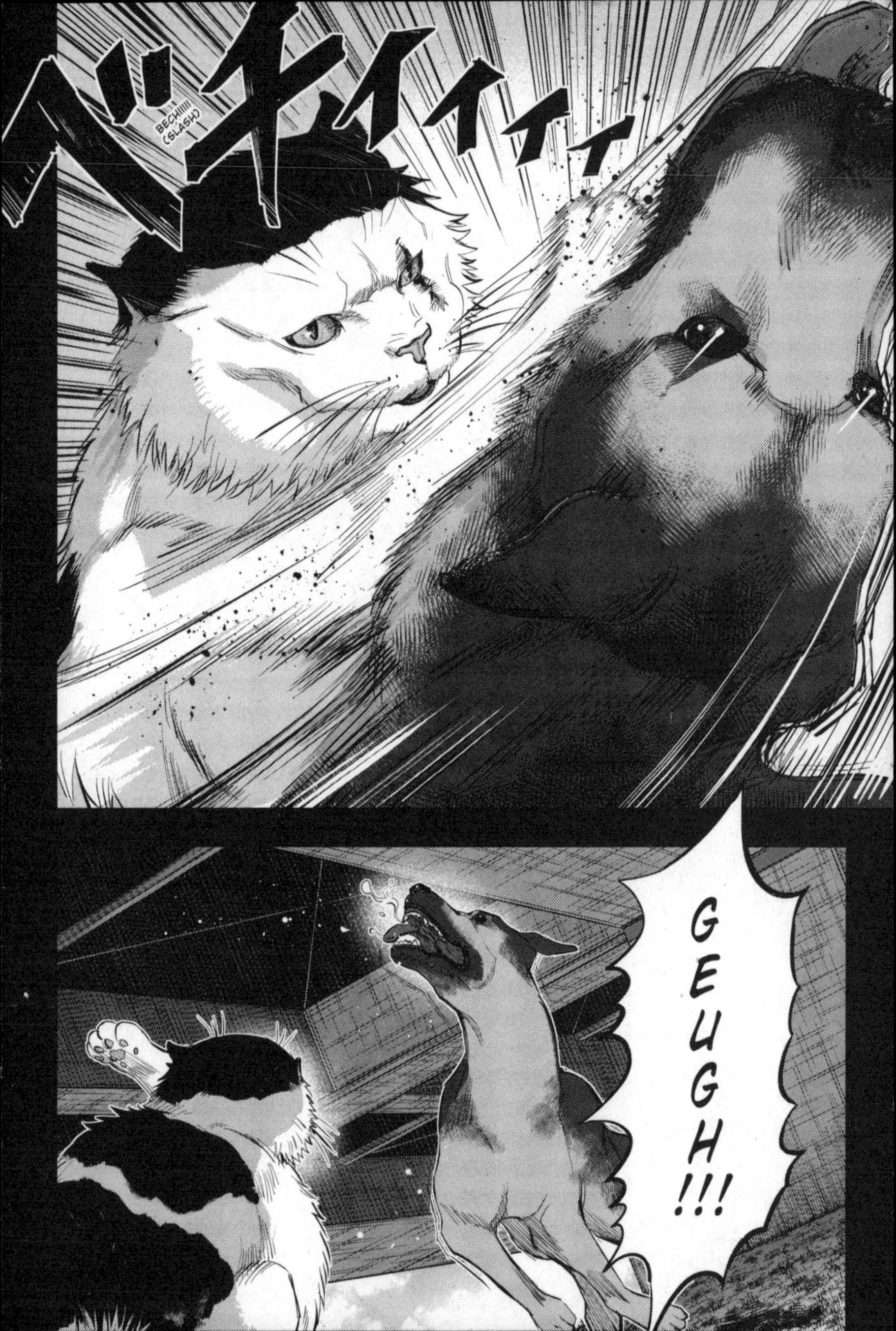
BECHIIIII (SLASH)
GEUGH!!!

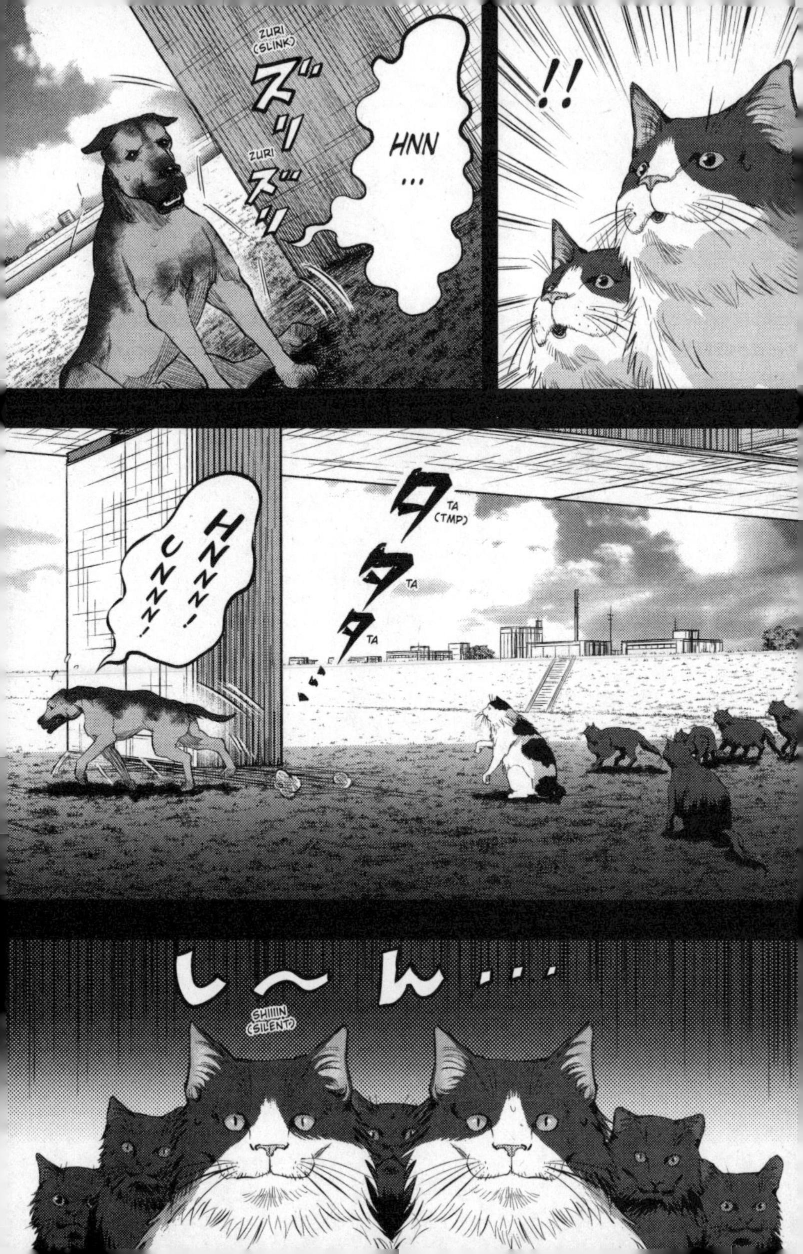
!!
ZURI (SLINK)
ZURI
HNN ...
TA (TMP)
TA
TA
HNNN! UNNN!
SHIIIIN (SILENT)

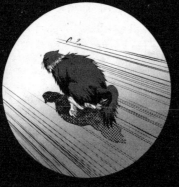

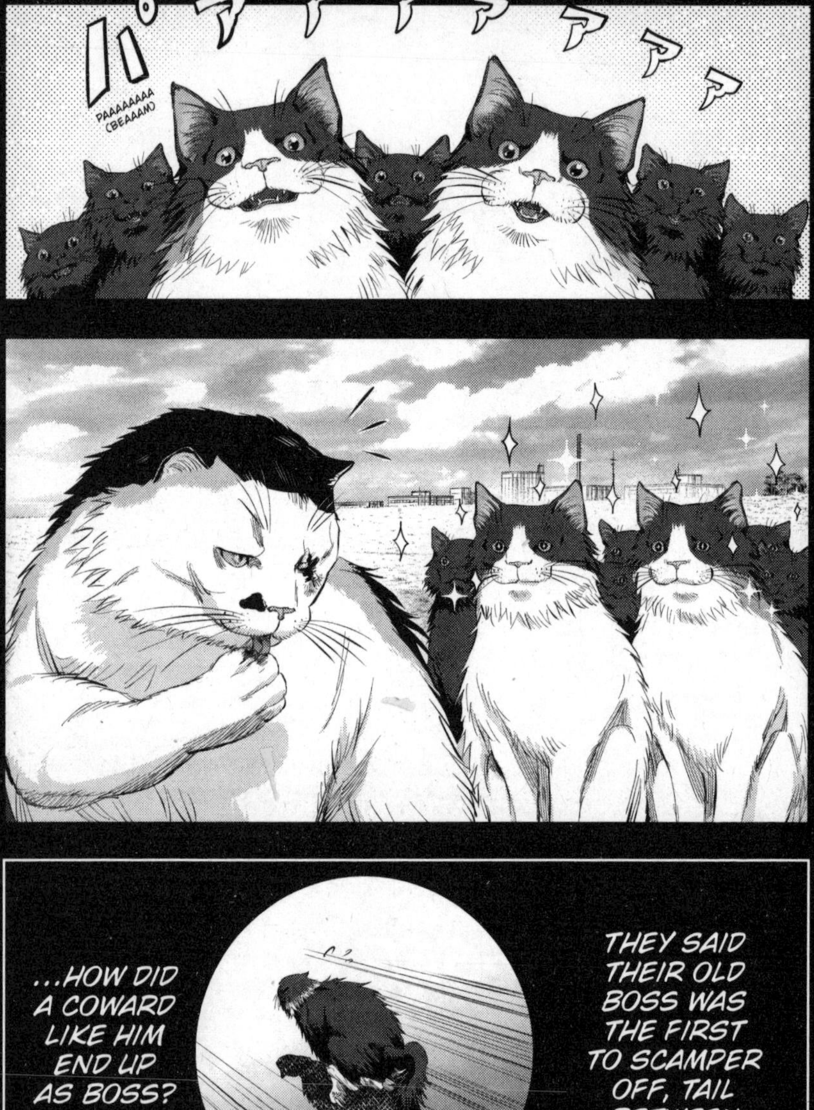
パアアアアアアア
PAAAAAAAA
(BEAAAM)
THEY SAID THEIR OLD BOSS WAS THE FIRST TO SCAMPER OFF, TAIL BETWEEN HIS LEGS.
...HOW DID A COWARD LIKE HIM END UP AS BOSS?

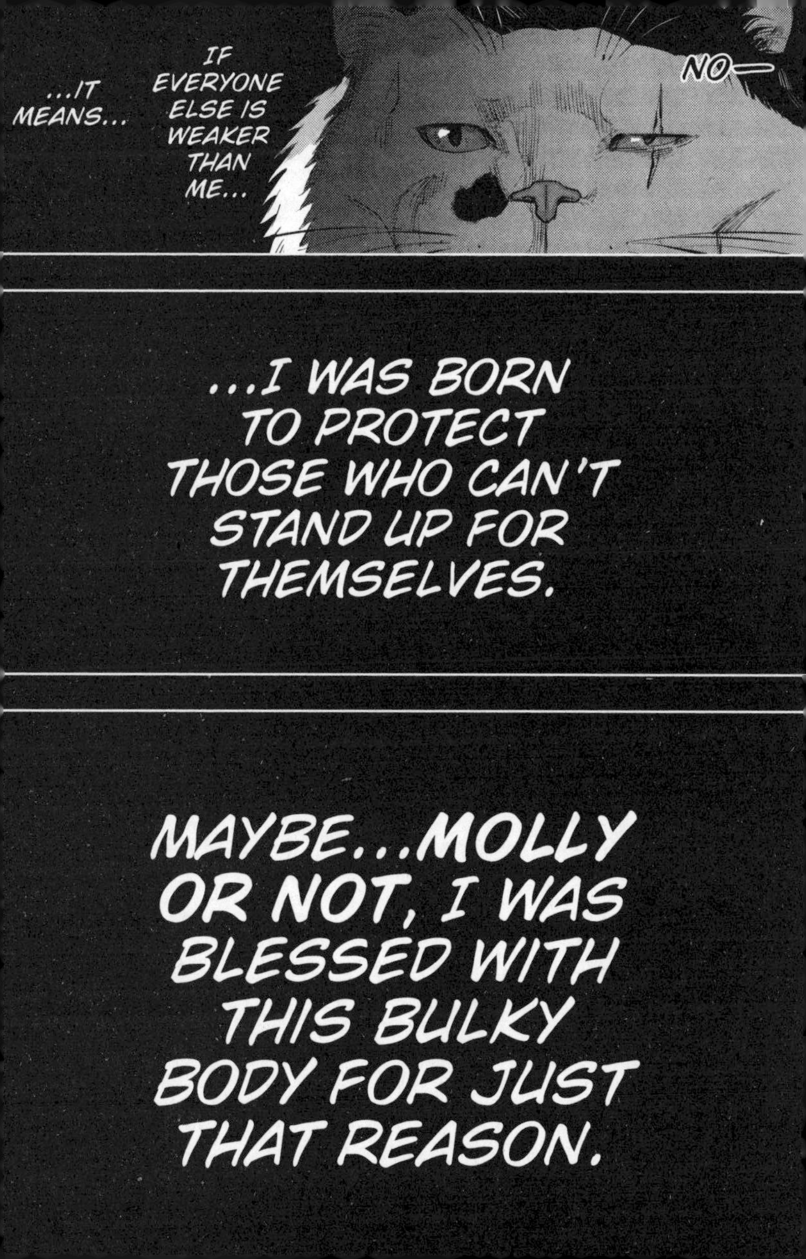
NO—
IF EVERYONE ELSE IS WEAKER THAN ME...
...IT MEANS...
...I WAS BORN TO PROTECT THOSE WHO CAN'T STAND UP FOR THEMSELVES.
MAYBE...**MOLLY OR NOT**, I WAS BLESSED WITH THIS BULKY BODY FOR JUST THAT REASON.

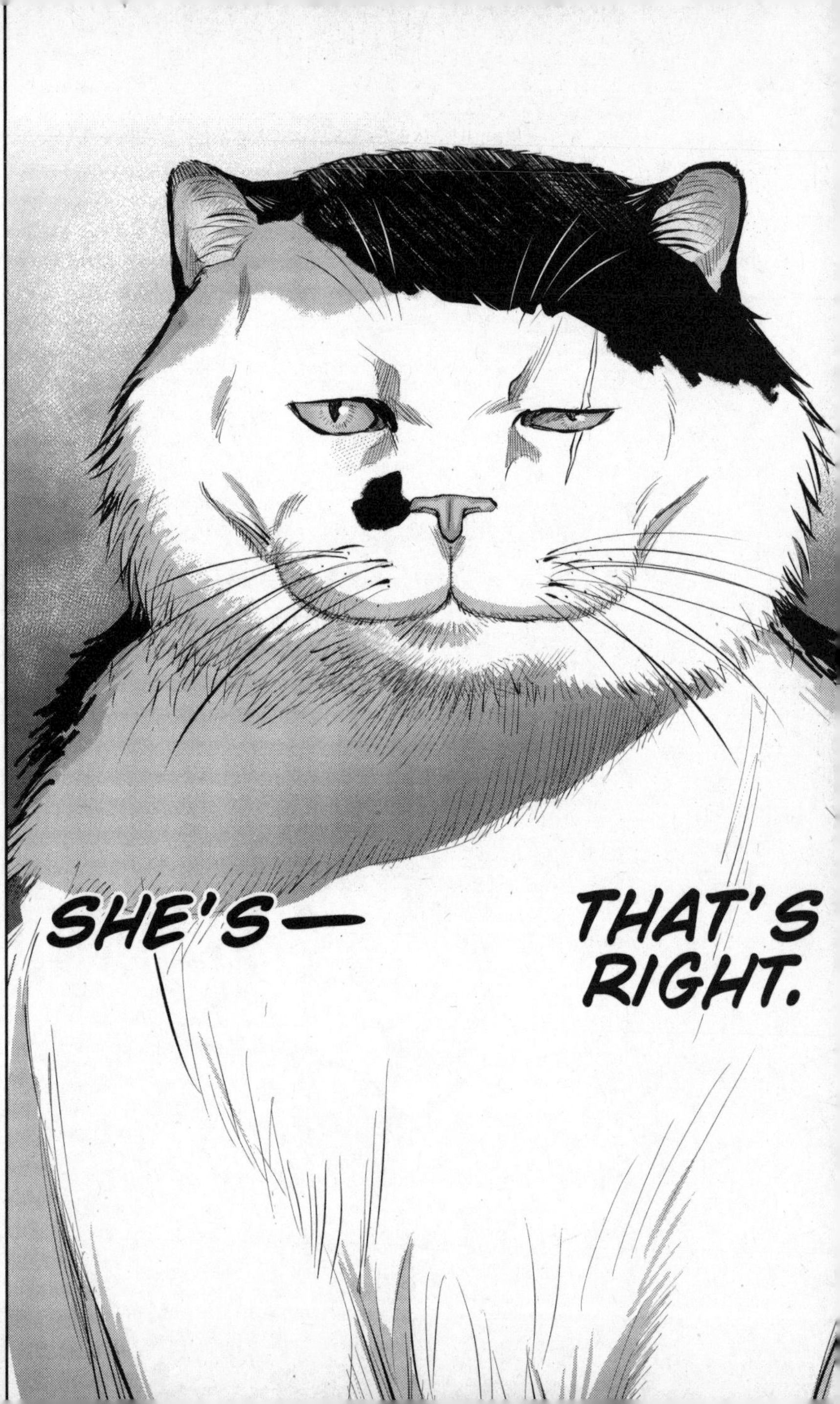
THAT'S RIGHT.
SHE'S—

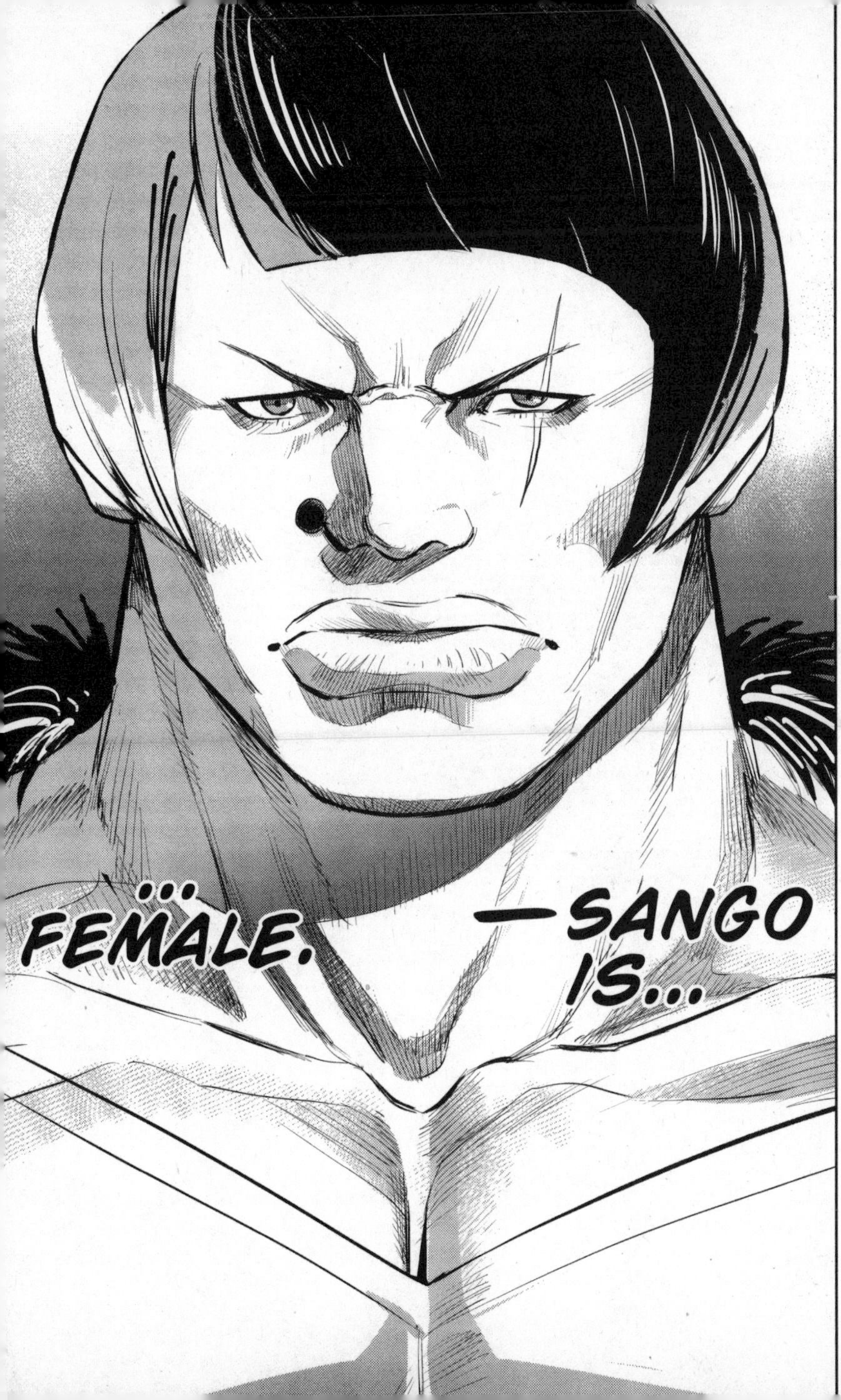
—SANGO IS...
...FEMALE.

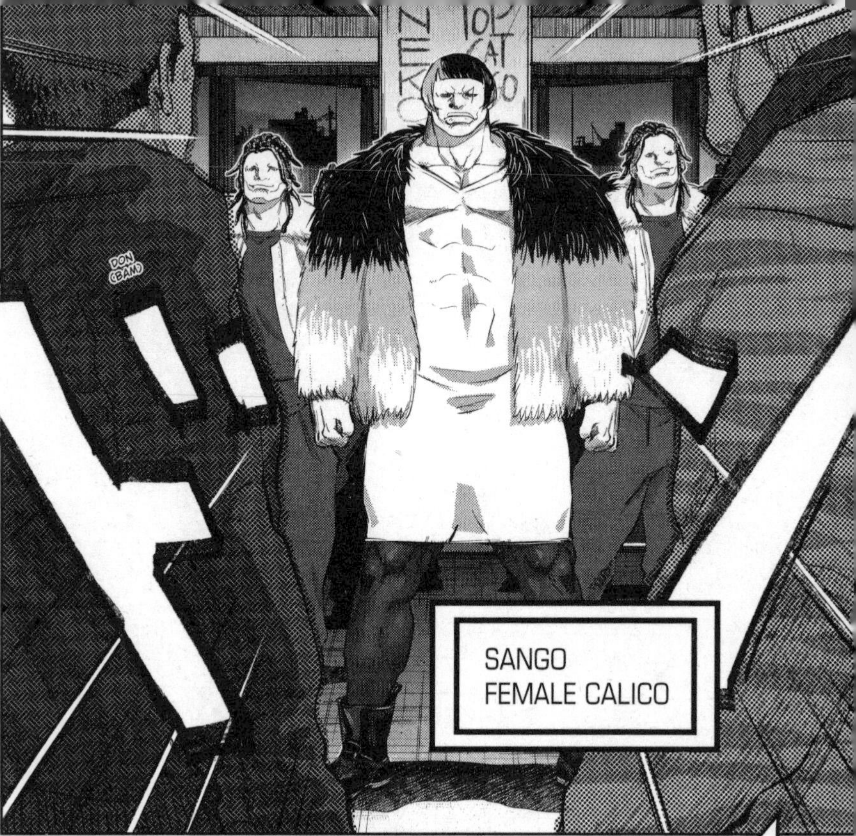
DON (BAM)
SANGO
FEMALE CALICO

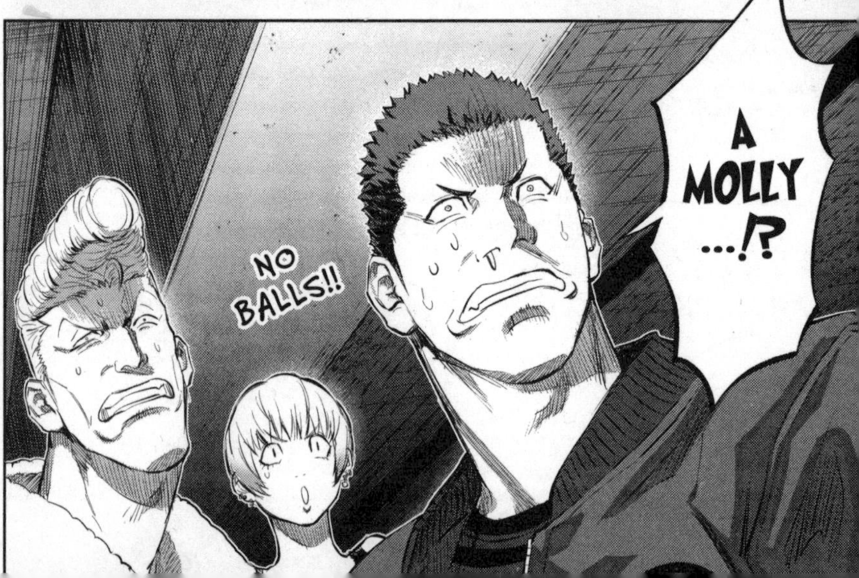
A MOLLY ...!?
NO BALLS!!

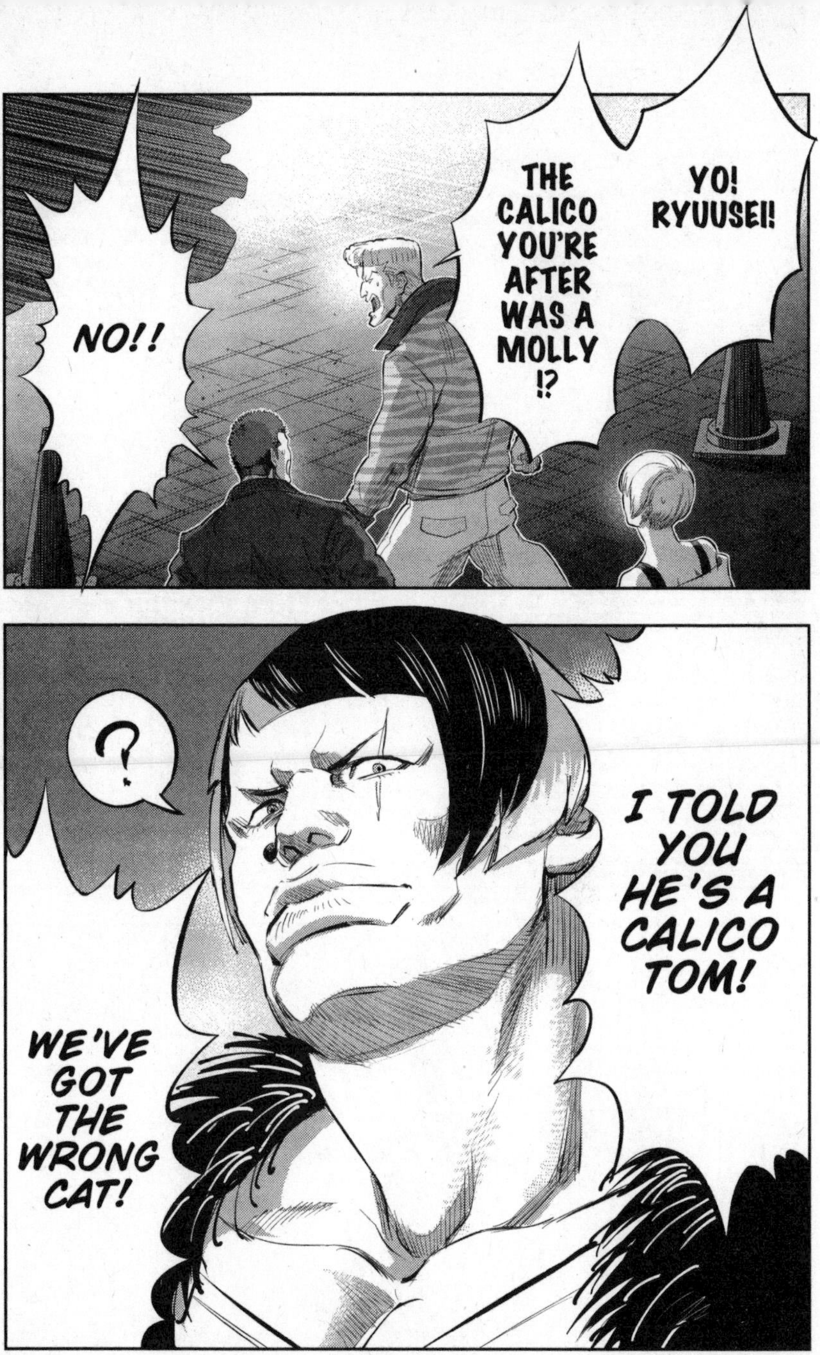
YO! RYUUSEI!
THE CALICO YOU'RE AFTER WAS A MOLLY !?
NO!!
I TOLD YOU HE'S A CALICO TOM!
?
WE'VE GOT THE WRONG CAT!

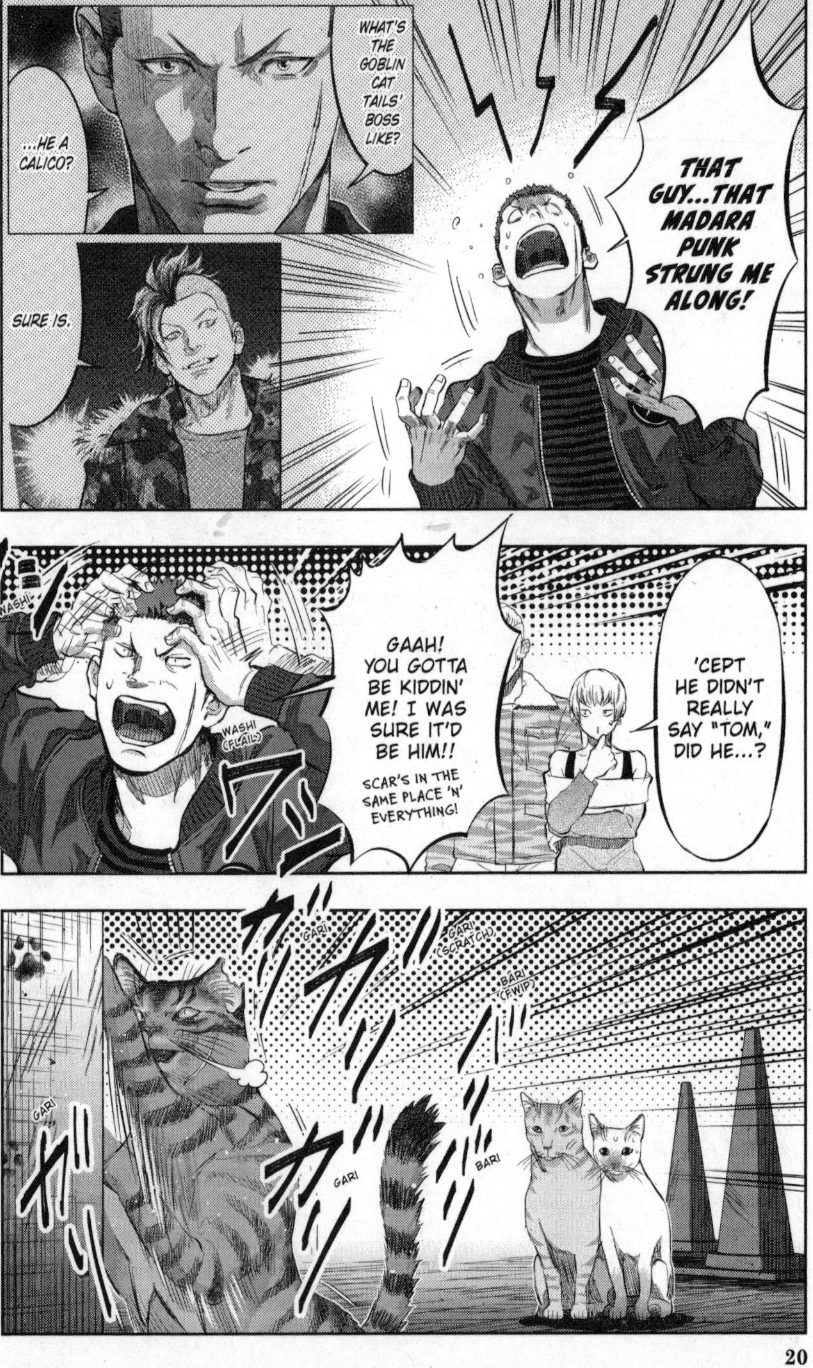
WHAT'S THE GOBLIN CAT TAILS' BOSS LIKE?
...HE A CALICO?
SURE IS.
THAT GUY...THAT MADARA PUNK STRUNG ME ALONG!
WASHI
WASHI (FLAIL)
GAAH! YOU GOTTA BE KIDDIN' ME! I WAS SURE IT'D BE HIM!!
SCAR'S IN THE SAME PLACE 'N' EVERYTHING!
'CEPT HE DIDN'T REALLY SAY "TOM," DID HE...?
GARI
GARI (SCRATCH)
BARI (FWIP)
GARI
GARI
BARI

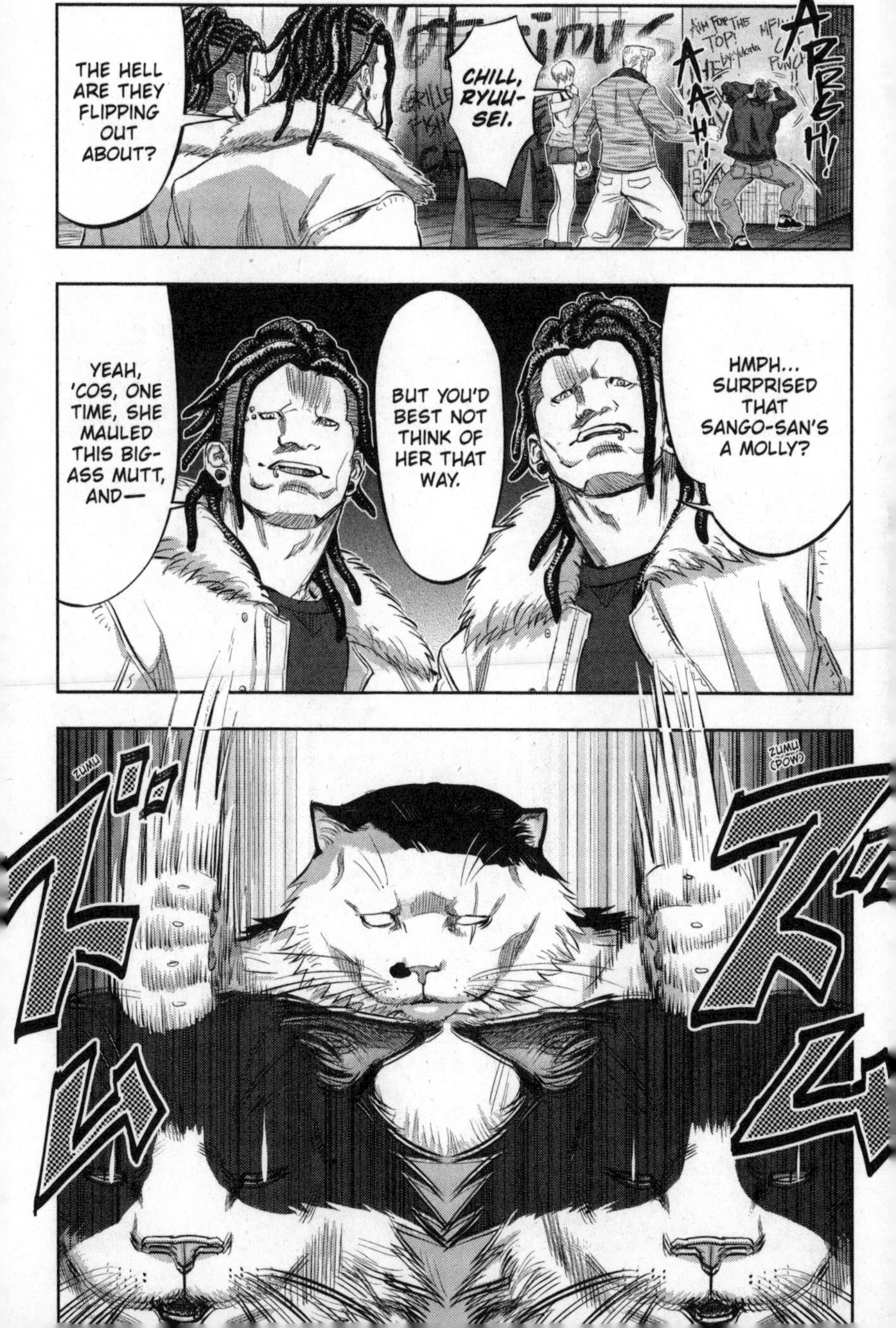
ARRGH!
AAAH!!
AIM FOR THE TOP!
PUNCH!!
CHILL, RYUU-SEI.
THE HELL ARE THEY FLIPPING OUT ABOUT?
HMPH... SURPRISED THAT SANGO-SAN'S A MOLLY?
BUT YOU'D BEST NOT THINK OF HER THAT WAY.
YEAH, 'COS, ONE TIME, SHE MAULED THIS BIG-ASS MUTT, AND—
ZUMU (POW)
ZUMU

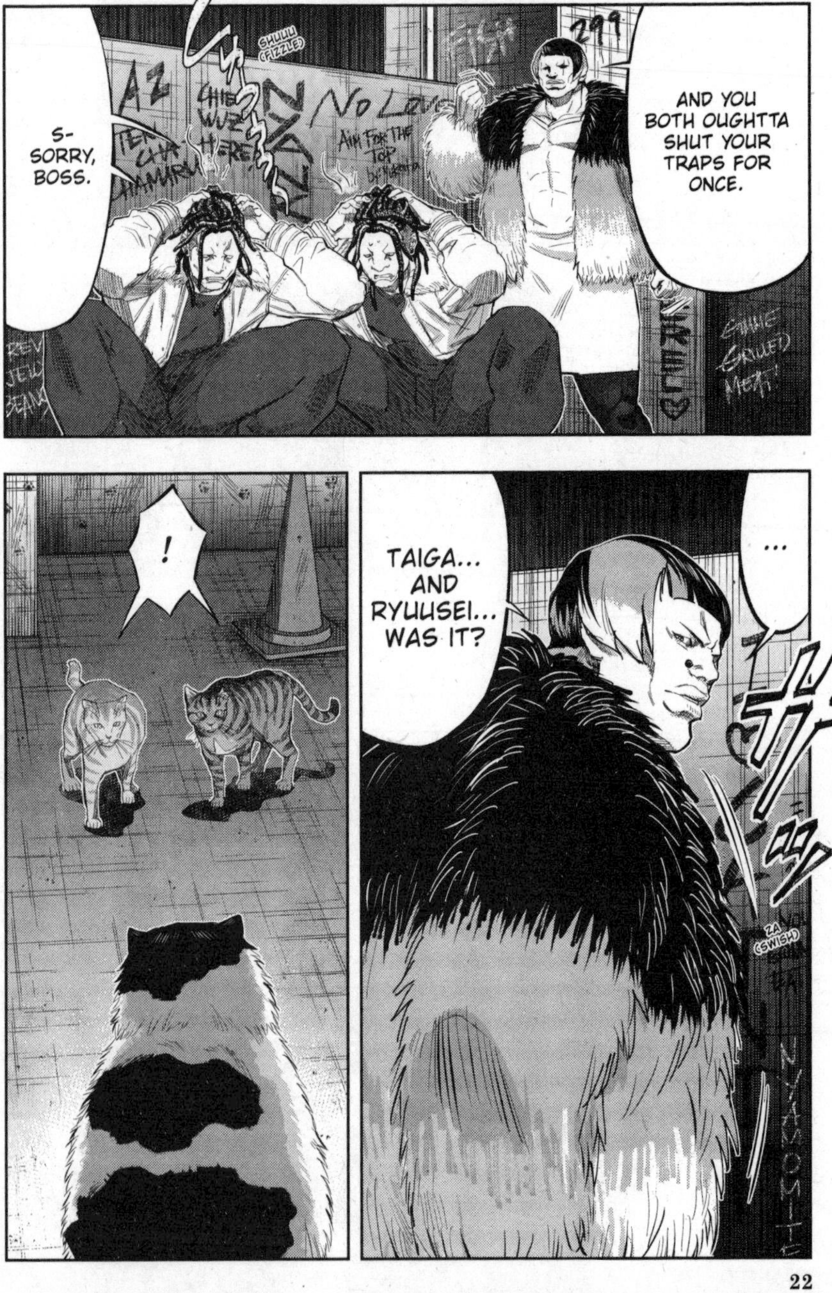
AND YOU BOTH OUGHTTA SHUT YOUR TRAPS FOR ONCE.
SHULLU (FIZZLE)
S-SORRY, BOSS.
...
TAIGA... AND RYUUSEI... WAS IT?
ZA (SWISH)
!

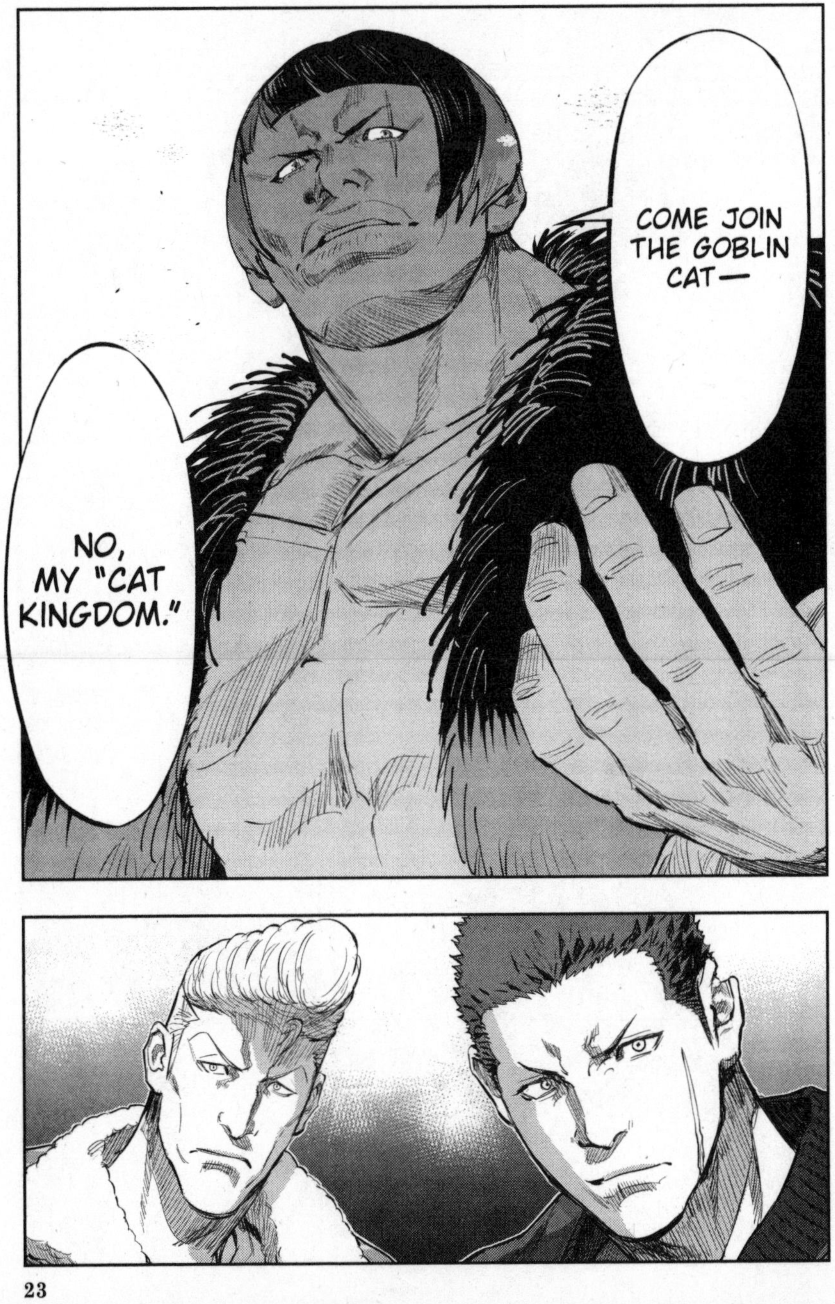
COME JOIN THE GOBLIN CAT—
NO, MY "CAT KINGDOM."

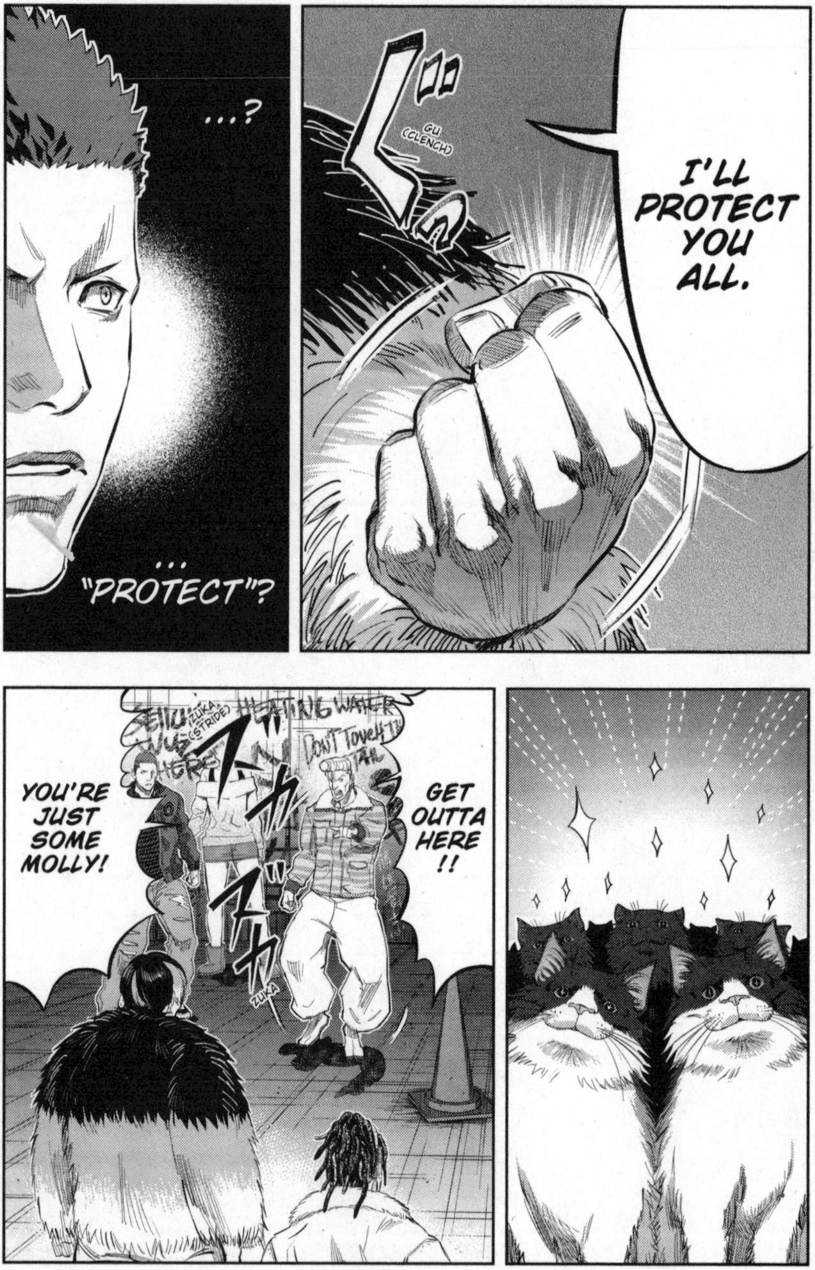
GU (CLENCH)
I'LL PROTECT YOU ALL.
...?
... "PROTECT"?
GET OUTTA HERE!!
HEATING WATER
DON'T TOUCH
ZUKA (STRIDE)
YOU'RE JUST SOME MOLLY!
ZUKA

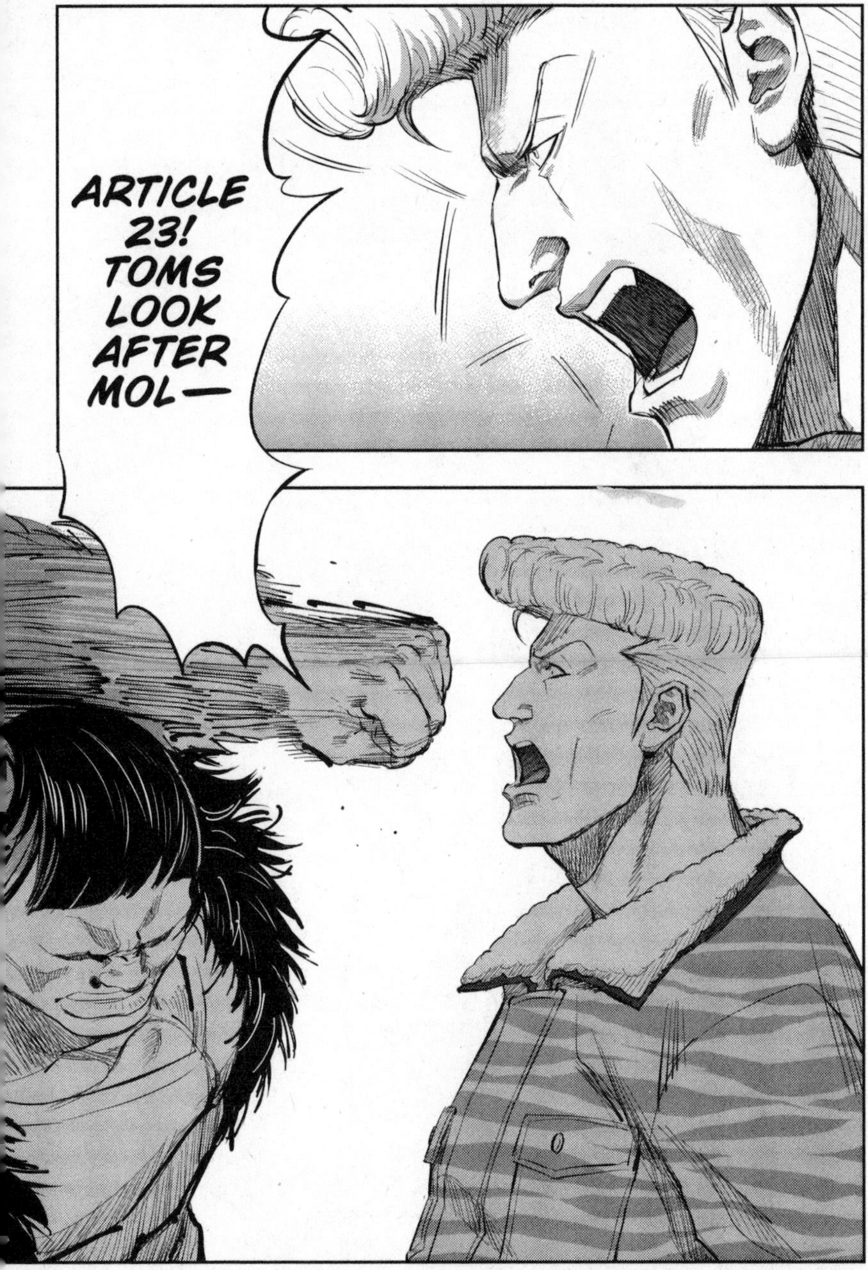
ARTICLE 23! TOMS LOOK AFTER MOL—

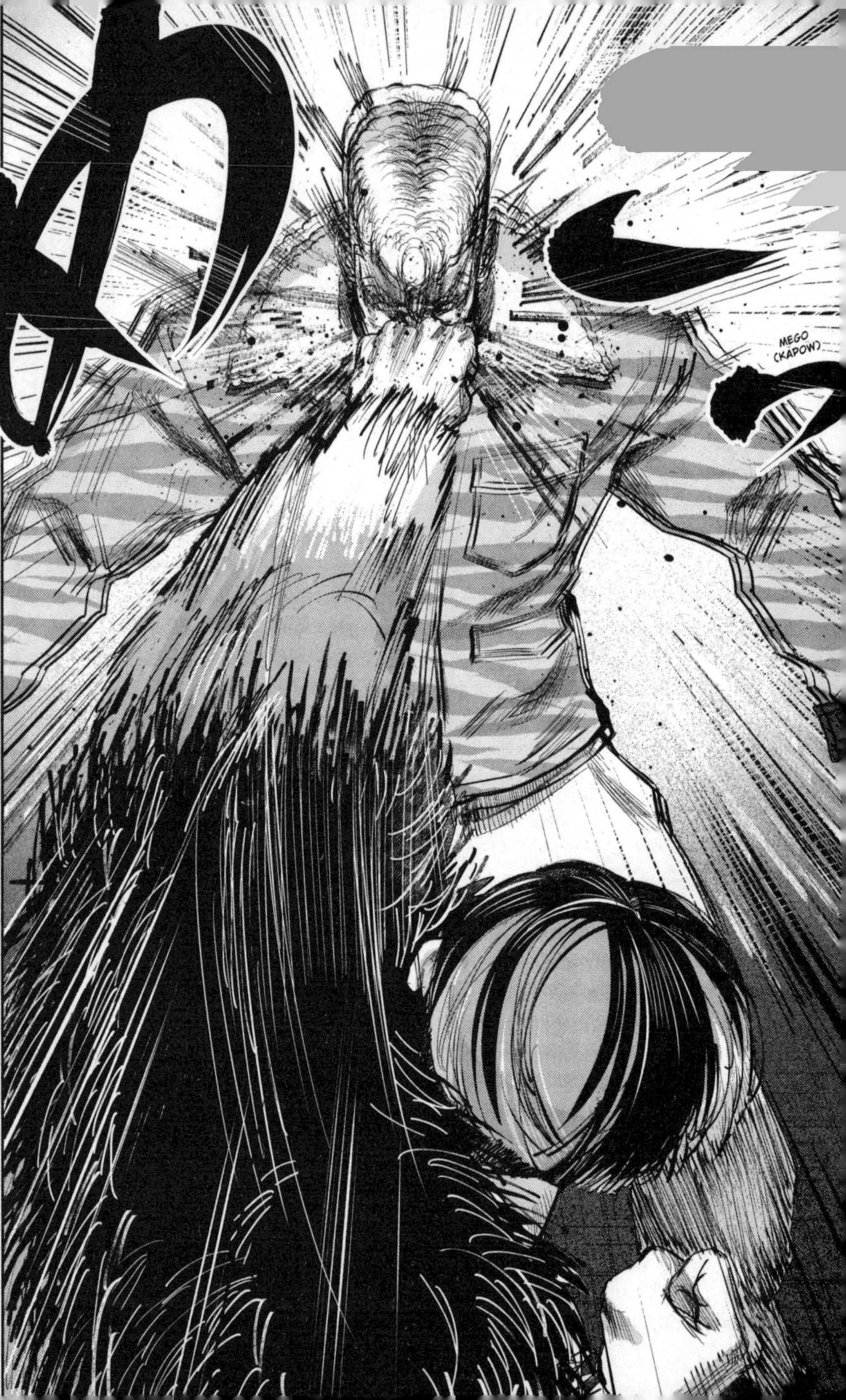

MEGO
(KAPOW)

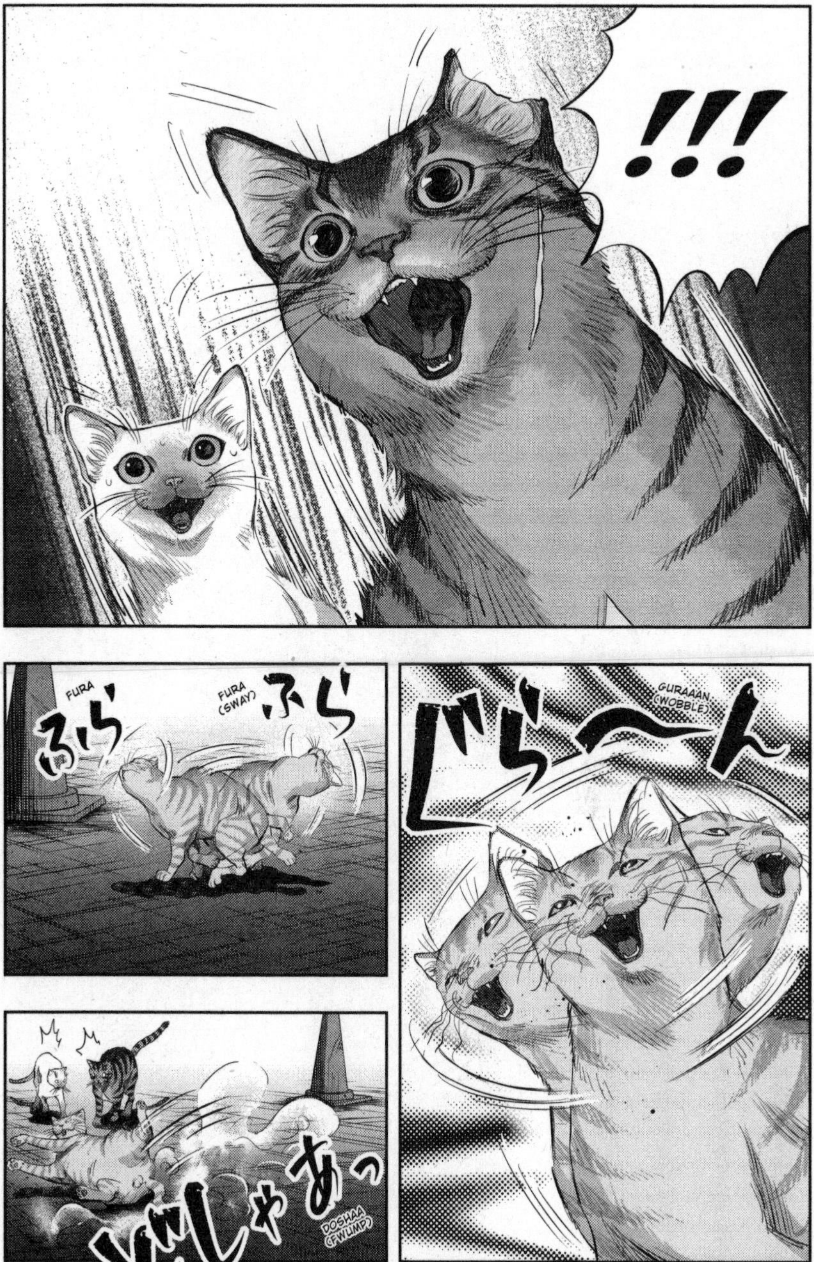
!!!
GURAAAN (WOBBLE)
ぐら〜ん
FURA (SWAY)
ふら
FURA
ふら
どしゃあっ
DOSHAA (FWUMP)

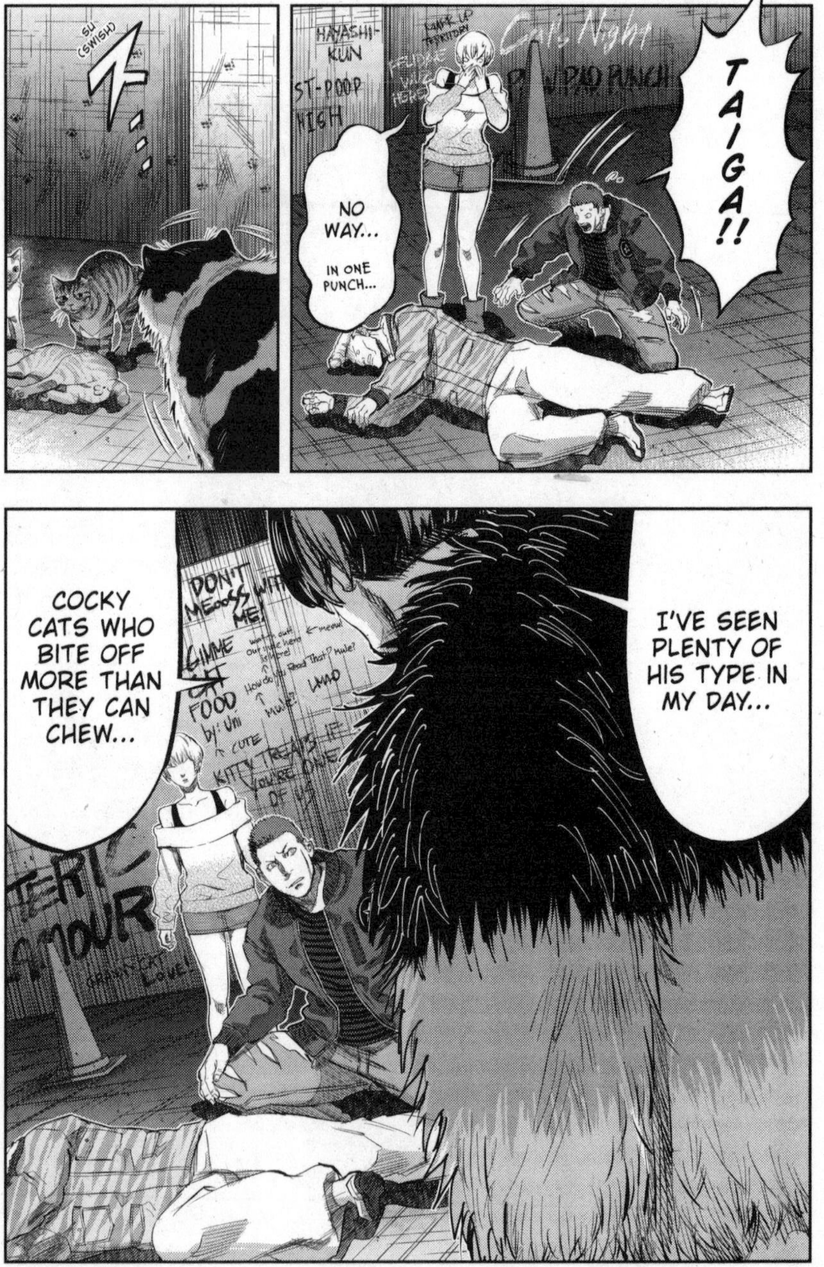
TAIGA!!
NO WAY...
IN ONE PUNCH...
SU (SWISH)
I'VE SEEN PLENTY OF HIS TYPE IN MY DAY...
COCKY CATS WHO BITE OFF MORE THAN THEY CAN CHEW...

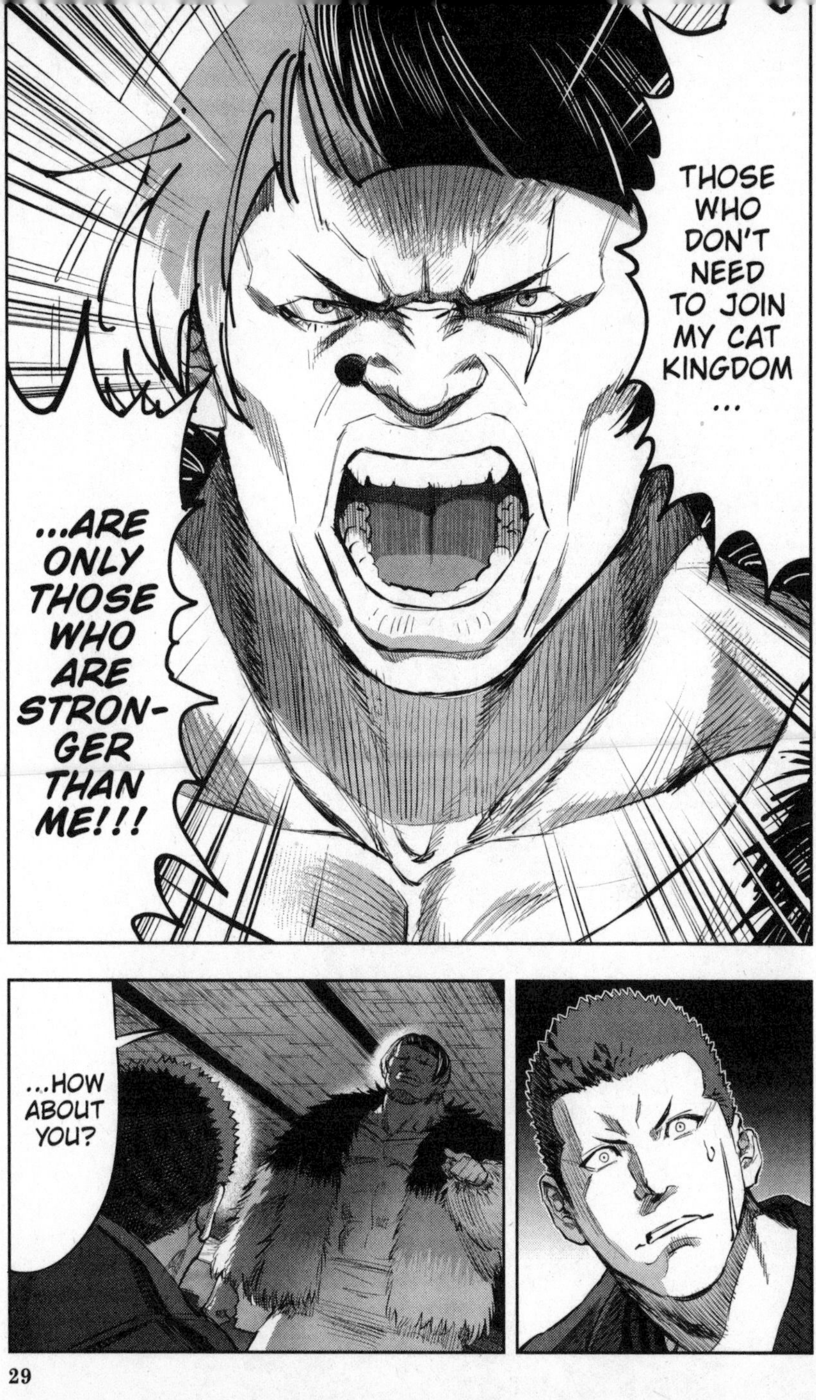
THOSE WHO DON'T NEED TO JOIN MY CAT KINGDOM ...
...ARE ONLY THOSE WHO ARE STRONGER THAN ME!!!
...HOW ABOUT YOU?

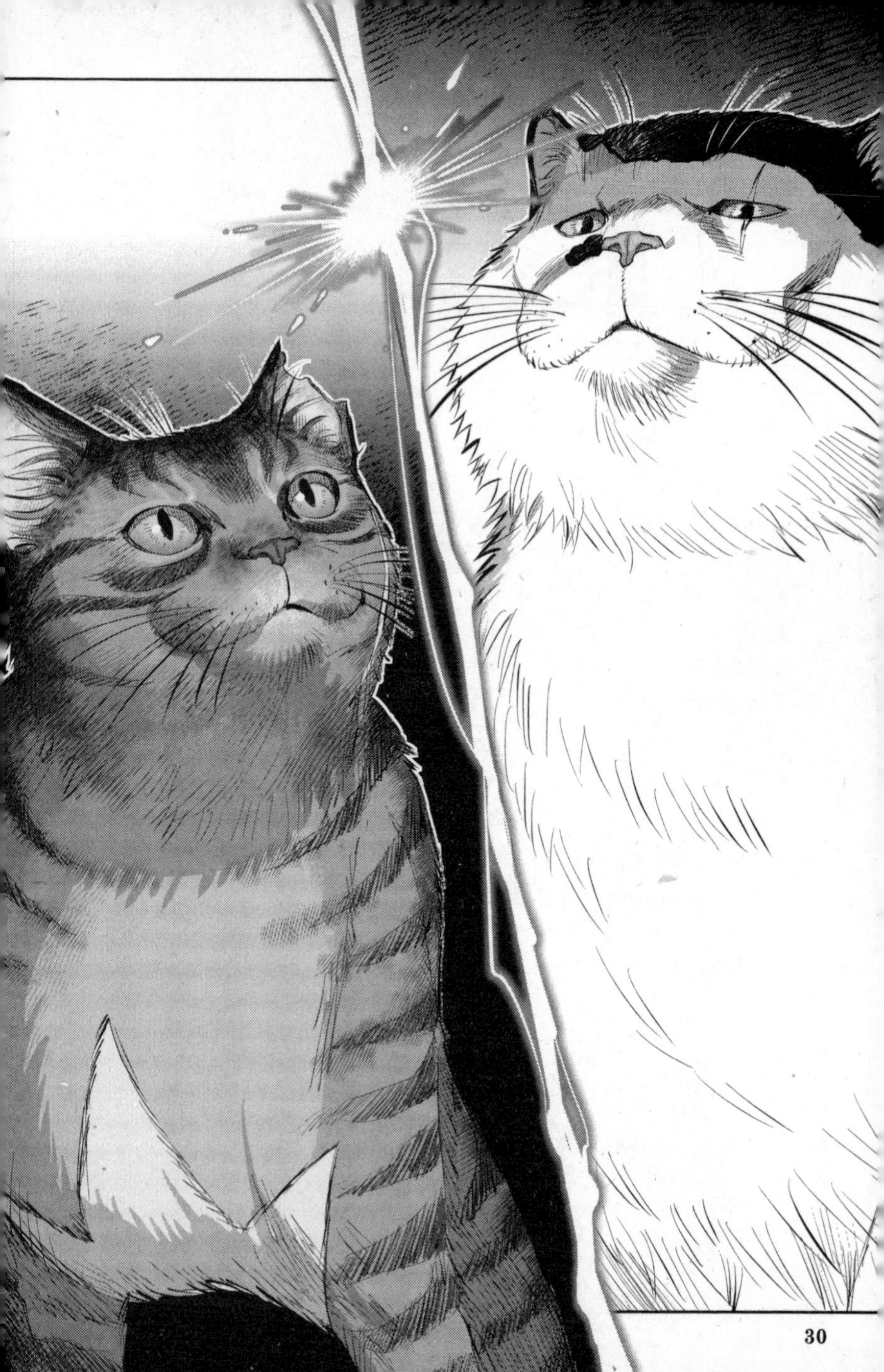

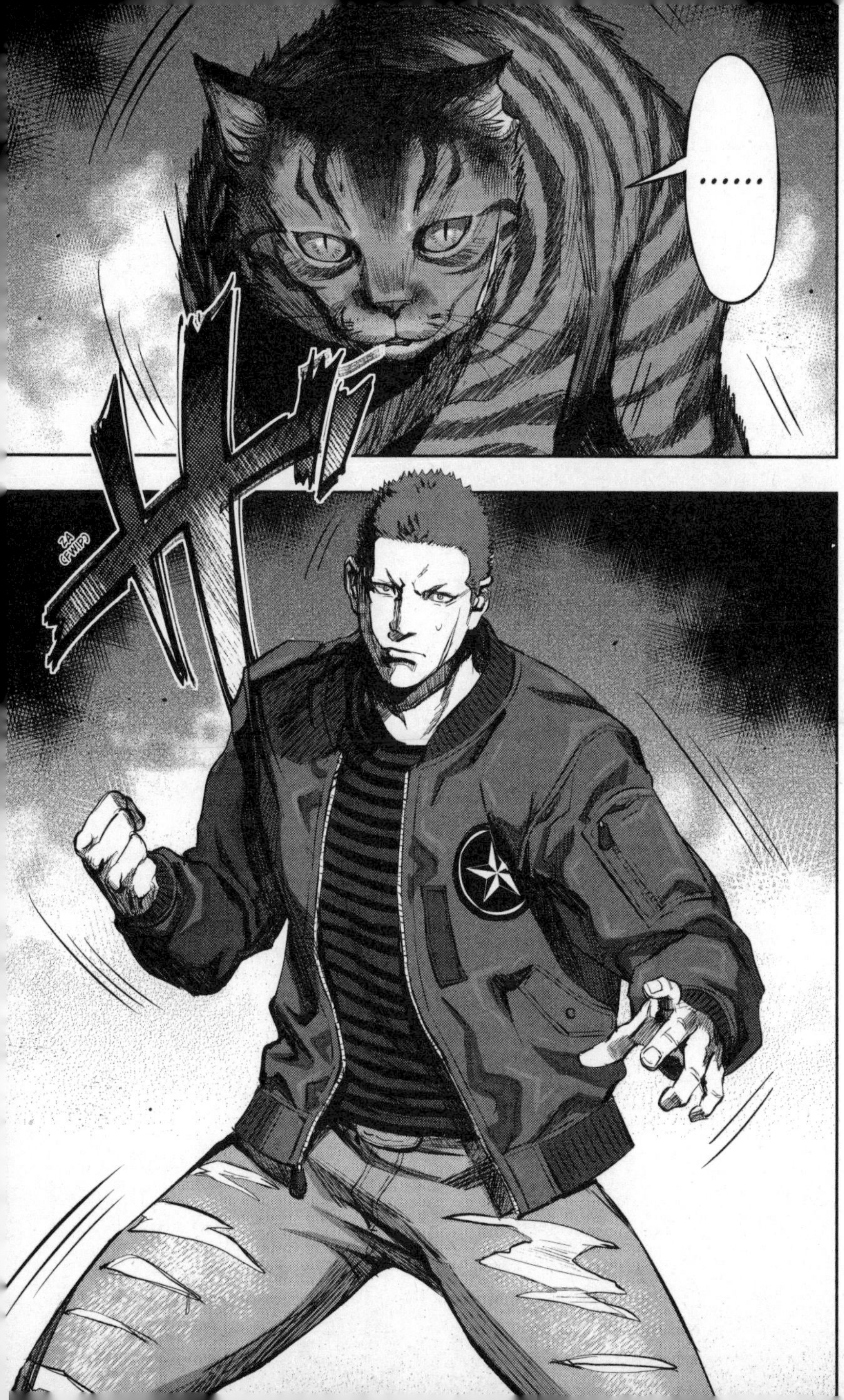
......
ZA
(FWIP)

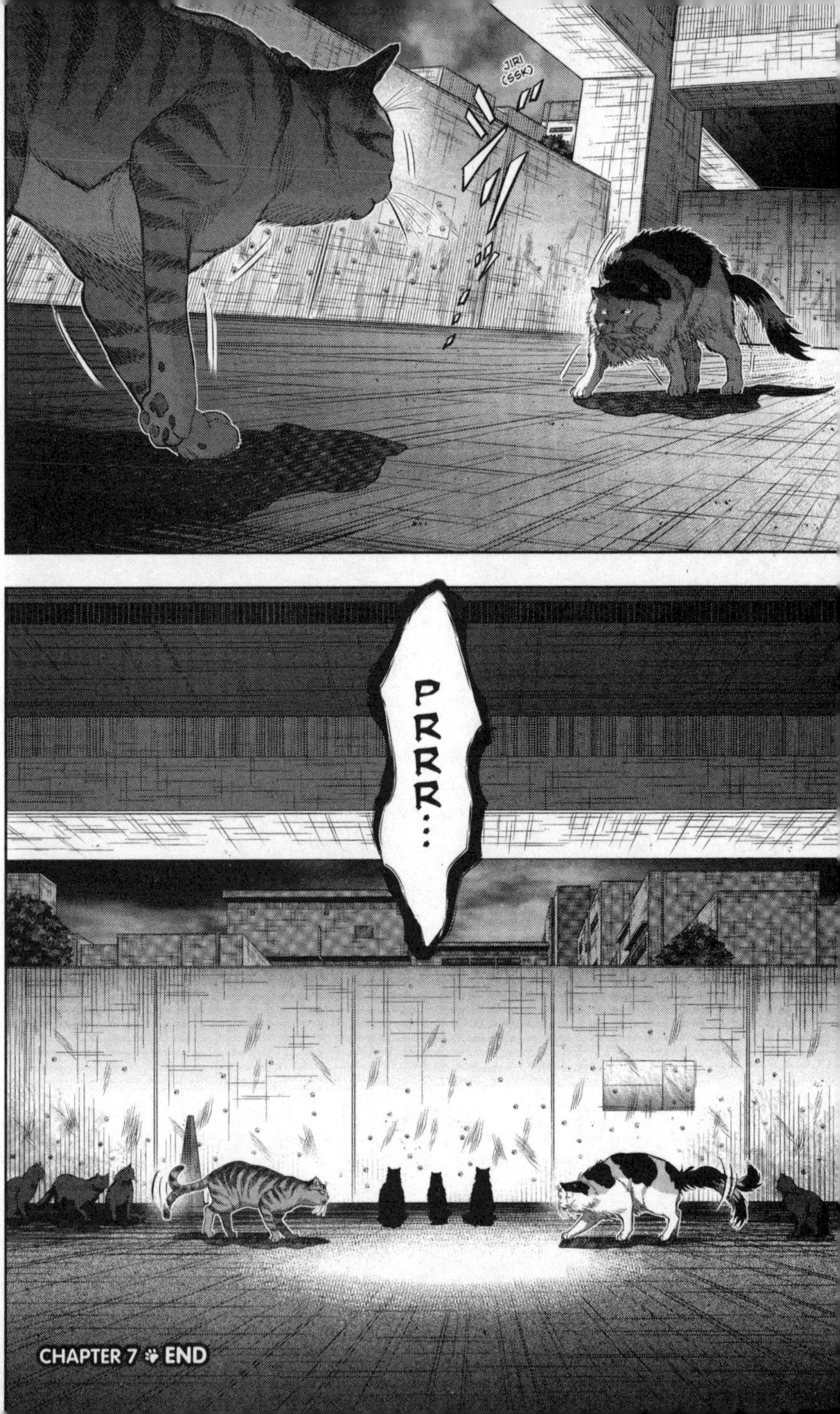
JIRI
(SSK)
PRRR...
CHAPTER 7 END

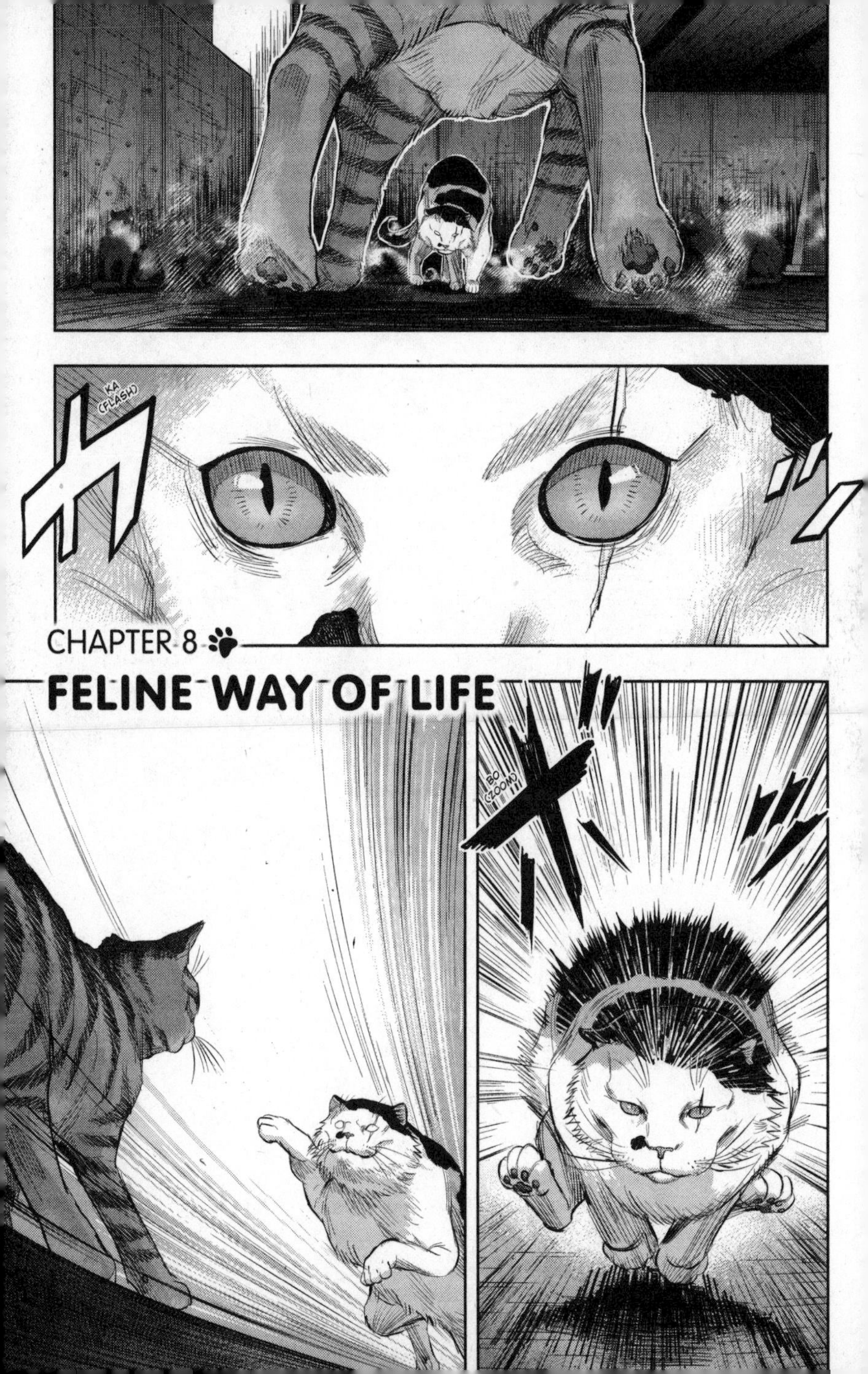
KA (FLASH)
CHAPTER 8
FELINE WAY OF LIFE
BO (ZOOM)

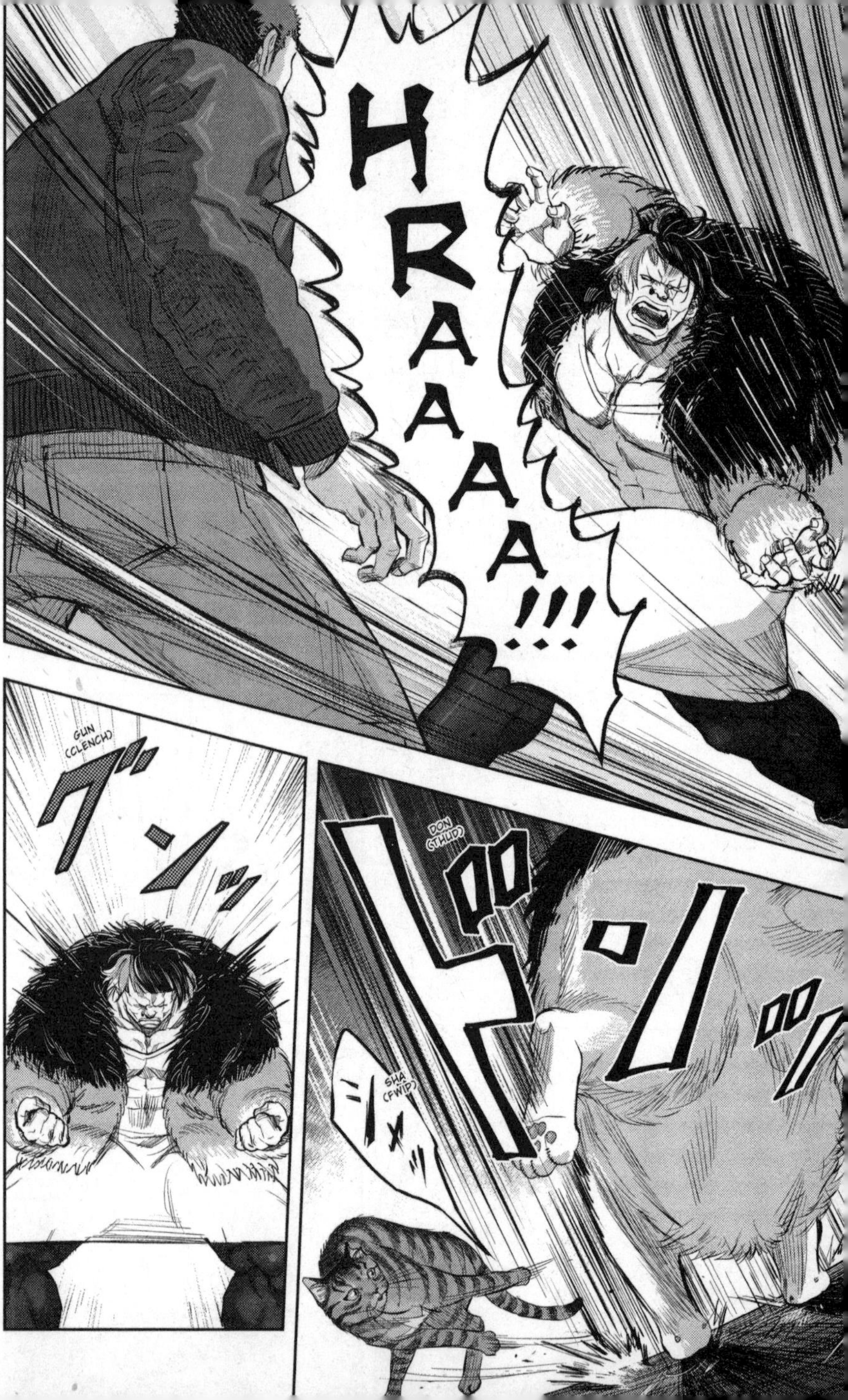
HRAAAA!!!
DON (THUD)
SHA (FWIP)
GUN (CLENCH)

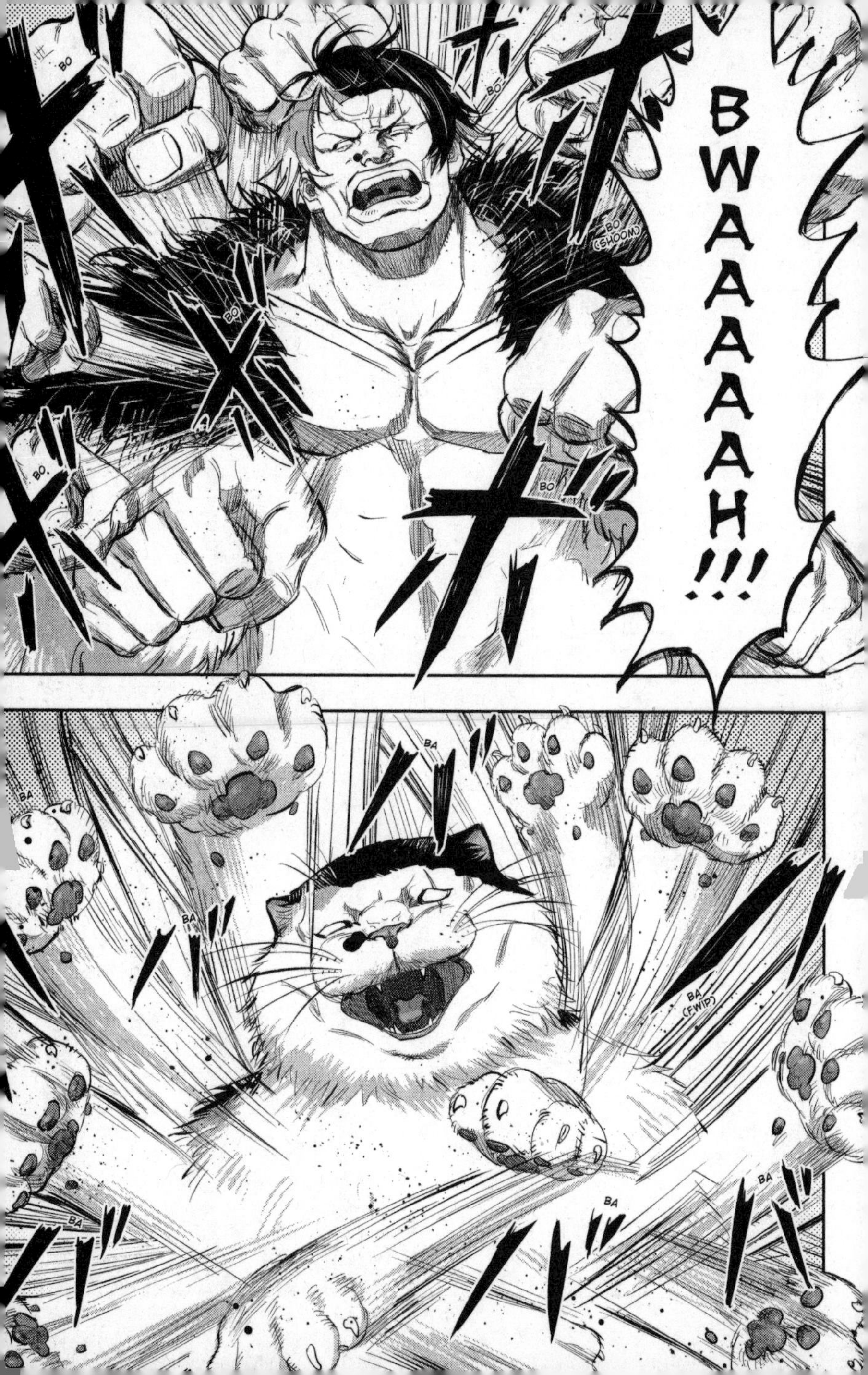
BWAAAAAAH!!!
BO
(SHOOM)
BO
BO
BO
BO
BO
BA
BA
(FWIP)
BA
BA
BA
BA
BA

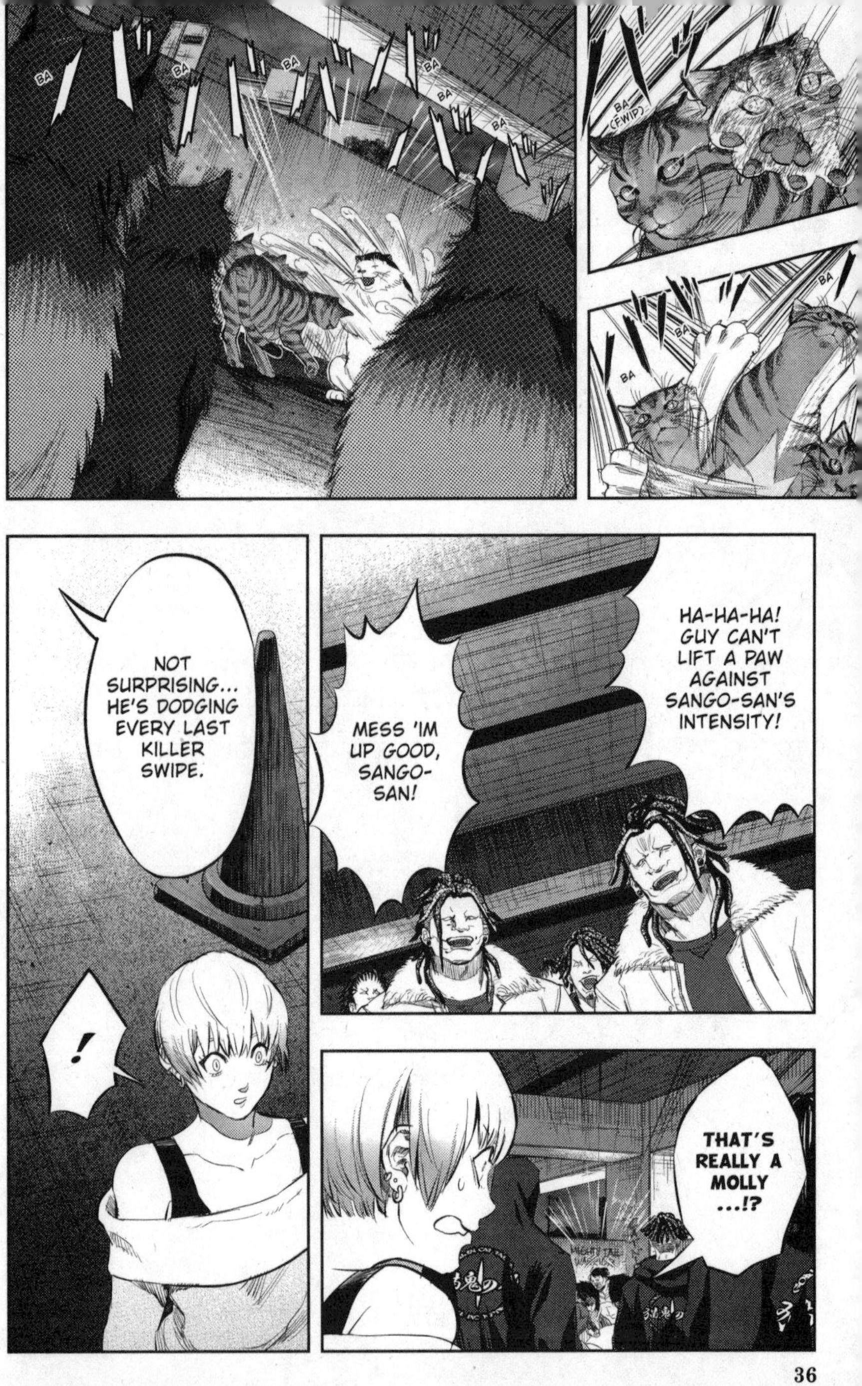
BA
(FWIP)
BA
BA
BA
BA
BA
BA
BA
BA
BA
HA-HA-HA! GUY CAN'T LIFT A PAW AGAINST SANGO-SAN'S INTENSITY!
MESS 'IM UP GOOD, SANGO-SAN!
THAT'S REALLY A MOLLY ...!?
NOT SURPRISING... HE'S DODGING EVERY LAST KILLER SWIPE.
!

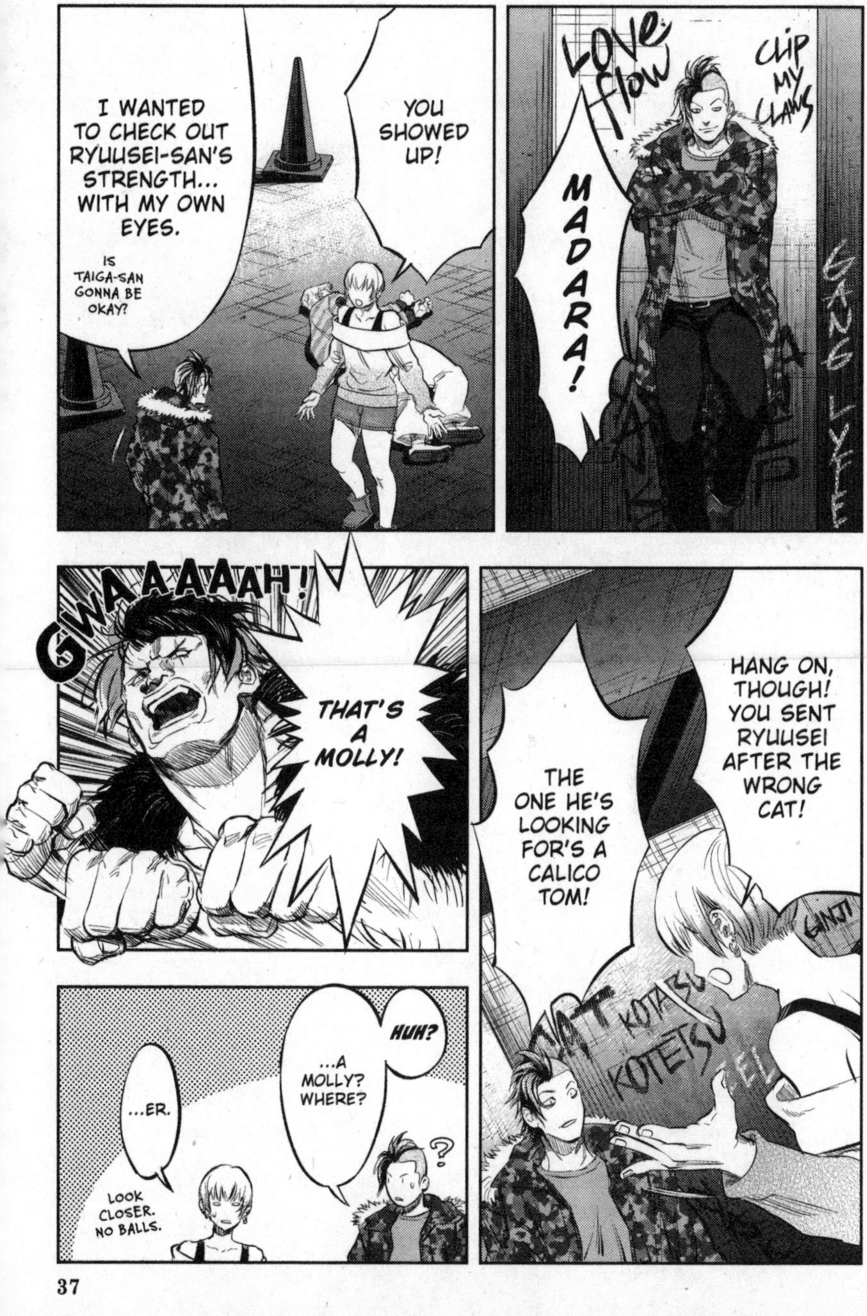
MADARA!
LOVE flow
Clip MY CLAWS
GANG LYFE
YOU SHOWED UP!
I WANTED TO CHECK OUT RYUUSEI-SAN'S STRENGTH... WITH MY OWN EYES.
IS TAIGA-SAN GONNA BE OKAY?
HANG ON, THOUGH! YOU SENT RYUUSEI AFTER THE WRONG CAT!
THE ONE HE'S LOOKING FOR'S A CALICO TOM!
GINJI
KOTATSU
KOTETSU
GWAAAAAH!
THAT'S A MOLLY!
HUH?
...A MOLLY? WHERE?
...ER.
LOOK CLOSER. NO BALLS.

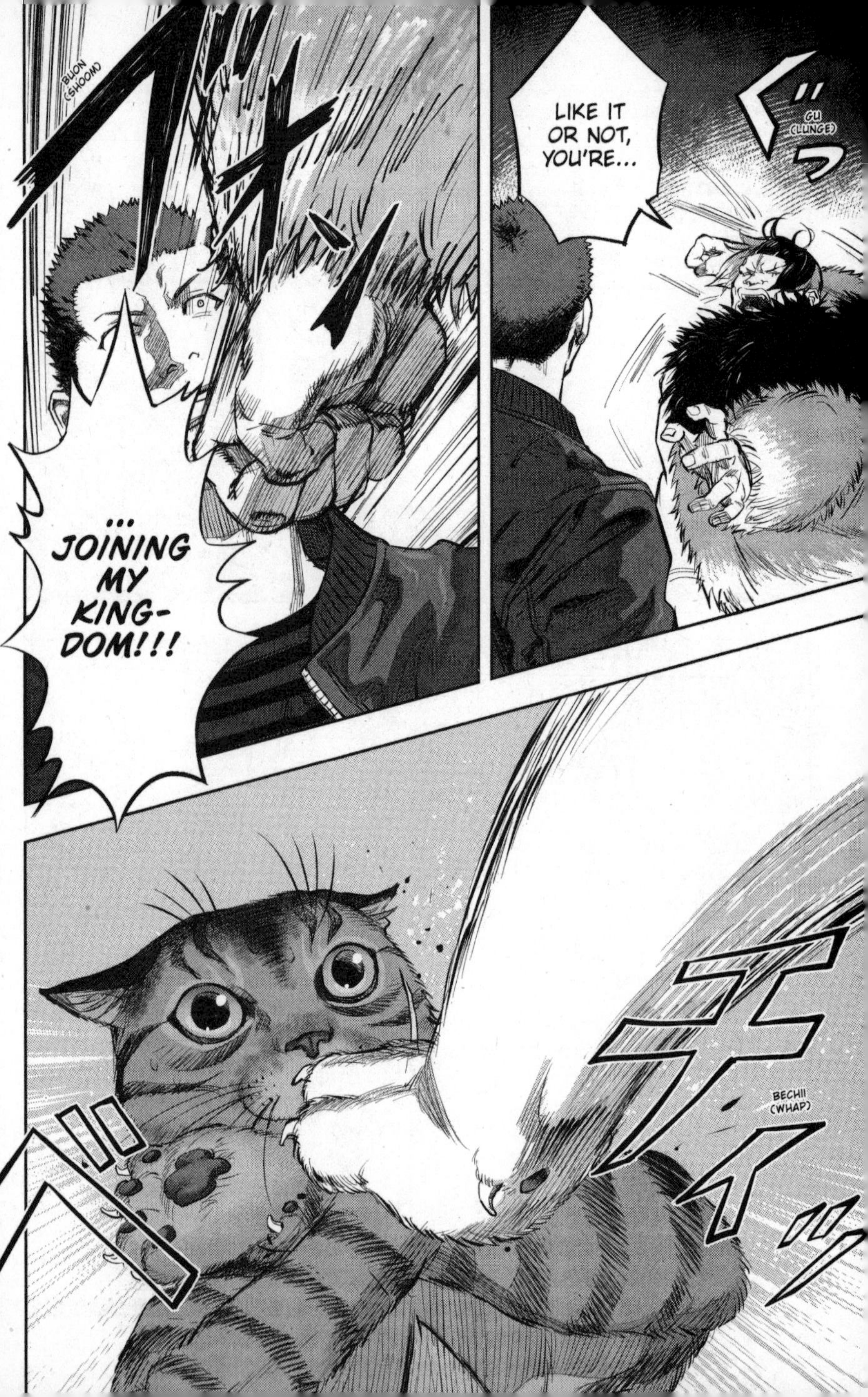
LIKE IT OR NOT, YOU'RE...
GU (LUNGE)
BUON (SHOOM)
...JOINING MY KINGDOM!!!
BECHII (WHAP)

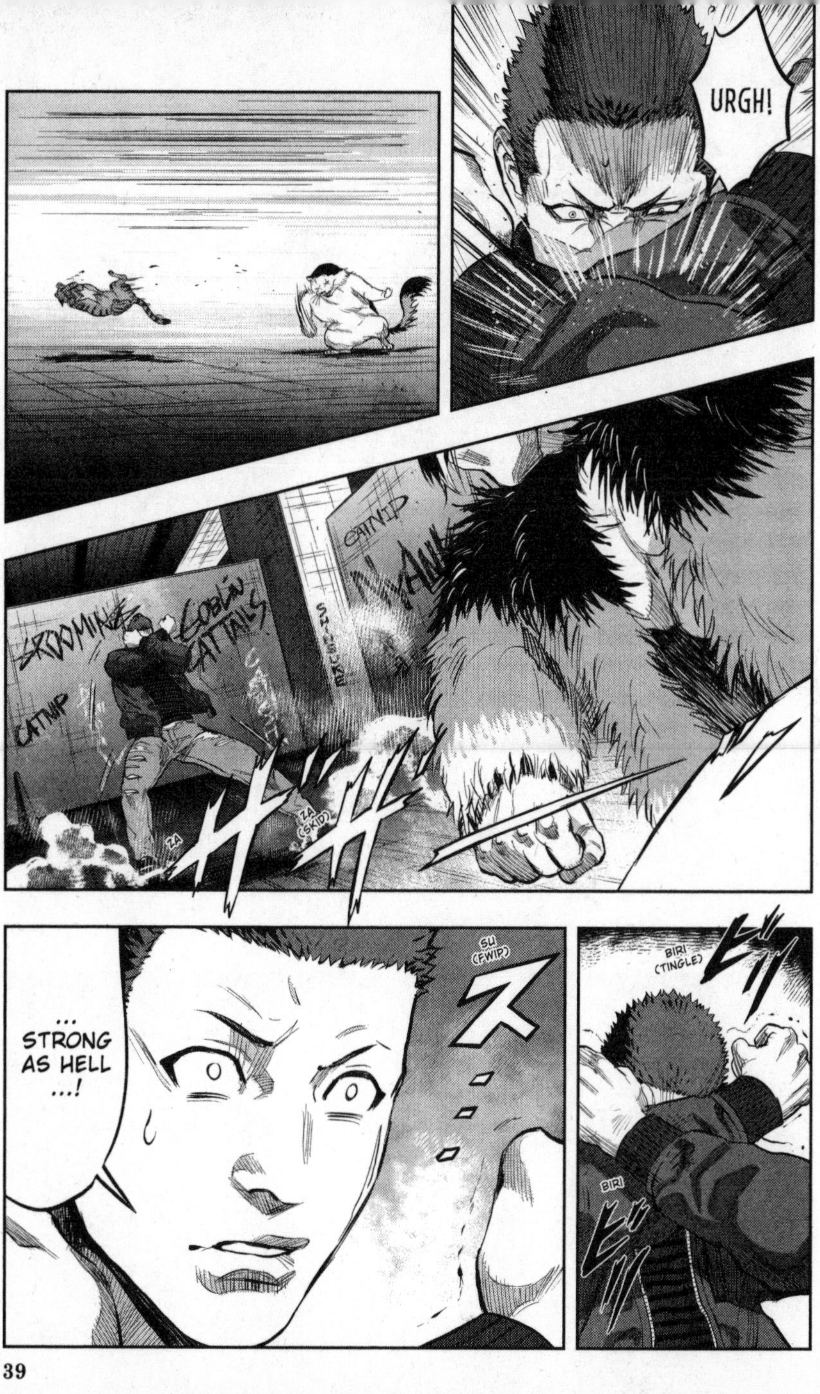
URGH!
CATNIP
GOBLIN CATTAILS
CATNIP
SHINSUKE
ZA (SKID)
ZA
BIRI (TINGLE)
BIRI
SU (FWIP)
... STRONG AS HELL ...!

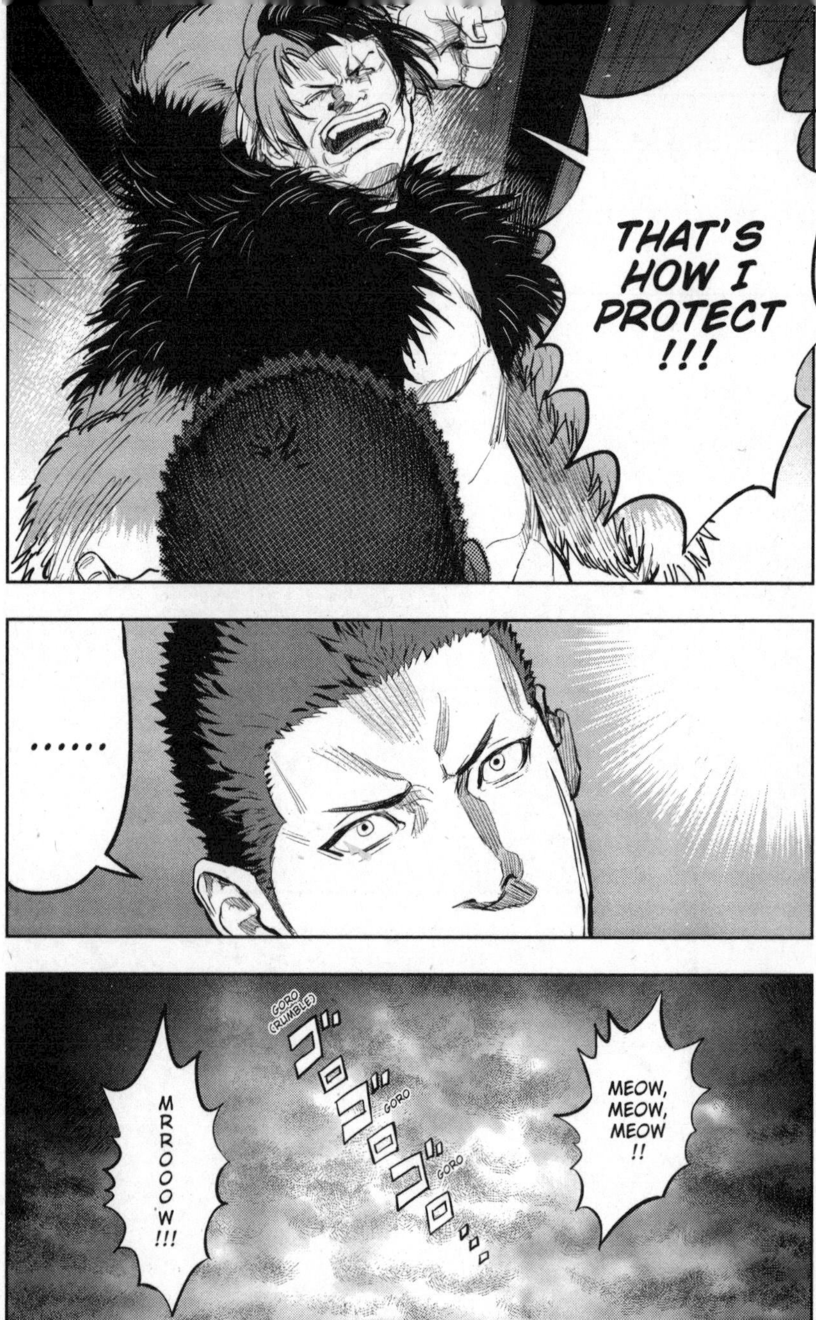
THAT'S HOW I PROTECT!!!
......
MEOW, MEOW, MEOW!!
GORO (RUMBLE)
GORO
GORO
MRROOOOW!!!

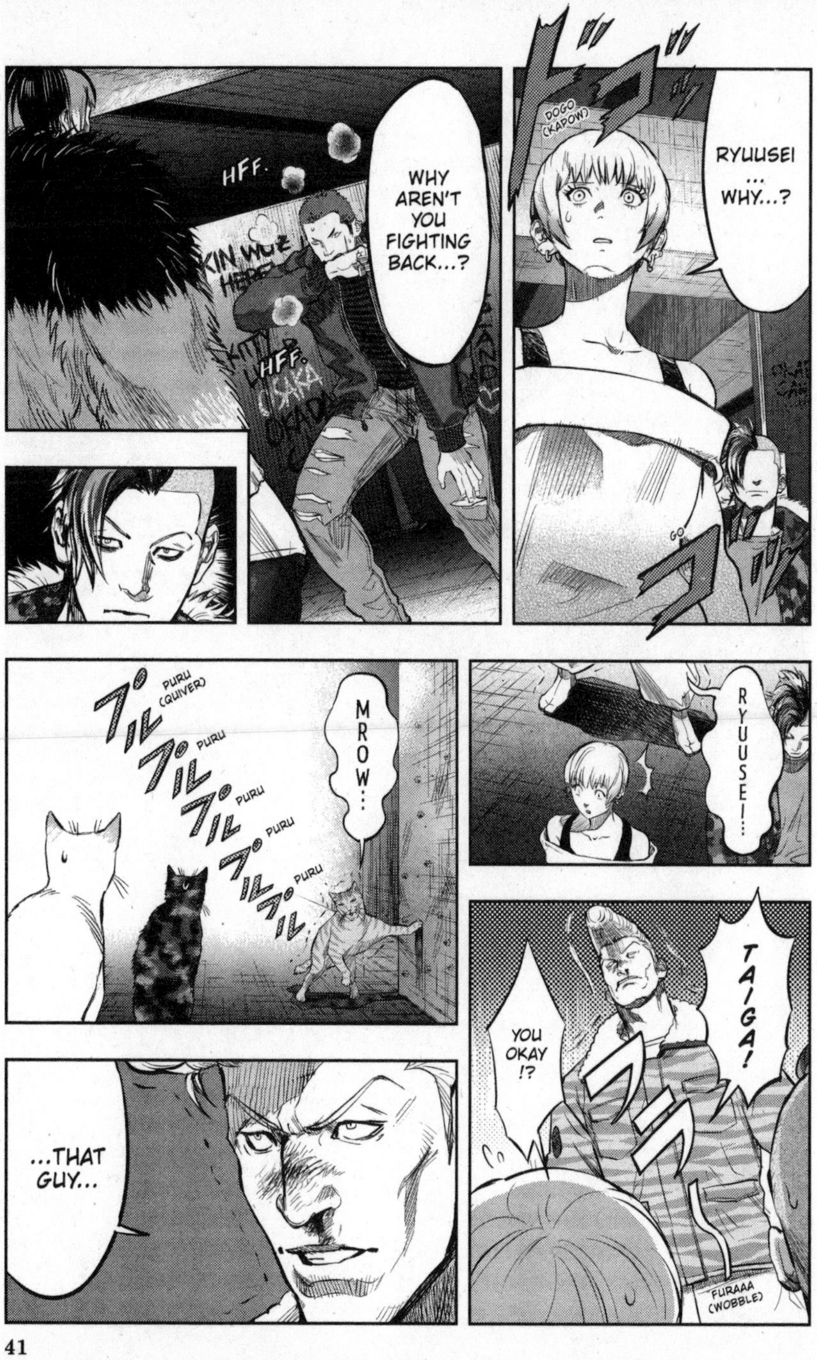
DOGO (KAPOW)
RYUUSEI ... WHY...?
GO
HFF.
WHY AREN'T YOU FIGHTING BACK...?
HFF.
RYUUSEI!...
PURU (QUIVER)
PURU
PURU
PURU
PURU
MROW...
TAIGA!
YOU OKAY!?
FURAAA (WOBBLE)
...THAT GUY...

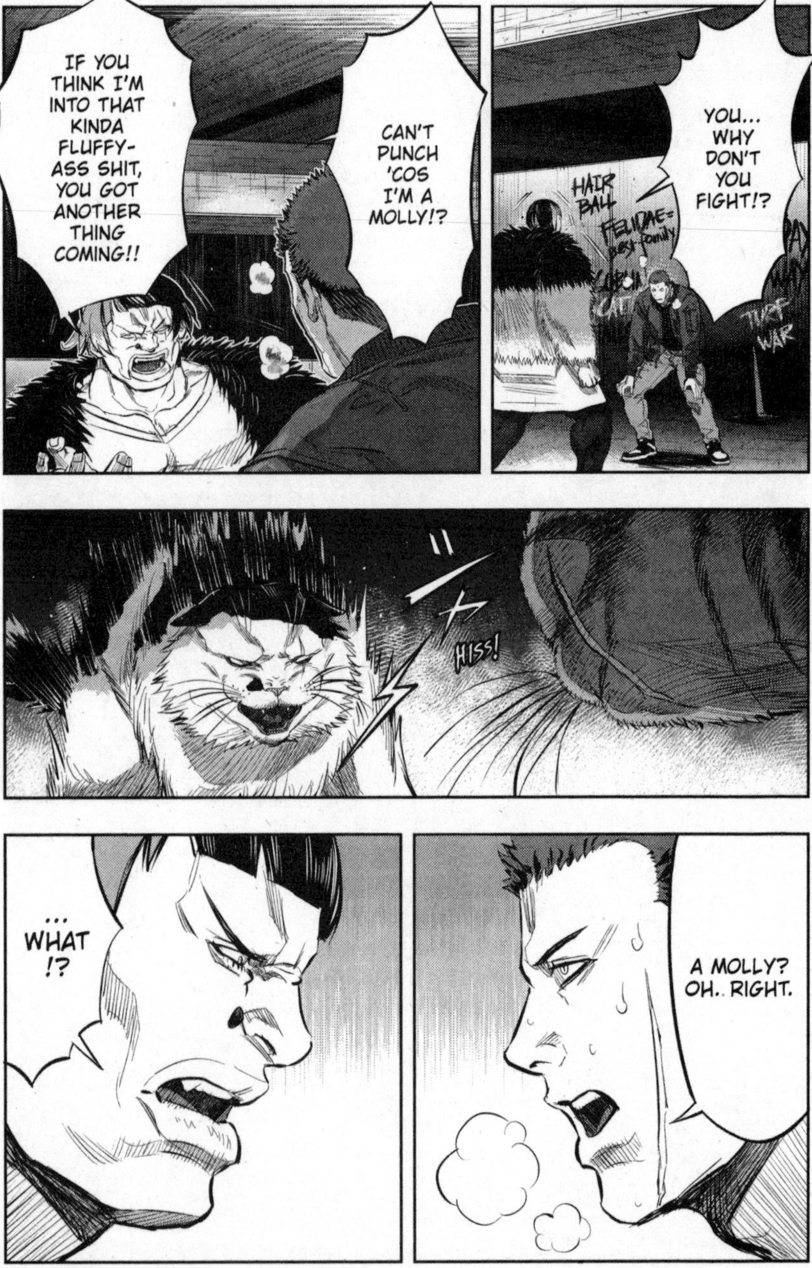
YOU... WHY DON'T YOU FIGHT!?
HAIR BALL
FELIDAE=
TURF WAR
CAN'T PUNCH 'COS I'M A MOLLY!?
IF YOU THINK I'M INTO THAT KINDA FLUFFY-ASS SHIT, YOU GOT ANOTHER THING COMING!!
HISS!
A MOLLY? OH.. RIGHT.
... WHAT !?

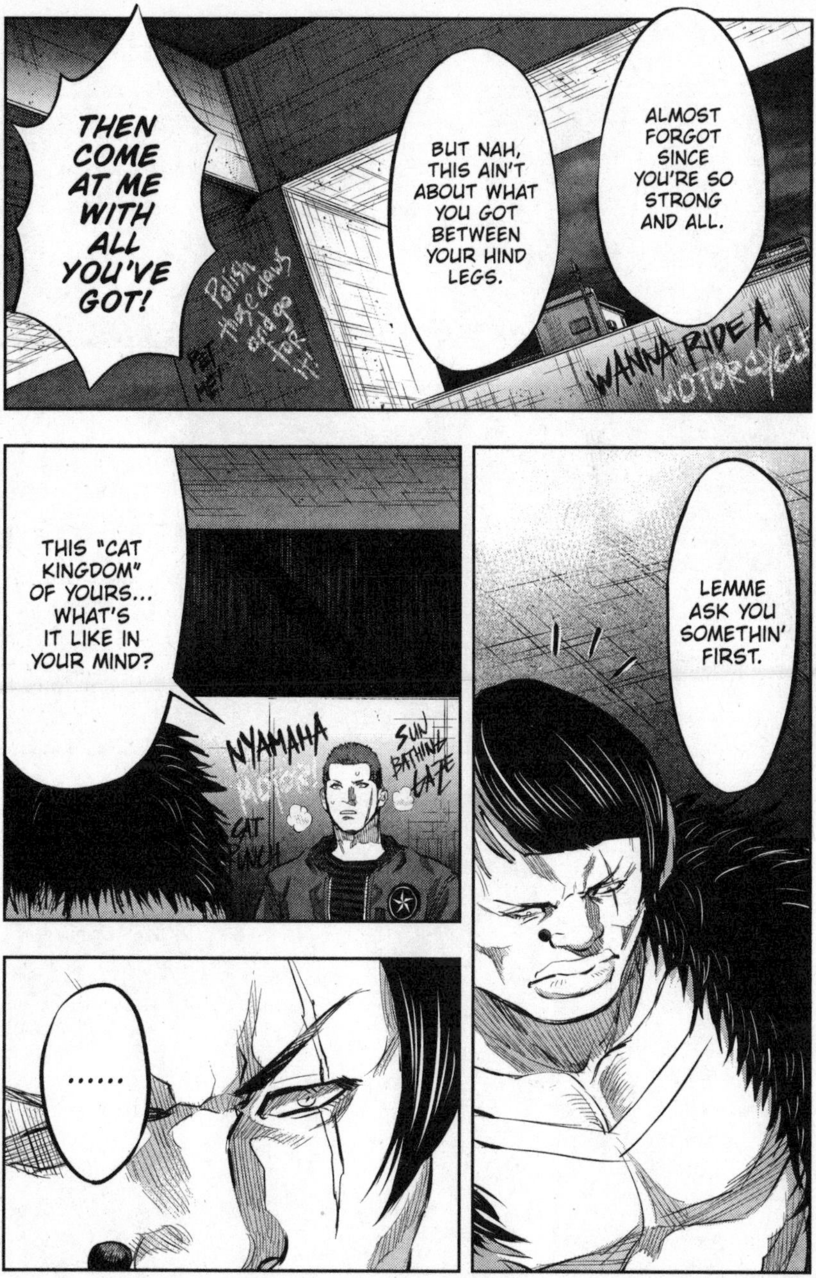
ALMOST FORGOT SINCE YOU'RE SO STRONG AND ALL.
BUT NAH, THIS AIN'T ABOUT WHAT YOU GOT BETWEEN YOUR HIND LEGS.
THEN COME AT ME WITH ALL YOU'VE GOT!
Polish those claws and go for it!
PET ME!
WANNA RIDE A
LEMME ASK YOU SOMETHIN' FIRST.
THIS "CAT KINGDOM" OF YOURS... WHAT'S IT LIKE IN YOUR MIND?
NYAMAHA
CAT PUNCH
......

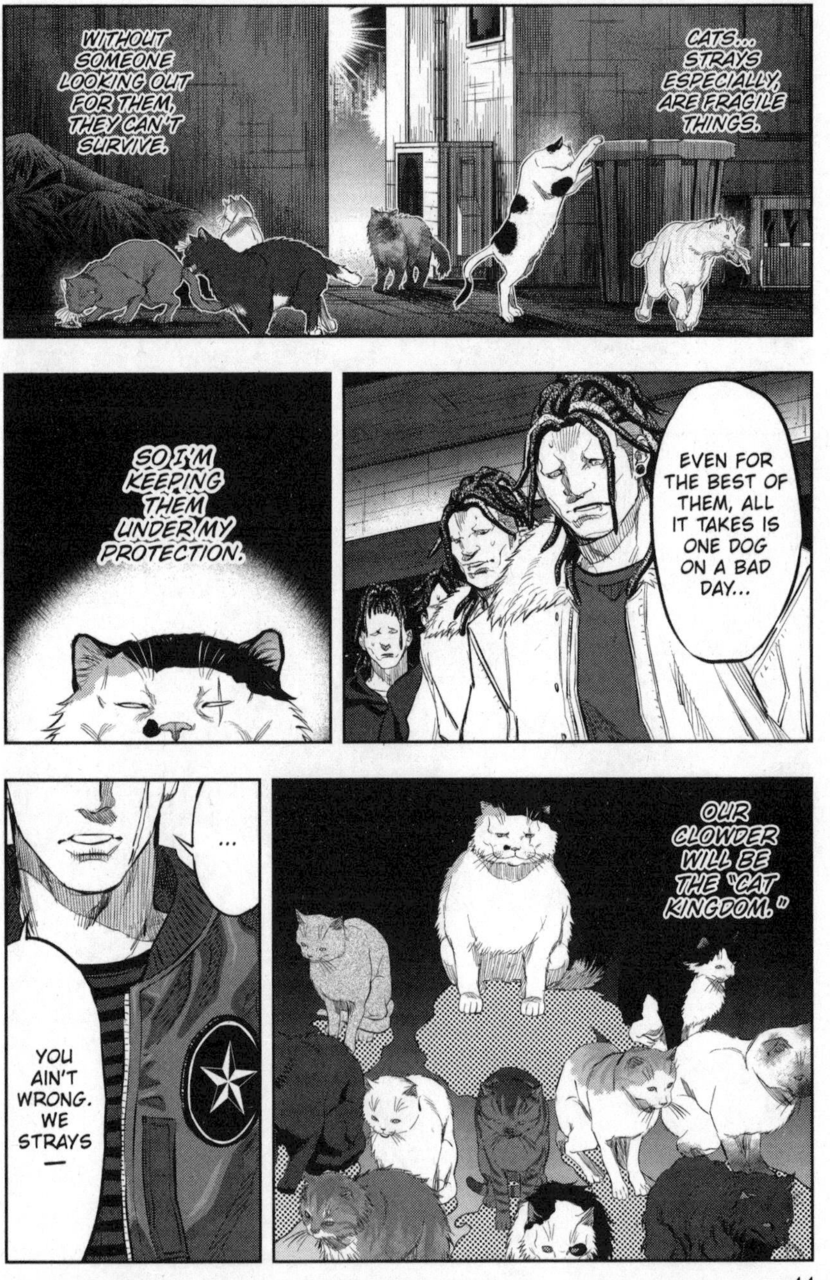
CATS... STRAYS ESPECIALLY, ARE FRAGILE THINGS.
WITHOUT SOMEONE LOOKING OUT FOR THEM, THEY CAN'T SURVIVE.
EVEN FOR THE BEST OF THEM, ALL IT TAKES IS ONE DOG ON A BAD DAY...
SO I'M KEEPING THEM UNDER MY PROTECTION.
OUR CLOWDER WILL BE THE "CAT KINGDOM."
...
YOU AIN'T WRONG. WE STRAYS—

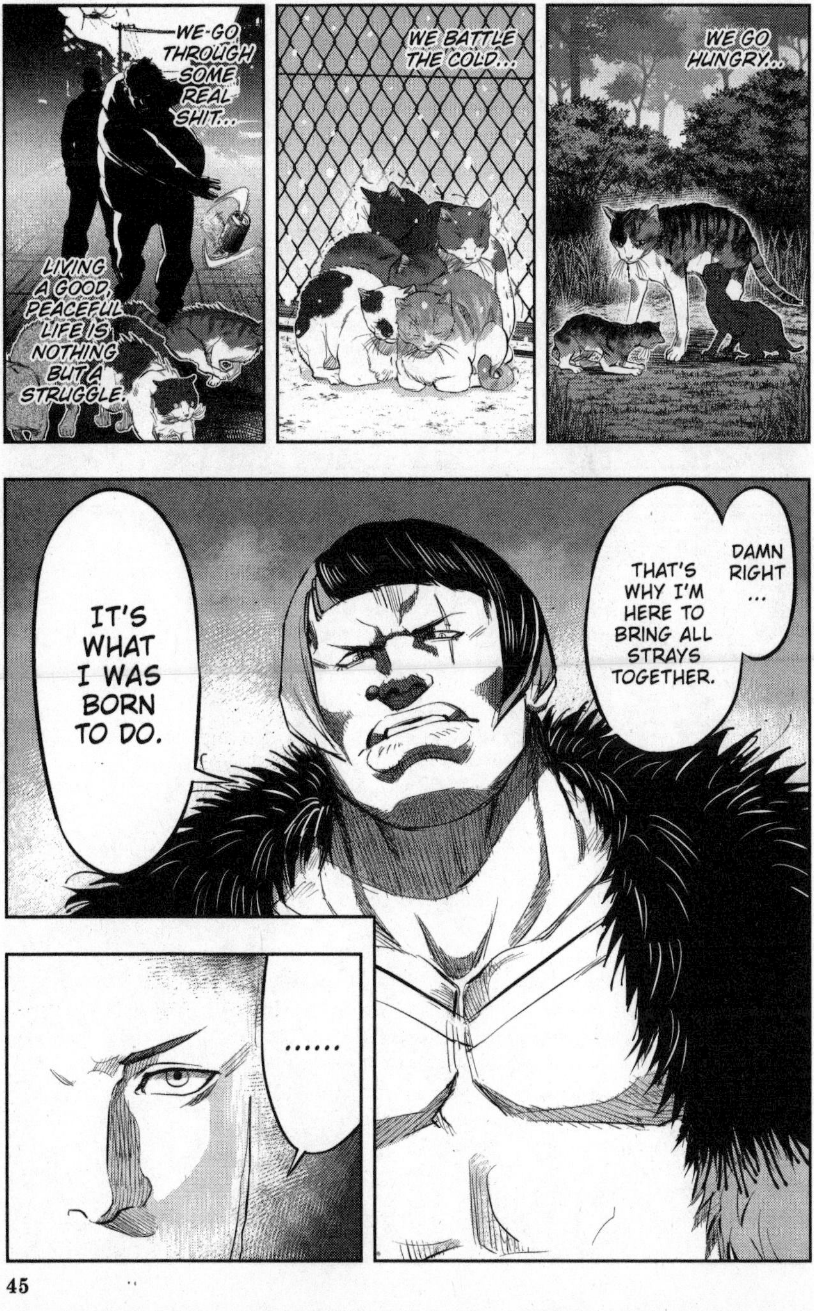
WE GO HUNGRY...
WE BATTLE THE COLD...
WE GO THROUGH SOME REAL SHIT...
LIVING A GOOD, PEACEFUL LIFE IS NOTHING BUT A STRUGGLE.
DAMN RIGHT...
THAT'S WHY I'M HERE TO BRING ALL STRAYS TOGETHER.
IT'S WHAT I WAS BORN TO DO.
......

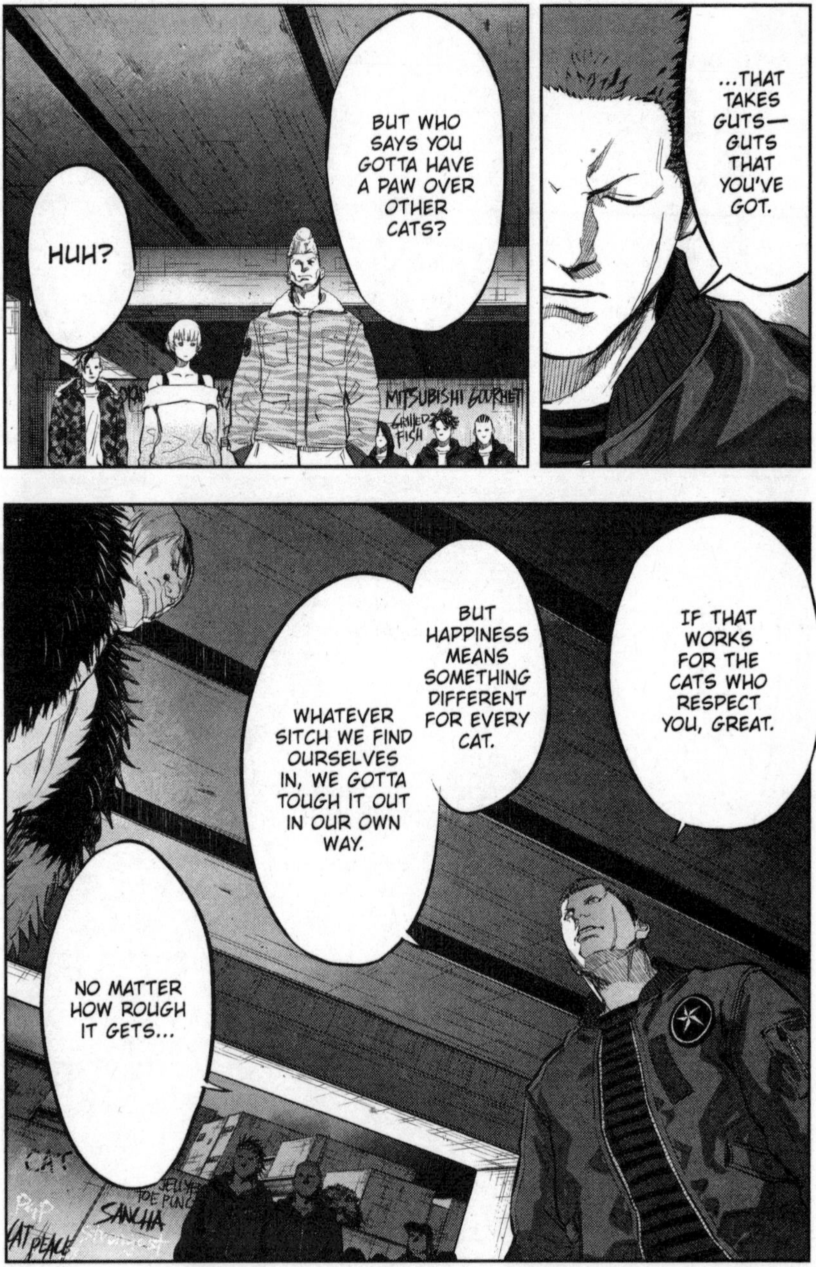
...THAT TAKES GUTS—GUTS THAT YOU'VE GOT.
BUT WHO SAYS YOU GOTTA HAVE A PAW OVER OTHER CATS?
HUH?
MITSUBISHI GOURMET
GRILLED FISH
IF THAT WORKS FOR THE CATS WHO RESPECT YOU, GREAT.
BUT HAPPINESS MEANS SOMETHING DIFFERENT FOR EVERY CAT.
WHATEVER SITCH WE FIND OURSELVES IN, WE GOTTA TOUGH IT OUT IN OUR OWN WAY.
NO MATTER HOW ROUGH IT GETS...
CAT
SANCHA

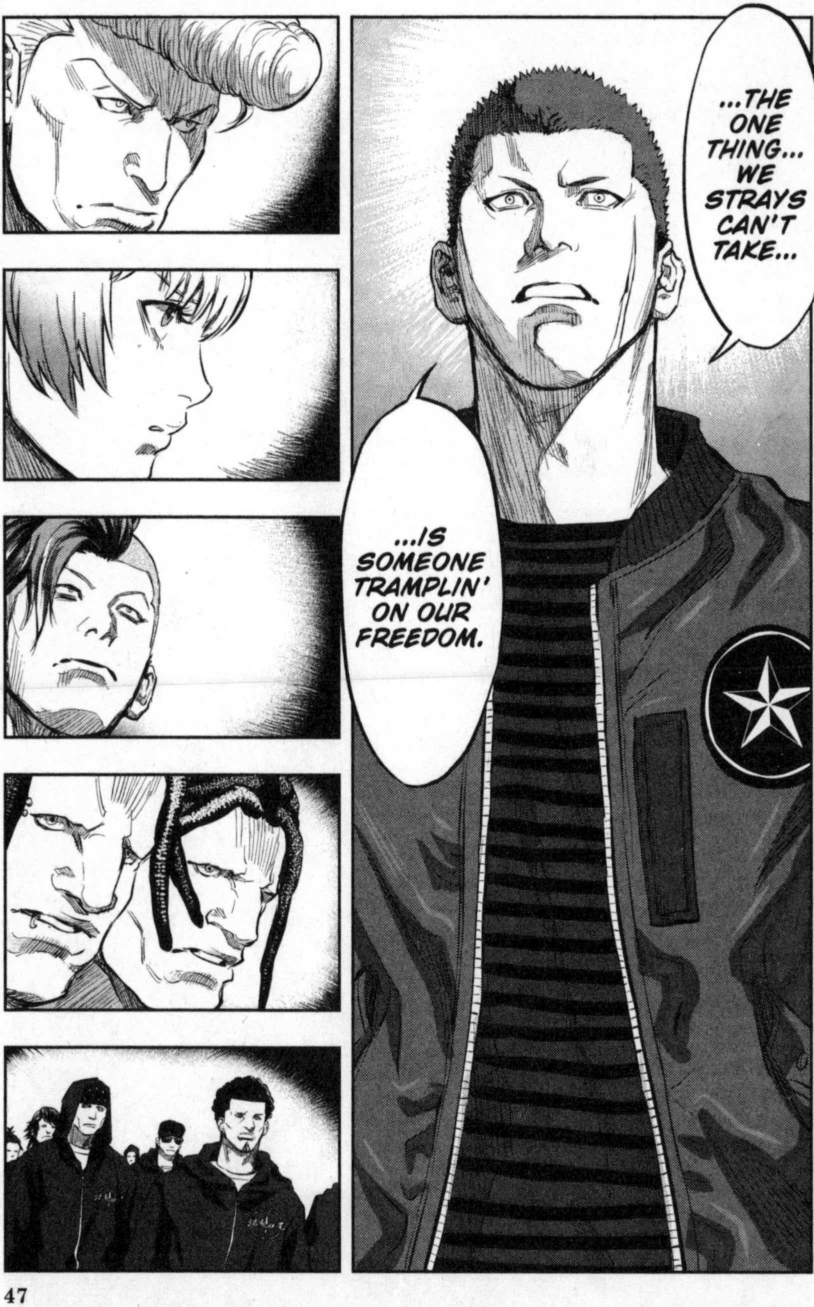
...THE ONE THING... WE STRAYS CAN'T TAKE...
...IS SOMEONE TRAMPLIN' ON OUR FREEDOM.

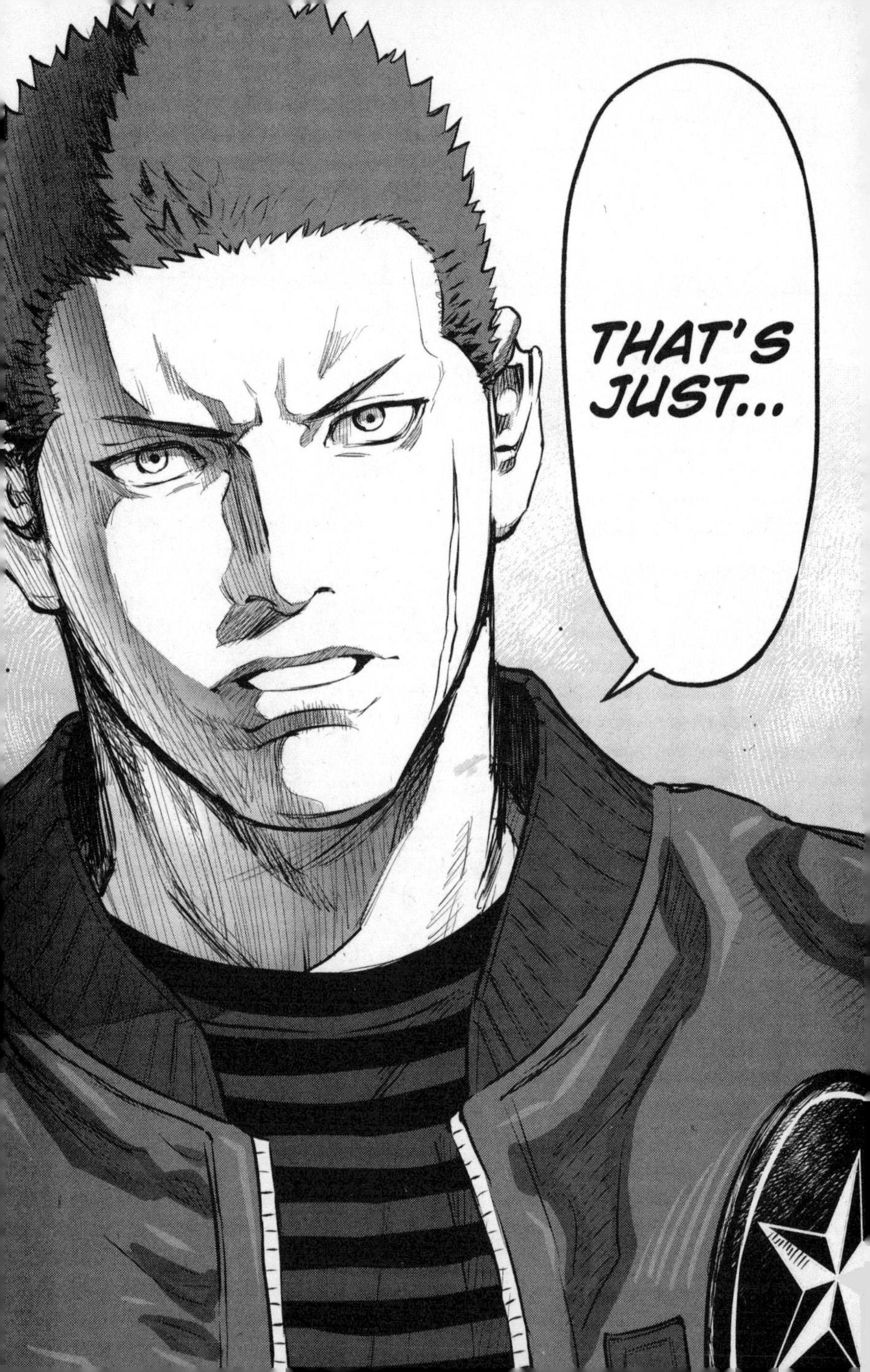
THAT'S JUST...

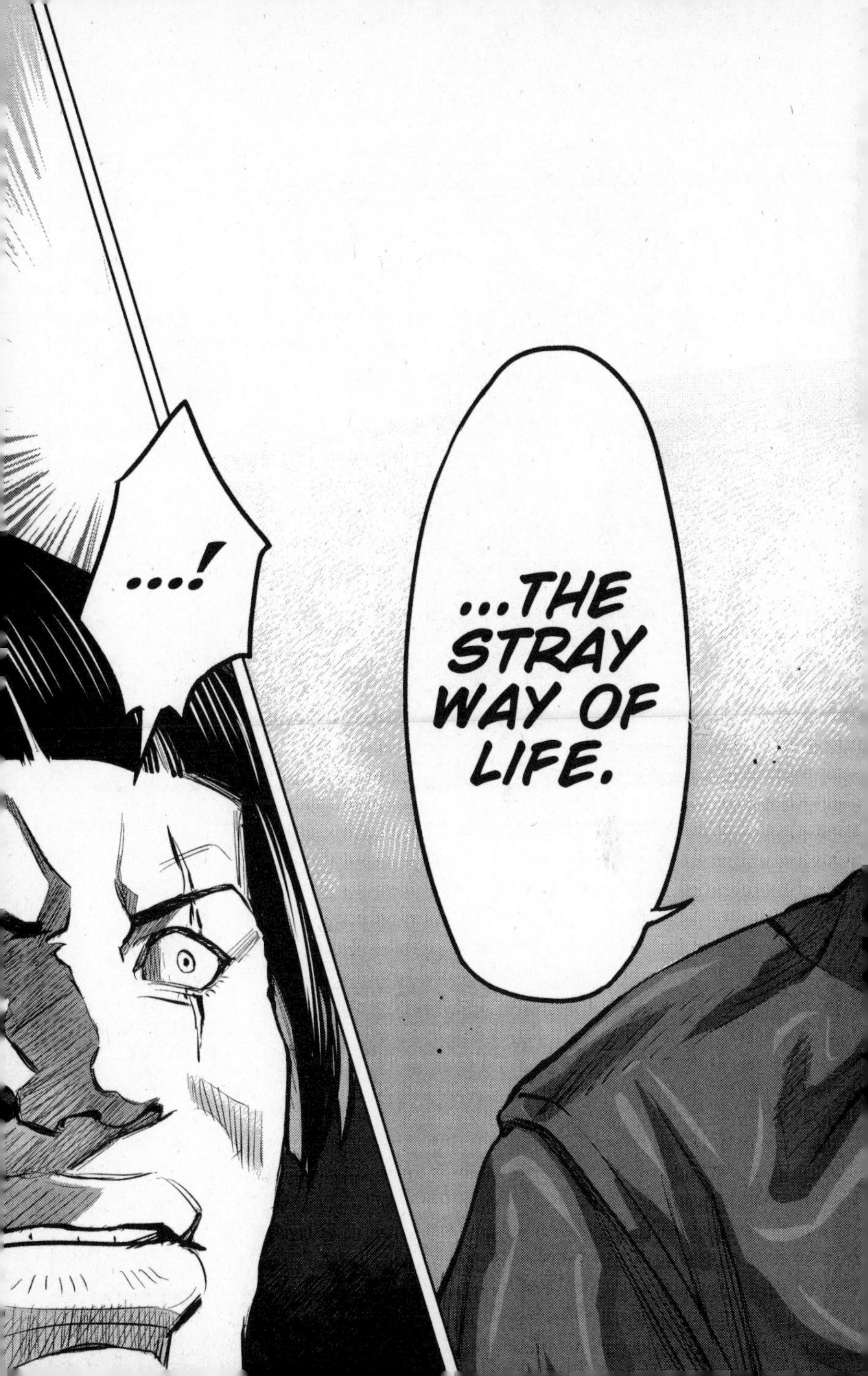
...THE STRAY WAY OF LIFE.
...!

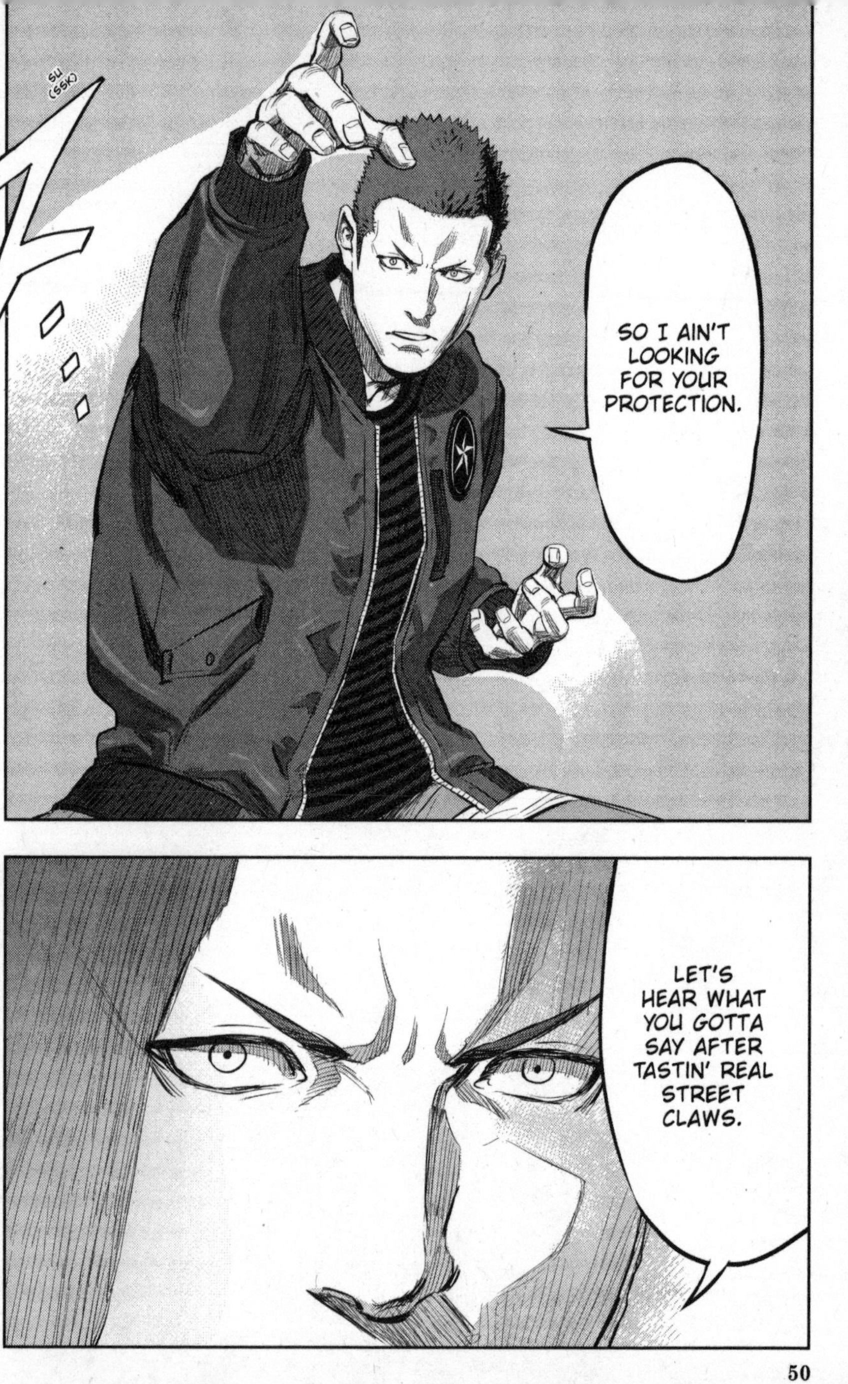
SU (SSK)
SO I AIN'T LOOKING FOR YOUR PROTECTION.
LET'S HEAR WHAT YOU GOTTA SAY AFTER TASTIN' REAL STREET CLAWS.

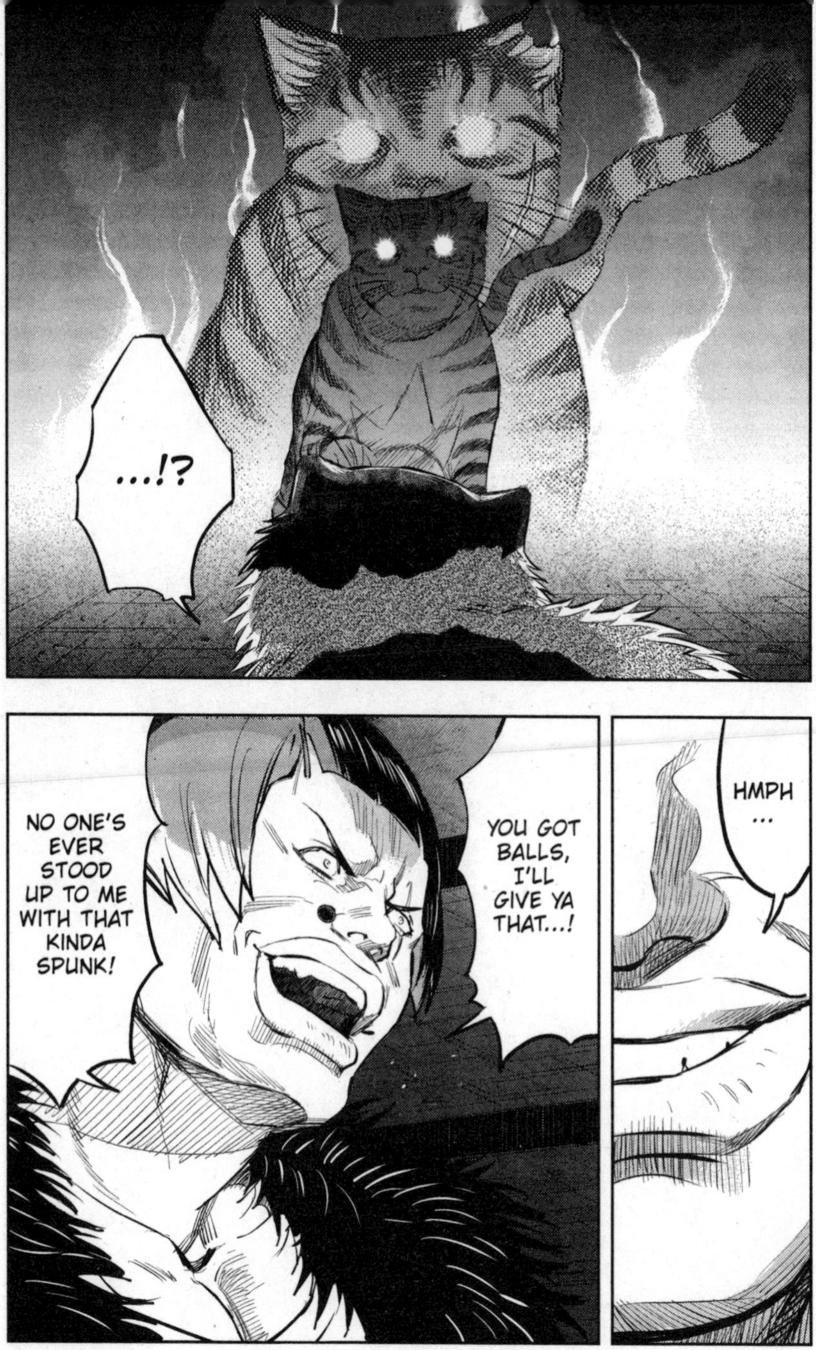
...!?
HMPH ...
YOU GOT BALLS, I'LL GIVE YA THAT...!
NO ONE'S EVER STOOD UP TO ME WITH THAT KINDA SPUNK!

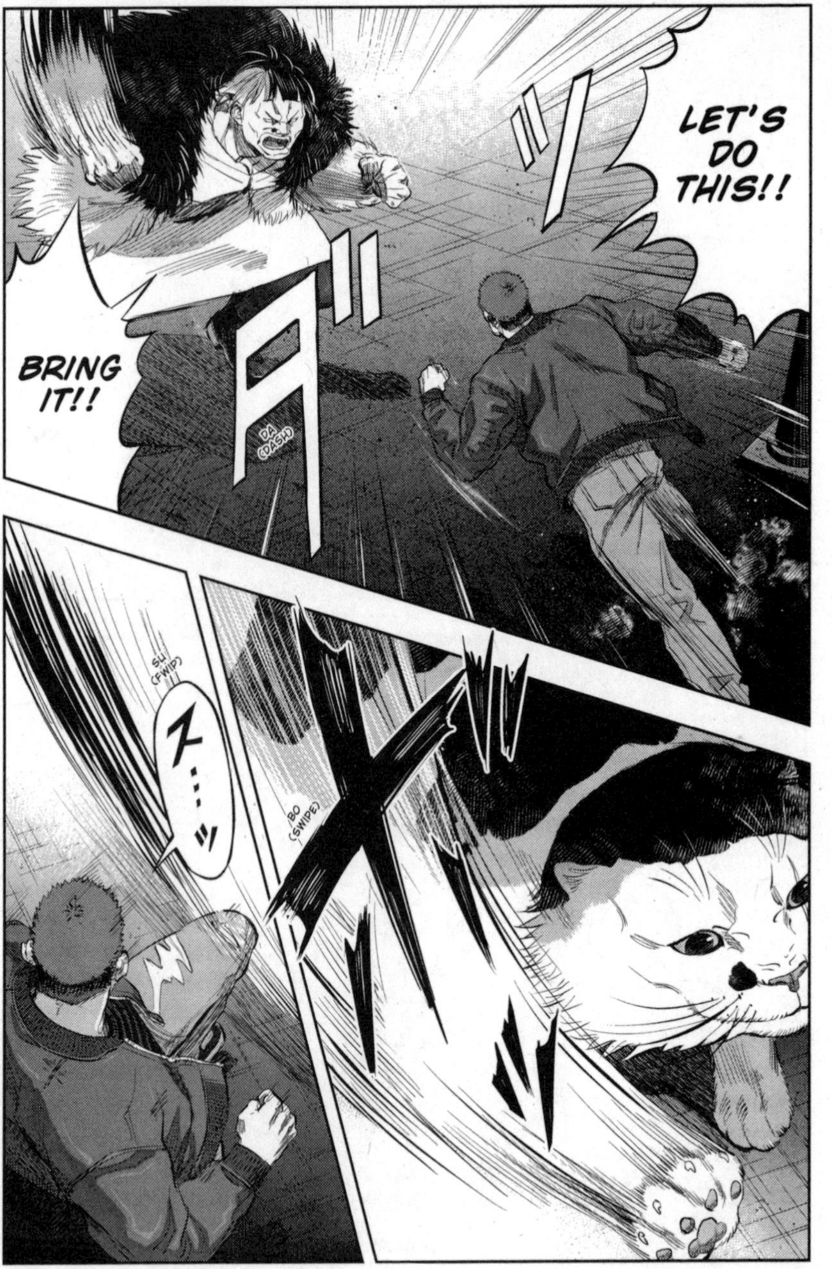
LET'S DO THIS!!
BRING IT!!
DA (DASH)
BO (SWIPE)
SU (FWIP)

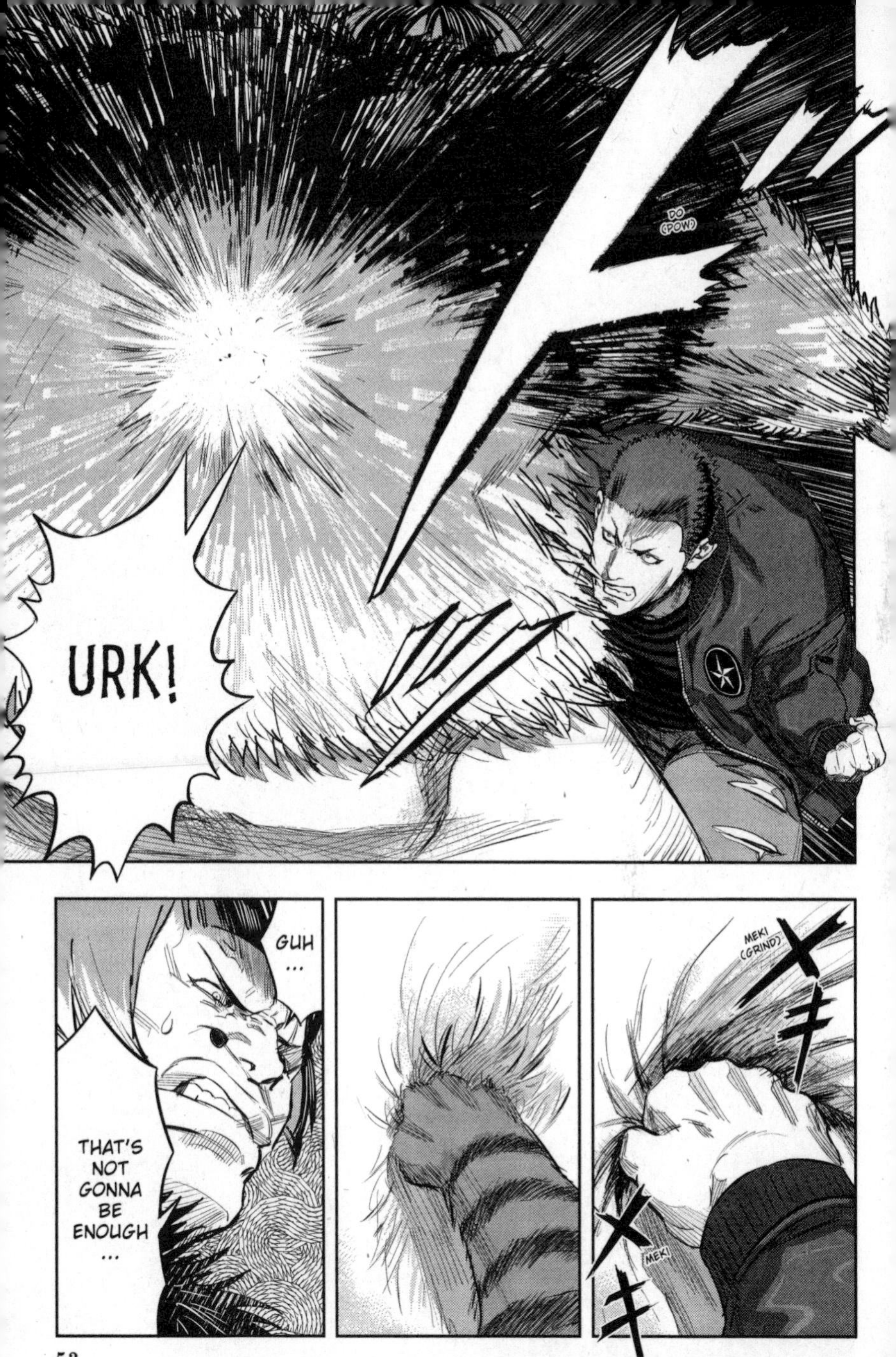
DO (POW)
URK!
MEKI (GRIND)
MEKI
GUH ...
THAT'S NOT GONNA BE ENOUGH ...

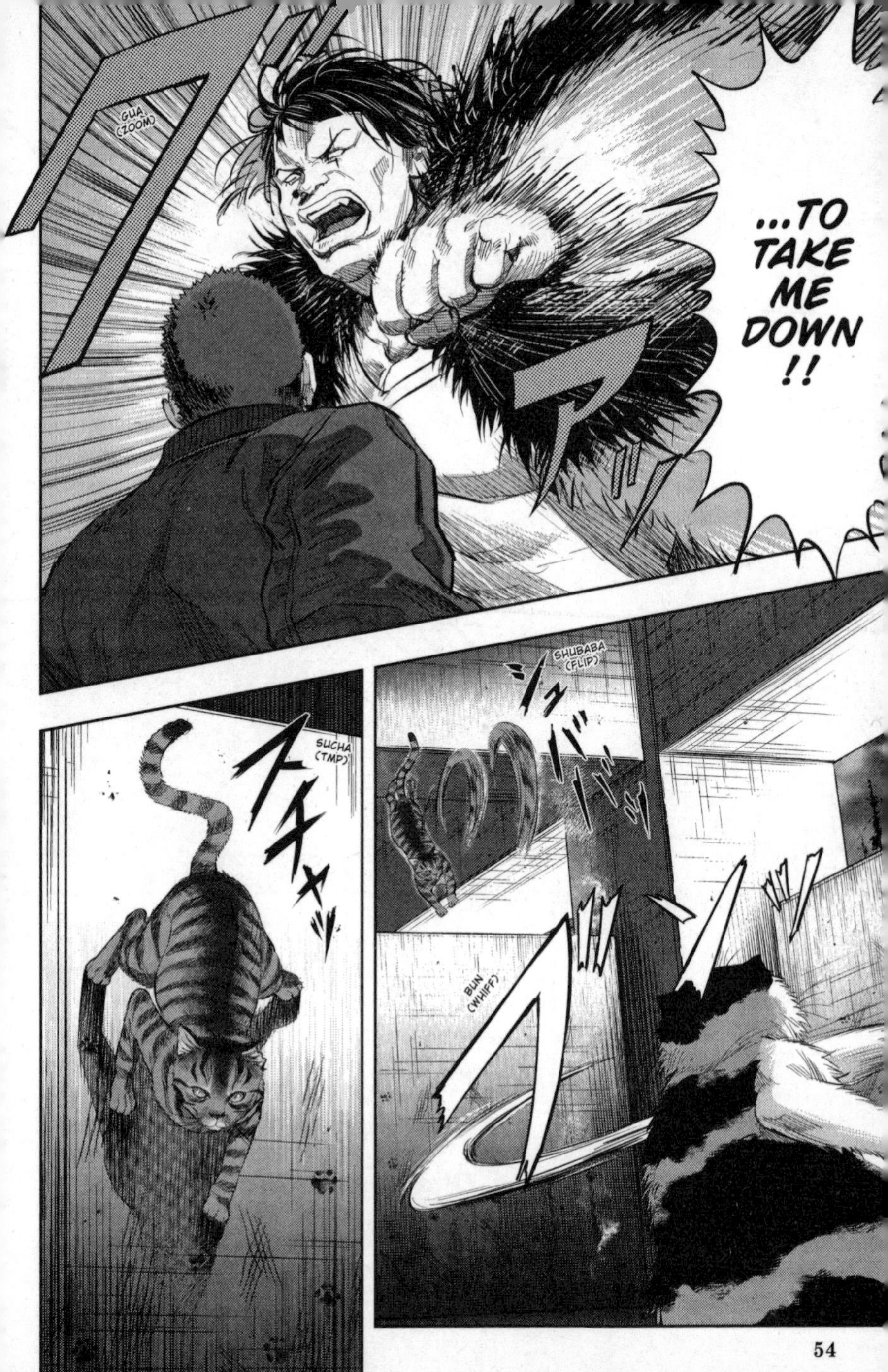
...TO TAKE ME DOWN!!
GUA (ZOOM)
SHUBABA (FLIP)
BUN (WHIFF)
SUCHA (TMP)

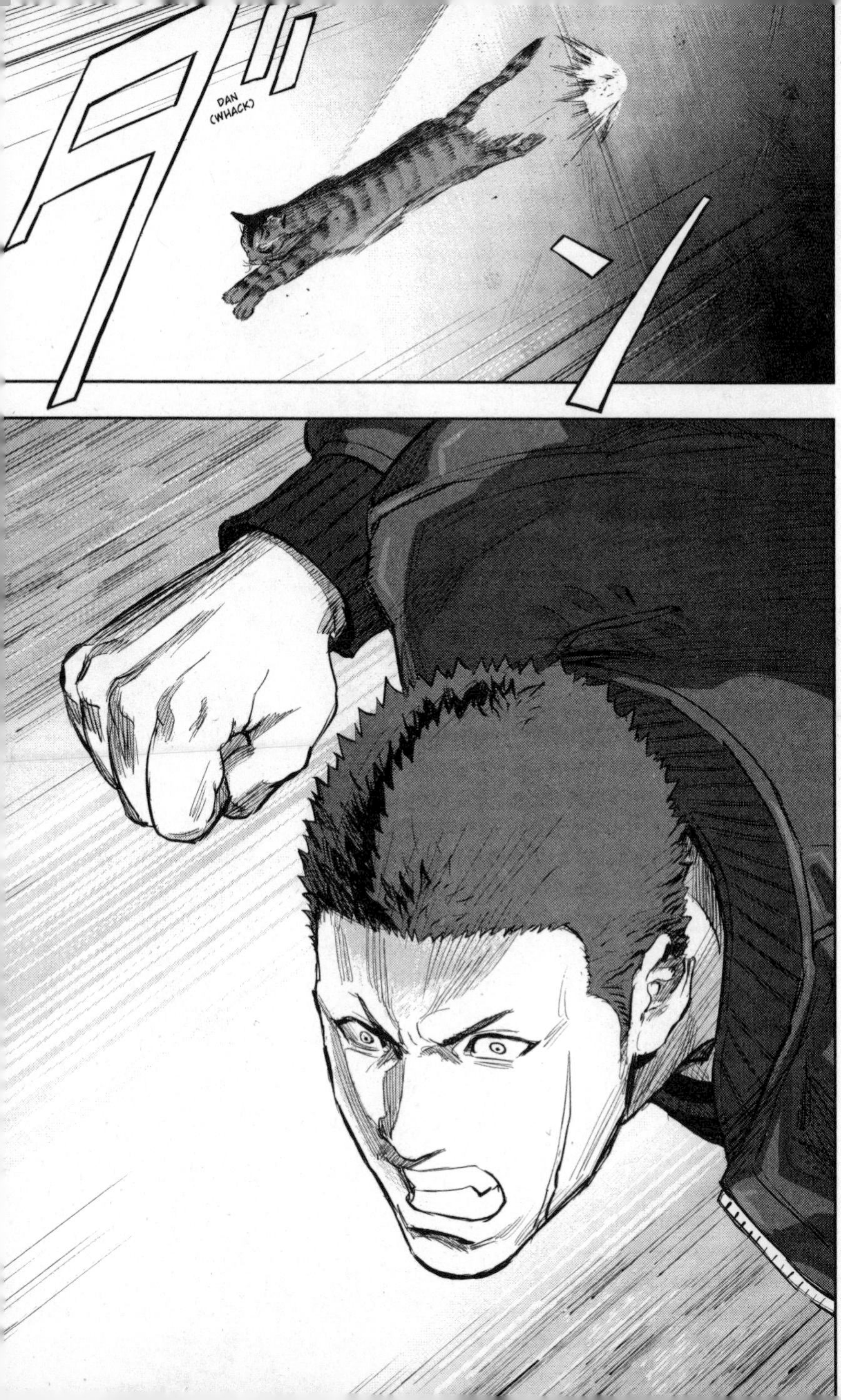
DAN
(WHACK)

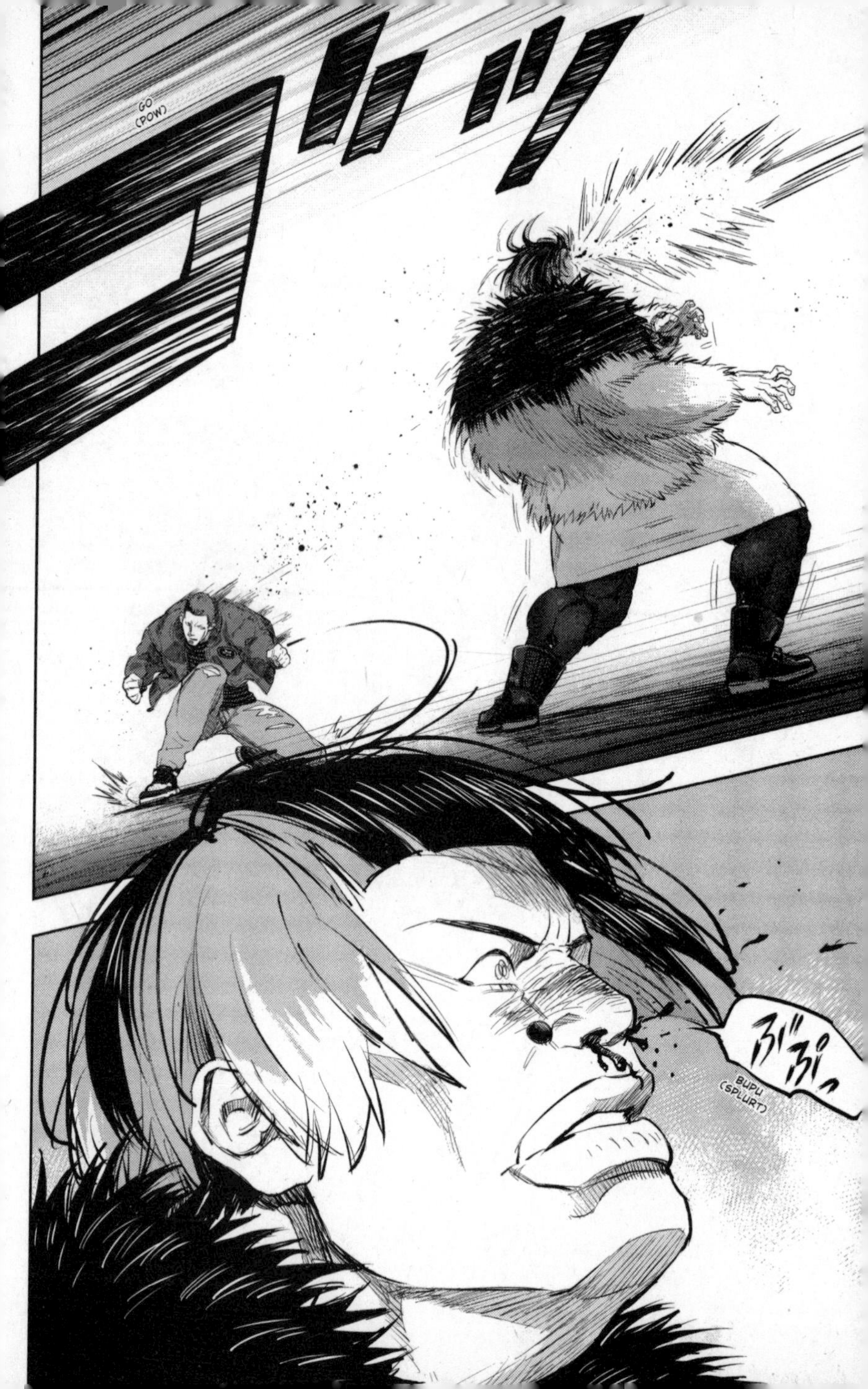
ゴッ!
GO (POW)
ぶぶっ
BUPU (SPLURT)

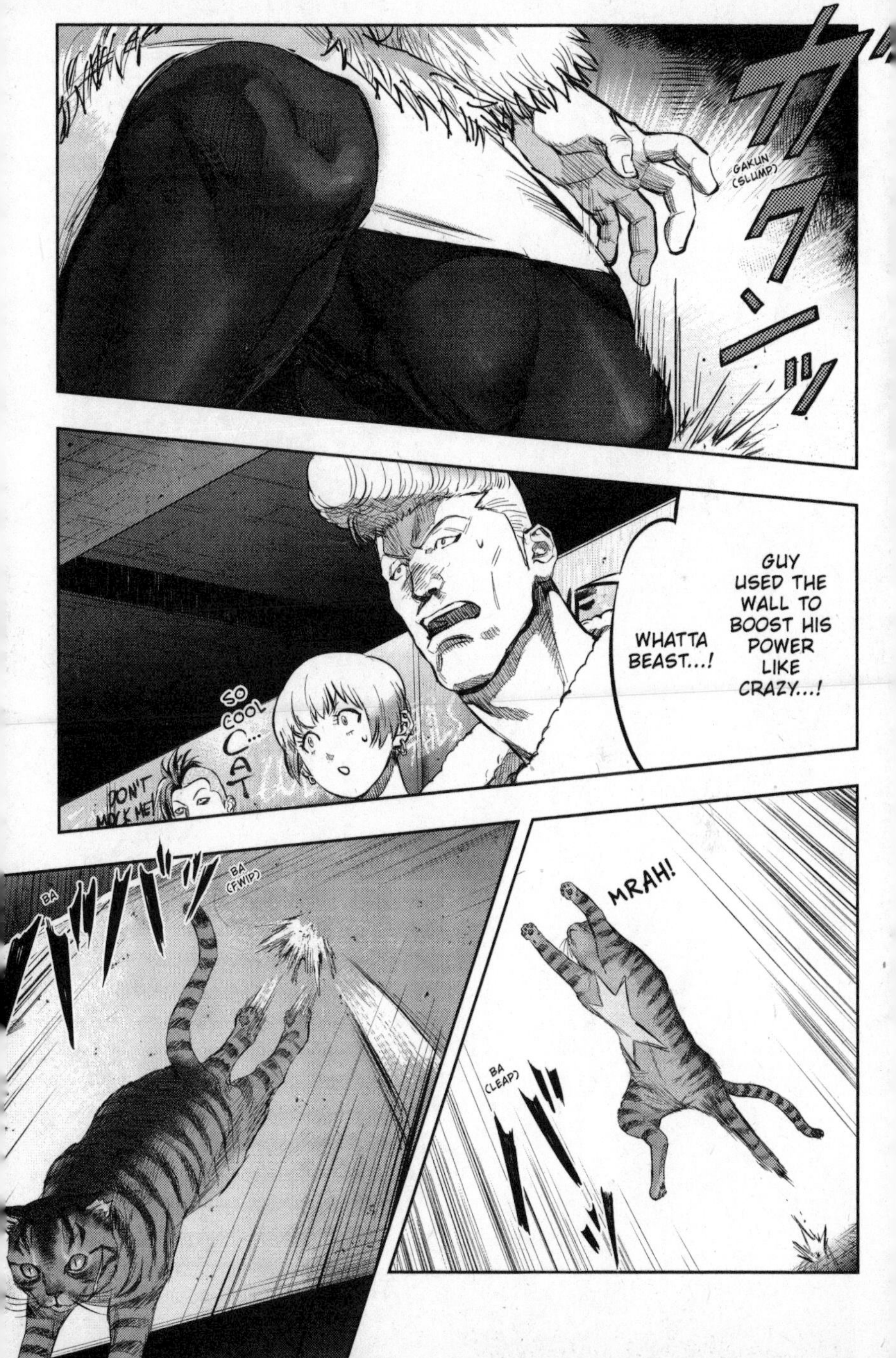

GAKUN (SLUMP)
GUY USED THE WALL TO BOOST HIS POWER LIKE CRAZY...!
WHATTA BEAST...!
SO COOL... CAT
DON'T MOCK ME!
MRAH!
BA (LEAP)
BA (FWIP)
BA

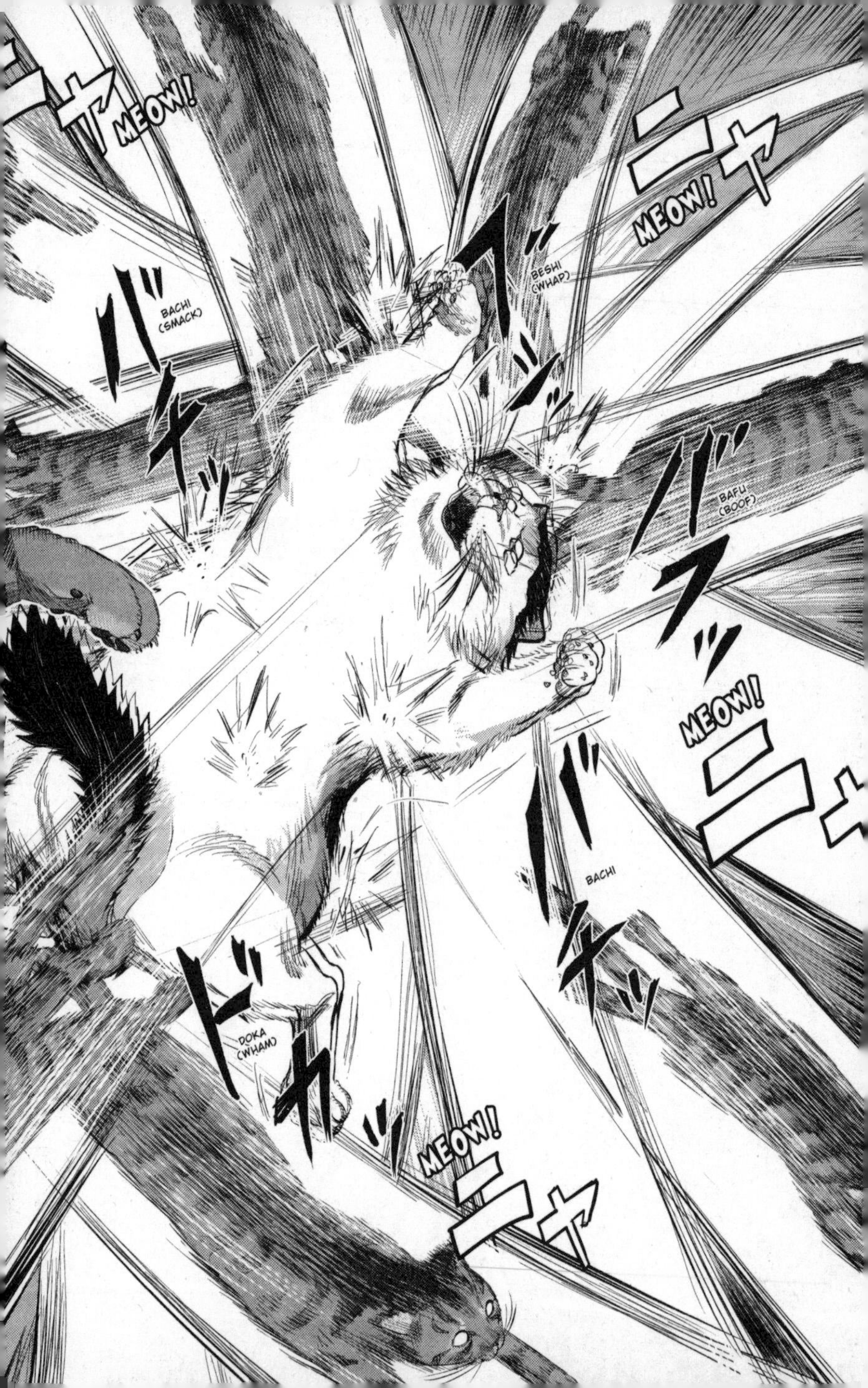
ニャ
MEOW!
BESHI (WHAP)
ニャ
MEOW!
BACHI (SMACK)
バチッ
BAFU (BOOF)
バフッ
MEOW!
ニャ
BACHI
バチッ
DOKA (WHAM)
ドカッ
MEOW!
ニャ

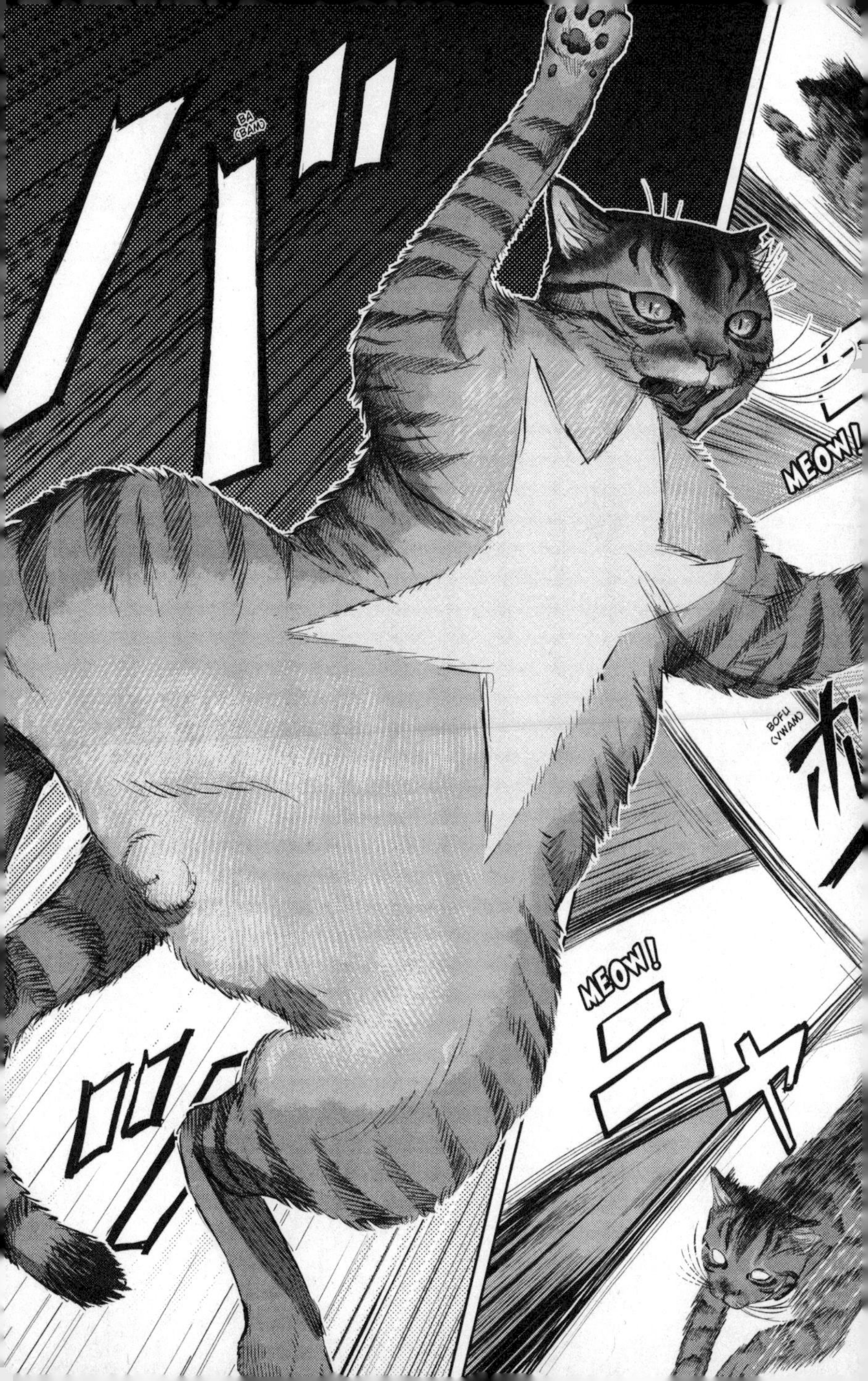
BA (BAM)
MEOW!
BOFU (VWAM)
MEOW!

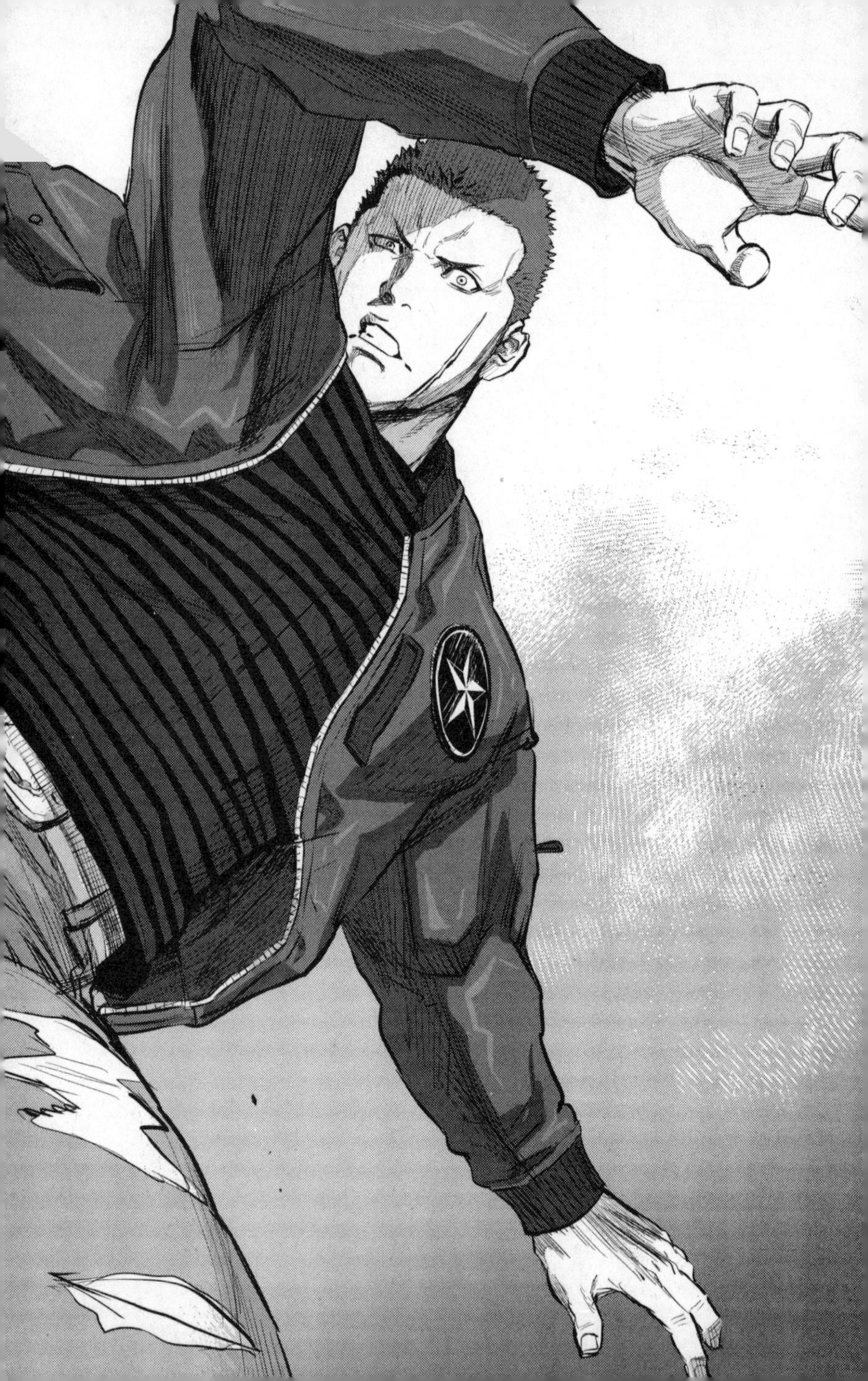

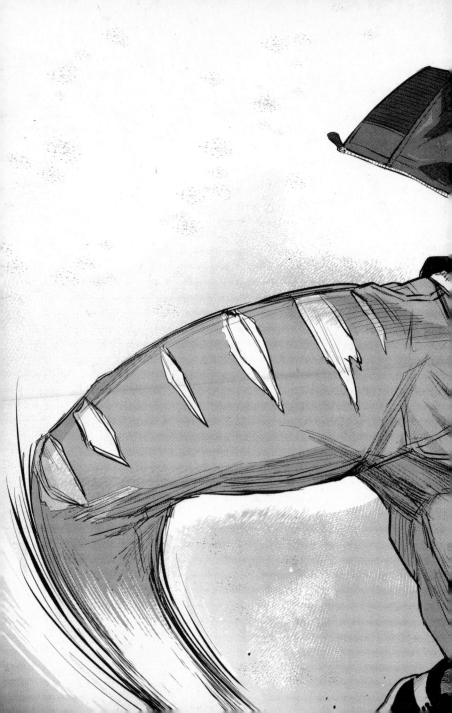

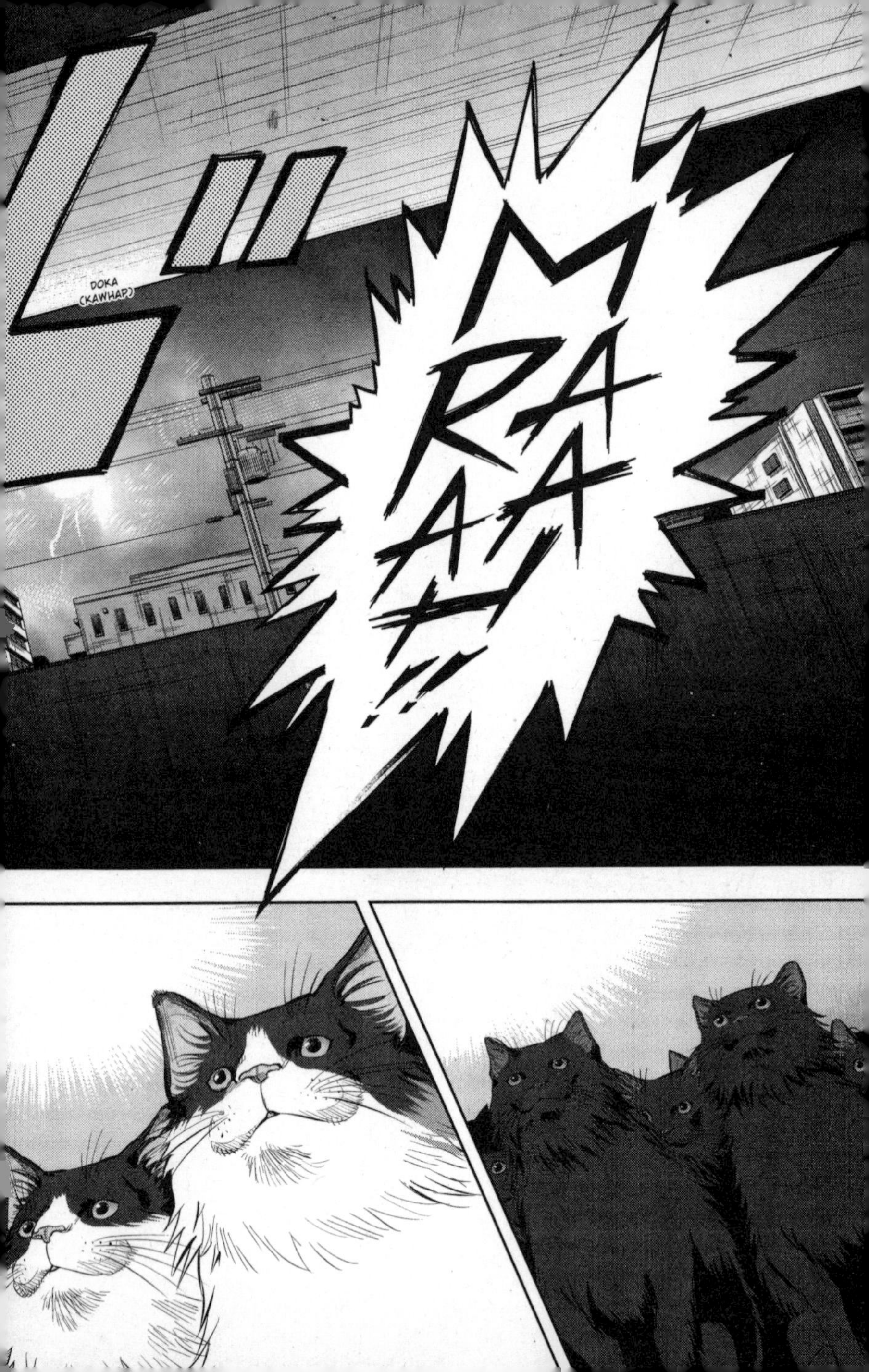
MRAAAH!!
DOKA
(KAWHAP)

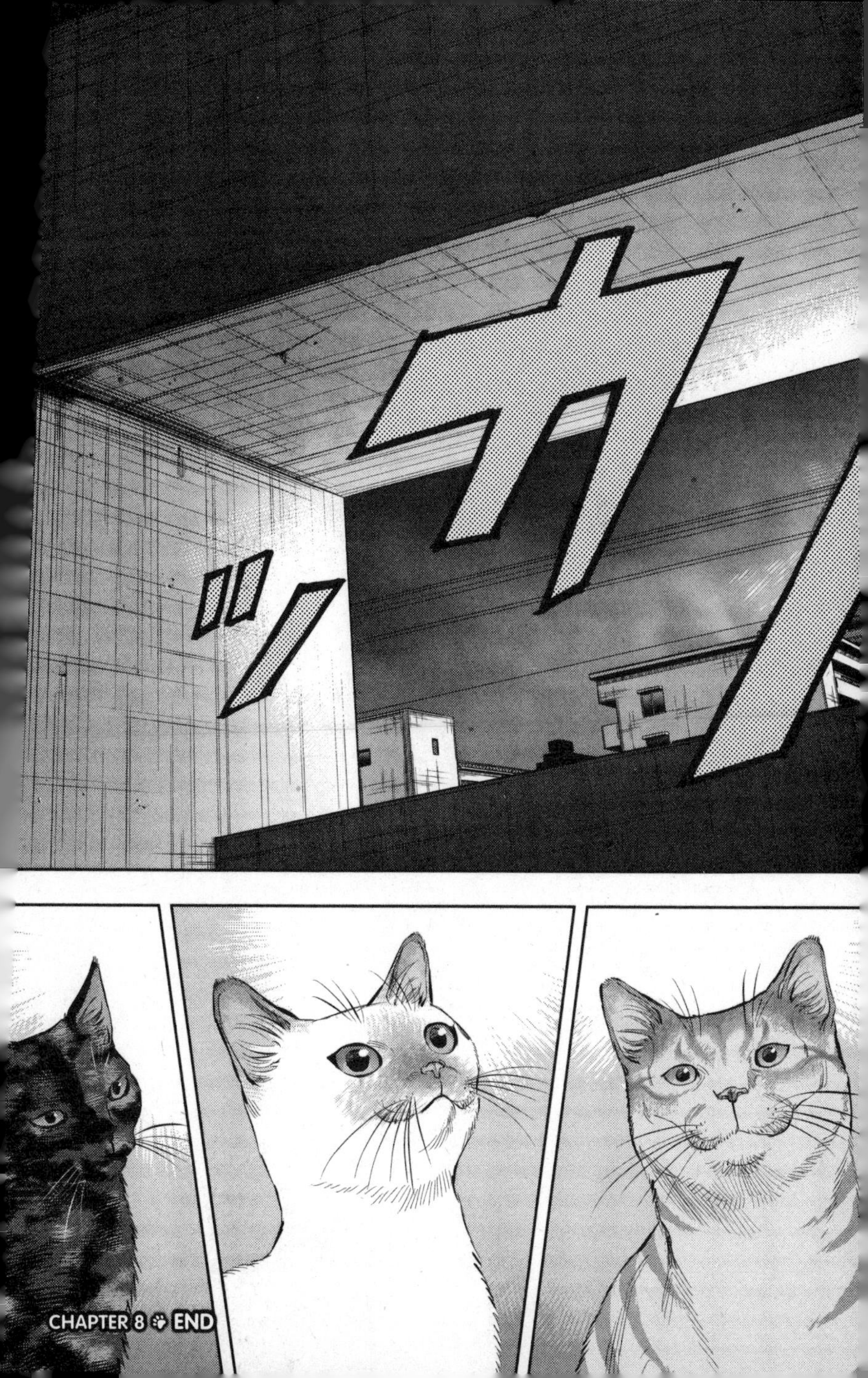
CHAPTER 8 END

NYANKEES 🐾

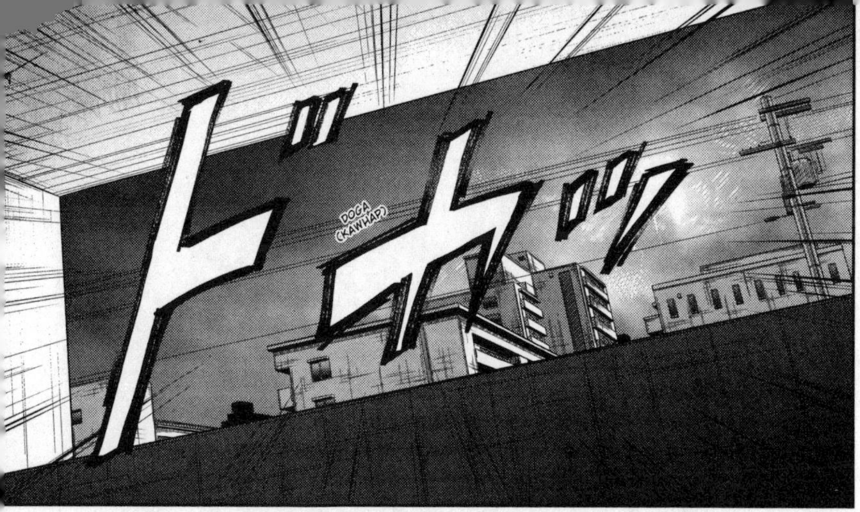
ドガッ
DOGA (KAWHAP)

CHAPTER 9 🐾 CONNYECTION

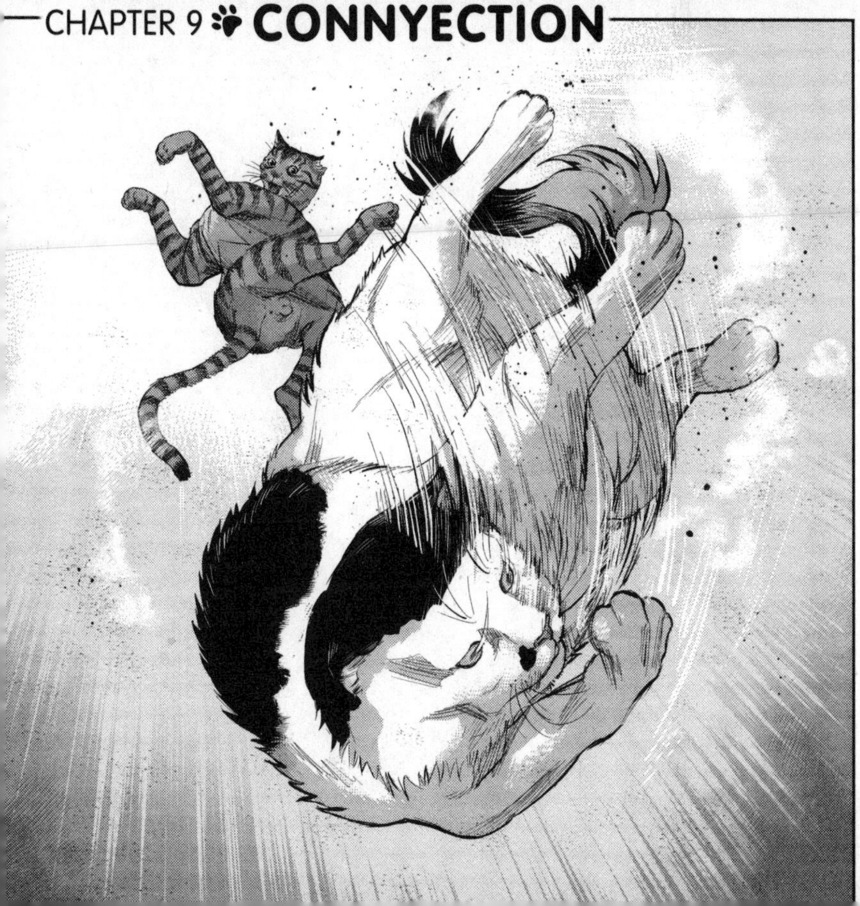

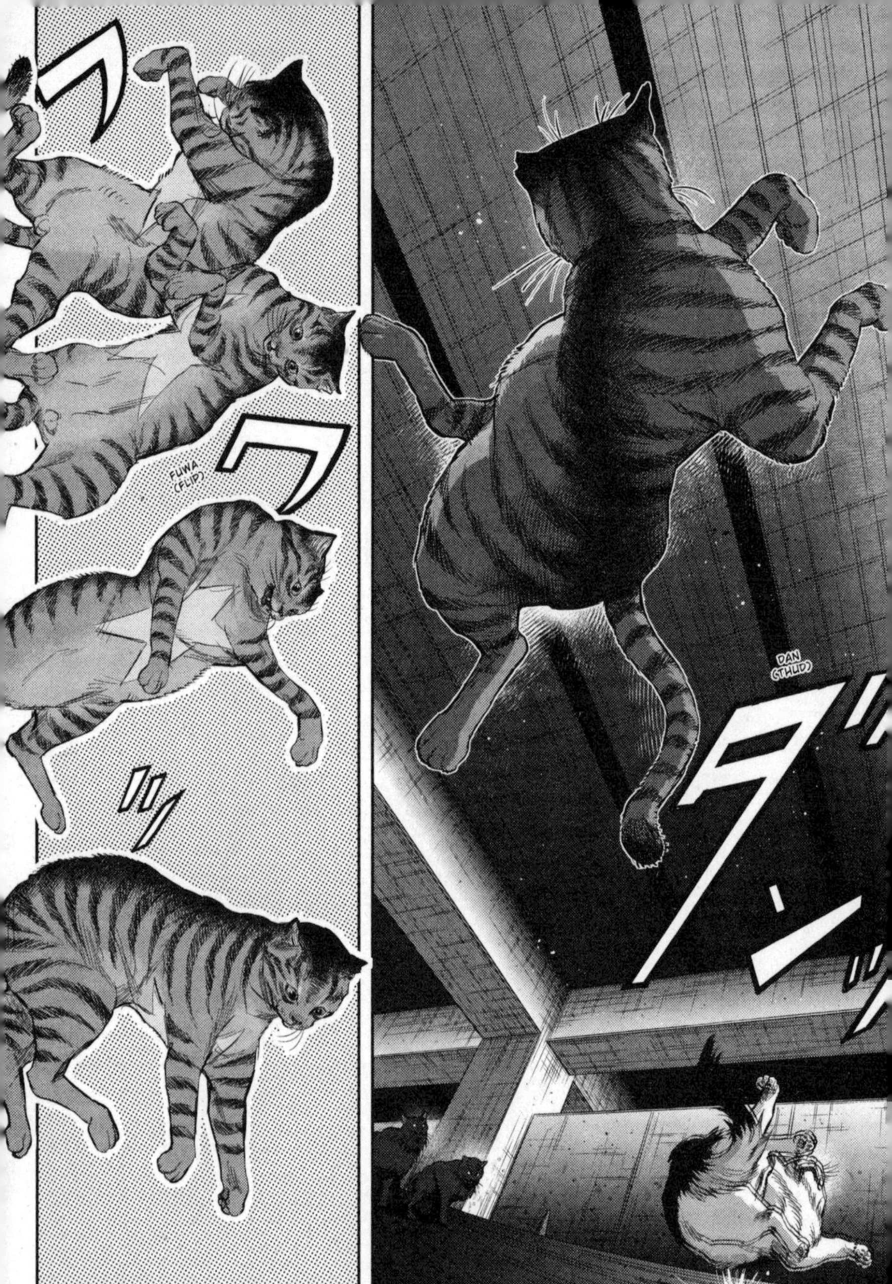
DAN (THUD)
FUWA (FLIP)

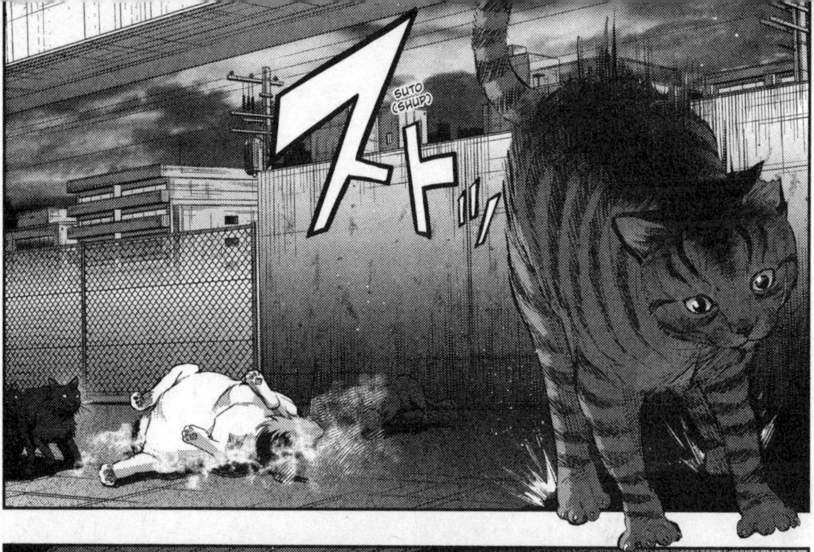
SUTO (SHUP)

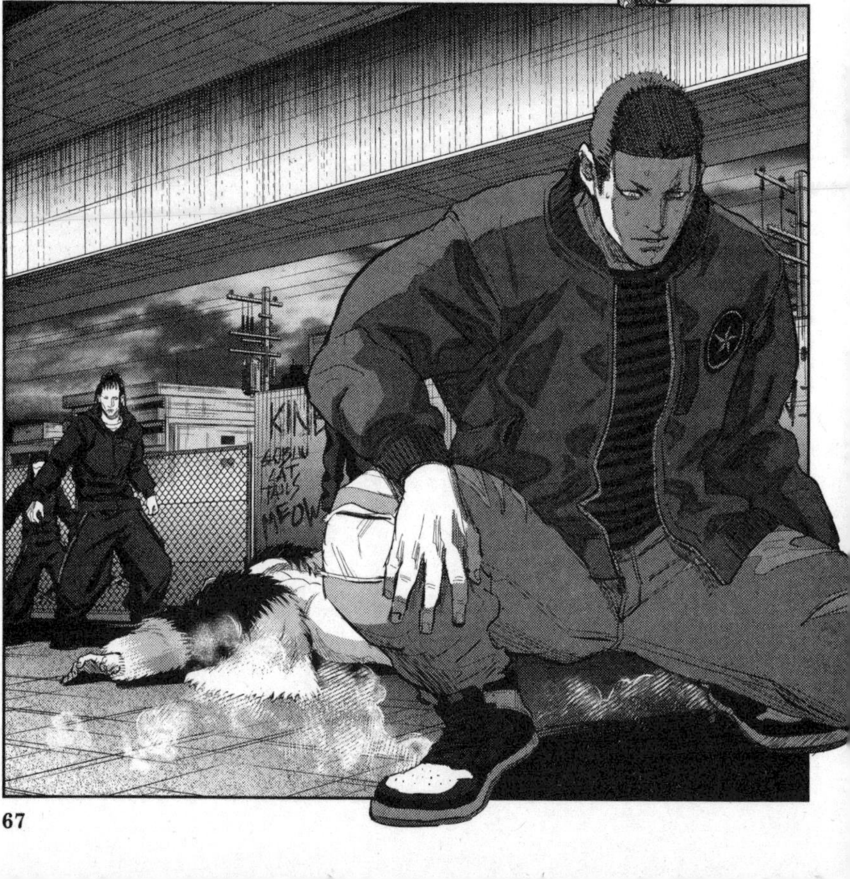
GOBLIN CAT TAILS
MEOW

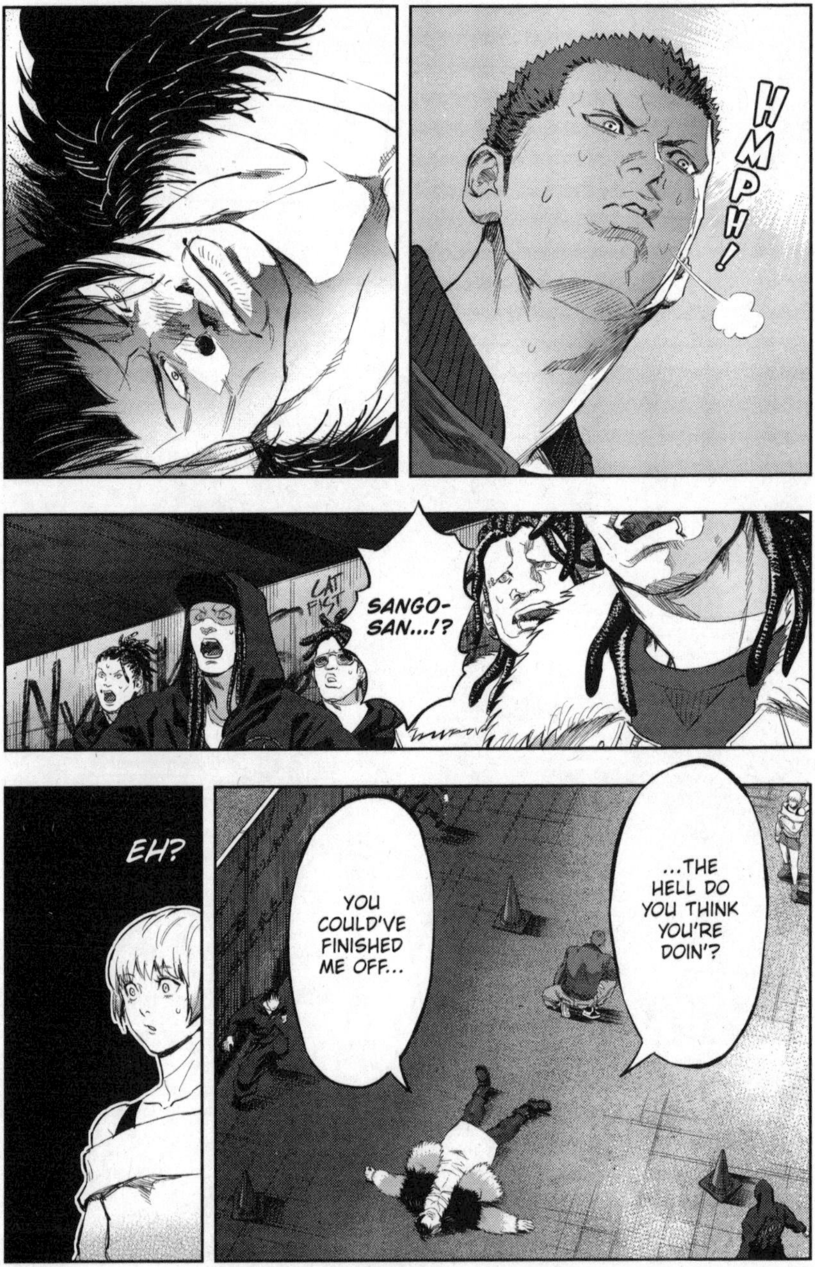
HMPH!
CAT FIST
SANGO-SAN...!?
...THE HELL DO YOU THINK YOU'RE DOIN'?
YOU COULD'VE FINISHED ME OFF...
EH?

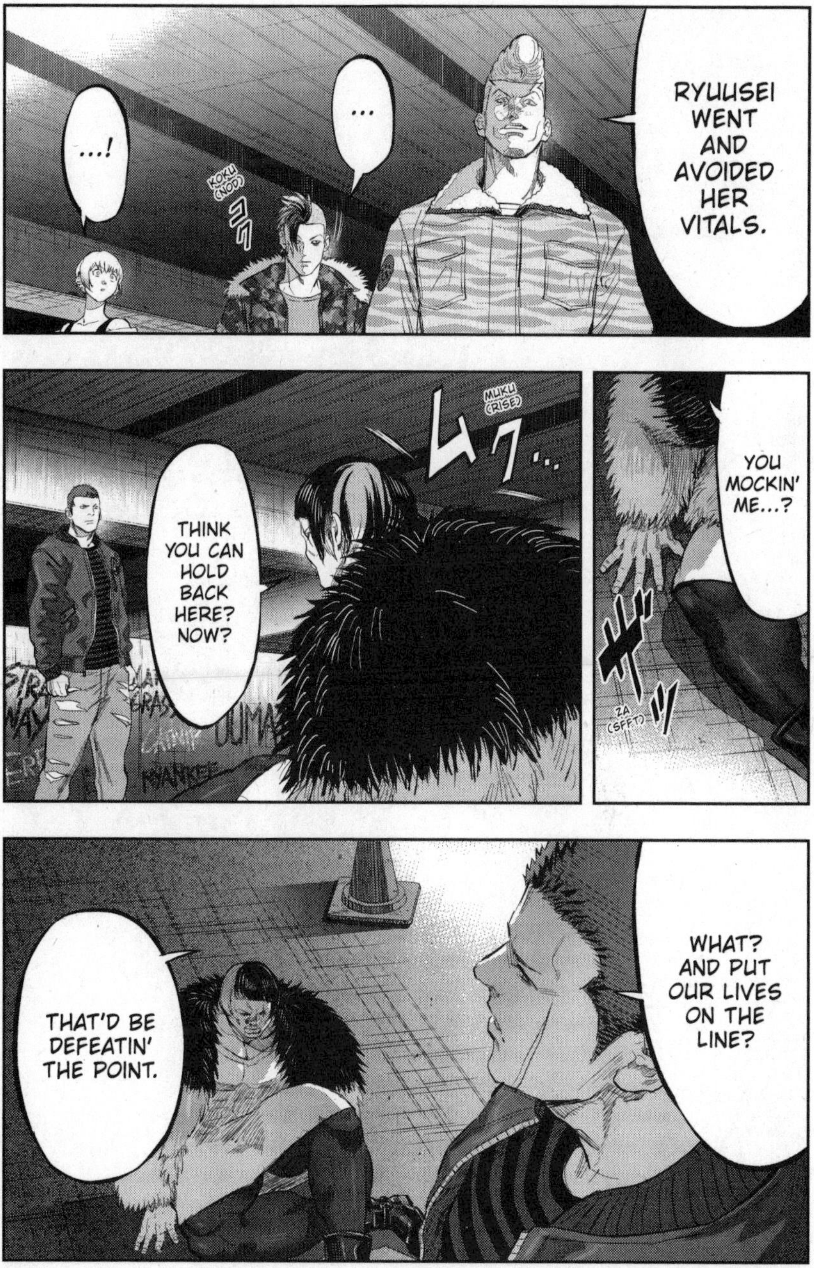
RYUUSEI WENT AND AVOIDED HER VITALS.
...
KOKU (NOD)
...!
YOU MOCKIN' ME...?
ZA (SFFT)
MUKU (RISE)
THINK YOU CAN HOLD BACK HERE? NOW?
WHAT? AND PUT OUR LIVES ON THE LINE?
THAT'D BE DEFEATIN' THE POINT.

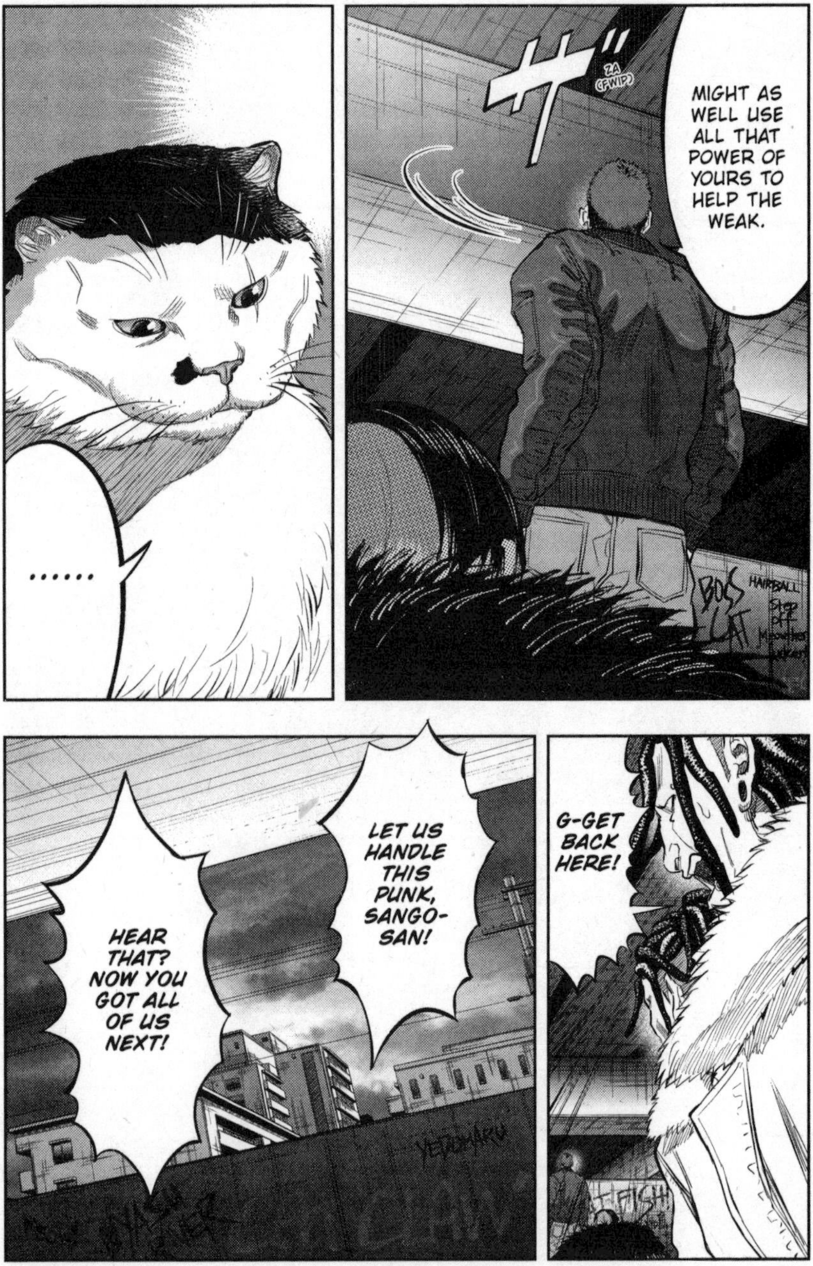
ZA (FWIP)
MIGHT AS WELL USE ALL THAT POWER OF YOURS TO HELP THE WEAK.
HAIRBALL
......
G-GET BACK HERE!
LET US HANDLE THIS PUNK, SANGO-SAN!
HEAR THAT? NOW YOU GOT ALL OF US NEXT!

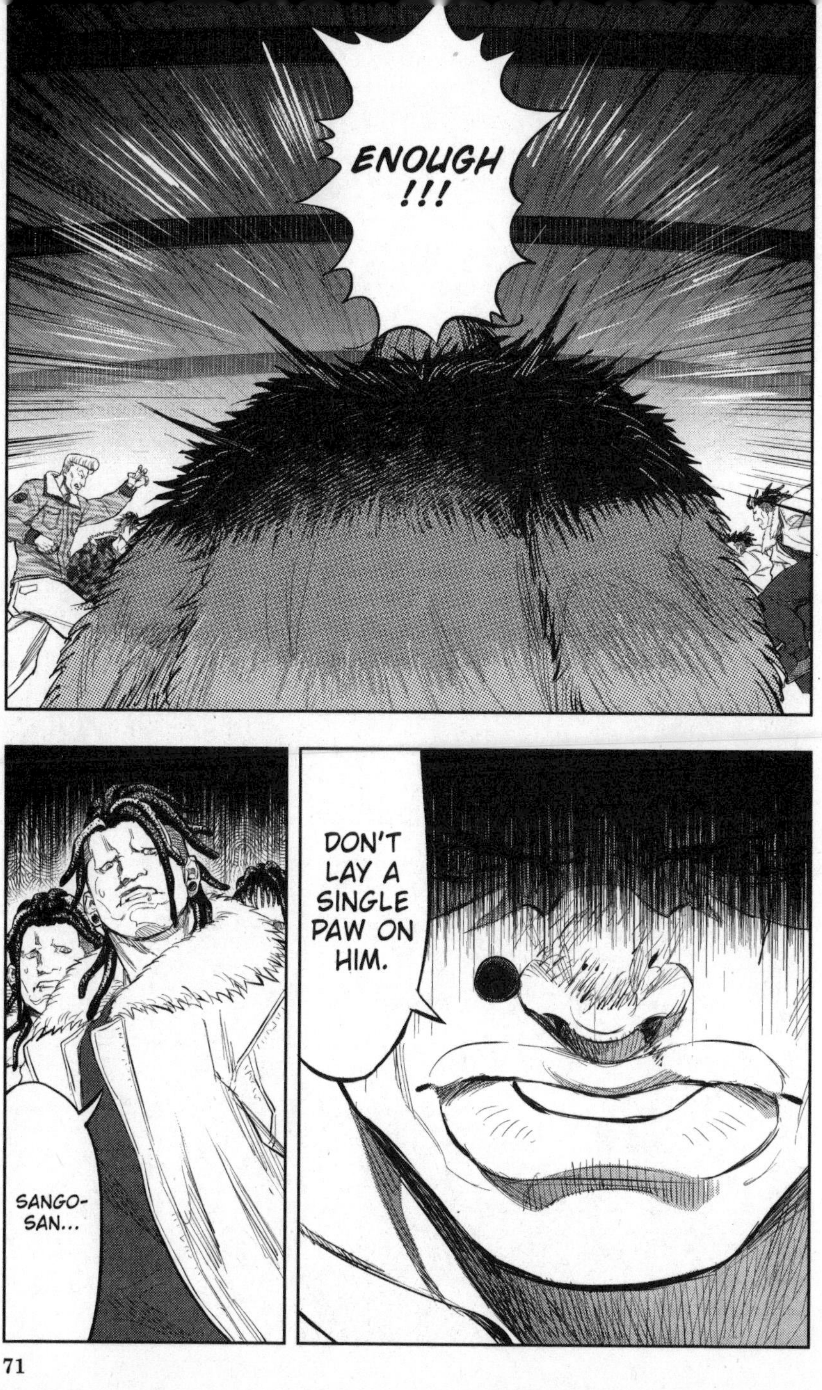
ENOUGH !!!
DON'T LAY A SINGLE PAW ON HIM.
SANGO-SAN...

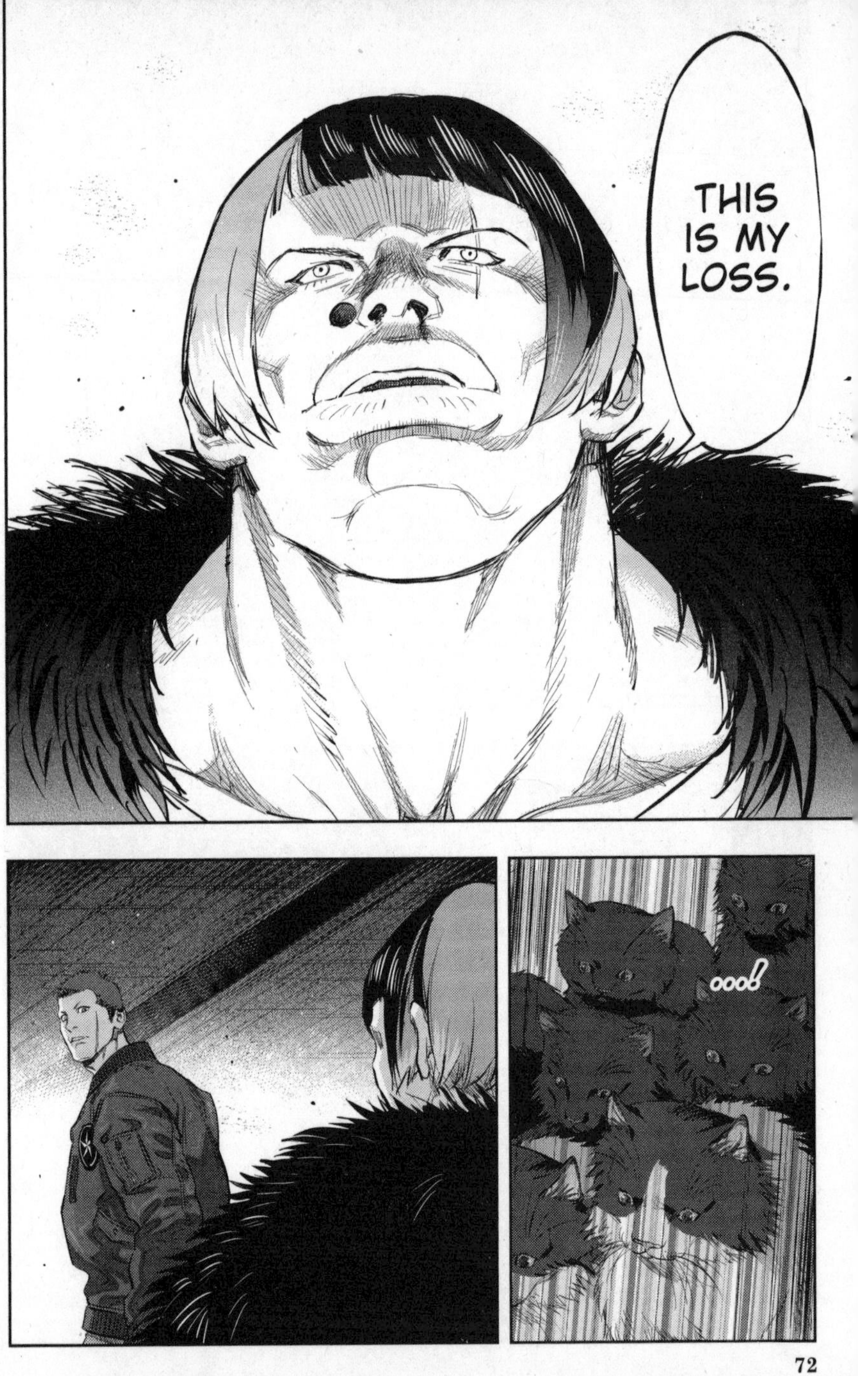
THIS IS MY LOSS.
OOOB

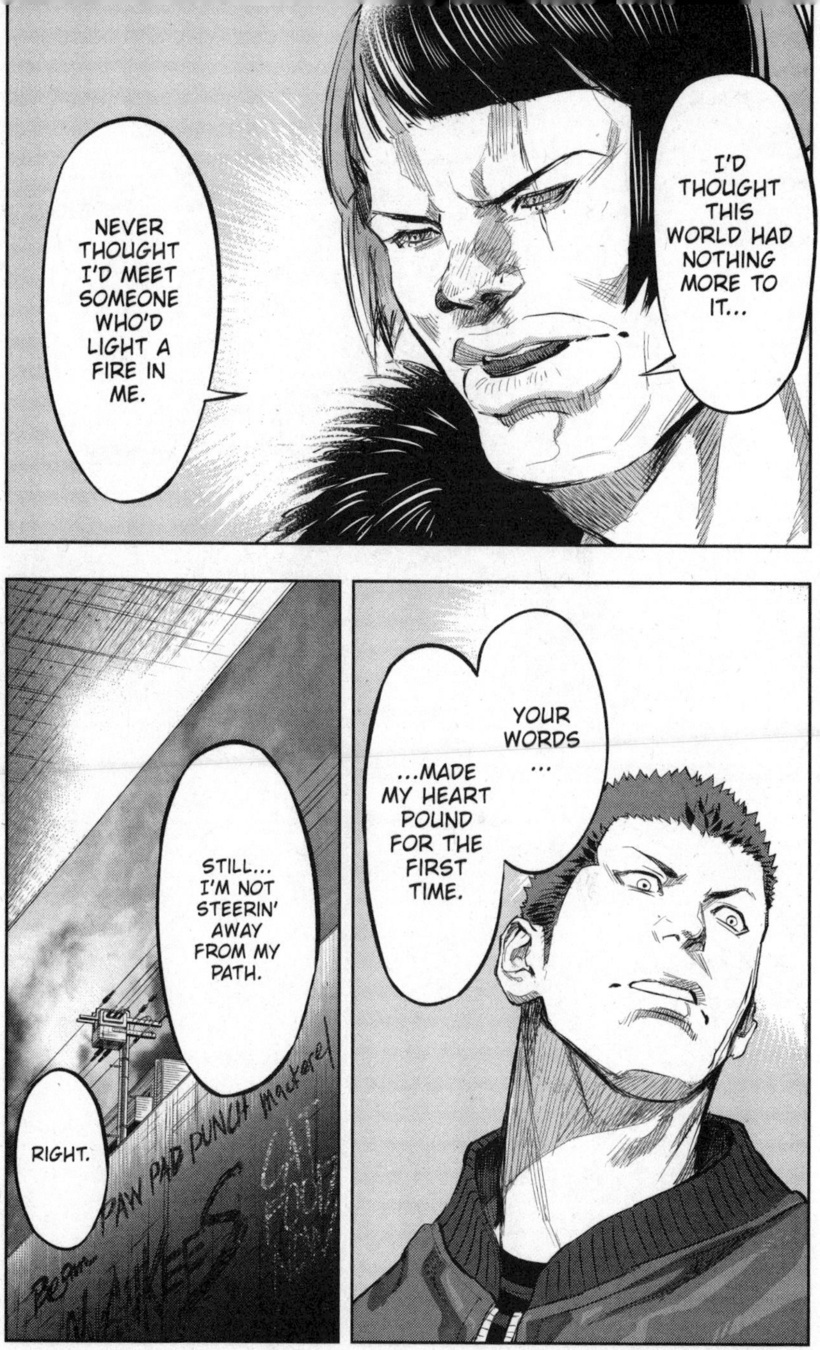

I'D THOUGHT THIS WORLD HAD NOTHING MORE TO IT...
NEVER THOUGHT I'D MEET SOMEONE WHO'D LIGHT A FIRE IN ME.
YOUR WORDS ...
...MADE MY HEART POUND FOR THE FIRST TIME.
STILL... I'M NOT STEERIN' AWAY FROM MY PATH.
RIGHT.
PAW PAD PUNCH

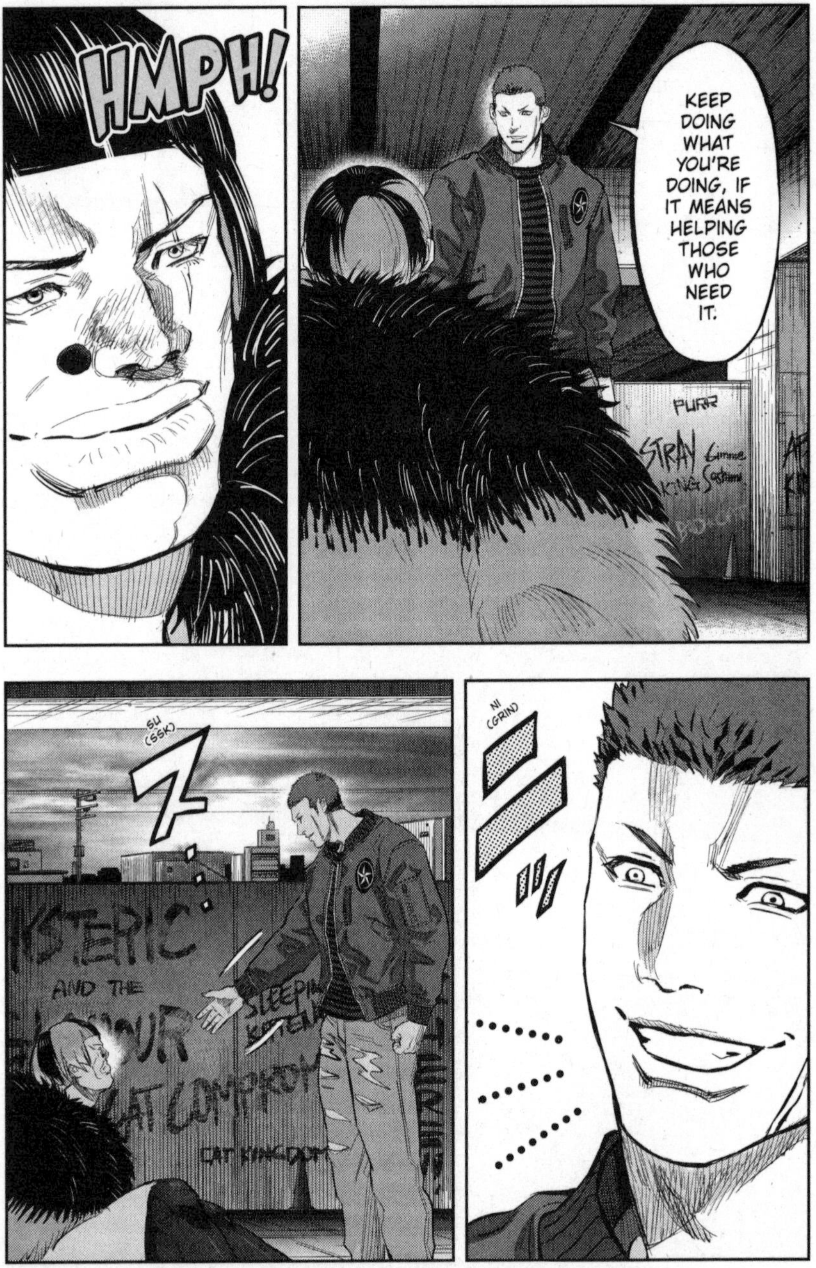
KEEP DOING WHAT YOU'RE DOING, IF IT MEANS HELPING THOSE WHO NEED IT.
PURR
STRAY
HMPH!
NI
(GRIN)
......
SU
(SSK)
AND THE
CAT KINGDOM

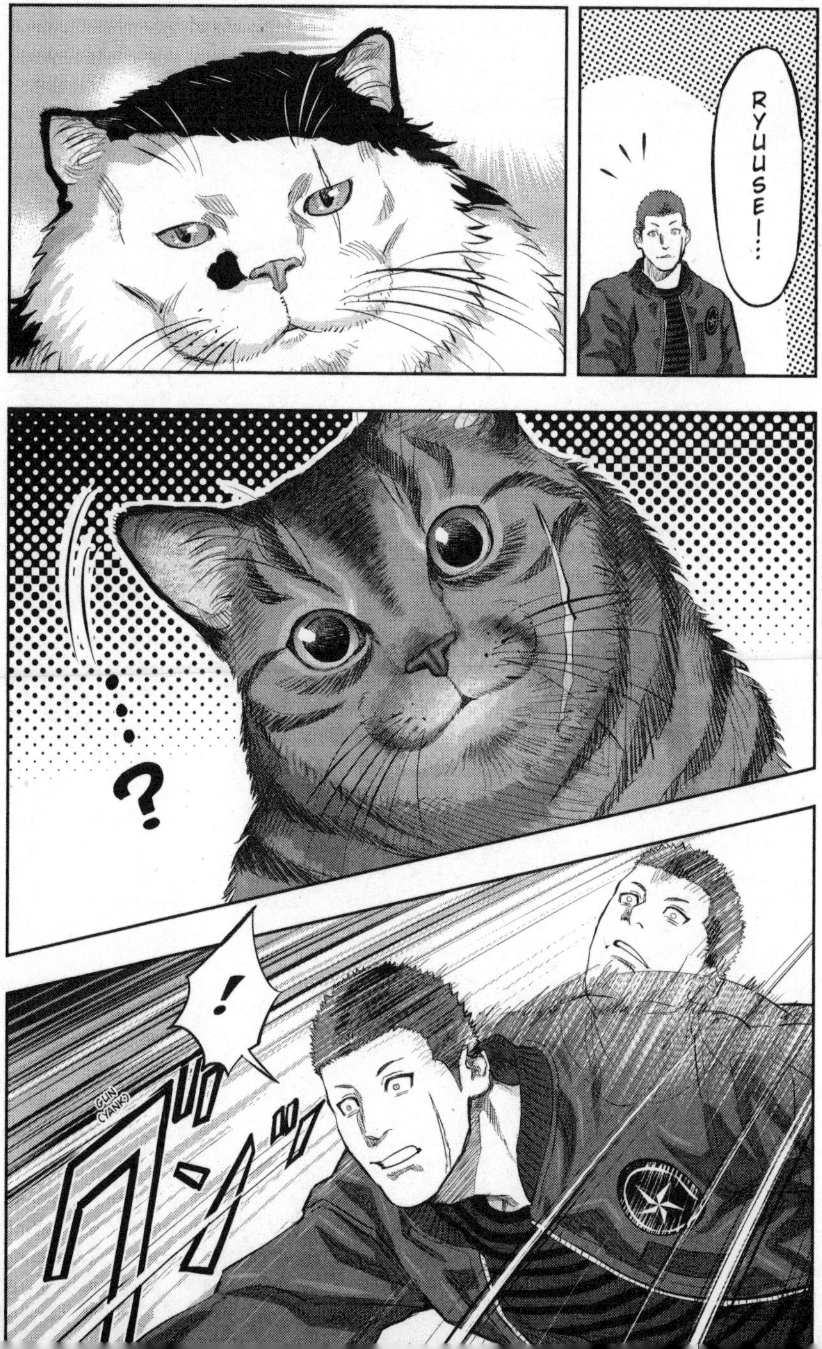
RYUUSEI...
...?
!
GUN (YANK)
グンッ

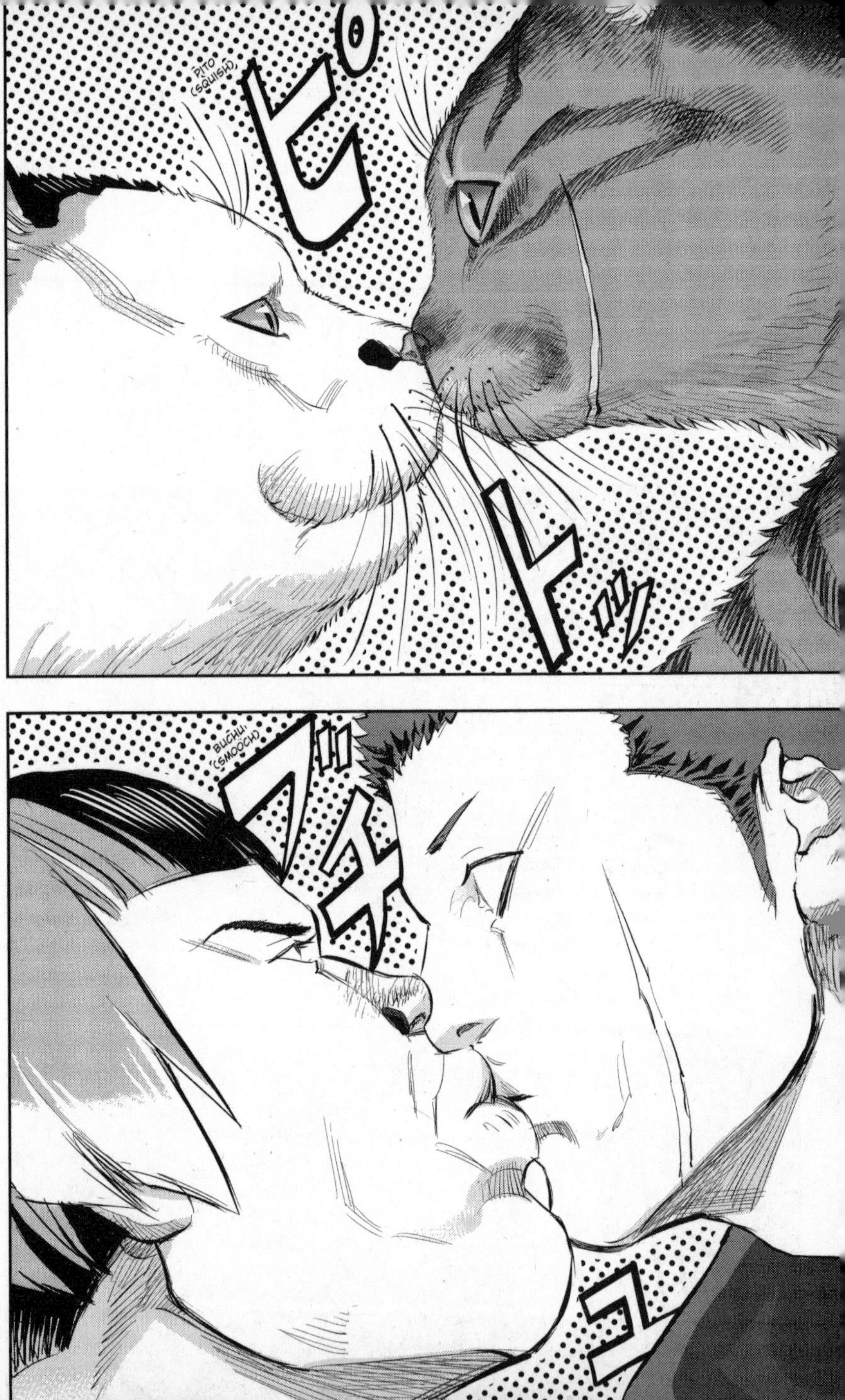
PITO (SQUISH)
BUCHU (SMOOCH)

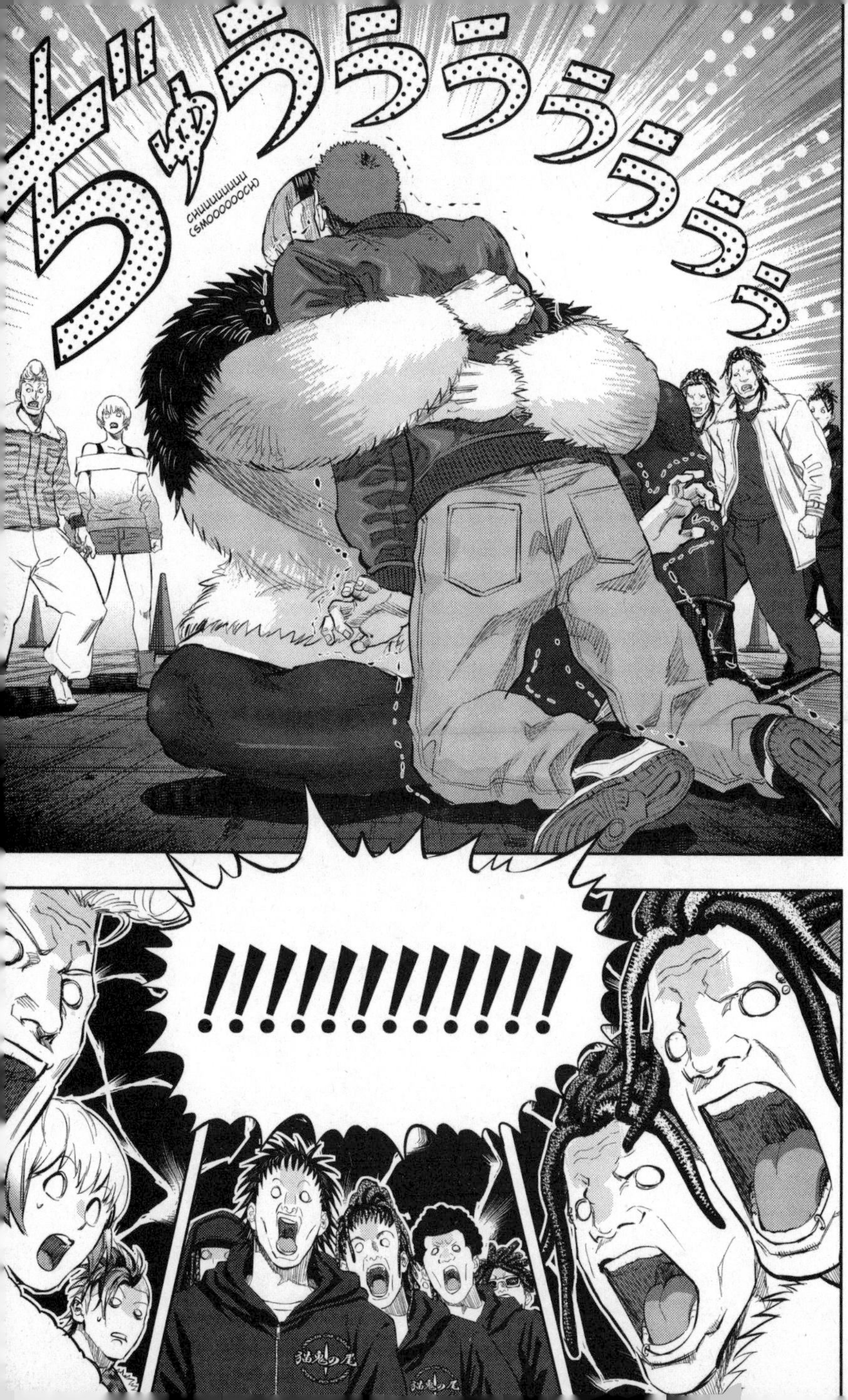
ぢゅううううううう
CHUUUUUUUUU
(SMOOOOOOOCH)
!!!!!!!!!!!!!!

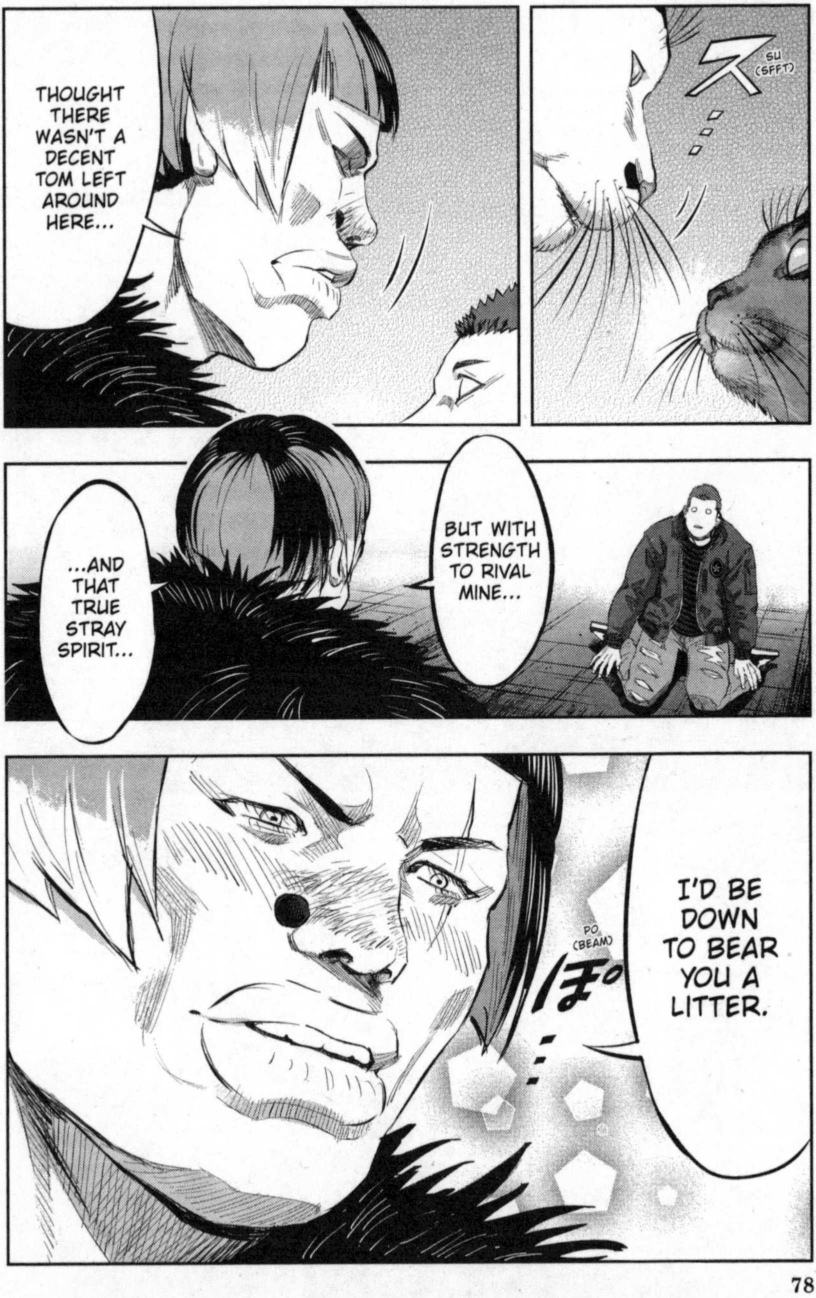
ス
SU (SFFT)
THOUGHT THERE WASN'T A DECENT TOM LEFT AROUND HERE...
BUT WITH STRENGTH TO RIVAL MINE...
...AND THAT TRUE STRAY SPIRIT...
I'D BE DOWN TO BEAR YOU A LITTER.
PO (BEAM)
ぽ

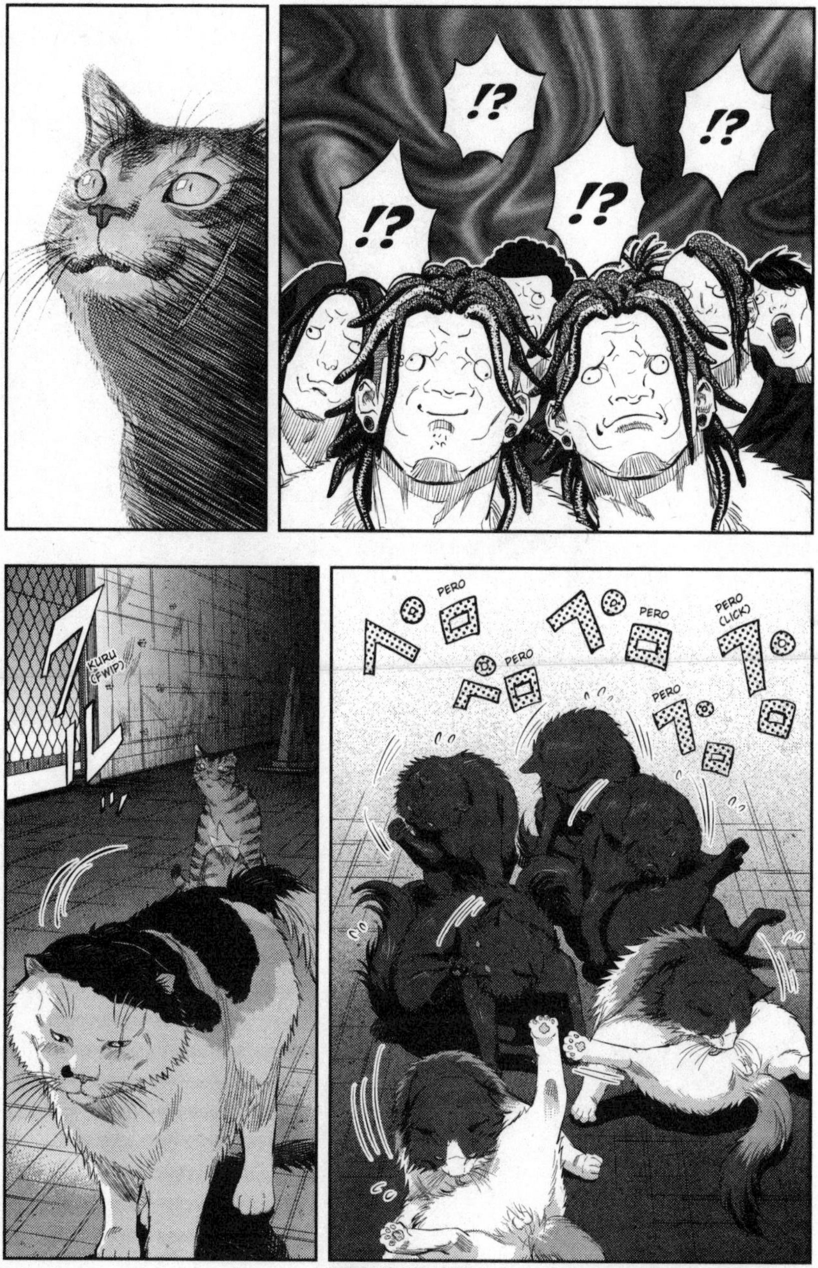
!?
!?
!?
!?
PERO (LICK)
PERO
PERO
PERO
PERO
KURU (FWIP)

※ WHEN AGITATED, CATS WILL GROOM THEMSELVES IN ORDER TO CALM DOWN.

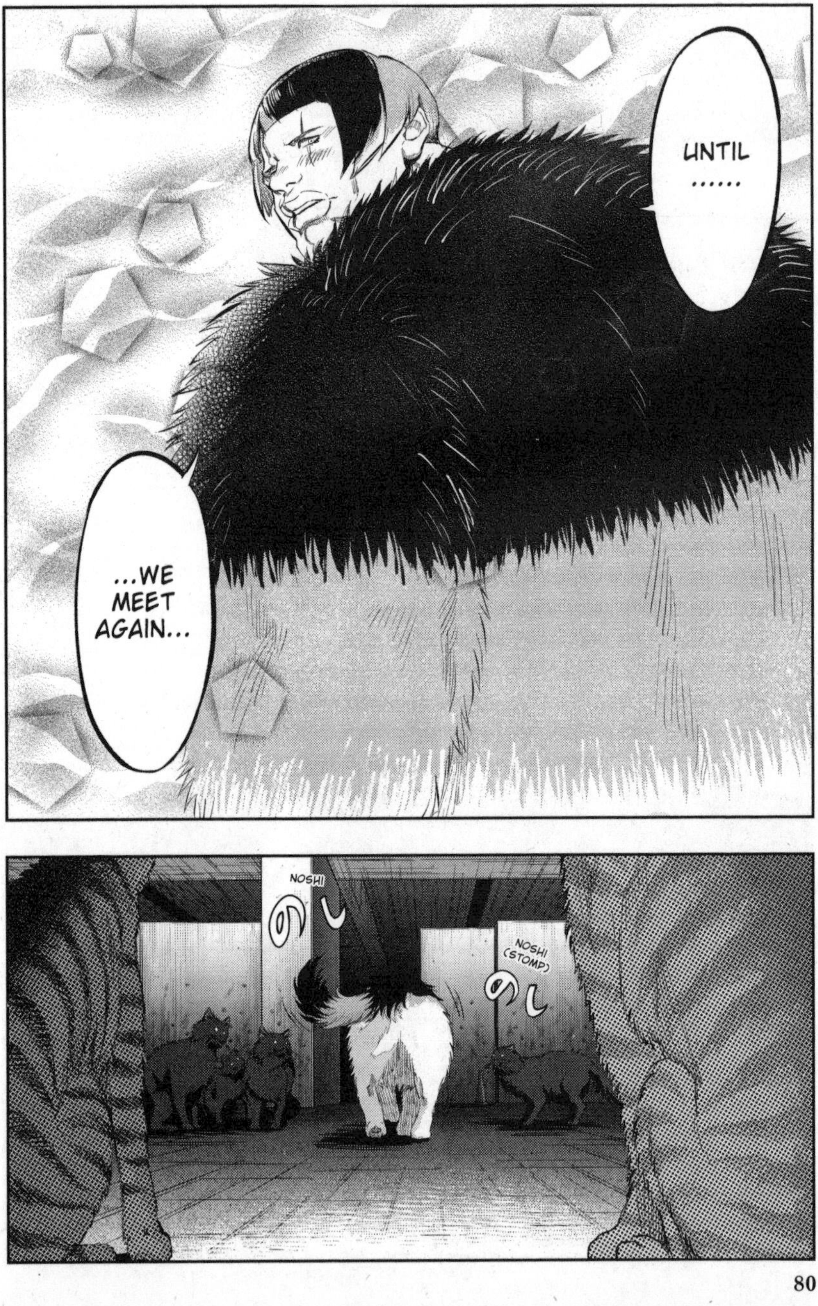
UNTIL ......
...WE MEET AGAIN...
NOSHI (STOMP)
のし
NOSHI
のし

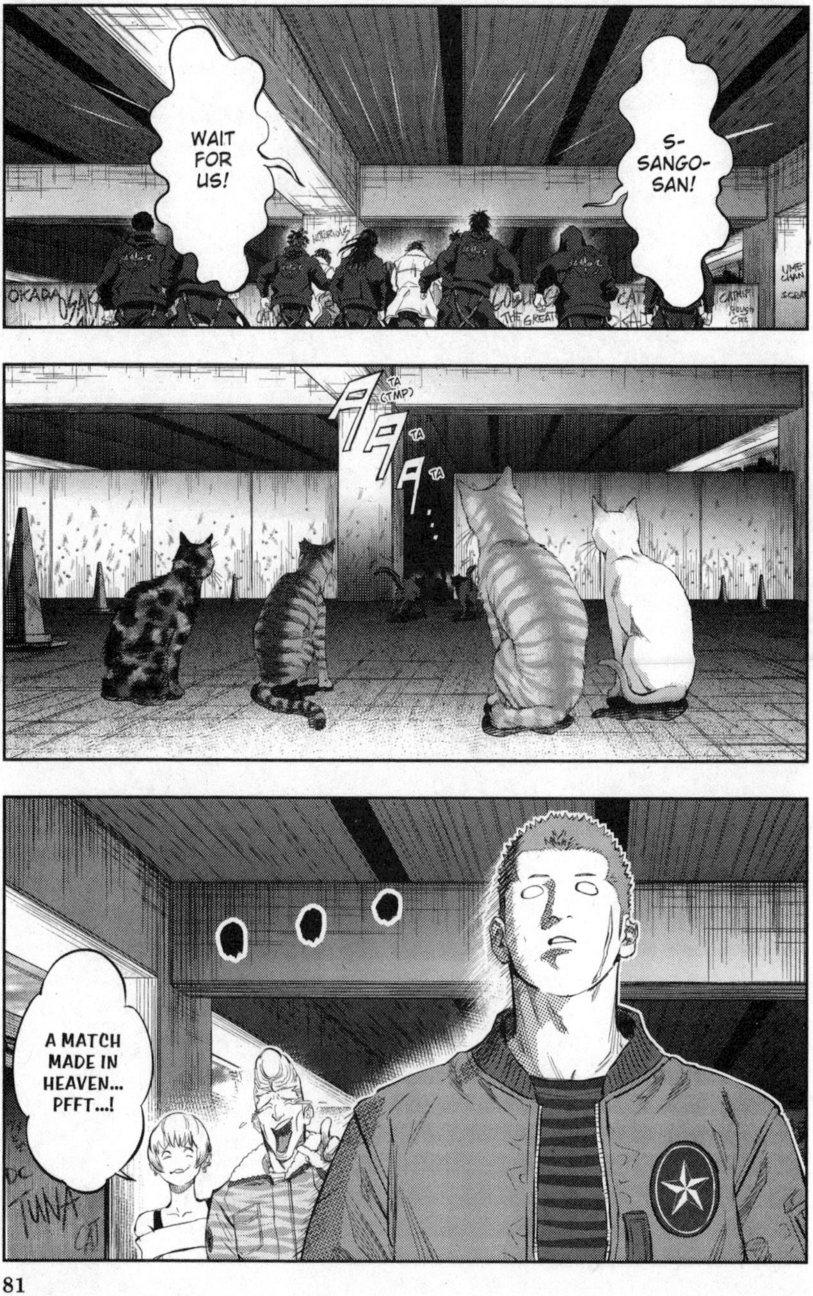
S-SANGO-SAN!
WAIT FOR US!
TA (TMP)
TA
TA
A MATCH MADE IN HEAVEN... PFFT...!
TUNA

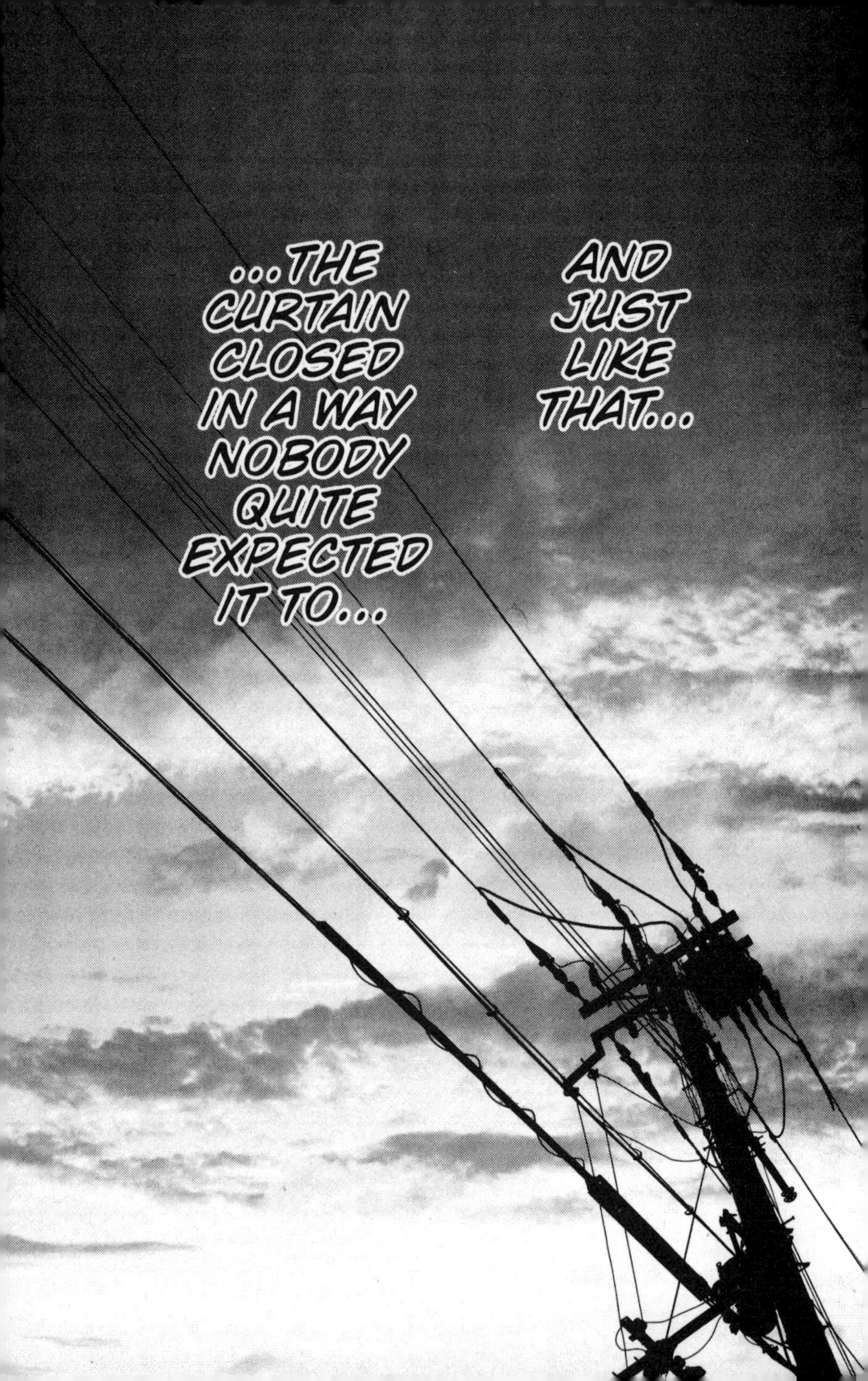
AND JUST LIKE THAT...
...THE CURTAIN CLOSED IN A WAY NOBODY QUITE EXPECTED IT TO...

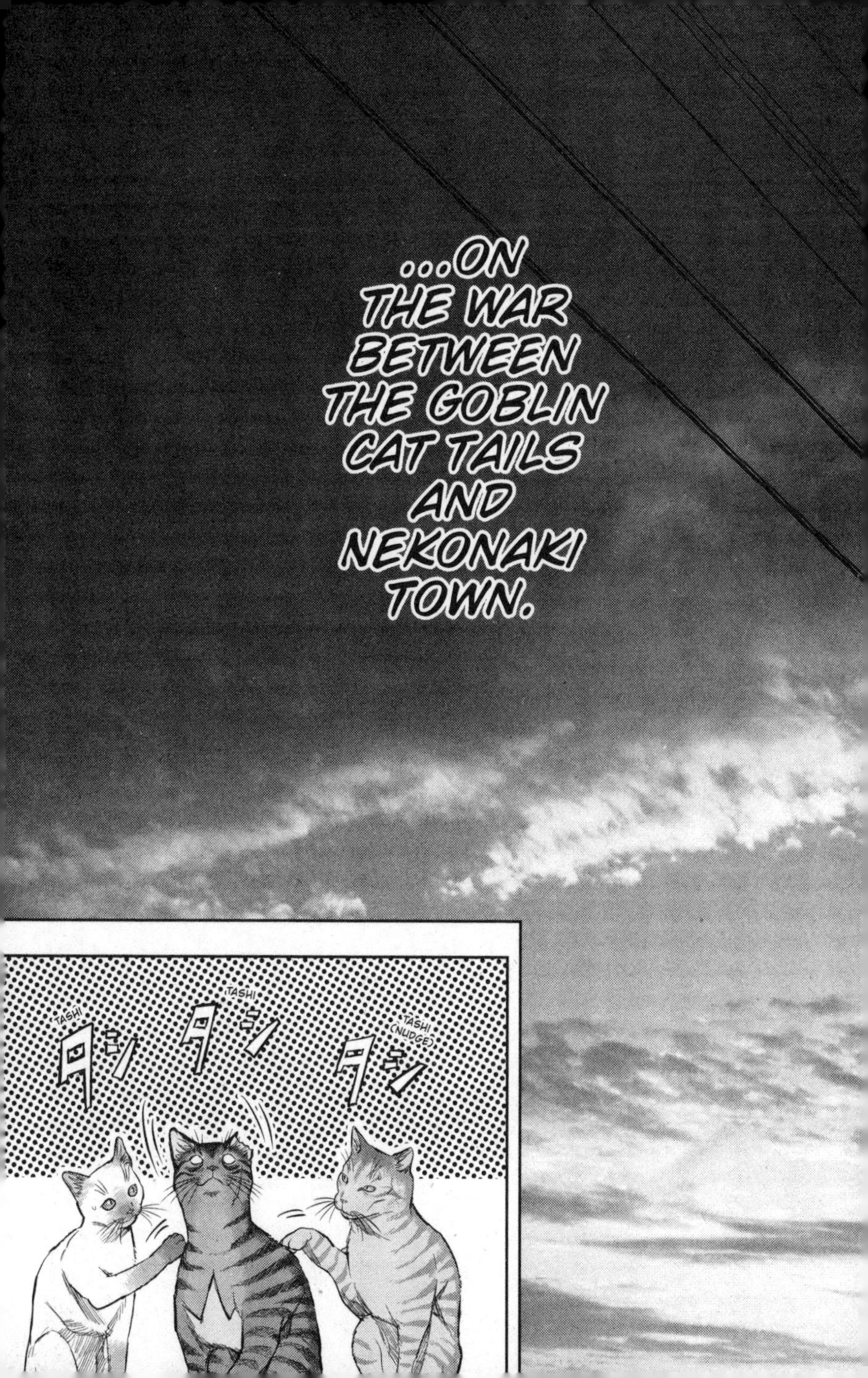
...ON THE WAR BETWEEN THE GOBLIN CAT TAILS AND NEKONAKI TOWN.
TASHI (NUDGE)
TASHI
TASHI

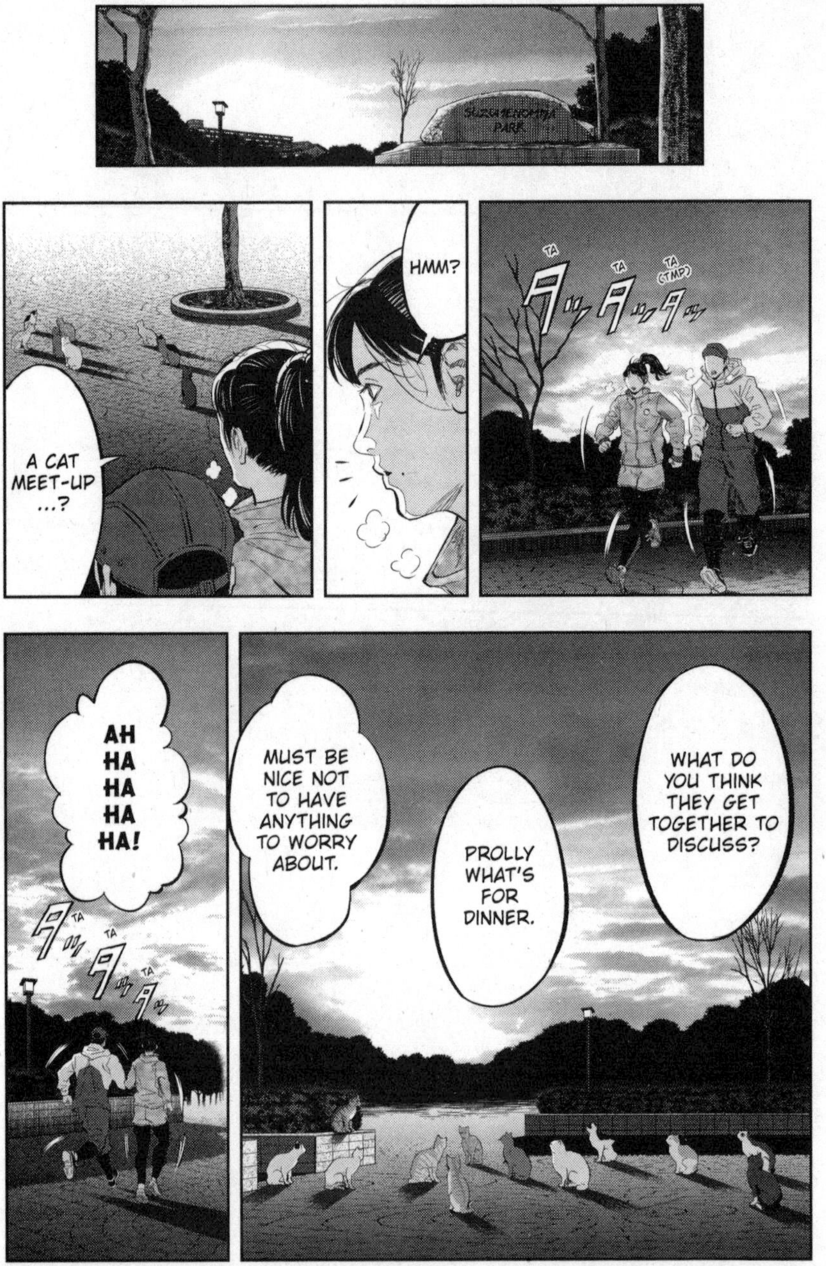
SUZUMENOMIYA PARK
TA TA TA (TMP)
HMM?
A CAT MEET-UP ...?
WHAT DO YOU THINK THEY GET TOGETHER TO DISCUSS?
PROLLY WHAT'S FOR DINNER.
MUST BE NICE NOT TO HAVE ANYTHING TO WORRY ABOUT.
AH HA HA HA HA!
TA TA TA

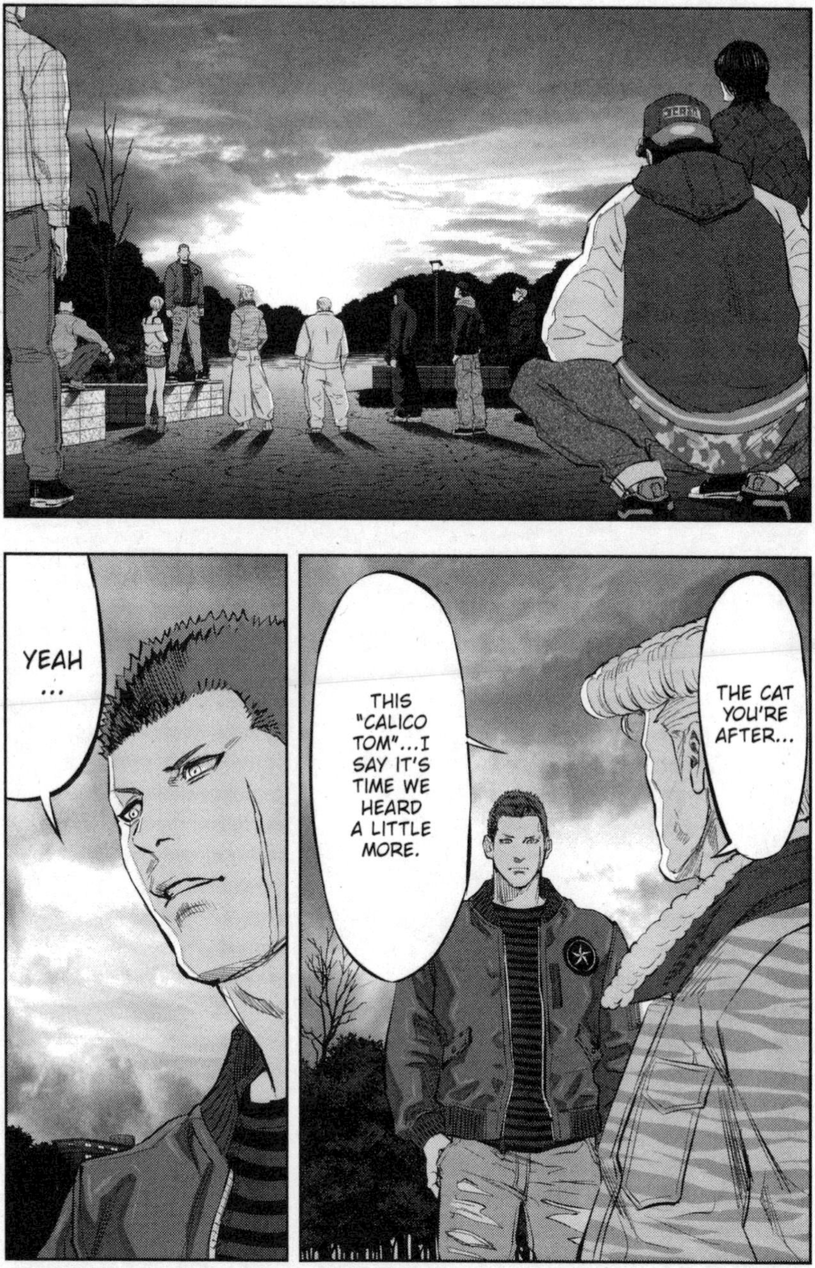
THE CAT YOU'RE AFTER...
THIS "CALICO TOM"...I SAY IT'S TIME WE HEARD A LITTLE MORE.
YEAH ...

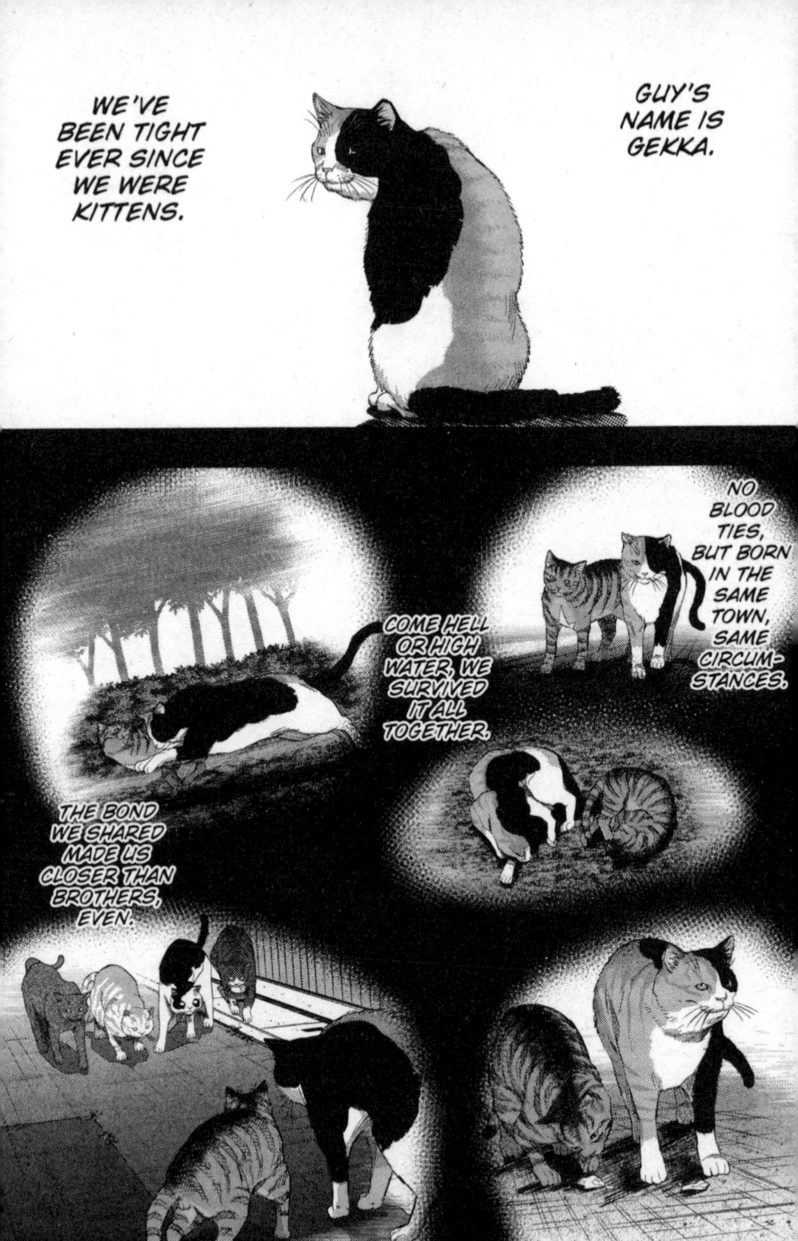
GUY'S NAME IS GEKKA.
WE'VE BEEN TIGHT EVER SINCE WE WERE KITTENS.
NO BLOOD TIES, BUT BORN IN THE SAME TOWN, SAME CIRCUM-STANCES.
COME HELL OR HIGH WATER, WE SURVIVED IT ALL TOGETHER.
THE BOND WE SHARED MADE US CLOSER THAN BROTHERS, EVEN.

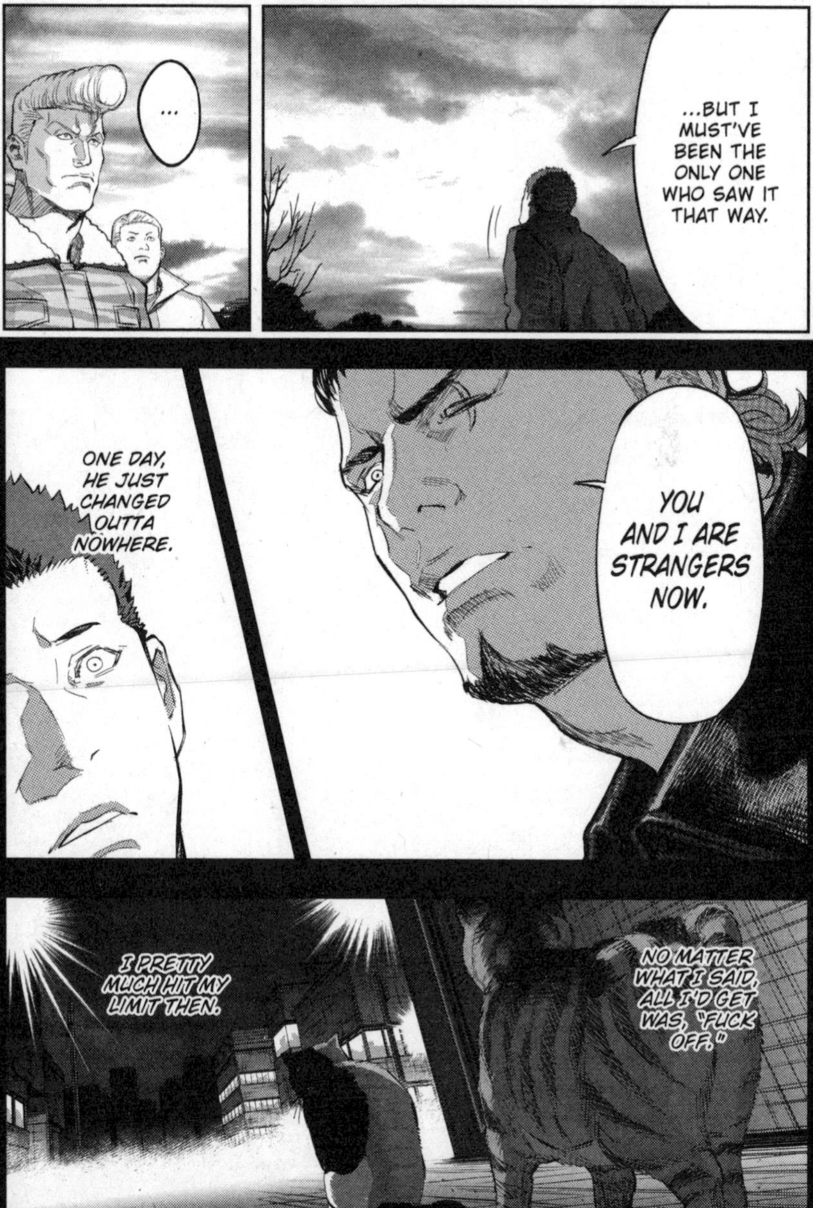
...BUT I MUST'VE BEEN THE ONLY ONE WHO SAW IT THAT WAY.
...
YOU AND I ARE STRANGERS NOW.
ONE DAY, HE JUST CHANGED OUTTA NOWHERE.
NO MATTER WHAT I SAID, ALL I'D GET WAS, "FUCK OFF."
I PRETTY MUCH HIT MY LIMIT THEN.

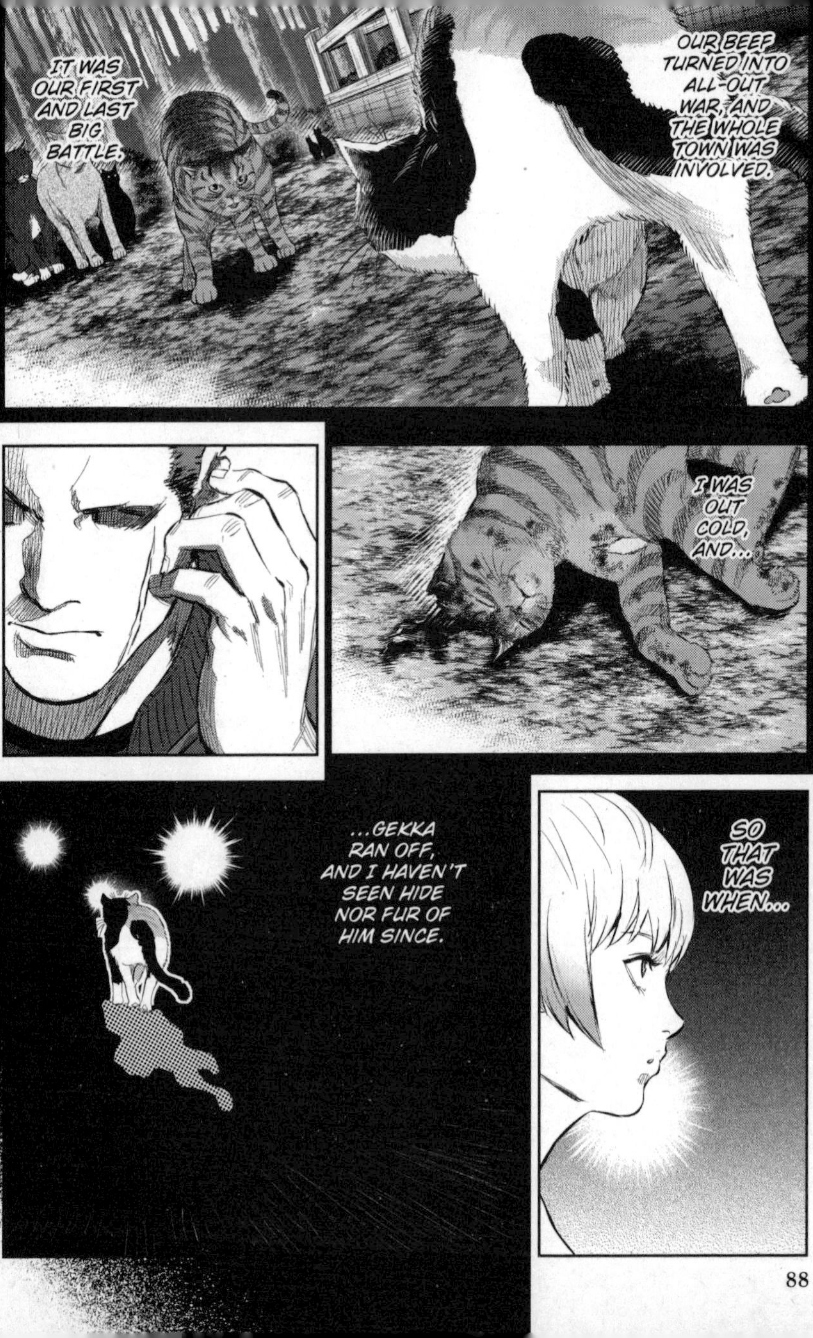
OUR BEEF TURNED INTO ALL-OUT WAR, AND THE WHOLE TOWN WAS INVOLVED.
IT WAS OUR FIRST AND LAST BIG BATTLE.
I WAS OUT COLD, AND...
SO THAT WAS WHEN...
...GEKKA RAN OFF, AND I HAVEN'T SEEN HIDE NOR FUR OF HIM SINCE.

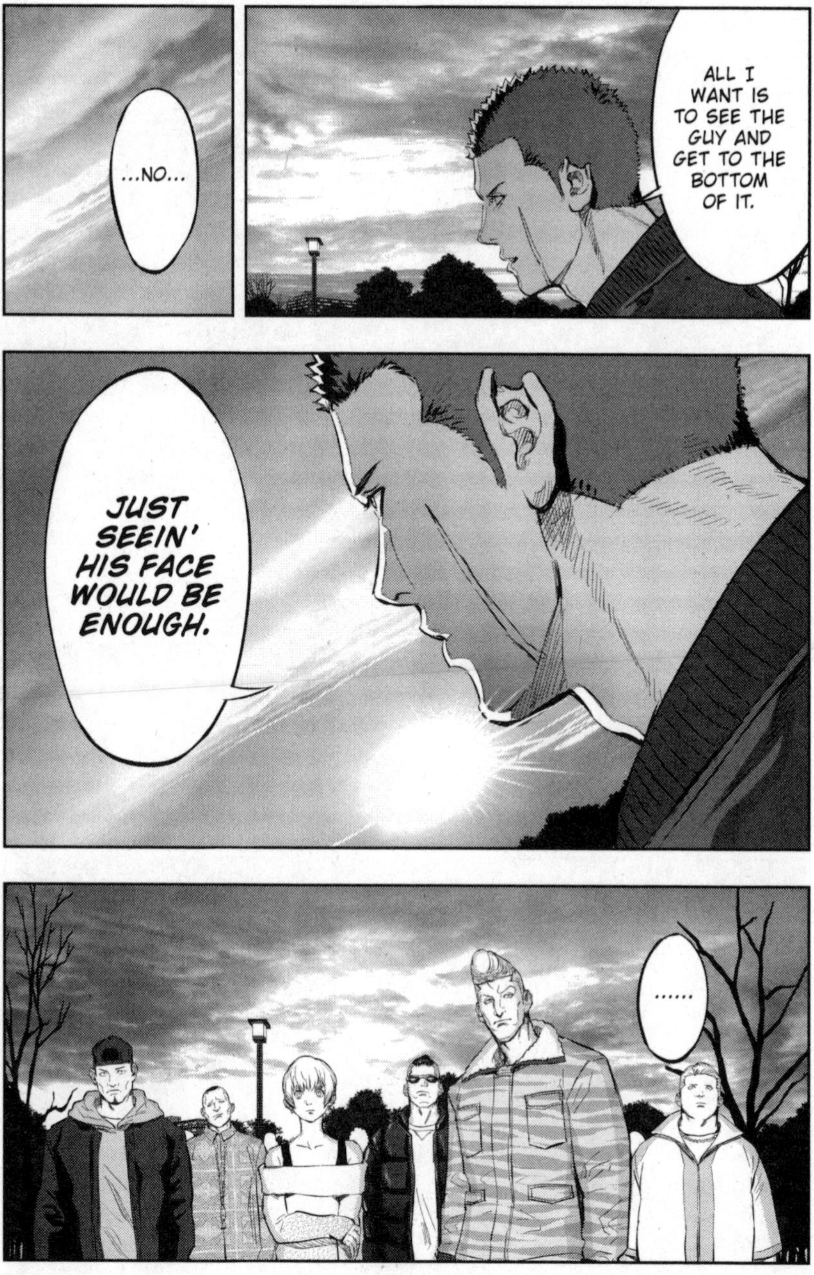
ALL I WANT IS TO SEE THE GUY AND GET TO THE BOTTOM OF IT.
...NO...
JUST SEEIN' HIS FACE WOULD BE ENOUGH.
......

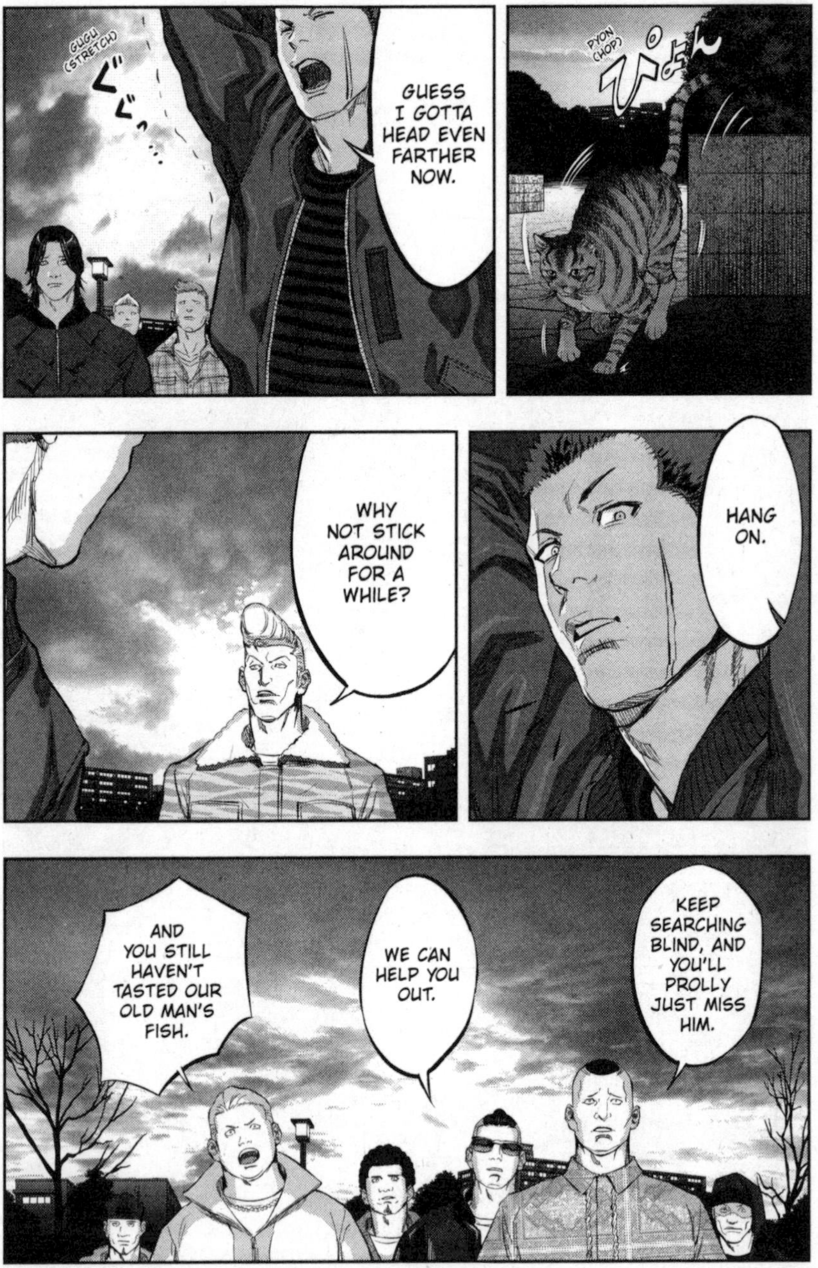
PYON (HOP)
ぴょん
GUGU (STRETCH)
ぐぐっ…
GUESS I GOTTA HEAD EVEN FARTHER NOW.
HANG ON.
WHY NOT STICK AROUND FOR A WHILE?
KEEP SEARCHING BLIND, AND YOU'LL PROLLY JUST MISS HIM.
WE CAN HELP YOU OUT.
AND YOU STILL HAVEN'T TASTED OUR OLD MAN'S FISH.

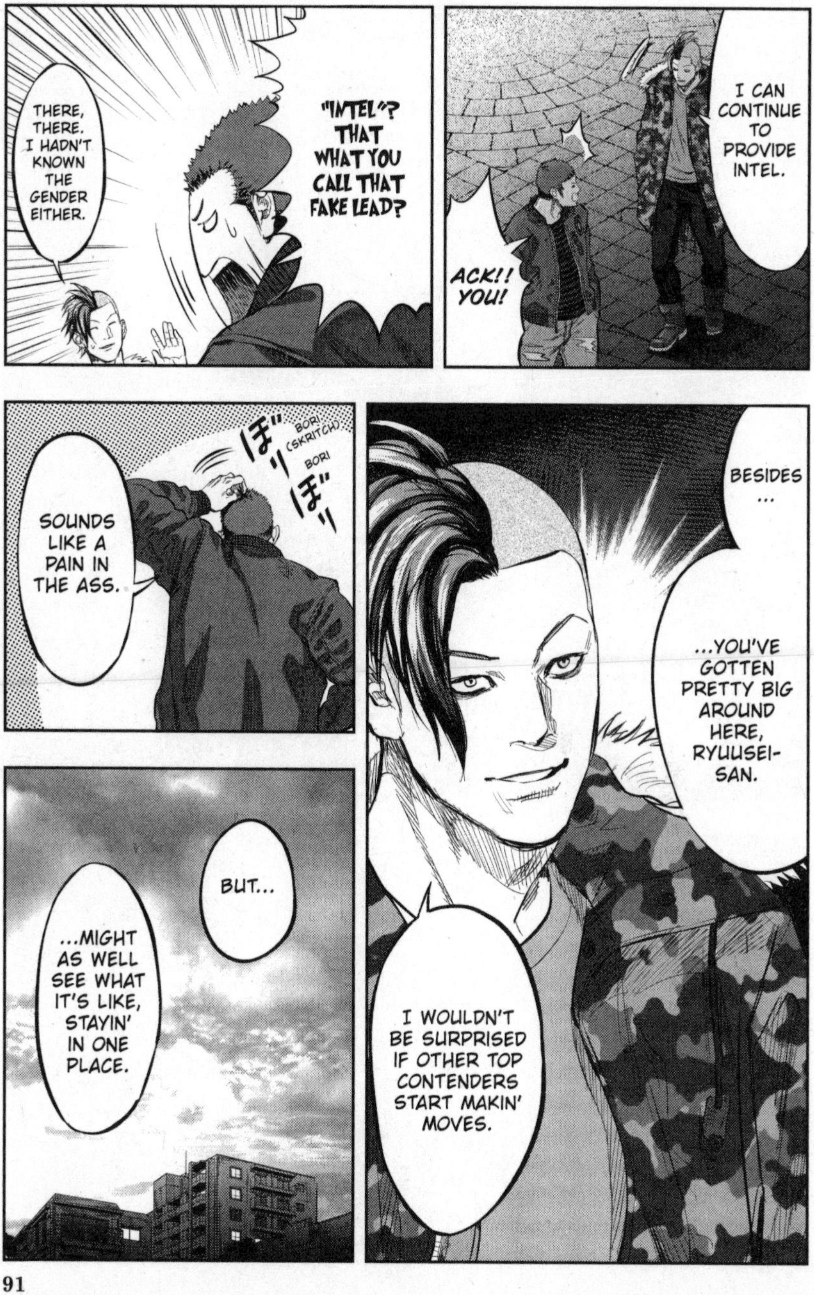
I CAN CONTINUE TO PROVIDE INTEL.
ACK!! YOU!
"INTEL"? THAT WHAT YOU CALL THAT FAKE LEAD?
THERE, THERE. I HADN'T KNOWN THE GENDER EITHER.
BESIDES...
...YOU'VE GOTTEN PRETTY BIG AROUND HERE, RYUUSEI-SAN.
I WOULDN'T BE SURPRISED IF OTHER TOP CONTENDERS START MAKIN' MOVES.
ぼり
BORI (SKRITCH)
ぼり
BORI
SOUNDS LIKE A PAIN IN THE ASS.
BUT...
...MIGHT AS WELL SEE WHAT IT'S LIKE, STAYIN' IN ONE PLACE.

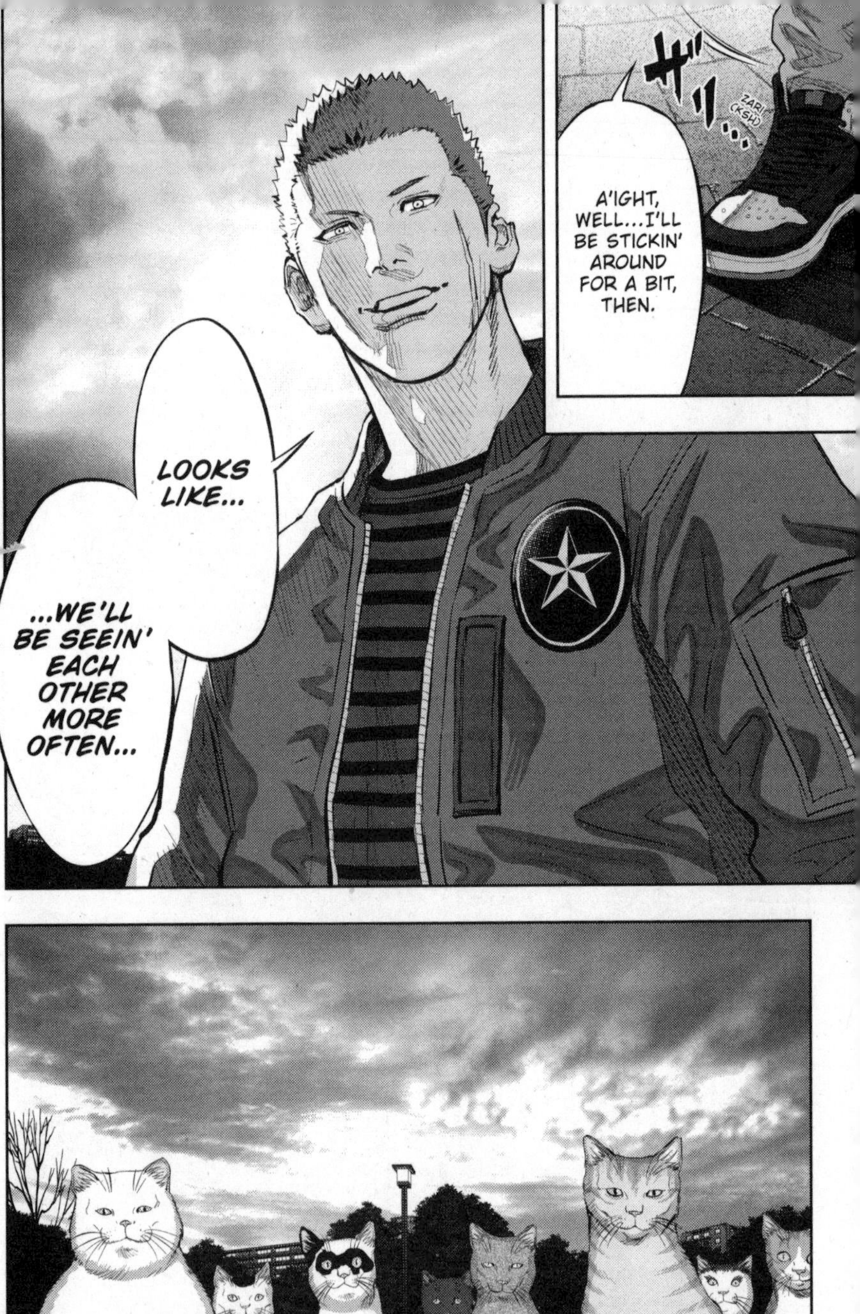
ザリ…
ZARI (KSH)
A'IGHT, WELL...I'LL BE STICKIN' AROUND FOR A BIT, THEN.
LOOKS LIKE...
...WE'LL BE SEEIN' EACH OTHER MORE OFTEN...

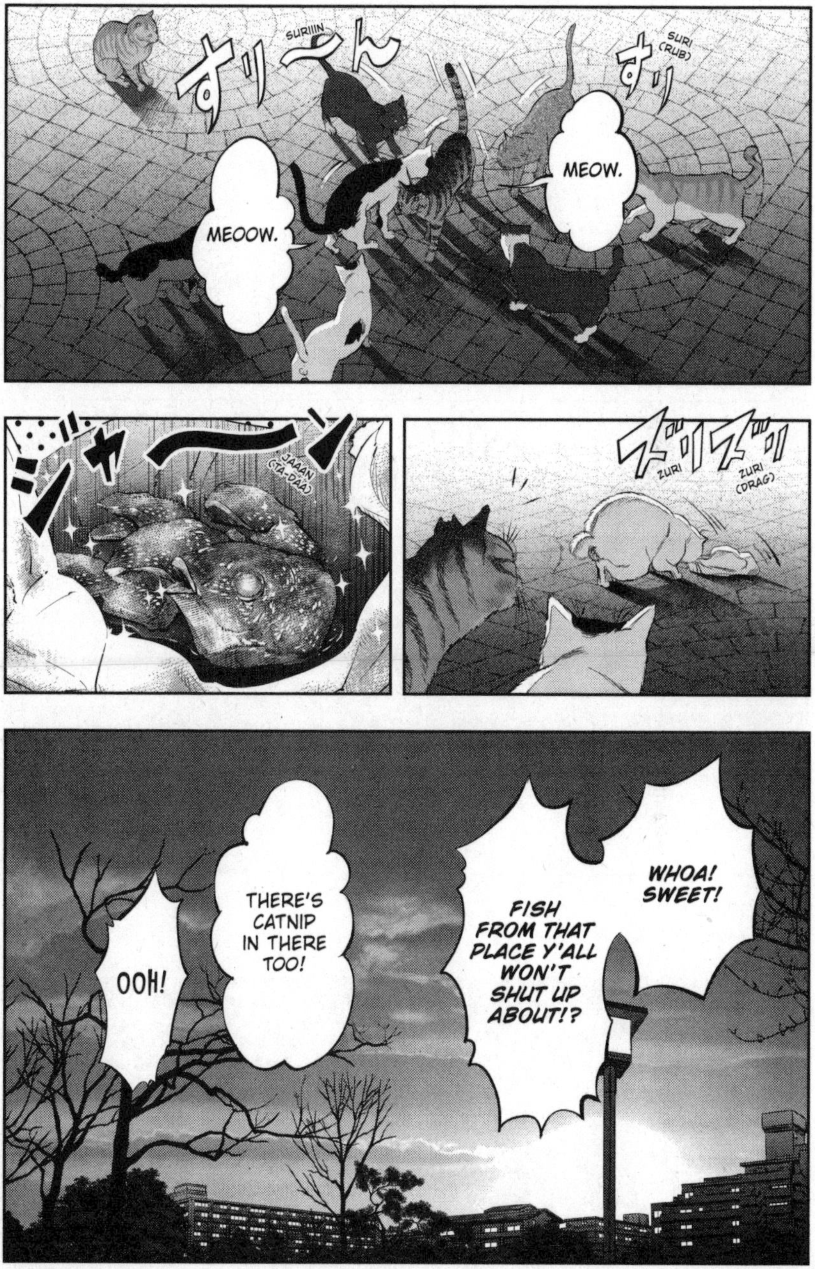
SURI (RUB)
SURIIIN
MEOW.
MEOOW.
ZURI
ZURI (DRAG)
JAAAN (TA-DAA)
WHOA! SWEET!
FISH FROM THAT PLACE Y'ALL WON'T SHUT UP ABOUT!?
THERE'S CATNIP IN THERE TOO!
OOH!

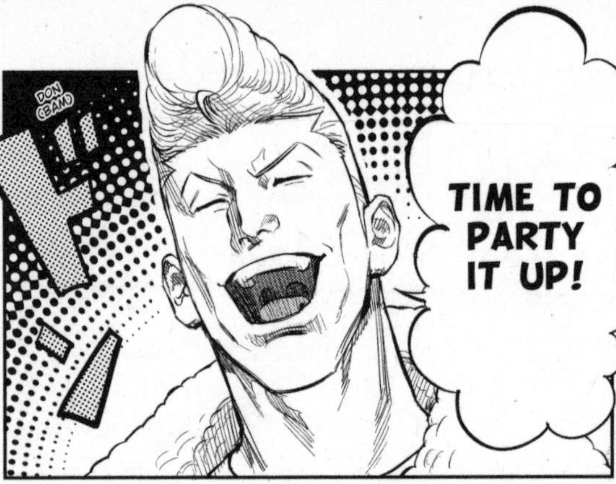
DON
(BAM)
TIME TO PARTY IT UP!
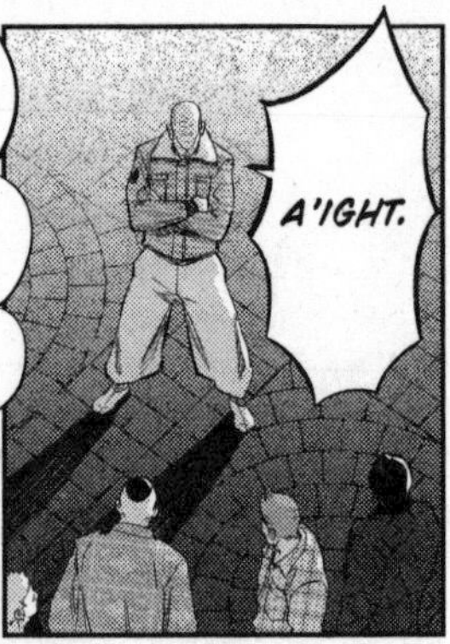
A'IGHT.
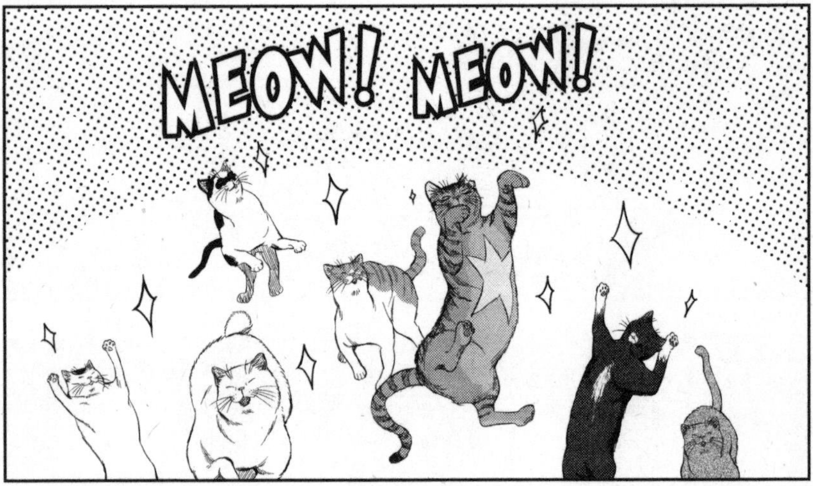
MEOW! MEOW!
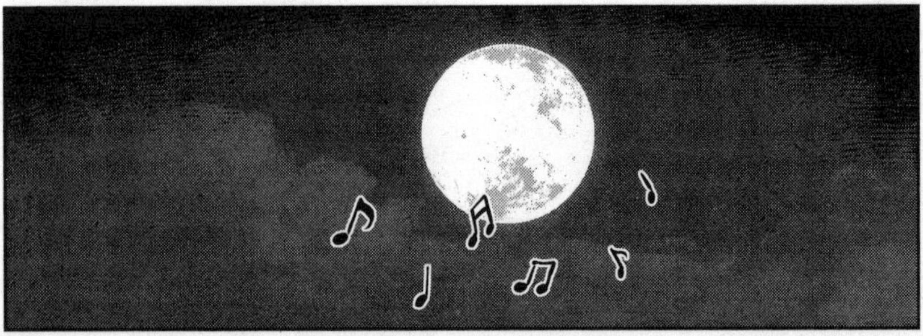

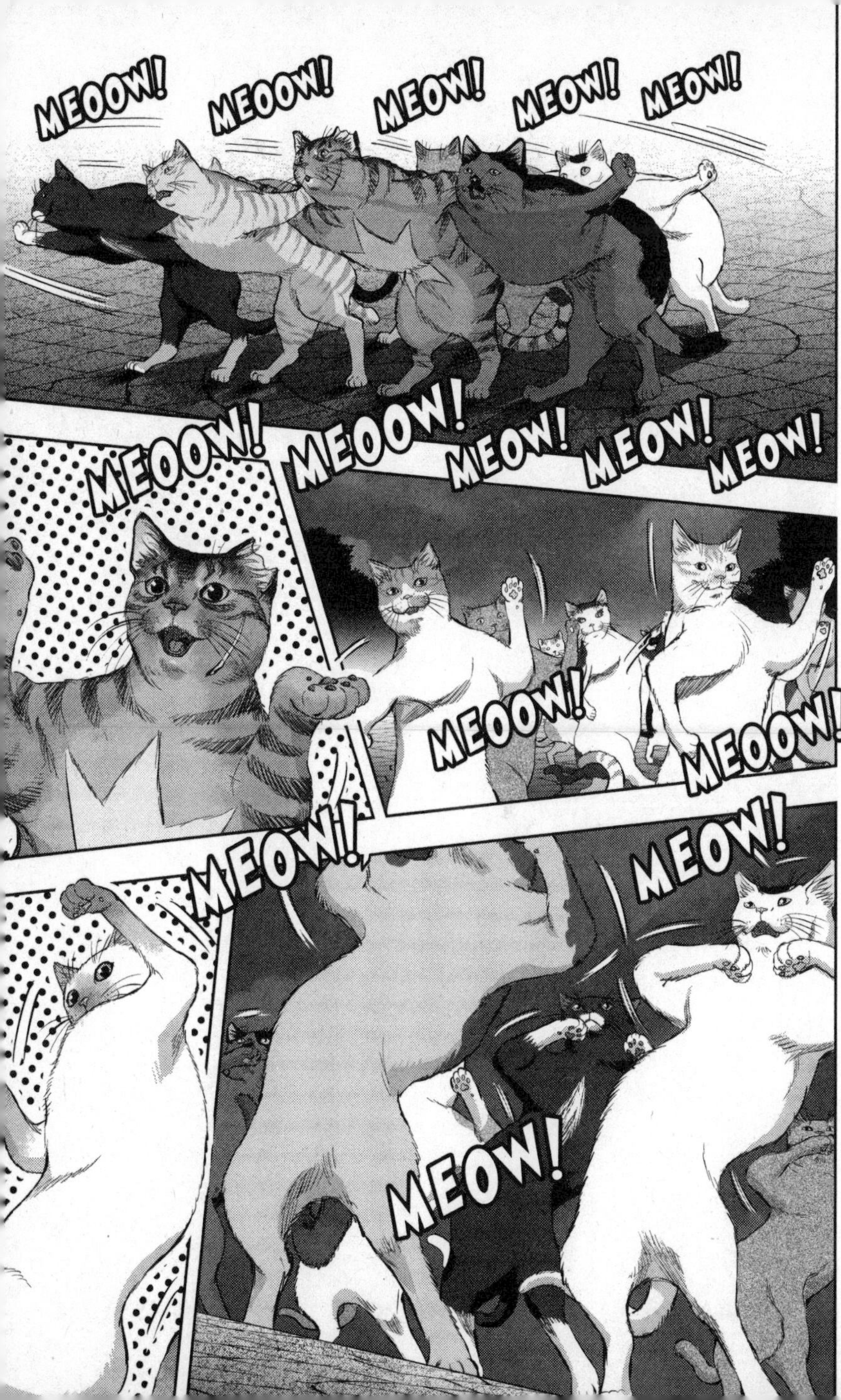
MEOW!
MEOW!
MEOW!
MEOOW!
MEOOW!
MEOW!
MEOW!
MEOW!
MEOOW!
MEOOW!
MEOOW!
MEOOW!
MEOW!
MEOW!
MEOW!

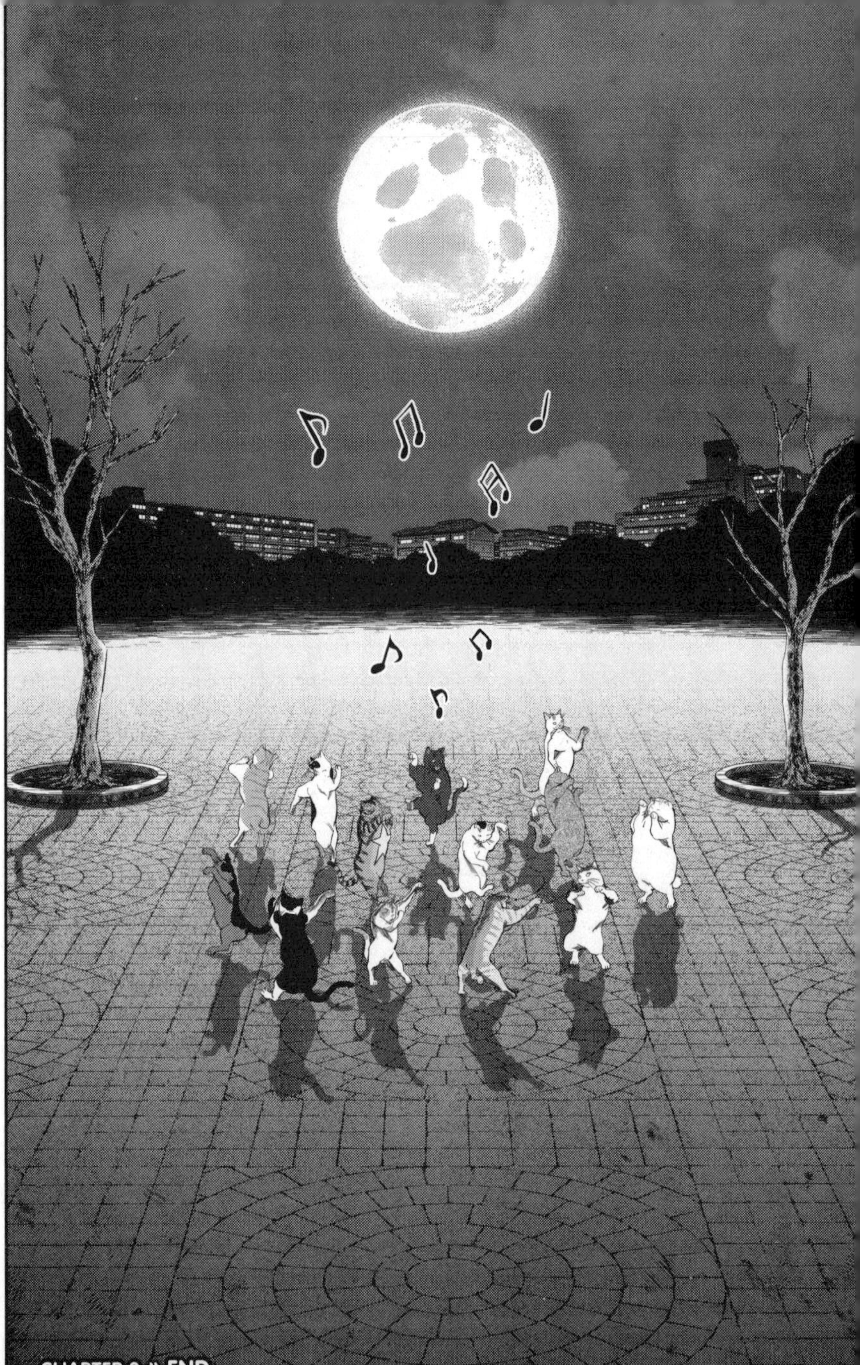

CHAPTER 9 END

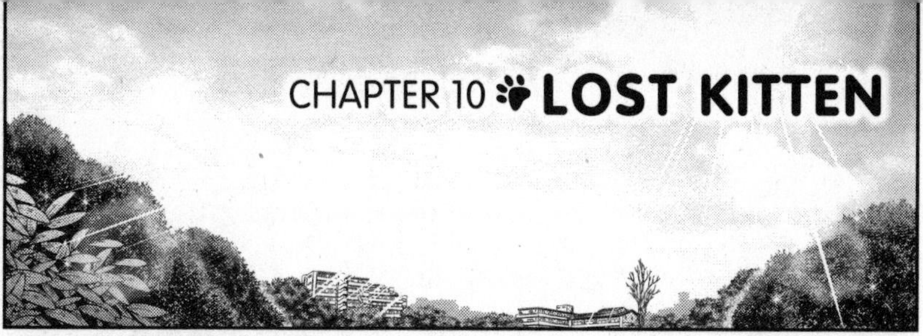
CHAPTER 10 LOST KITTEN

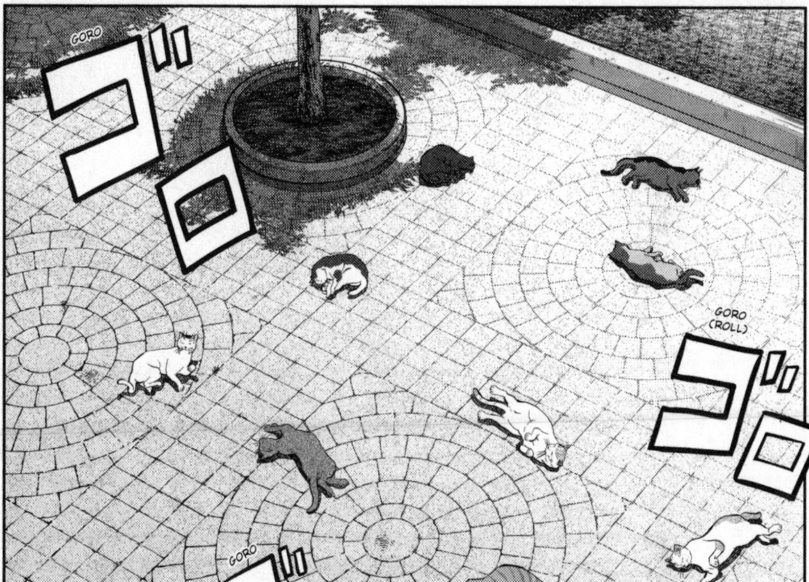
GORO
ゴロ
GORO (ROLL)
ゴロ
GORO
ゴロ

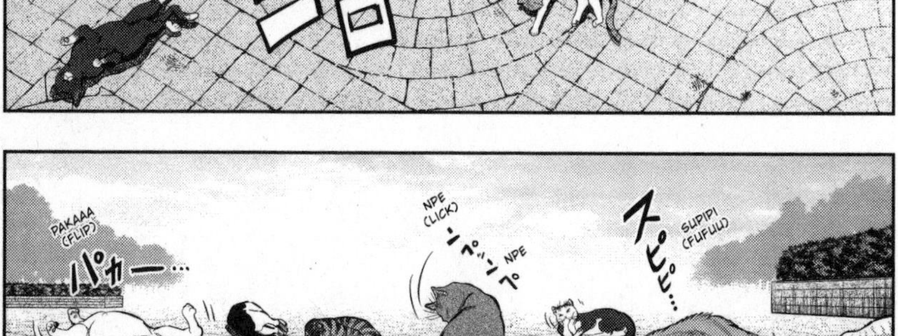
SUPIPI (FUFUU)
スピピ…
NPE (LICK)
ンペ
NPE
ンペ
PAKAAA (FLIP)
パカー…

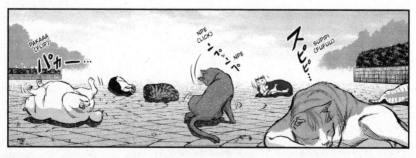

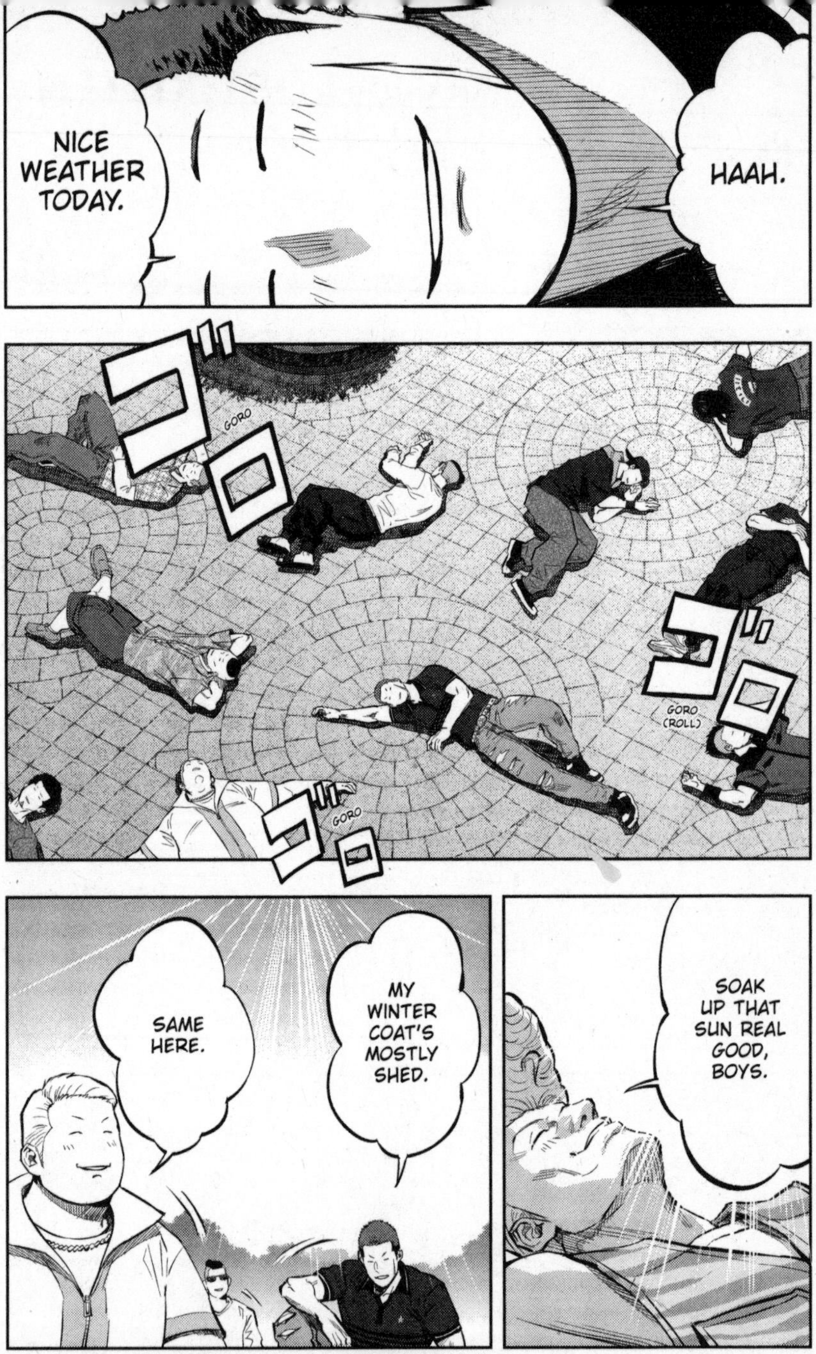
HAAH.
NICE WEATHER TODAY.
GORO (ROLL)
GORO
GORO
SOAK UP THAT SUN REAL GOOD, BOYS.
MY WINTER COAT'S MOSTLY SHED.
SAME HERE.

※ *MANY CLAIM THAT DIRECT SUNLIGHT HAS POSITIVE EFFECTS ON CAT HEALTH.*

SPRING'S REALLY SPRUNG, HUH?

SAWA (WHOOSH)

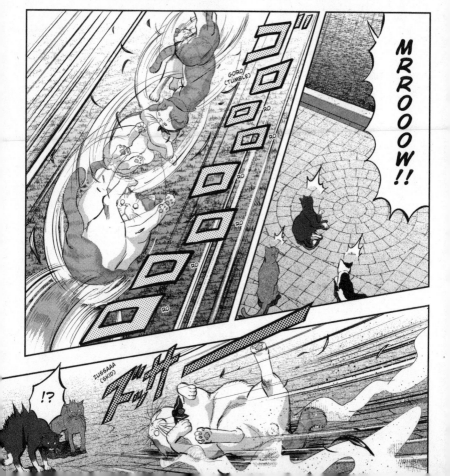

MRROOOW!!

GORO (TUMBLE)

RO RO RO RO RO RO RO

!?

ZUSSAAA (SKID)

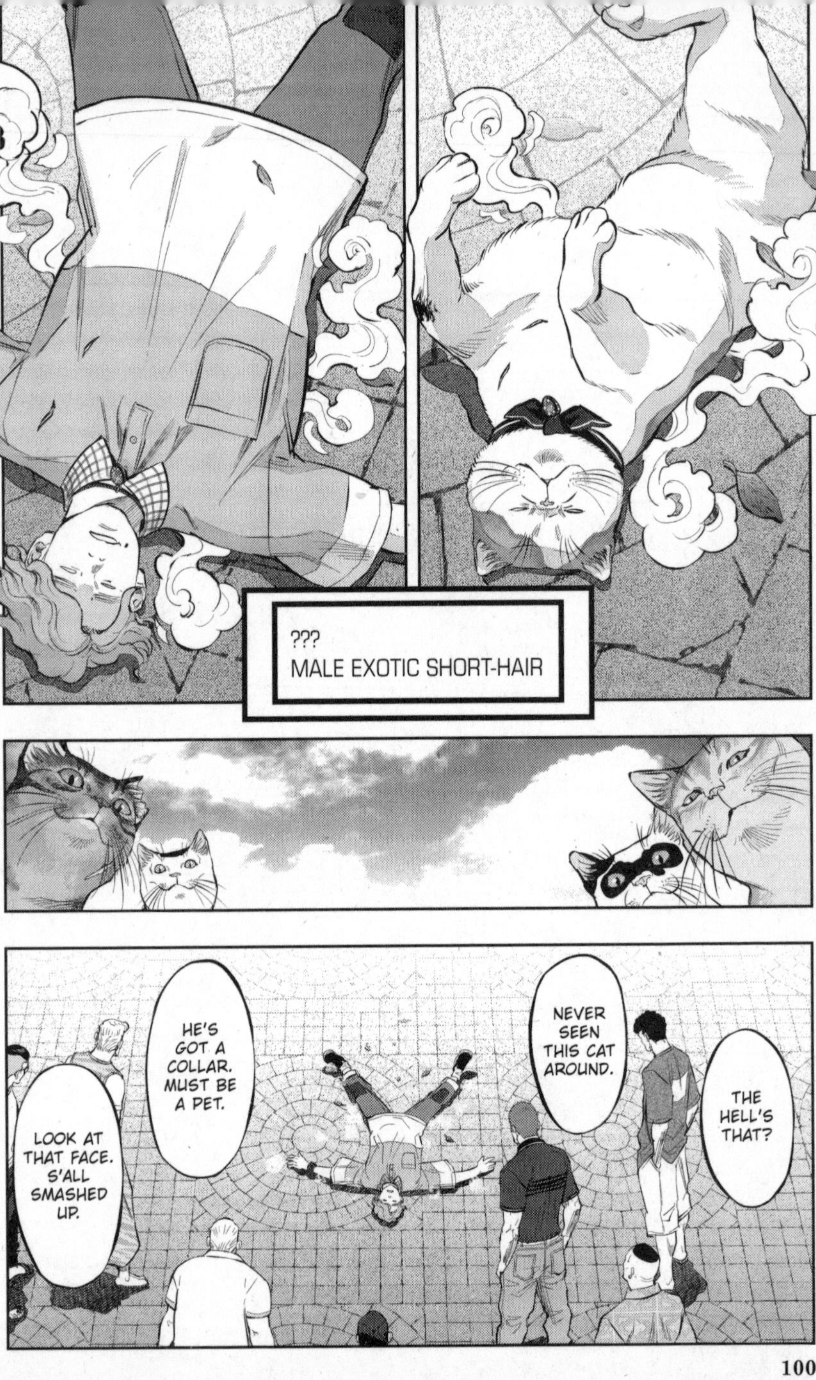
???
MALE EXOTIC SHORT-HAIR
THE HELL'S THAT?
NEVER SEEN THIS CAT AROUND.
HE'S GOT A COLLAR. MUST BE A PET.
LOOK AT THAT FACE. S'ALL SMASHED UP.

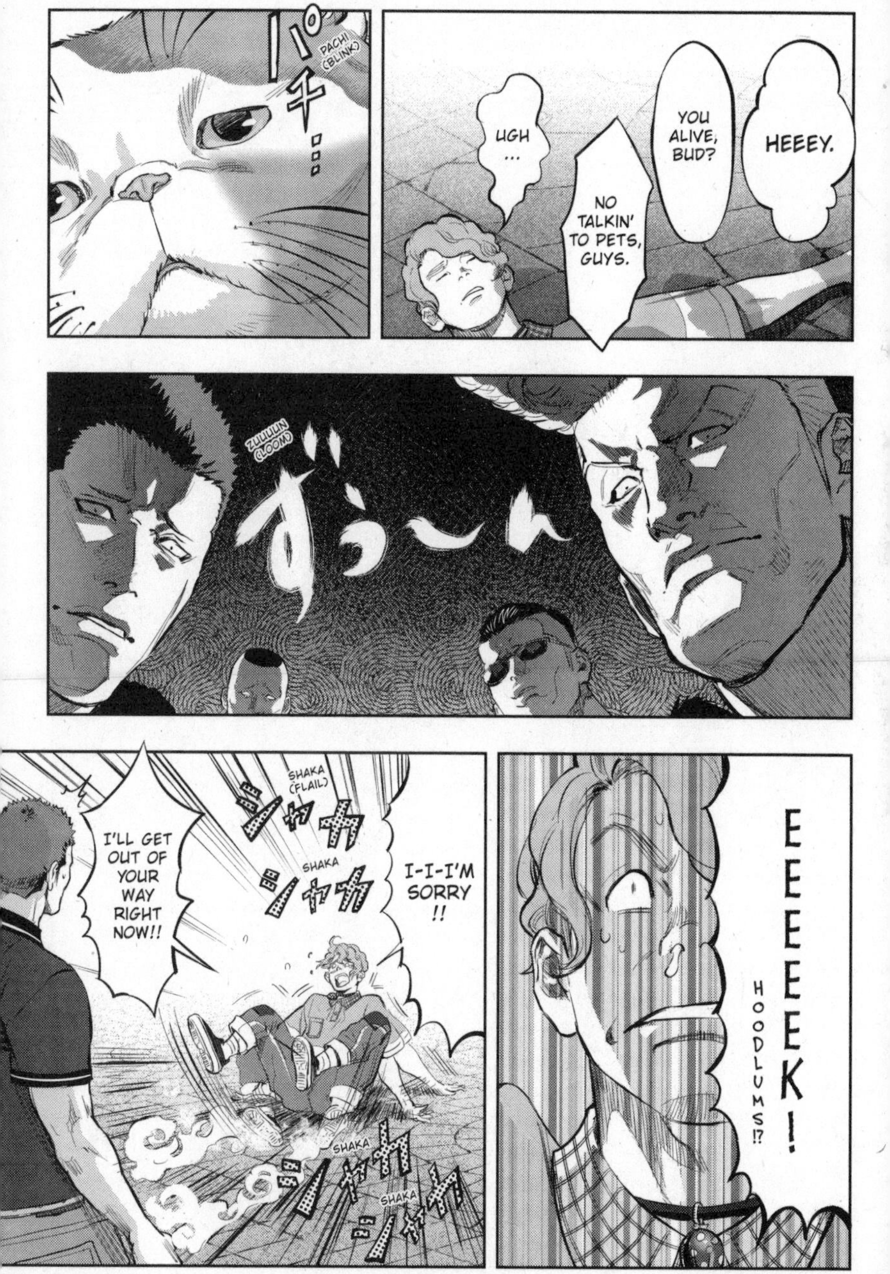
HEEEY.
YOU ALIVE, BUD?
NO TALKIN' TO PETS, GUYS.
UGH ...
PACHI (BLINK)
ZUUUUN (LOOM)
EEEEEEK!
HOODLUMS!?
I-I-I'M SORRY !!
SHAKA (FLAIL)
SHAKA
I'LL GET OUT OF YOUR WAY RIGHT NOW!!
SHAKA
SHAKA

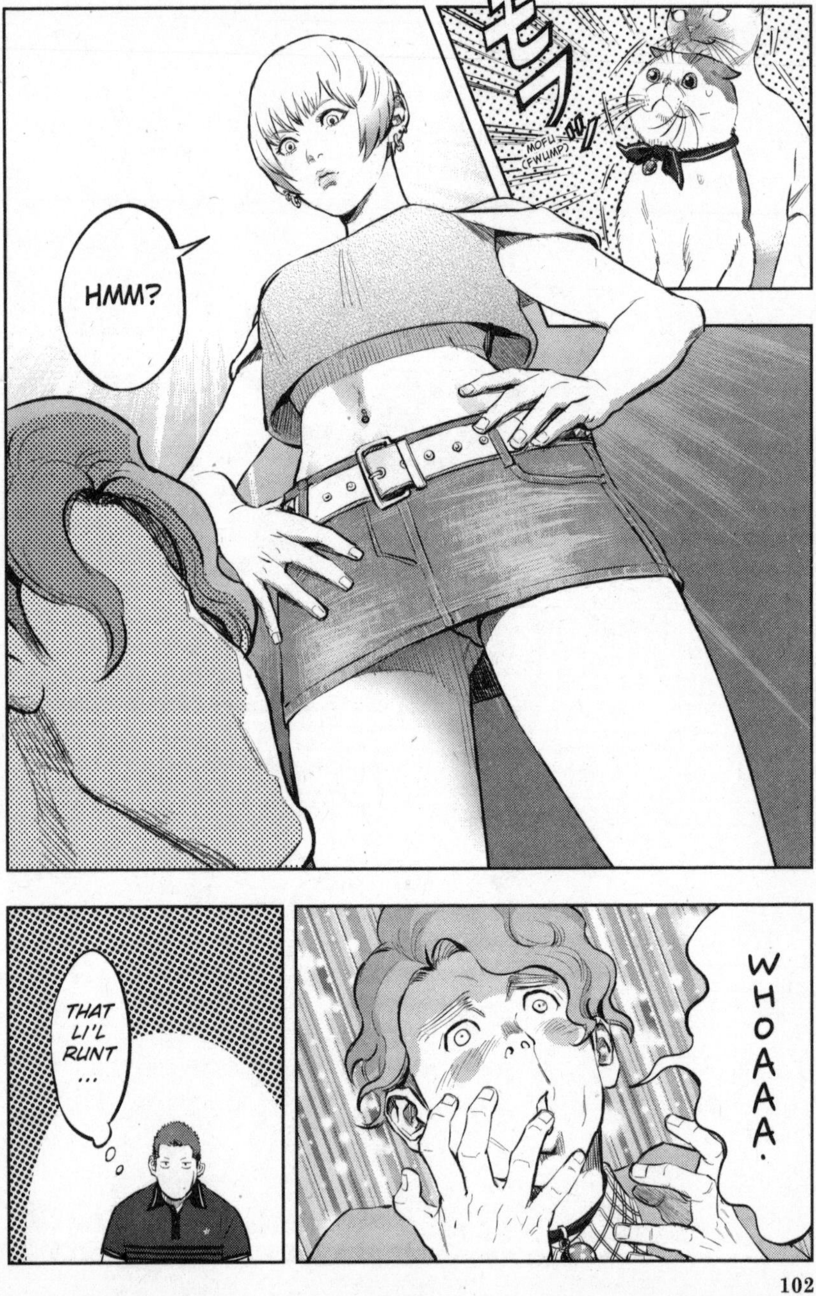
モフ
MOFU (FWUMP)
HMM?
WHOAAA.
THAT LI'L RUNT ...

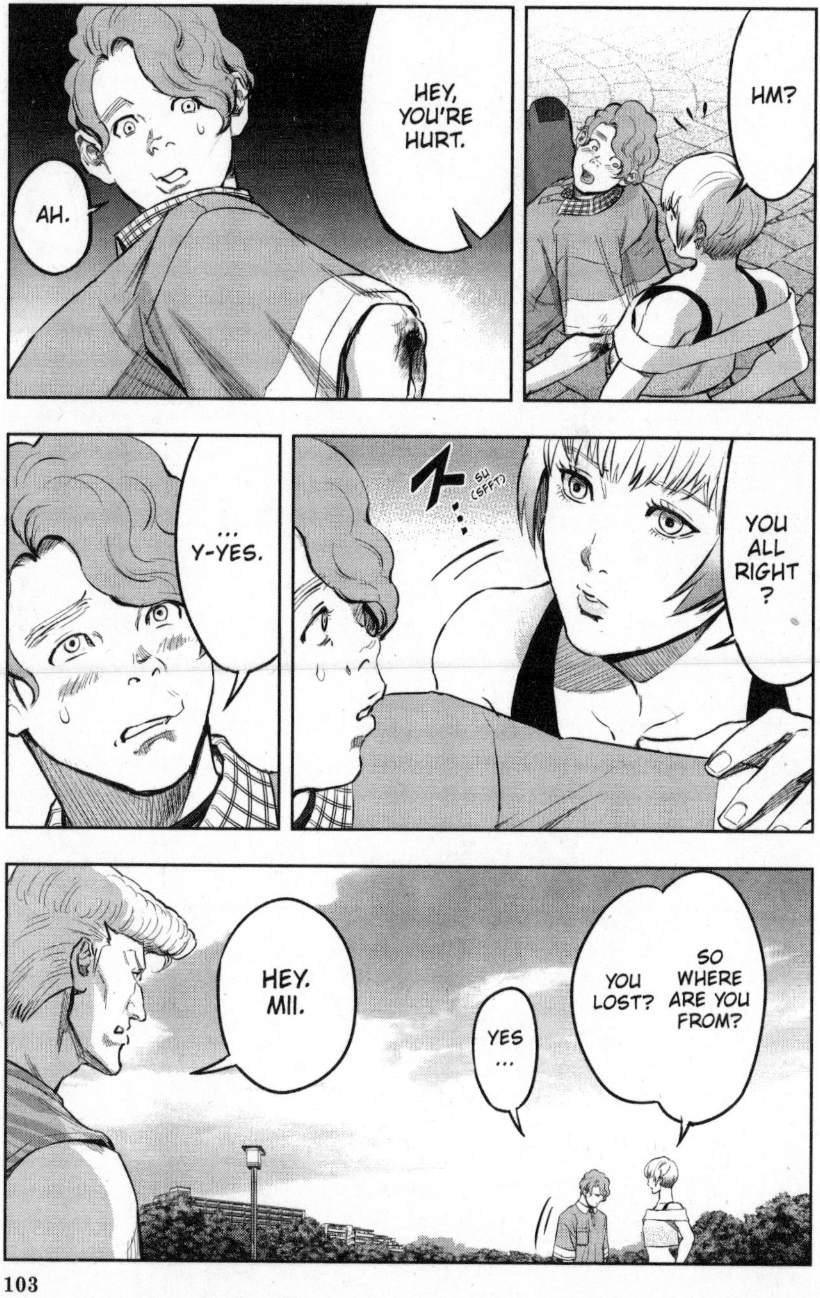
HM?
HEY, YOU'RE HURT.
AH.
SU (SFFT)
YOU ALL RIGHT?
... Y-YES.
SO WHERE ARE YOU FROM?
YOU LOST?
YES ...
HEY. MII.

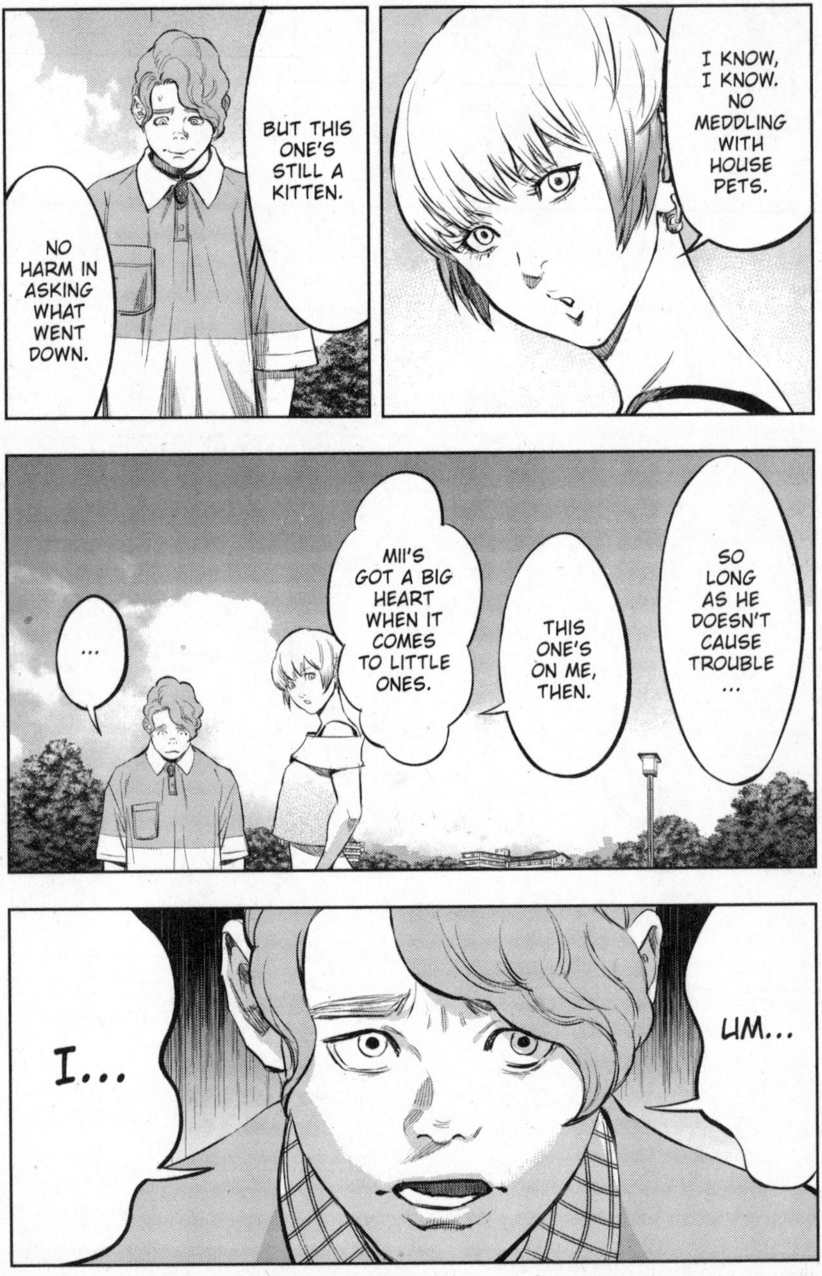

I KNOW, I KNOW. NO MEDDLING WITH HOUSE PETS.
BUT THIS ONE'S STILL A KITTEN.
NO HARM IN ASKING WHAT WENT DOWN.
SO LONG AS HE DOESN'T CAUSE TROUBLE ...
THIS ONE'S ON ME, THEN.
MII'S GOT A BIG HEART WHEN IT COMES TO LITTLE ONES.
...
UM...
I...

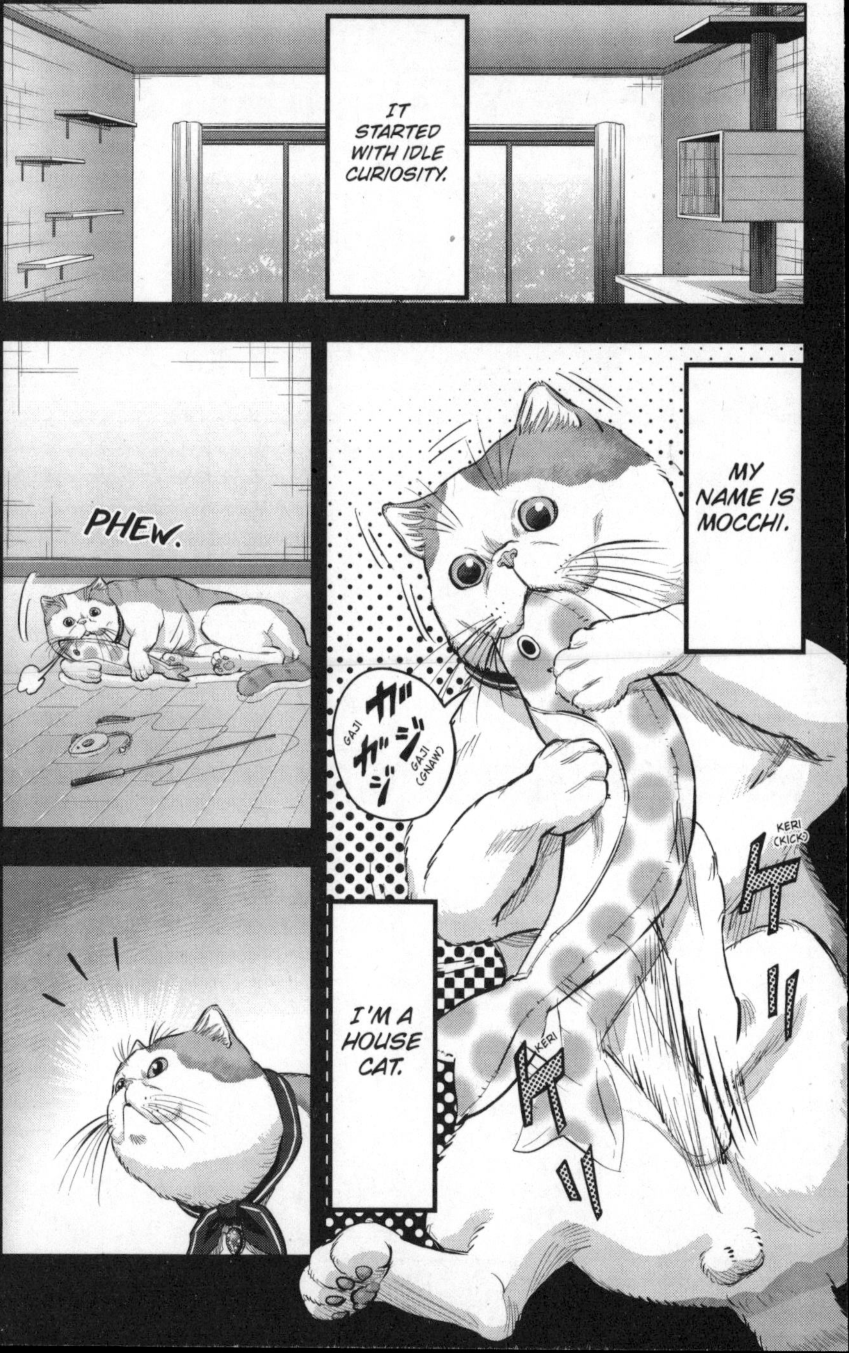
IT STARTED WITH IDLE CURIOSITY.
MY NAME IS MOCCHI.
GAJI GAJI (GNAW)
KERI (KICK)
I'M A HOUSE CAT.
KERI
PHEW.

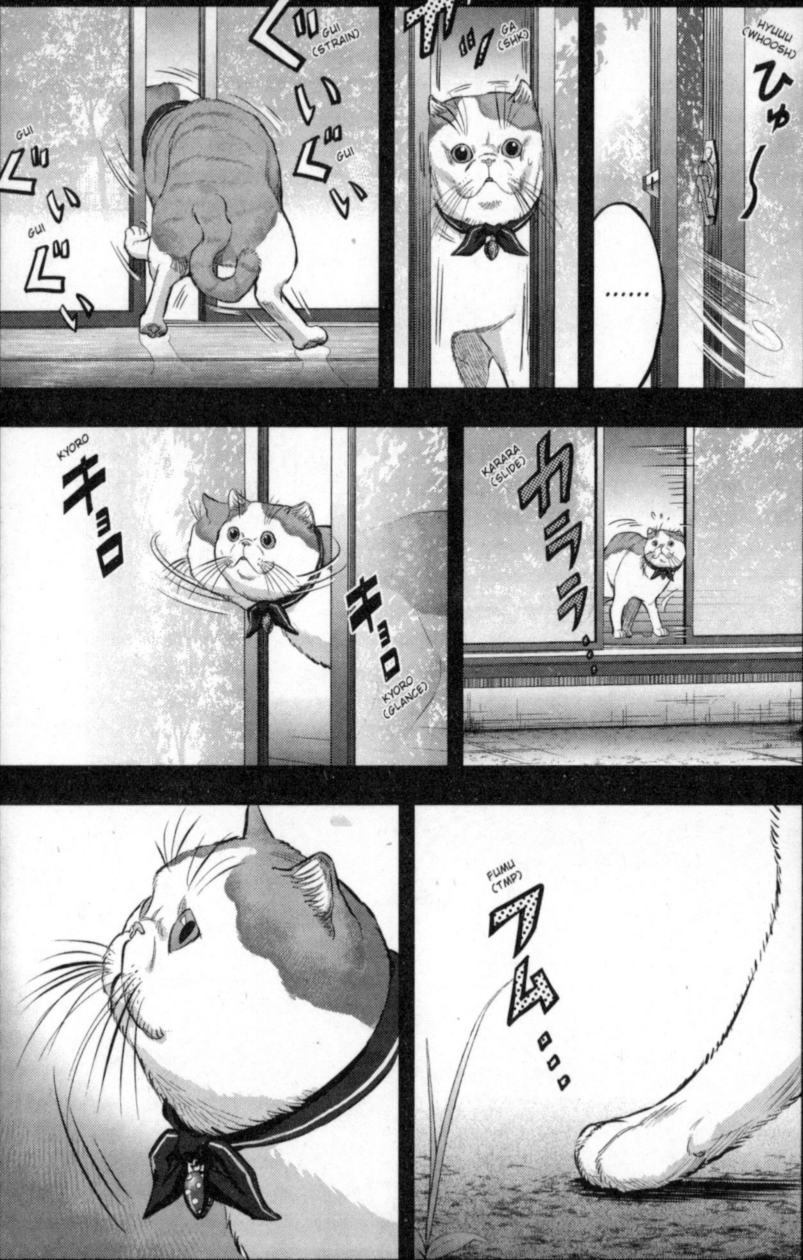
HYUUU (WHOOSH)
ひゅ〜〜
……
ガッ
GA (SHK)
ぐい
GUI (STRAIN)
ぐい
GUI
ぐい
GUI
ぐい
GUI
KARARA (SLIDE)
カララ
キョロ
KYORO (GLANCE)
キョロ
KYORO
FUMU (TMP)
フム…

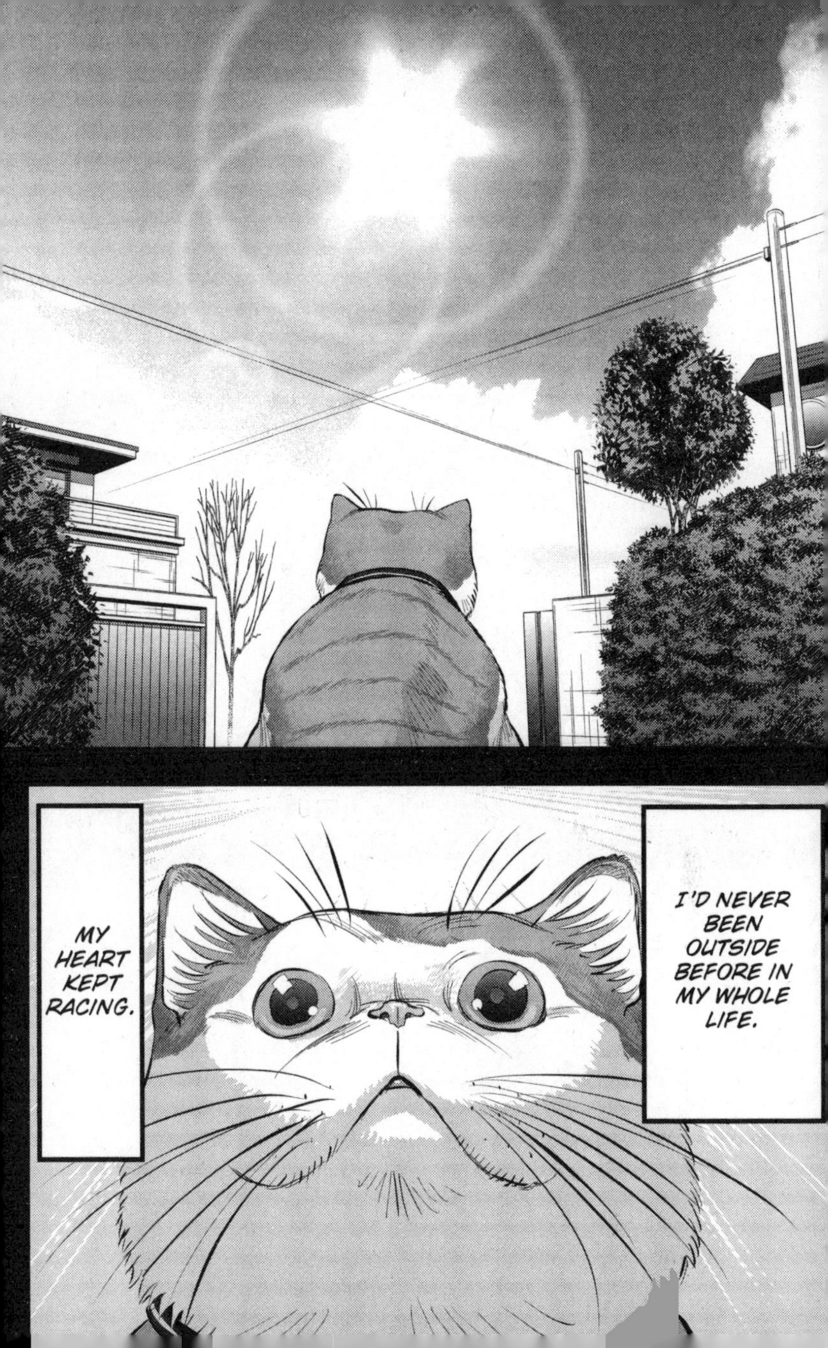
I'D NEVER BEEN OUTSIDE BEFORE IN MY WHOLE LIFE.
MY HEART KEPT RACING.

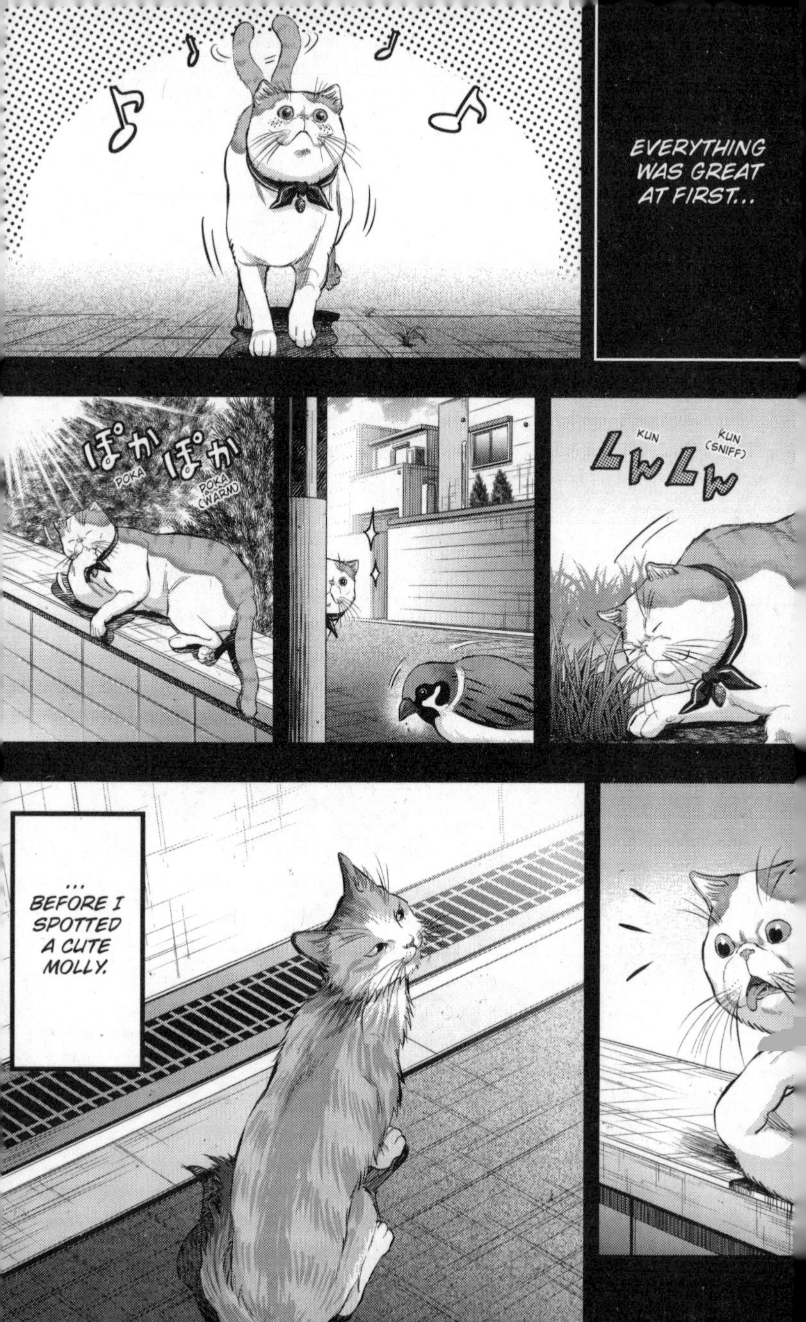
EVERYTHING WAS GREAT AT FIRST...
くんくん
KUN KUN (SNIFF)
ぽかぽか
POKA POKA (WARM)
... BEFORE I SPOTTED A CUTE MOLLY.

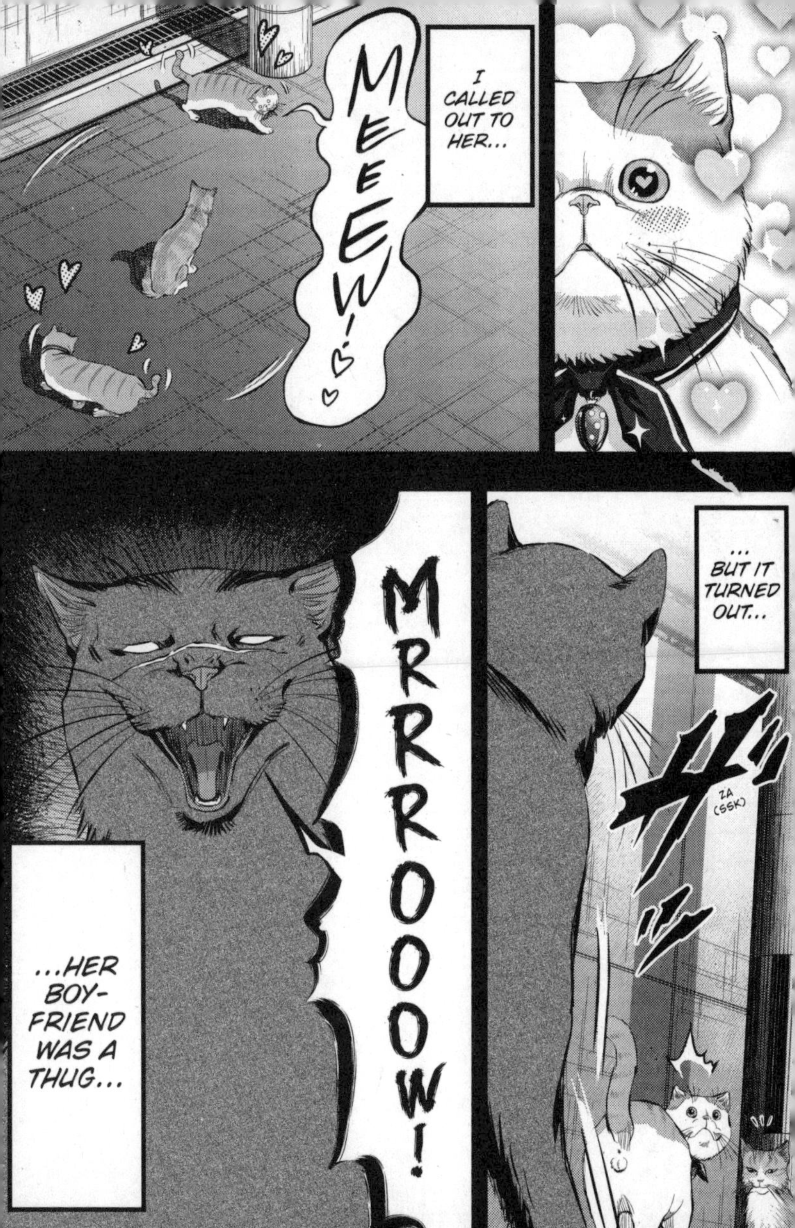
I CALLED OUT TO HER...
MEEEEW!
... BUT IT TURNED OUT...
ZA (SSK)
MRRROOOOW!
...HER BOY-FRIEND WAS A THUG...

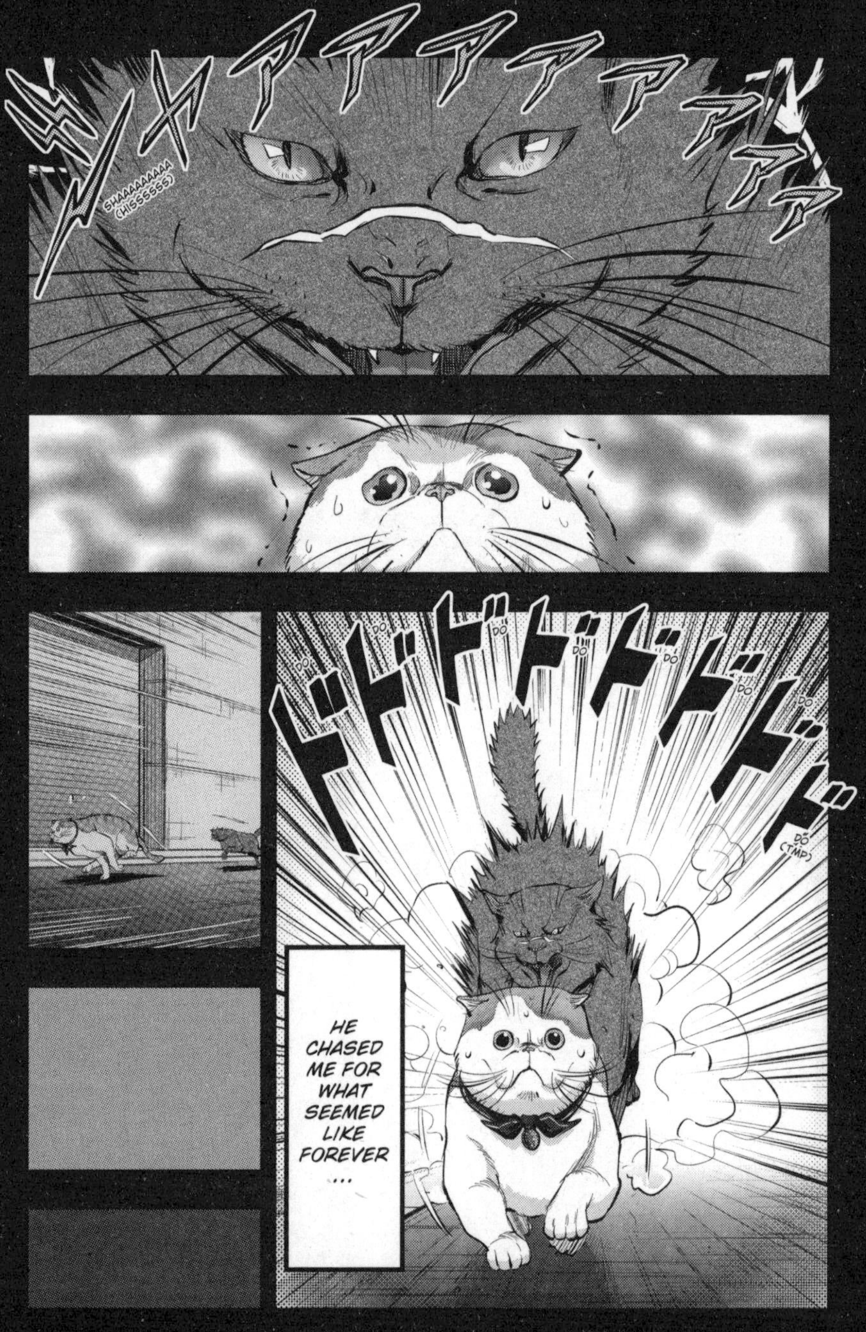
SHAAAAAAAAA (HISSSSSS)
DO DO DO DO DO DO DO DO (TMP)
HE CHASED ME FOR WHAT SEEMED LIKE FOREVER...

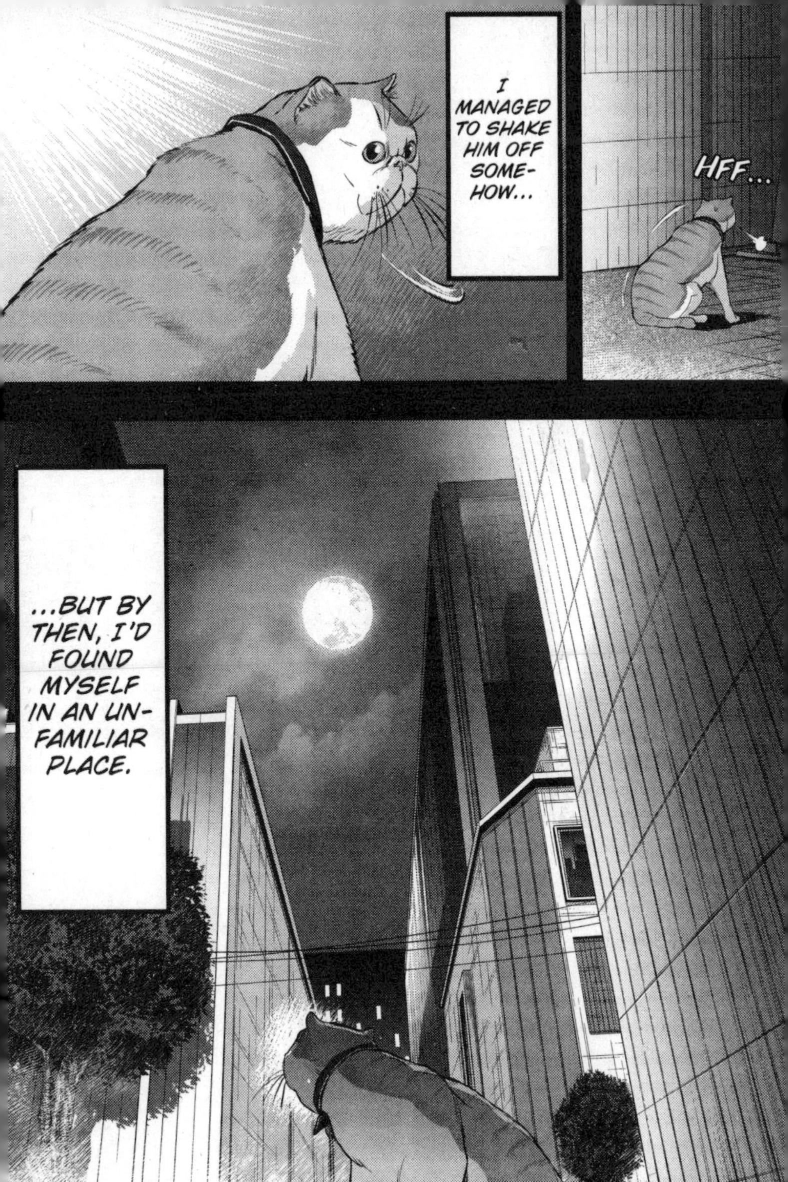
HFF...
I MANAGED TO SHAKE HIM OFF SOME-HOW...
...BUT BY THEN, I'D FOUND MYSELF IN AN UN-FAMILIAR PLACE.

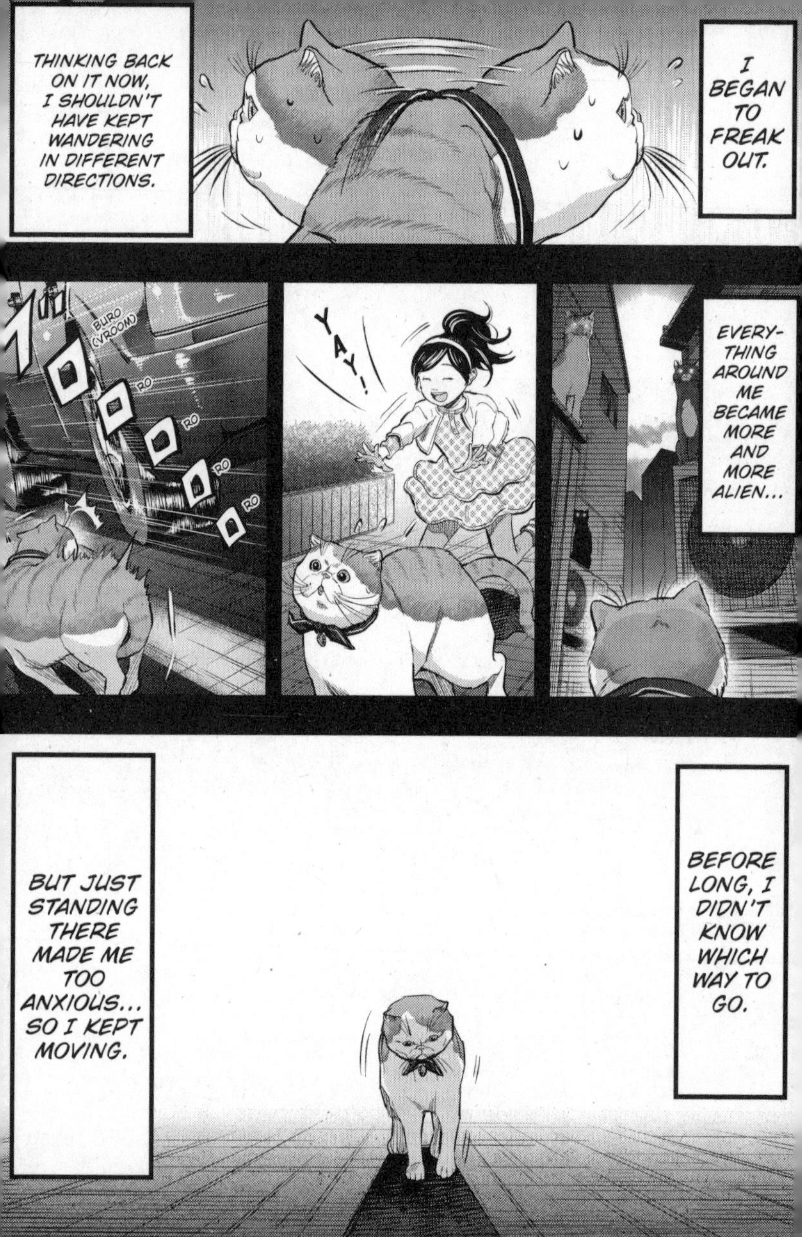
I BEGAN TO FREAK OUT.
THINKING BACK ON IT NOW, I SHOULDN'T HAVE KEPT WANDERING IN DIFFERENT DIRECTIONS.
EVERYTHING AROUND ME BECAME MORE AND MORE ALIEN...
YAY!
BURO (VROOM)
RO
RO
RO
RO
BEFORE LONG, I DIDN'T KNOW WHICH WAY TO GO.
BUT JUST STANDING THERE MADE ME TOO ANXIOUS... SO I KEPT MOVING.

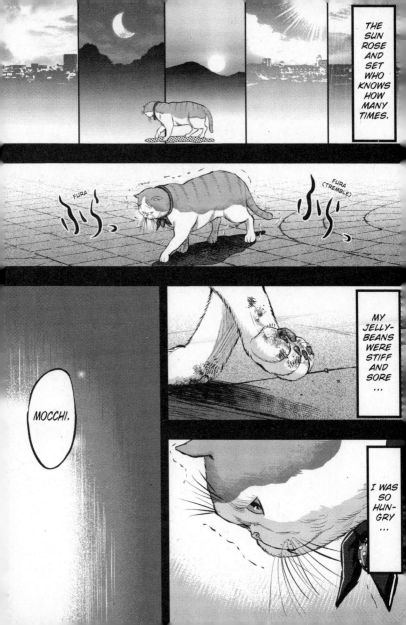

THE SUN ROSE AND SET WHO KNOWS HOW MANY TIMES.

FURA

FURA (TREMBLE)

MY JELLY-BEANS WERE STIFF AND SORE ...

MOCCHI.

I WAS SO HUN-GRY ...

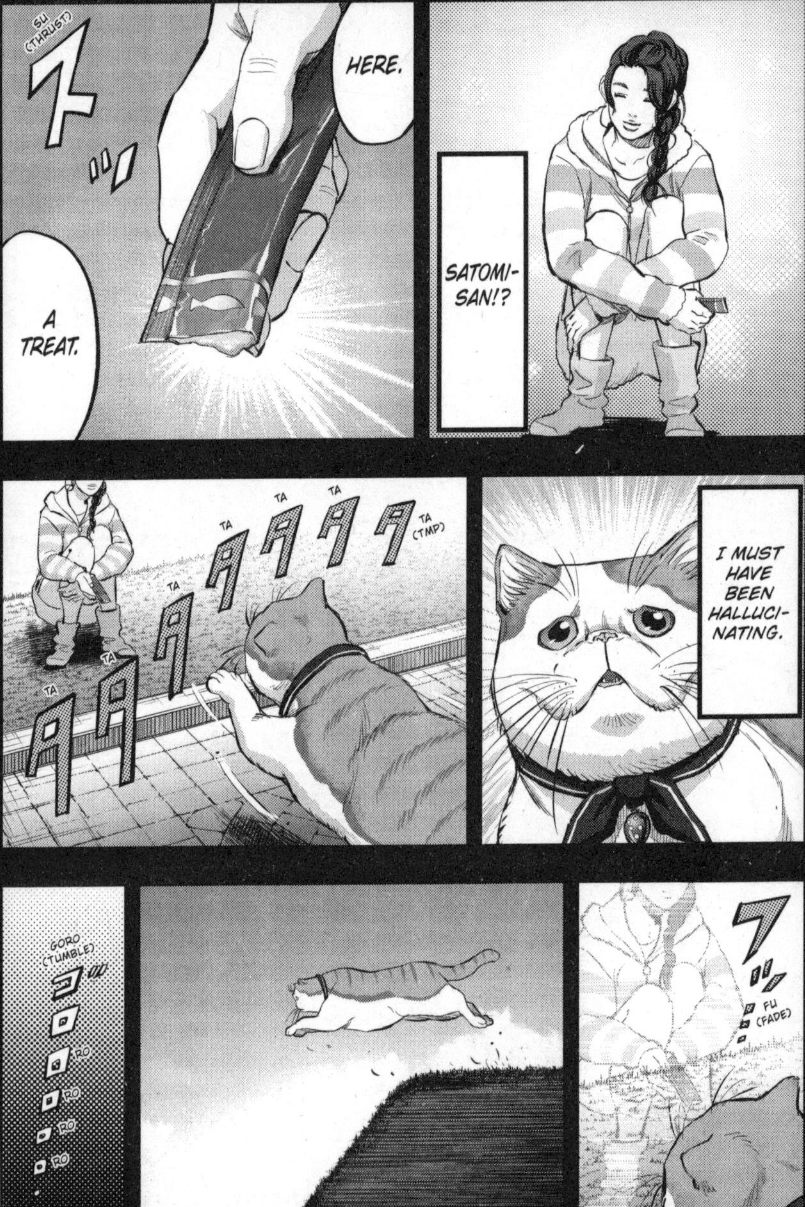
SATOMI-SAN!?
HERE.
SU (THRUST)
A TREAT.
I MUST HAVE BEEN HALLUCINATING.
TA (TMP)
TA
TA
TA
TA
TA
TA
FU (FADE)
GORO (TUMBLE)
RO
RO
RO
RO

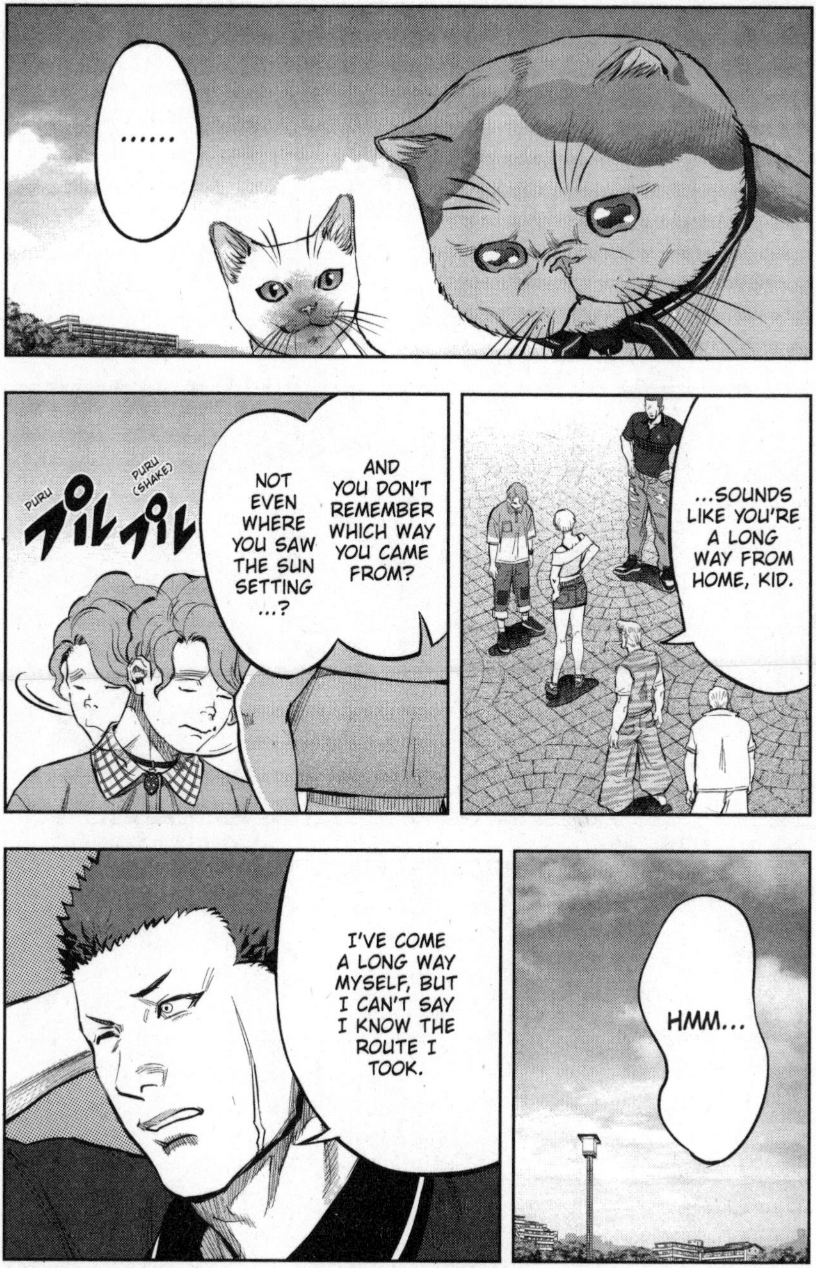
......
...SOUNDS LIKE YOU'RE A LONG WAY FROM HOME, KID.
AND YOU DON'T REMEMBER WHICH WAY YOU CAME FROM?
NOT EVEN WHERE YOU SAW THE SUN SETTING ...?
PURU プル PURU (SHAKE) プル
HMM...
I'VE COME A LONG WAY MYSELF, BUT I CAN'T SAY I KNOW THE ROUTE I TOOK.

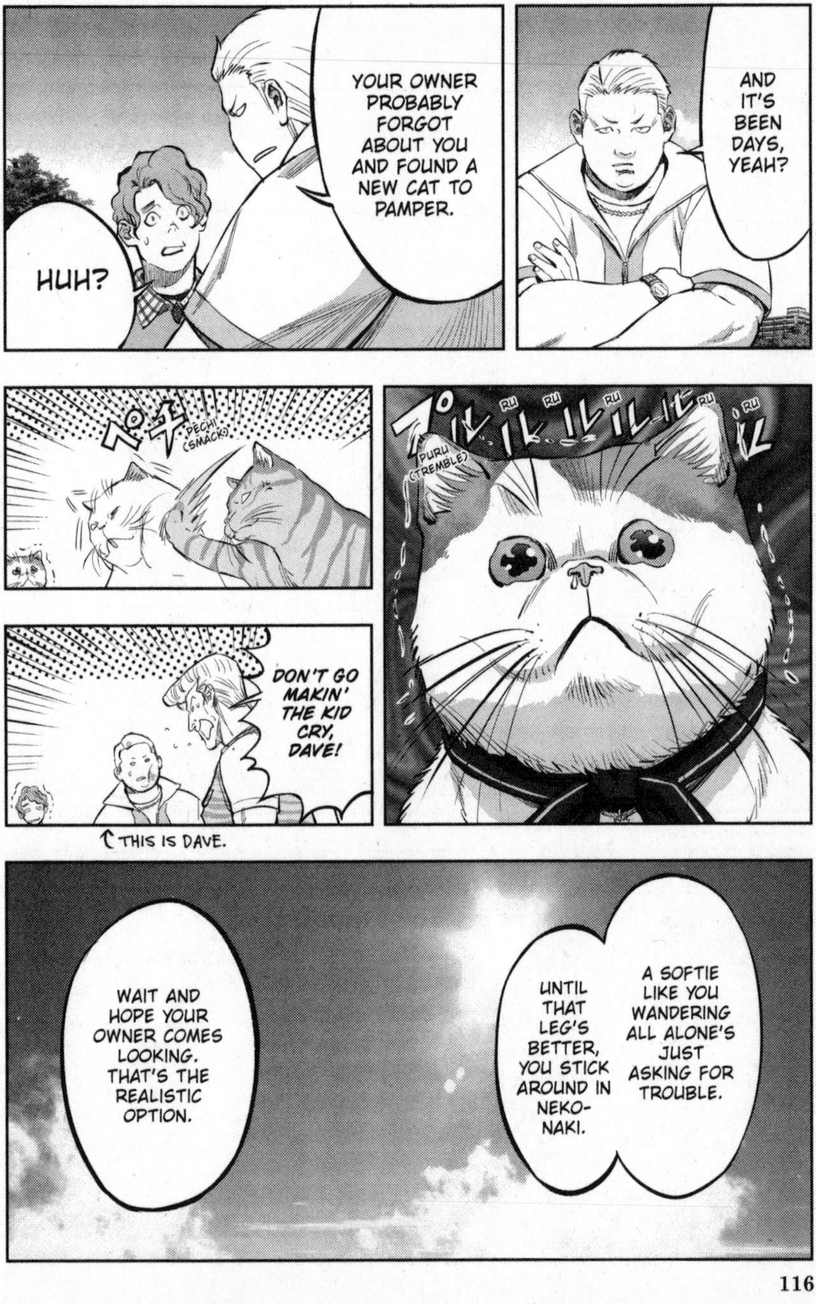
AND IT'S BEEN DAYS, YEAH?
YOUR OWNER PROBABLY FORGOT ABOUT YOU AND FOUND A NEW CAT TO PAMPER.
HUH?
PURU RU RU RU RU RU (TREMBLE)
PECHI (SMACK)
DON'T GO MAKIN' THE KID CRY, DAVE!
THIS IS DAVE.
A SOFTIE LIKE YOU WANDERING ALL ALONE'S JUST ASKING FOR TROUBLE.
UNTIL THAT LEG'S BETTER, YOU STICK AROUND IN NEKO-NAKI.
WAIT AND HOPE YOUR OWNER COMES LOOKING. THAT'S THE REALISTIC OPTION.

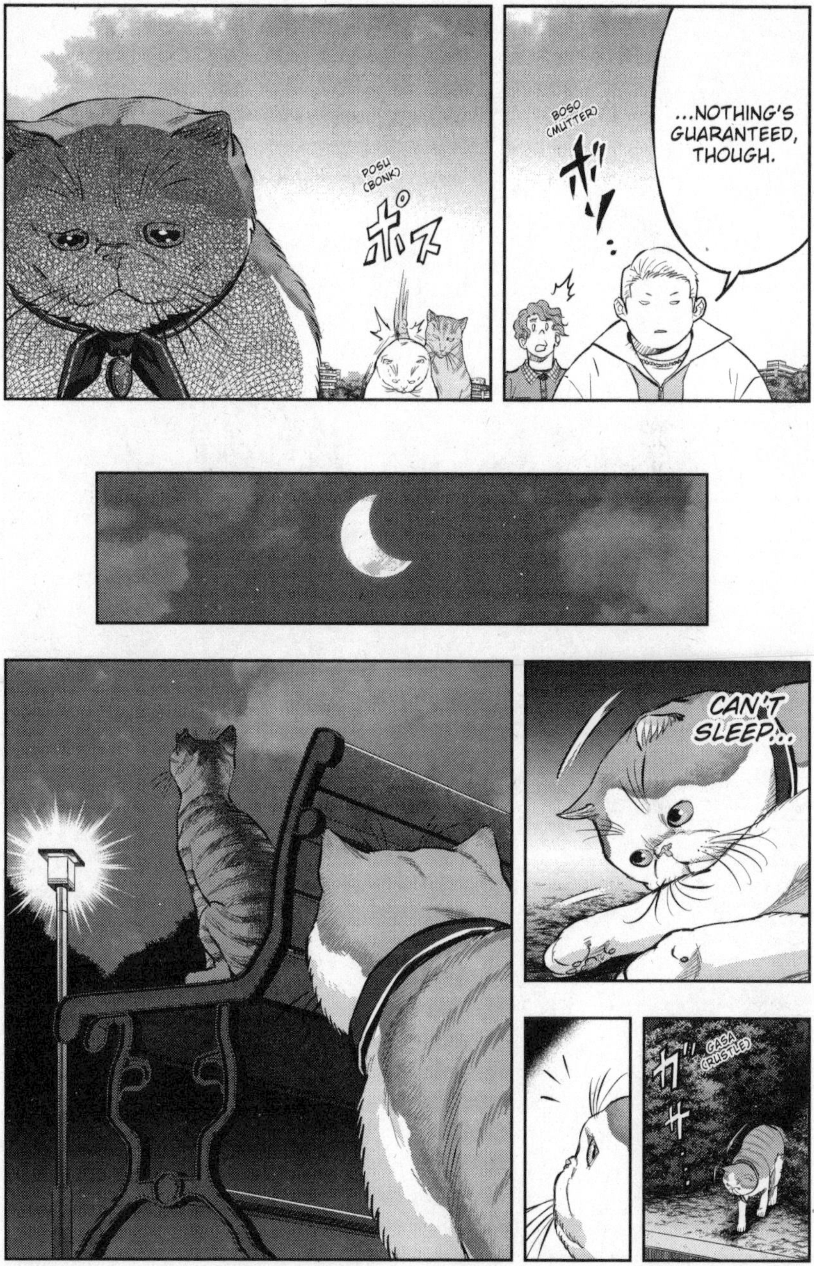
BOSO (MUTTER)
ボソ
...NOTHING'S GUARANTEED, THOUGH.
POSU (BONK)
ポス
CAN'T SLEEP...
GASA (RUSTLE)
ガサ

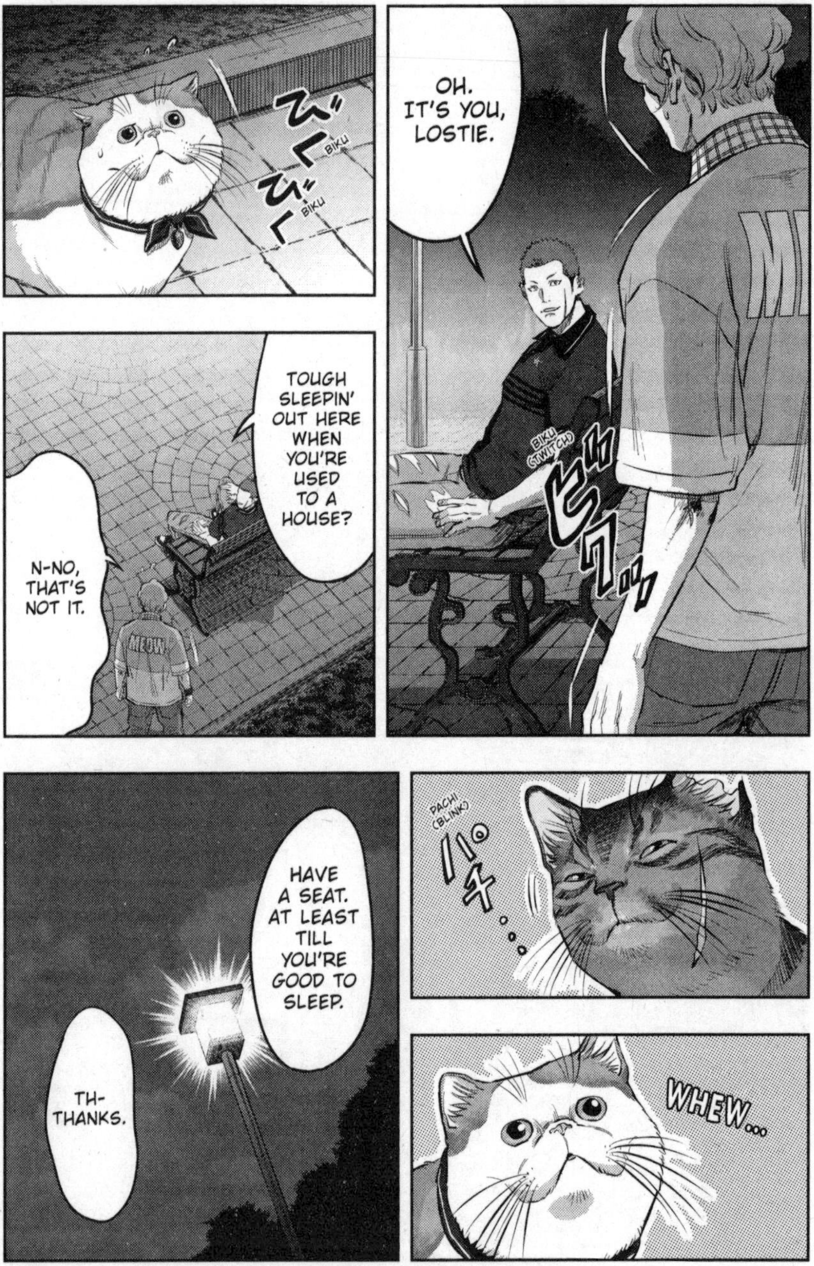
OH. IT'S YOU, LOSTIE.
BIKU (TWITCH)
BIKU
BIKU
TOUGH SLEEPIN' OUT HERE WHEN YOU'RE USED TO A HOUSE?
N-NO, THAT'S NOT IT.
PACHI (BLINK)
WHEW...
HAVE A SEAT. AT LEAST TILL YOU'RE GOOD TO SLEEP.
TH-THANKS.
MEOW

※ CATS WILL BLINK SLOWLY TO INDICATE A LACK OF HOSTILITY

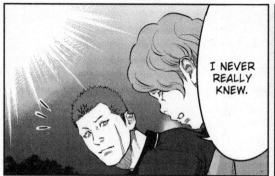

I NEVER REALLY KNEW.
HOW HARD YOU OUTDOOR CATS HAVE IT, I MEAN.
IT SEEMS LIKE A STRUGGLE ...
MEOW
WELL, NOT ALL CATS ARE BORN THE SAME.
THE STRAY LIFE JUST SUITS ME, THAT'S ALL.
......

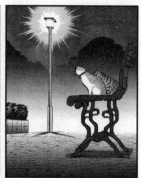

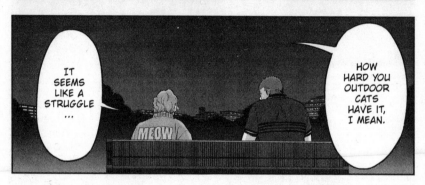

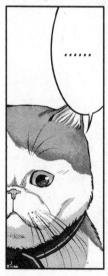

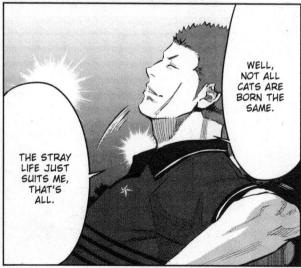

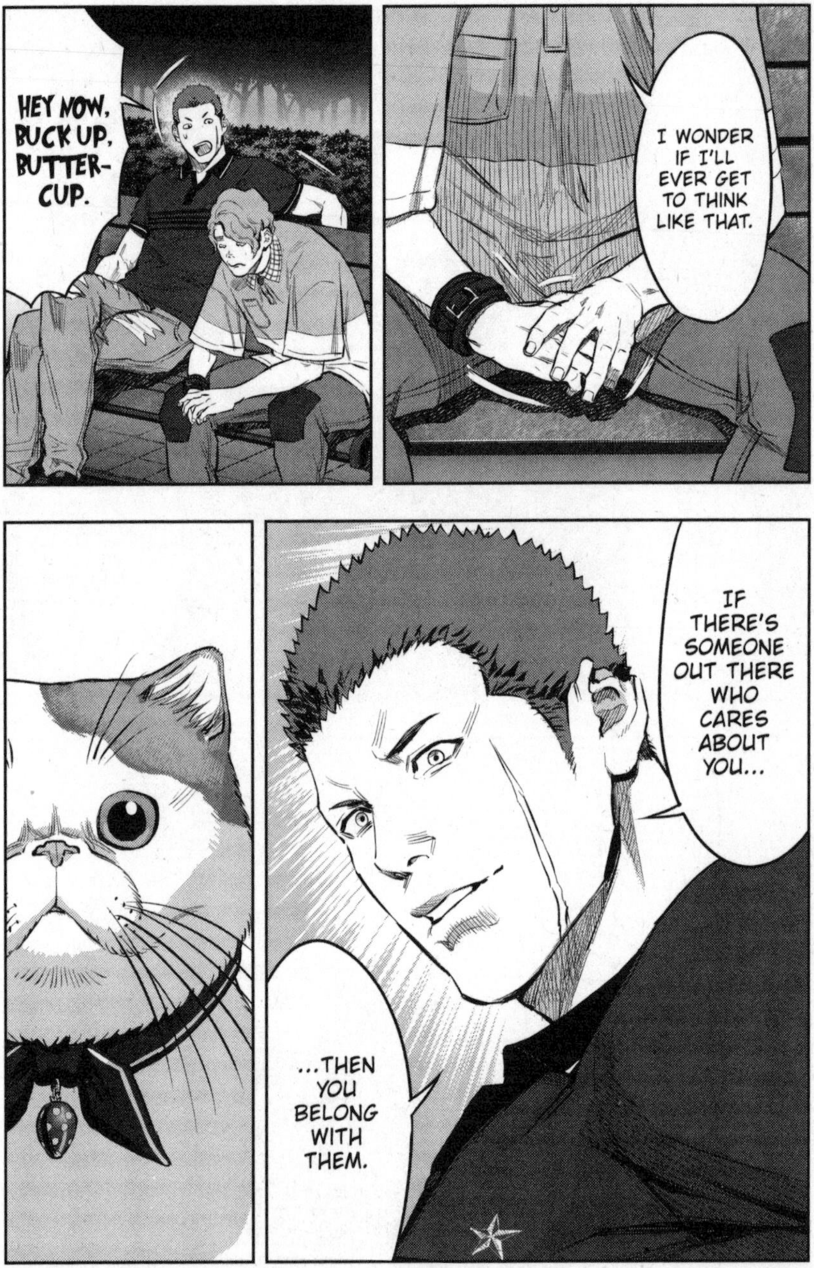
I WONDER IF I'LL EVER GET TO THINK LIKE THAT.
HEY NOW, BUCK UP, BUTTER-CUP.
IF THERE'S SOMEONE OUT THERE WHO CARES ABOUT YOU...
...THEN YOU BELONG WITH THEM.

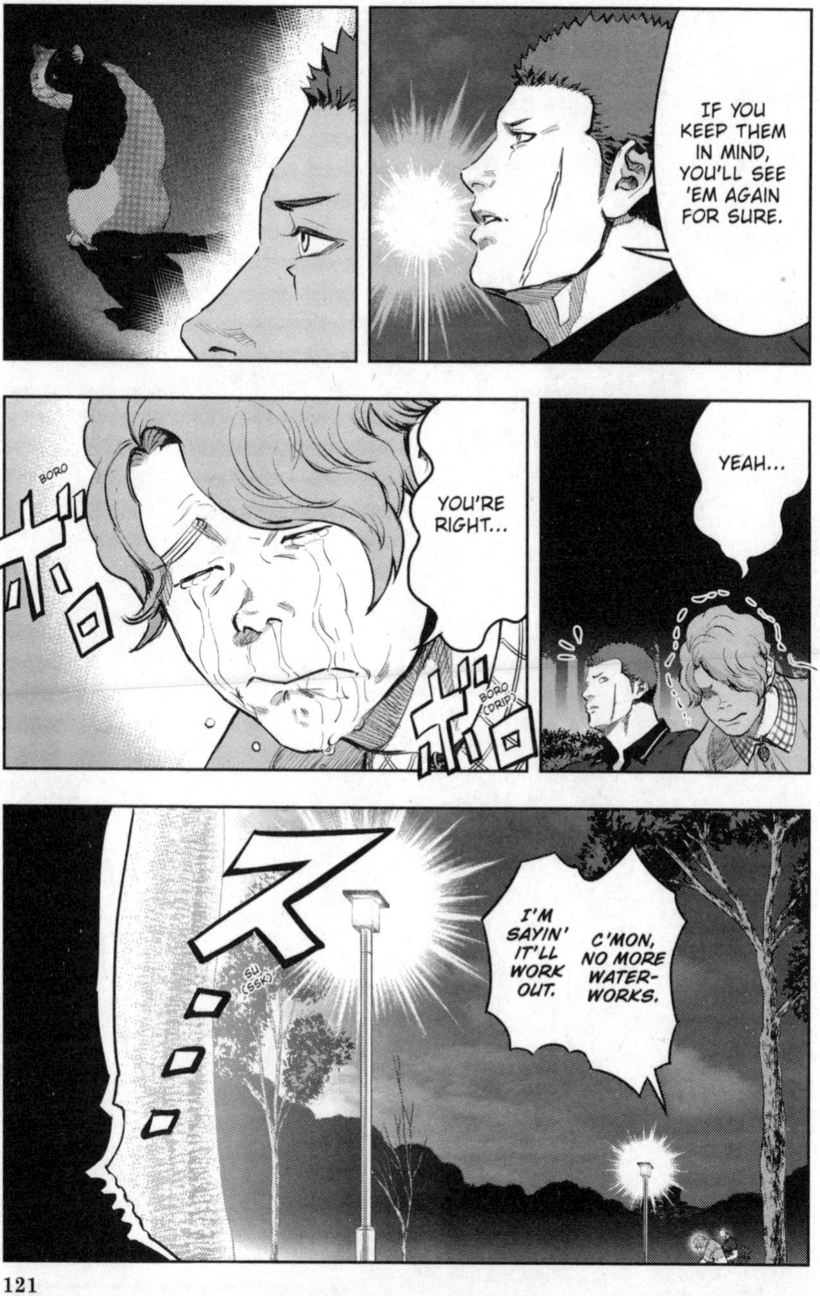
IF YOU KEEP THEM IN MIND, YOU'LL SEE 'EM AGAIN FOR SURE.
YEAH...
YOU'RE RIGHT...
BORO (DRIP)
BORO
C'MON, NO MORE WATER-WORKS.
I'M SAYIN' IT'LL WORK OUT.
SU (SSK)

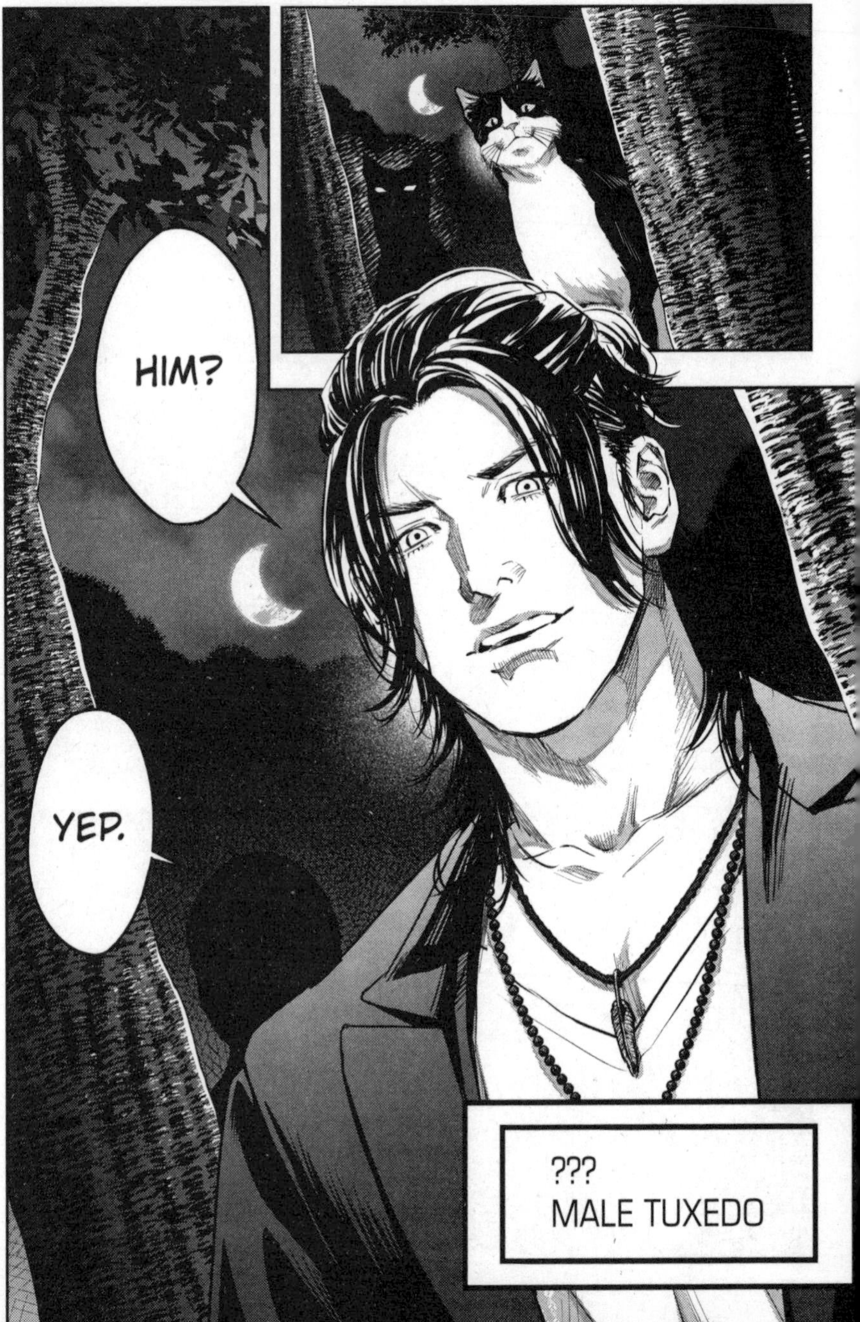
HIM?
YEP.
???
MALE TUXEDO

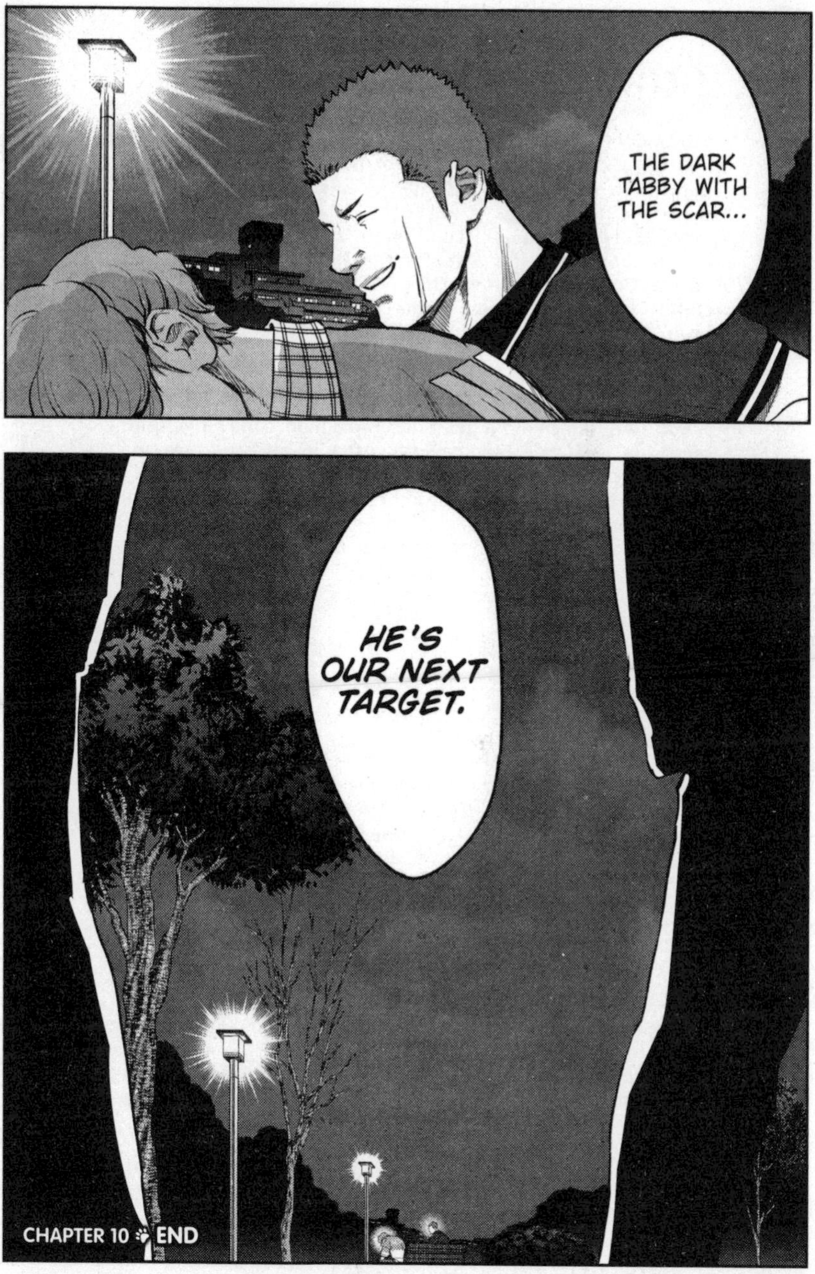
THE DARK TABBY WITH THE SCAR...
HE'S OUR NEXT TARGET.
CHAPTER 10 END

TRANSLATION NOTES

COMMON HONORIFICS
no honorific: Indicates familiarity or closeness; if used without permission or reason, addressing someone in this manner would constitute an insult.
-san: The Japanese equivalent of Mr./Mrs./Miss. If a situation calls for politeness, this is the fail-safe honorific.
-sama: Conveys great respect; may also indicate that the social status of the speaker is lower than that of the addressee.
-kun: Used most often when referring to boys, this indicates affection or familiarity. Occasionally used by older men among their peers, but it may also be used by anyone referring to a person of lower standing.
-chan: An affectionate honorific indicating familiarity used mostly in reference to girls; also used in reference to cute persons or animals of either gender.
-senpai: A suffix used to address upperclassmen or more experienced coworkers.
-kouhai: A suffix used to address underclassmen or less experienced coworkers.
-sensei: A respectful term for teachers, artists, or high-level professionals.

PAGE 6
The word "stray," or *nora*, is made up of the characters for "fields," or "farm" (*no*), and "skilled" (*ra*) in Japanese.

PAGE 101
In Japan, young high school thugs or rebels are usually referred to as *yankiis* or *yankees*. (The title *Nyankees* consists of both this word and *nya*—the Japanese onomatopoeia for a cat's meow.) In popular media, they are usually characterized as having blonde and orange hair, altered uniforms, and motorcycle jackets.

PAGE 160
An *izakaya* is a Japanese-style pub that serves a variety of side dishes and alcohol. It is popular for casual parties and social gatherings among young students and working adults.

Suzumenomiya literally translates to "a sparrow's palace." *Suzu* means "sparrow," and *miya* means palace or residence.

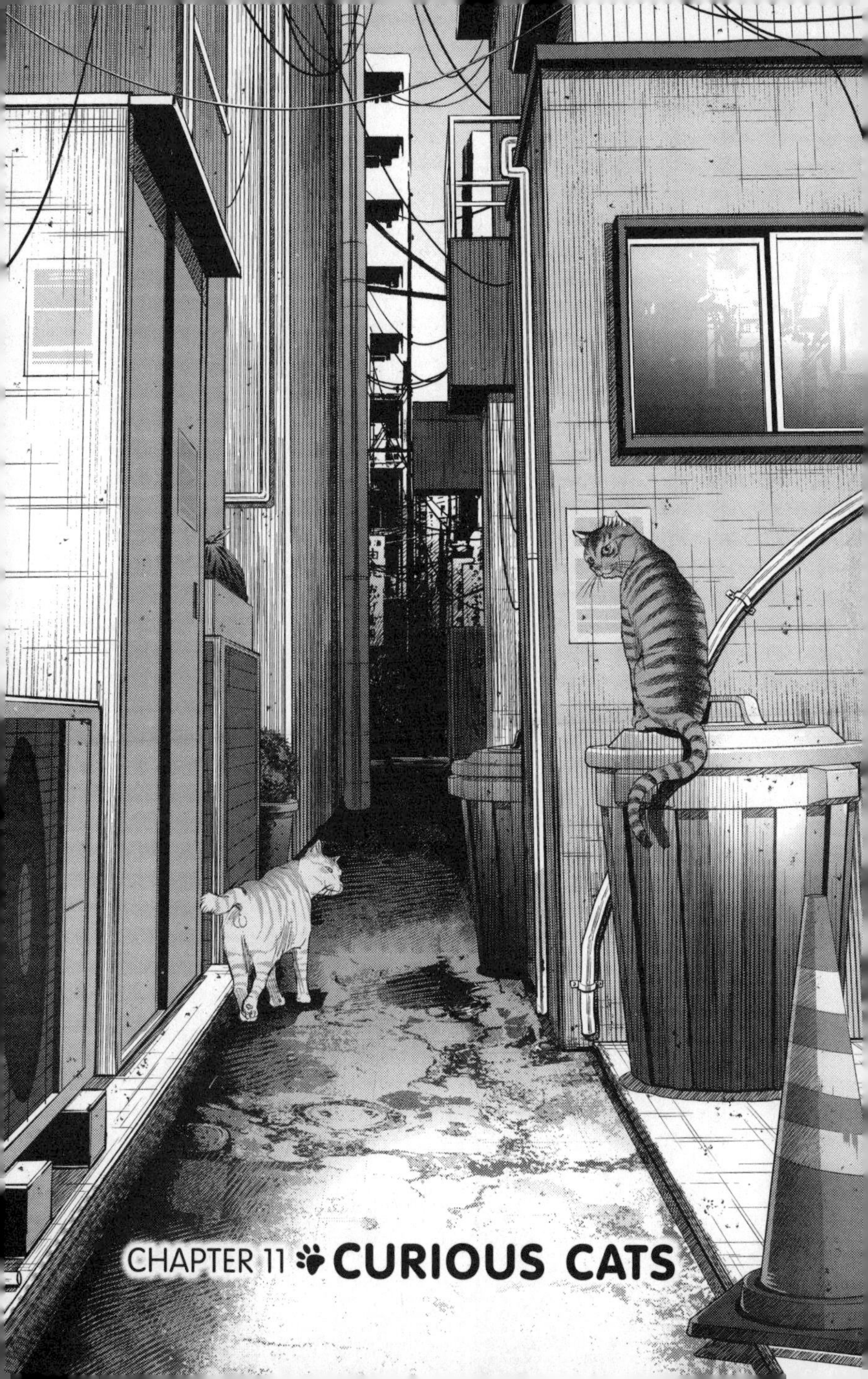
CHAPTER 11 CURIOUS CATS

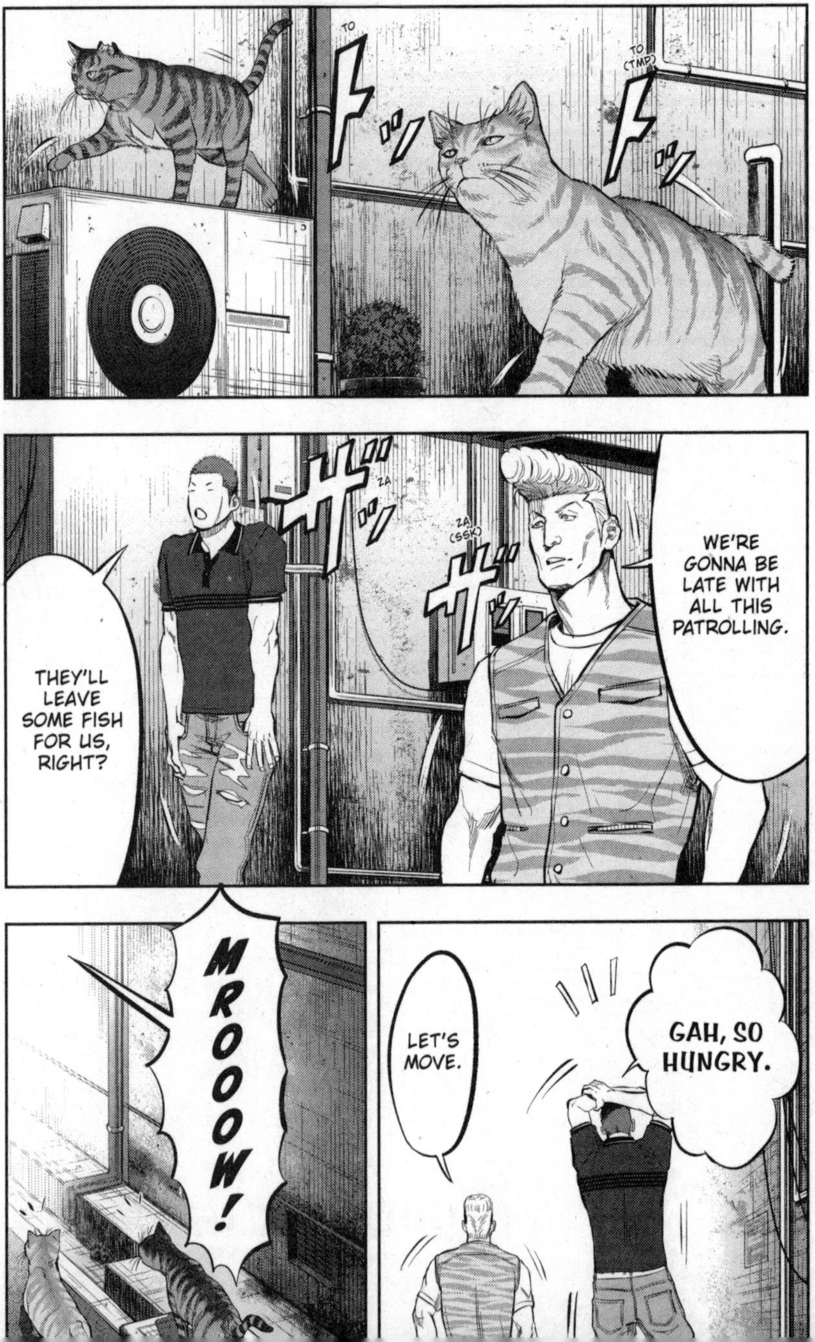
TO
(TMP)
TO
WE'RE GONNA BE LATE WITH ALL THIS PATROLLING.
ZA
(SSK)
ZA
THEY'LL LEAVE SOME FISH FOR US, RIGHT?
GAH, SO HUNGRY.
LET'S MOVE.
MROOOOW!

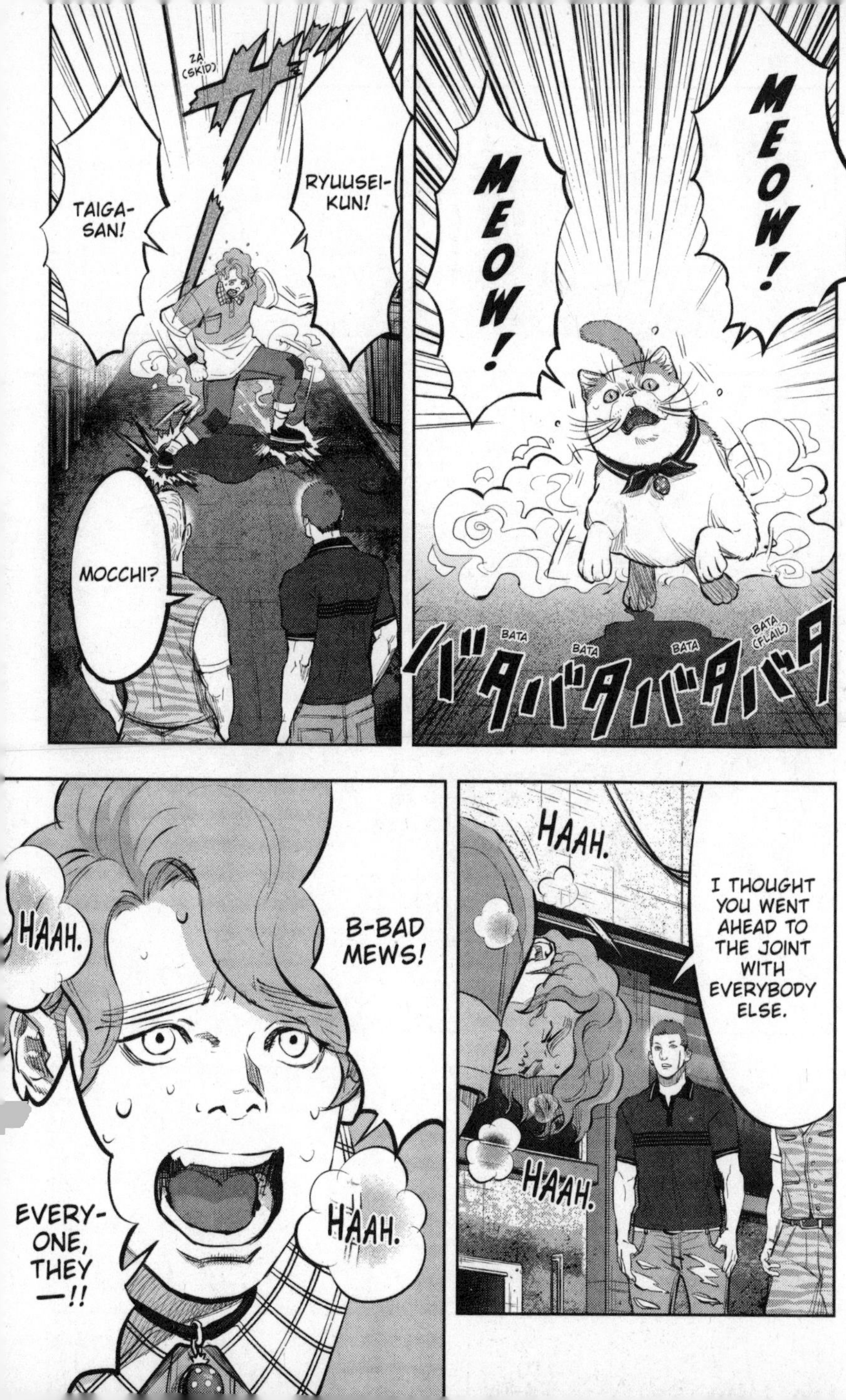
MEOW!
MEOW!
BATA BATA BATA BATA (FLAIL)
ZA (SKID)
RYUUSEI-KUN!
TAIGA-SAN!
MOCCHI?
HAAH.
I THOUGHT YOU WENT AHEAD TO THE JOINT WITH EVERYBODY ELSE.
HAAH.
B-BAD MEWS!
HAAH.
HAAH.
EVERY-ONE, THEY —!!

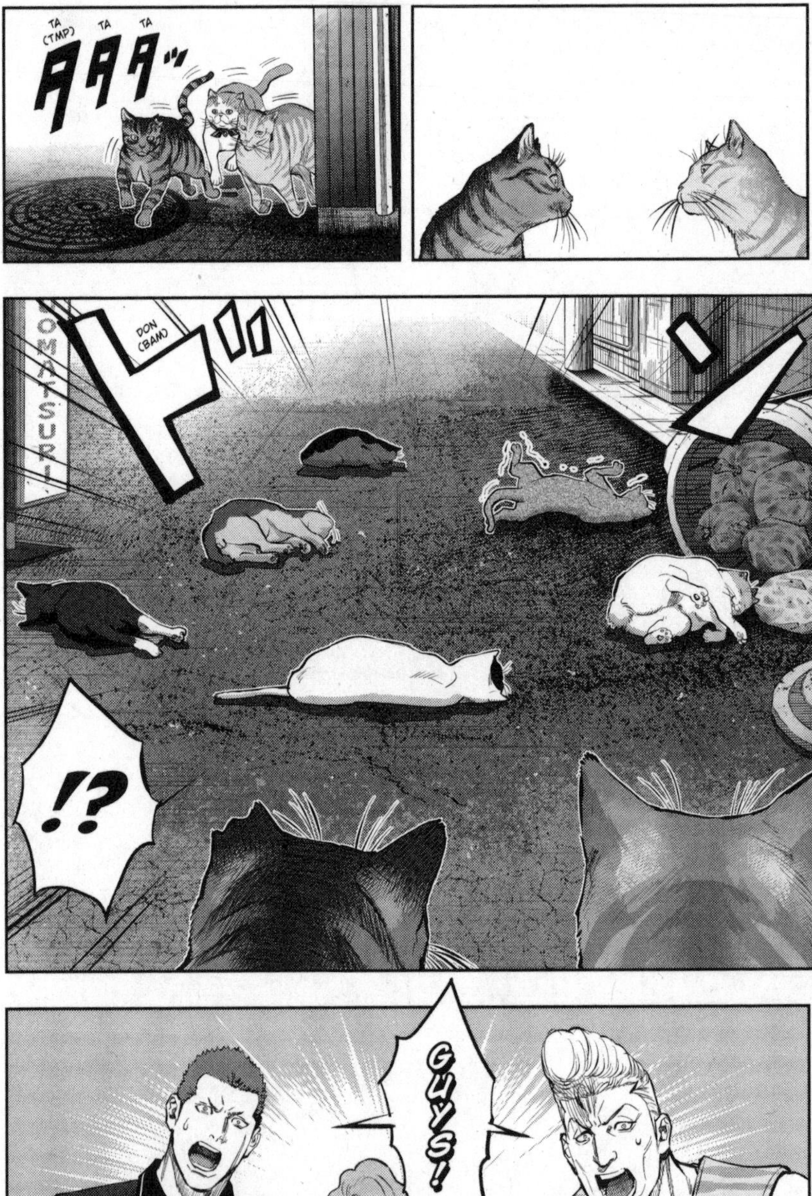
TA (TMP) TA TA
OMATSURI
DON (BAM)
!?
GUYS!

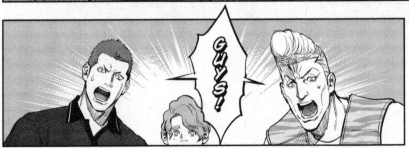

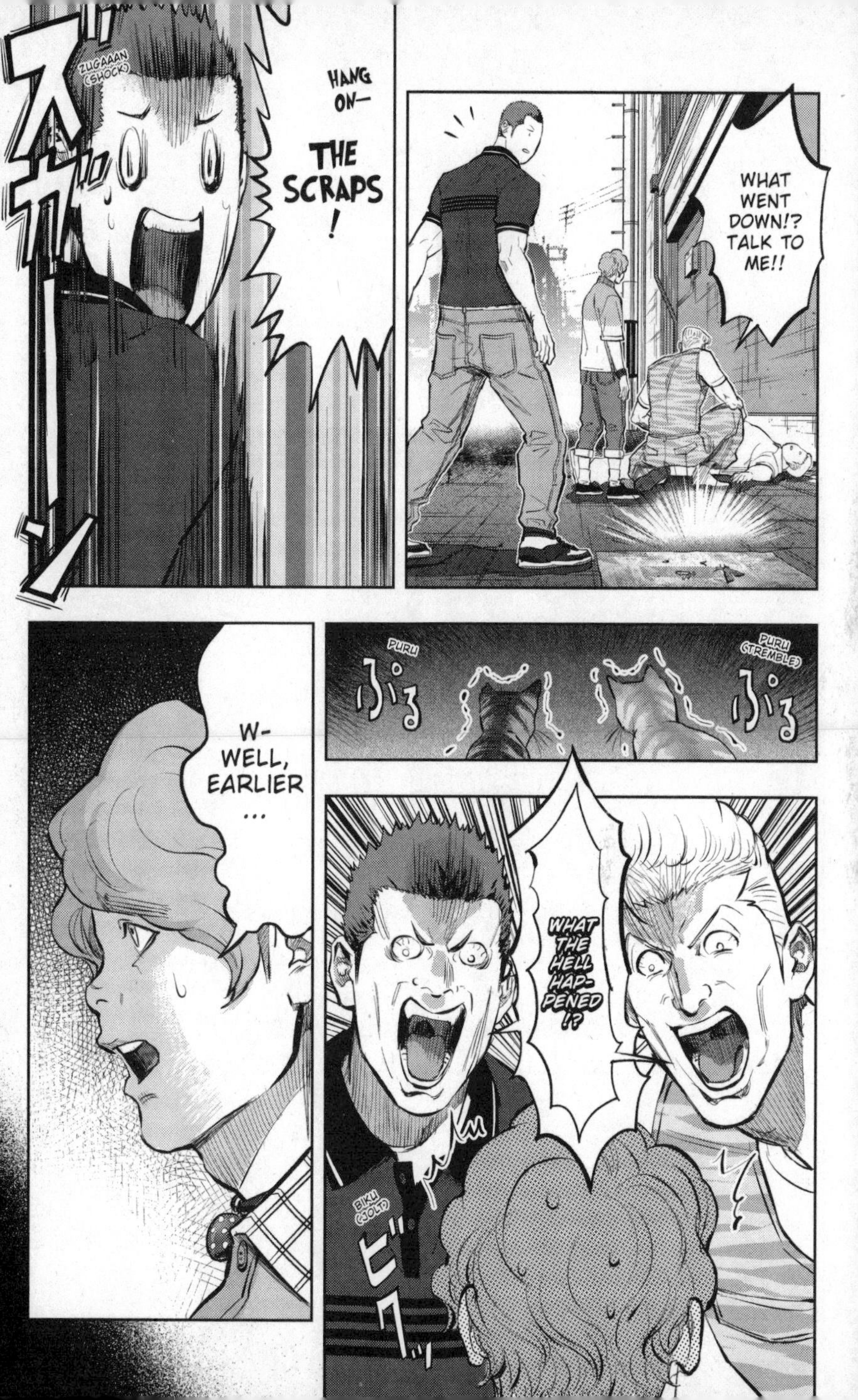
WHAT WENT DOWN!? TALK TO ME!!
ZUGAAAN (SHOCK)
HANG ON—
THE SCRAPS!
PURU (TREMBLE)
PURU
WHAT THE HELL HAPPENED!?
BIKU (JOLT)
W-WELL, EARLIER...

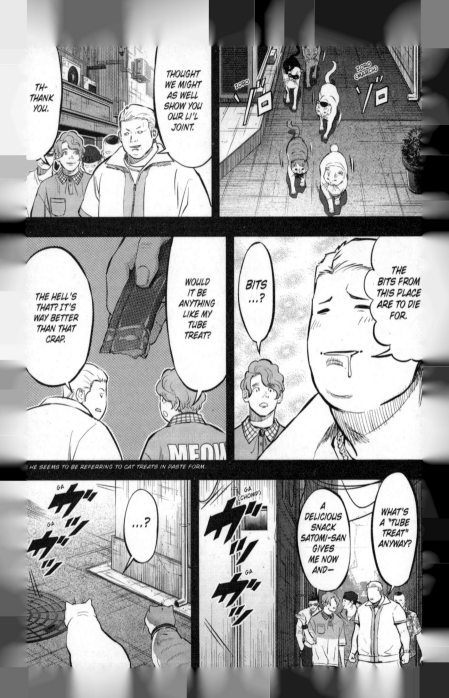

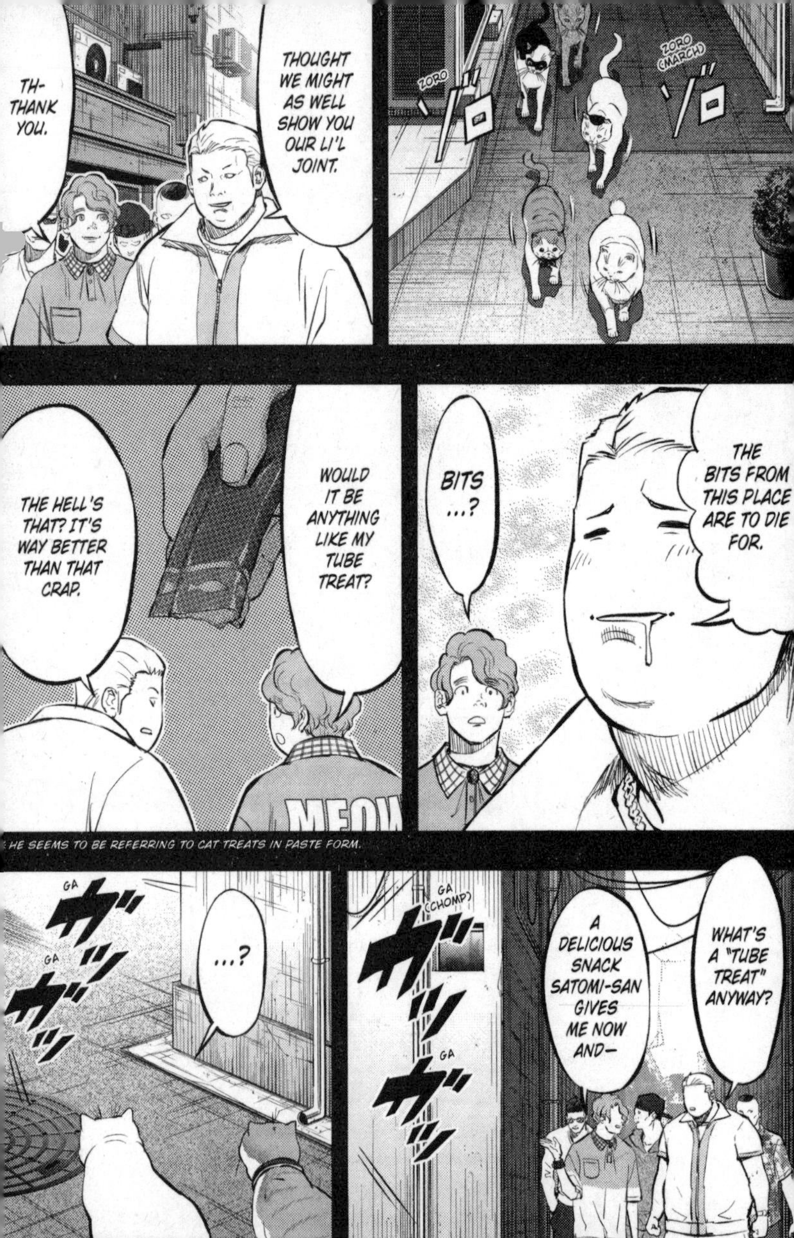
ZORO
ZORO (MARCH)
THOUGHT WE MIGHT AS WELL SHOW YOU OUR LI'L JOINT.
TH-THANK YOU.
THE BITS FROM THIS PLACE ARE TO DIE FOR.
BITS ...?
WOULD IT BE ANYTHING LIKE MY TUBE TREAT?
THE HELL'S THAT? IT'S WAY BETTER THAN THAT CRAP.
MEOW
HE SEEMS TO BE REFERRING TO CAT TREATS IN PASTE FORM.
WHAT'S A "TUBE TREAT" ANYWAY?
A DELICIOUS SNACK SATOMI-SAN GIVES ME NOW AND—
GA (CHOMP)
GA
...?
GA
GA

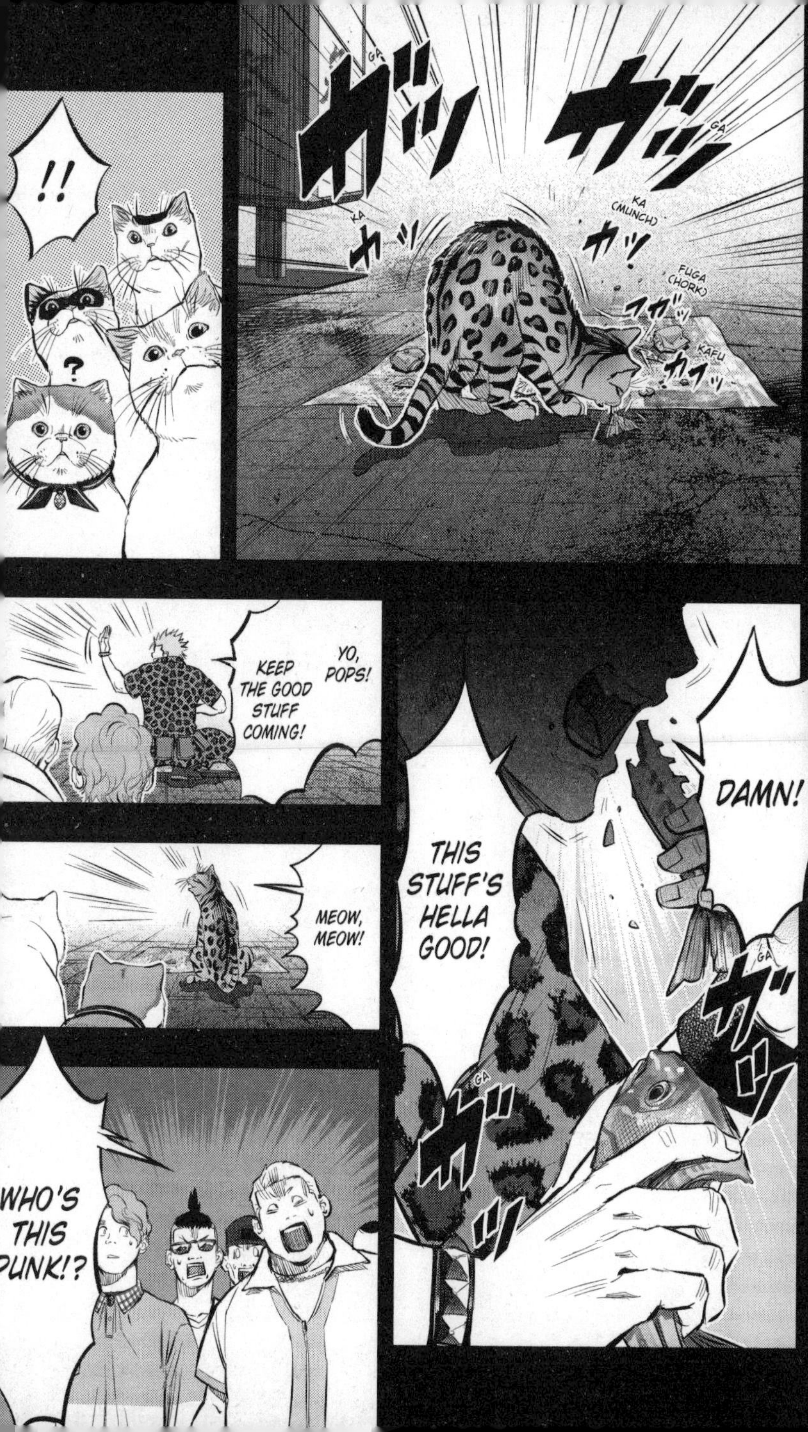
GA
GA
KA (MUNCH)
KA
FUGA (HORK)
KAFU
!!
?
DAMN!
THIS STUFF'S HELLA GOOD!
GA
GA
YO, POPS!
KEEP THE GOOD STUFF COMING!
MEOW, MEOW!
WHO'S THIS PUNK!?

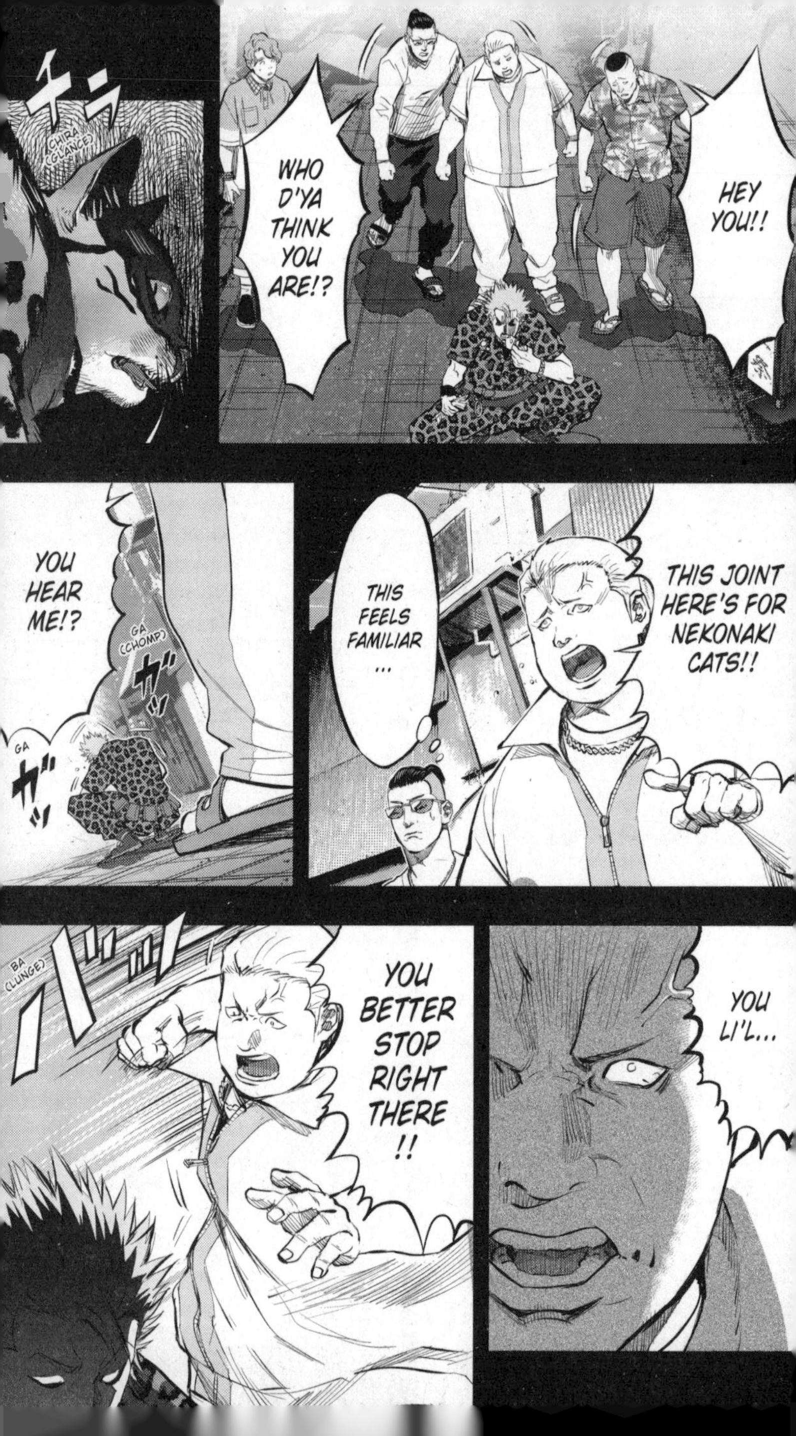
HEY YOU!!
WHO D'YA THINK YOU ARE!?
CHIRA (GLANCE)
THIS JOINT HERE'S FOR NEKONAKI CATS!!
THIS FEELS FAMILIAR ...
YOU HEAR ME!?
GA (CHOMP)
GA
YOU LI'L...
YOU BETTER STOP RIGHT THERE !!
BA (LUNGE)

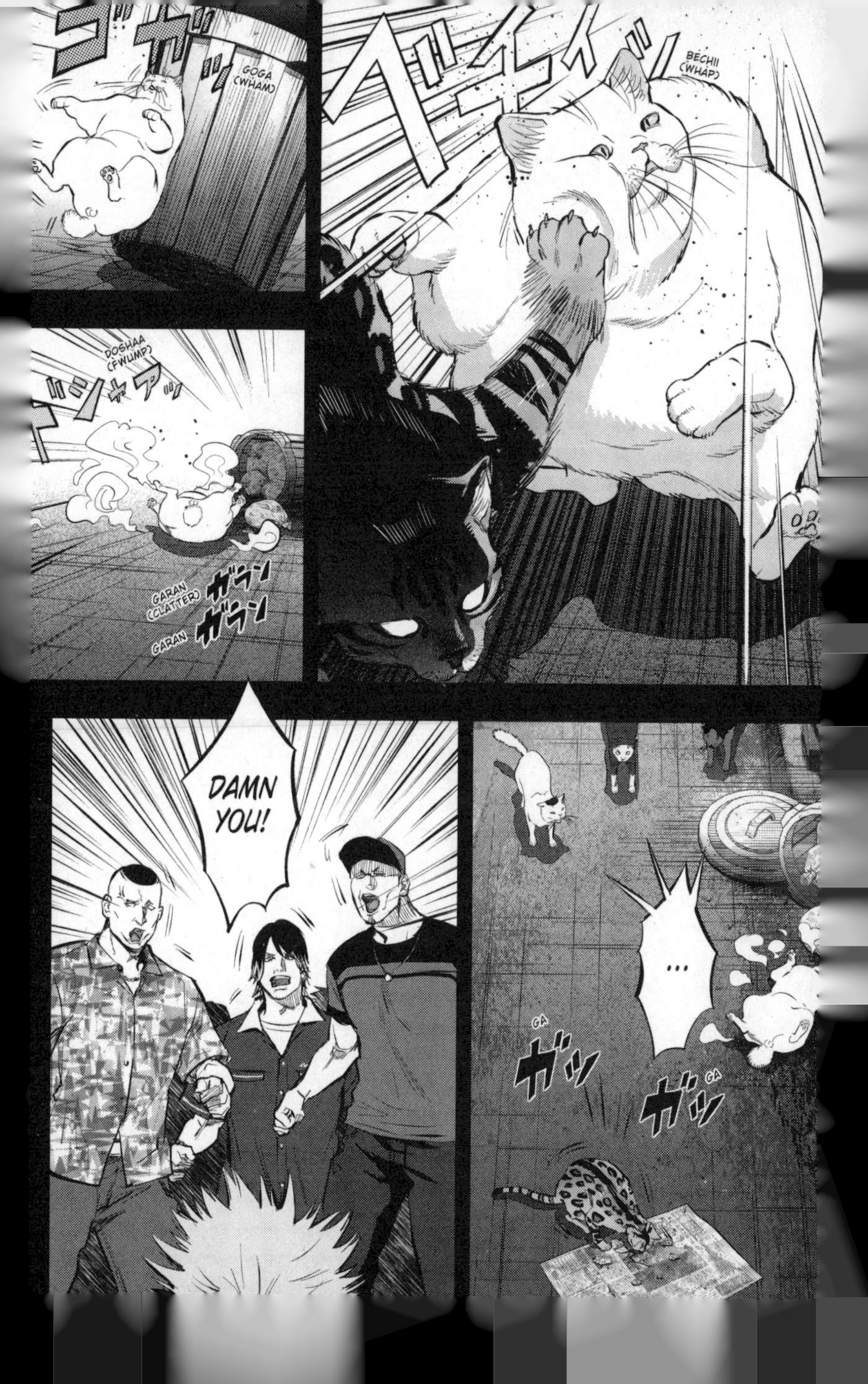
BECHII (WHAP)
GOGA (WHAM)
DOSHAA (FWUMP)
GARAN (CLATTER)
GARAN
...
GA
GA
DAMN YOU!

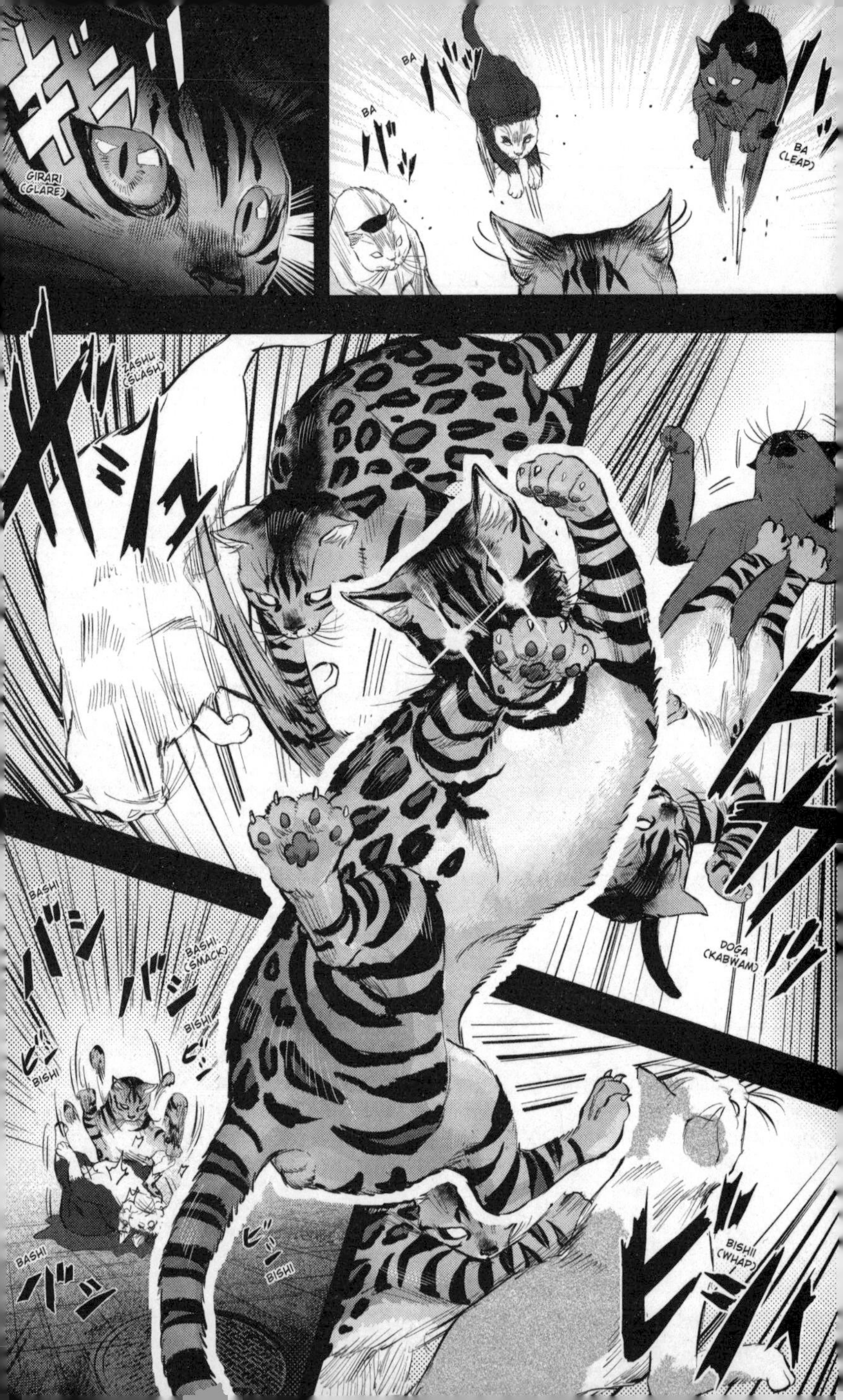
BA (LEAP)
BA
BA
GIRARI (GLARE)
DOGA (KABWAM)
ZASHU (SLASH)
BISHII (WHAP)
BISHI
BISHI
BASHI (SMACK)
BASHI
BISHI
BASHI

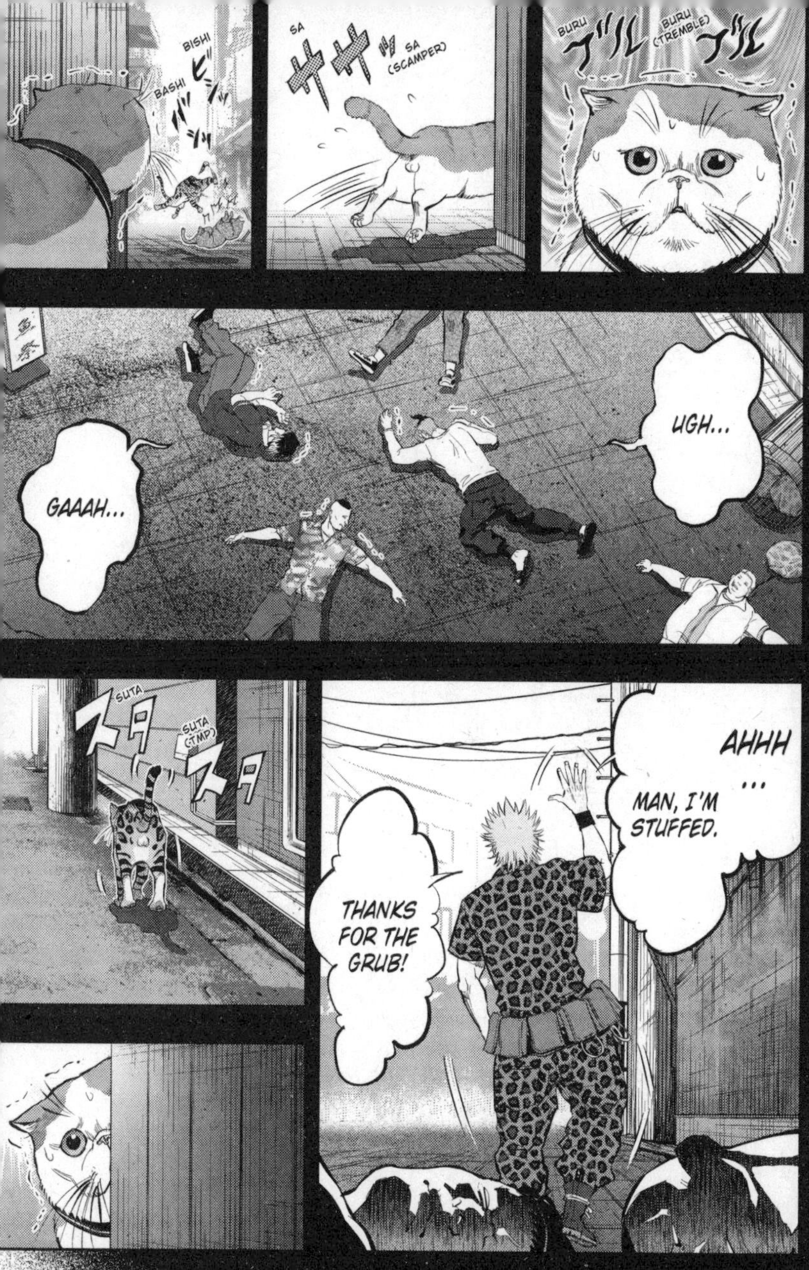
BURU
BURU (TREMBLE)
SA
SA (SCAMPER)
BISHI
BASHI
UGH...
GAAAH...
AHHH...
MAN, I'M STUFFED.
THANKS FOR THE GRUB!
SUTA
SUTA (TMP)

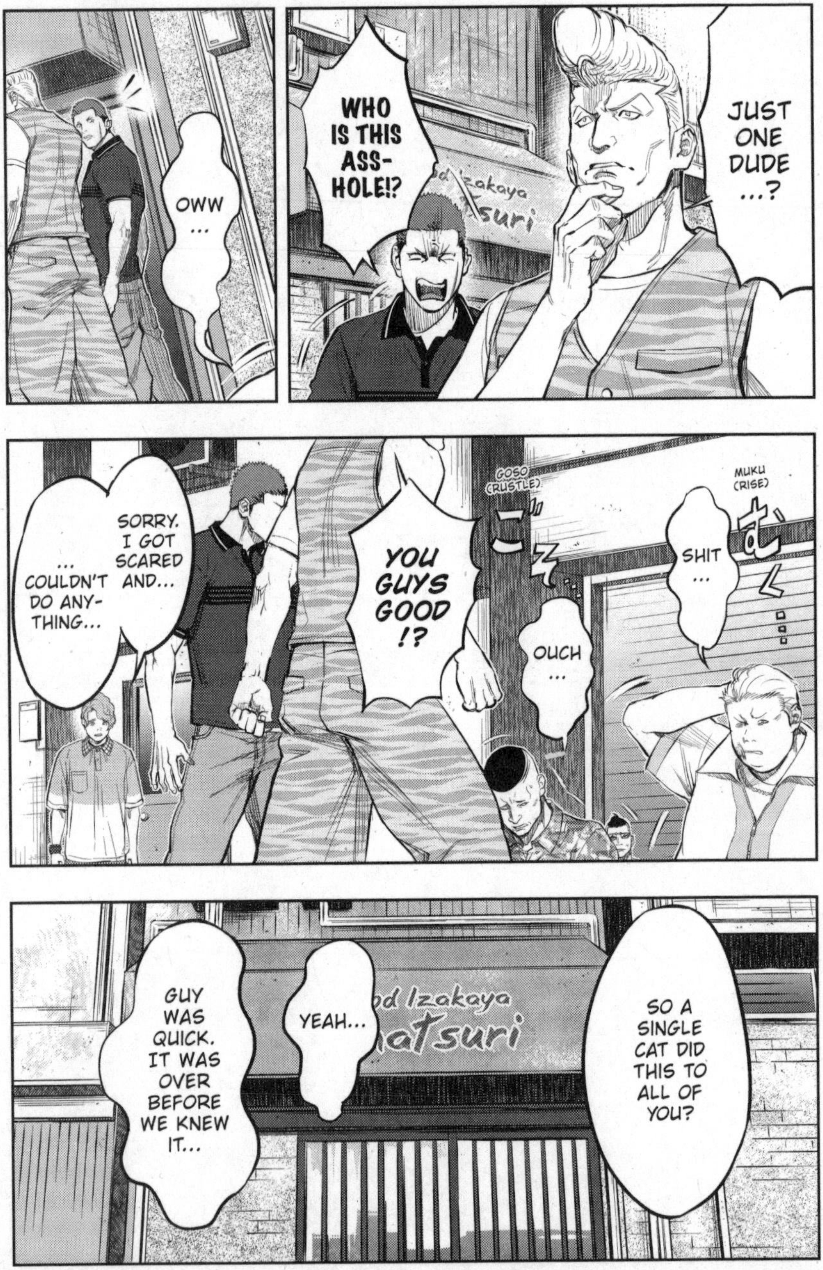
JUST ONE DUDE ...?
WHO IS THIS ASS-HOLE!?
OWW ...
MUKU (RISE)
SHIT ...
GOSO (RUSTLE)
OUCH ...
YOU GUYS GOOD !?
SORRY. I GOT SCARED AND...
... COULDN'T DO ANY-THING...
SO A SINGLE CAT DID THIS TO ALL OF YOU?
YEAH...
GUY WAS QUICK. IT WAS OVER BEFORE WE KNEW IT...

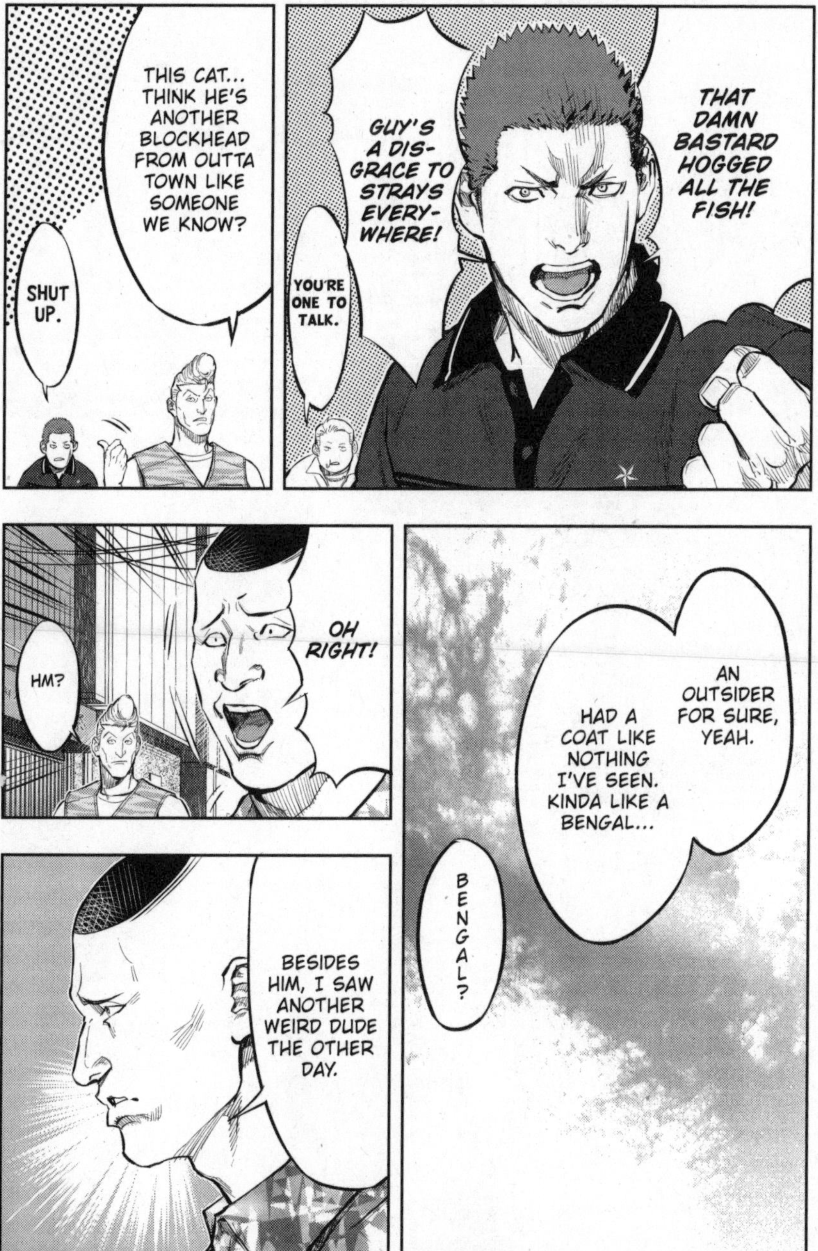
THAT DAMN BASTARD HOGGED ALL THE FISH!
GUY'S A DISGRACE TO STRAYS EVERYWHERE!
YOU'RE ONE TO TALK.
THIS CAT... THINK HE'S ANOTHER BLOCKHEAD FROM OUTTA TOWN LIKE SOMEONE WE KNOW?
SHUT UP.
AN OUTSIDER FOR SURE, YEAH.
HAD A COAT LIKE NOTHING I'VE SEEN. KINDA LIKE A BENGAL...
BENGAL?
OH RIGHT!
HM?
BESIDES HIM, I SAW ANOTHER WEIRD DUDE THE OTHER DAY.

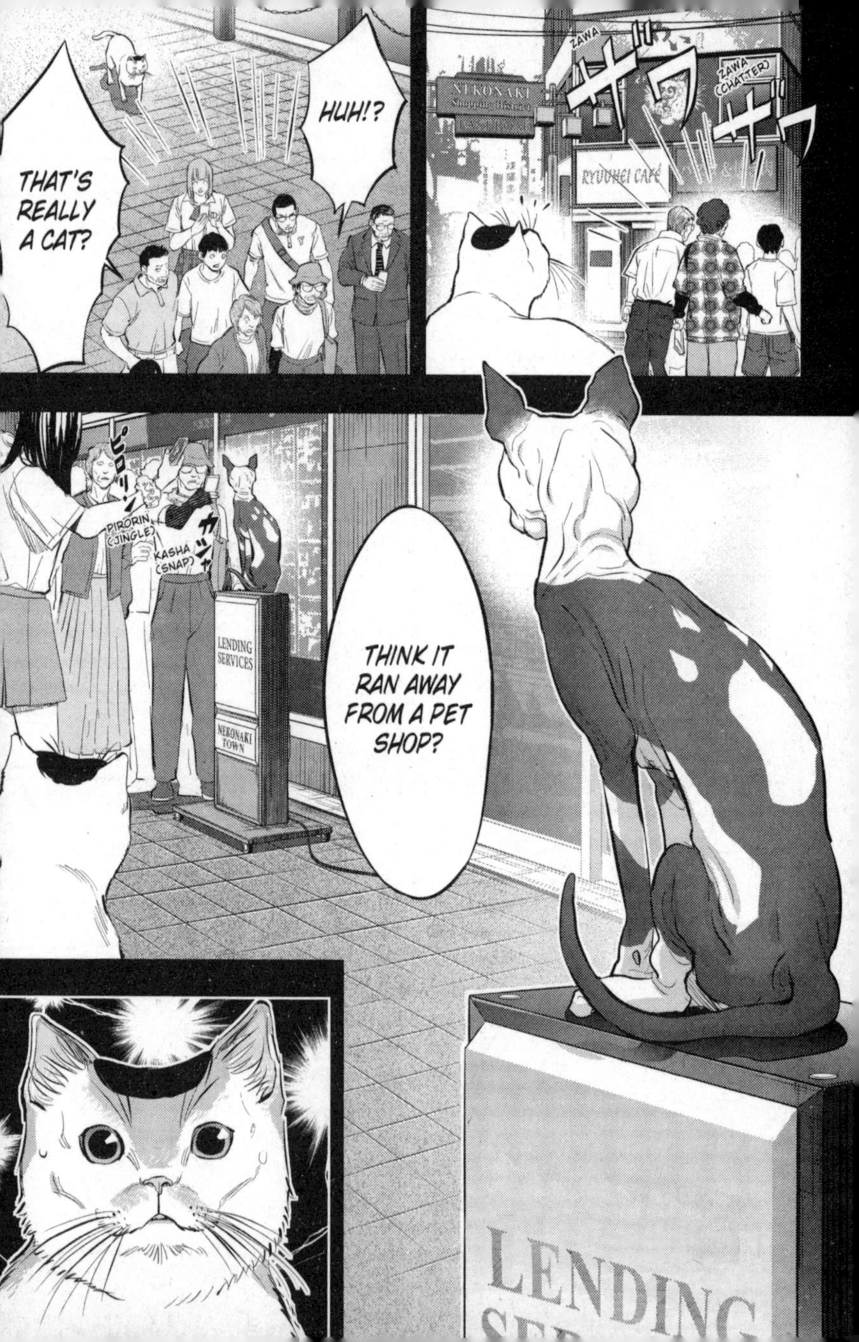
ZAWA
ZAWA (CHATTER)
NEKONAKI Shopping District
RYUUHEI CAFÉ
HUH!?
THAT'S REALLY A CAT?
THINK IT RAN AWAY FROM A PET SHOP?
PIRORIN (JINGLE)
KASHA (SNAP)
LENDING SERVICES
NEKONAKI TOWN
LENDING

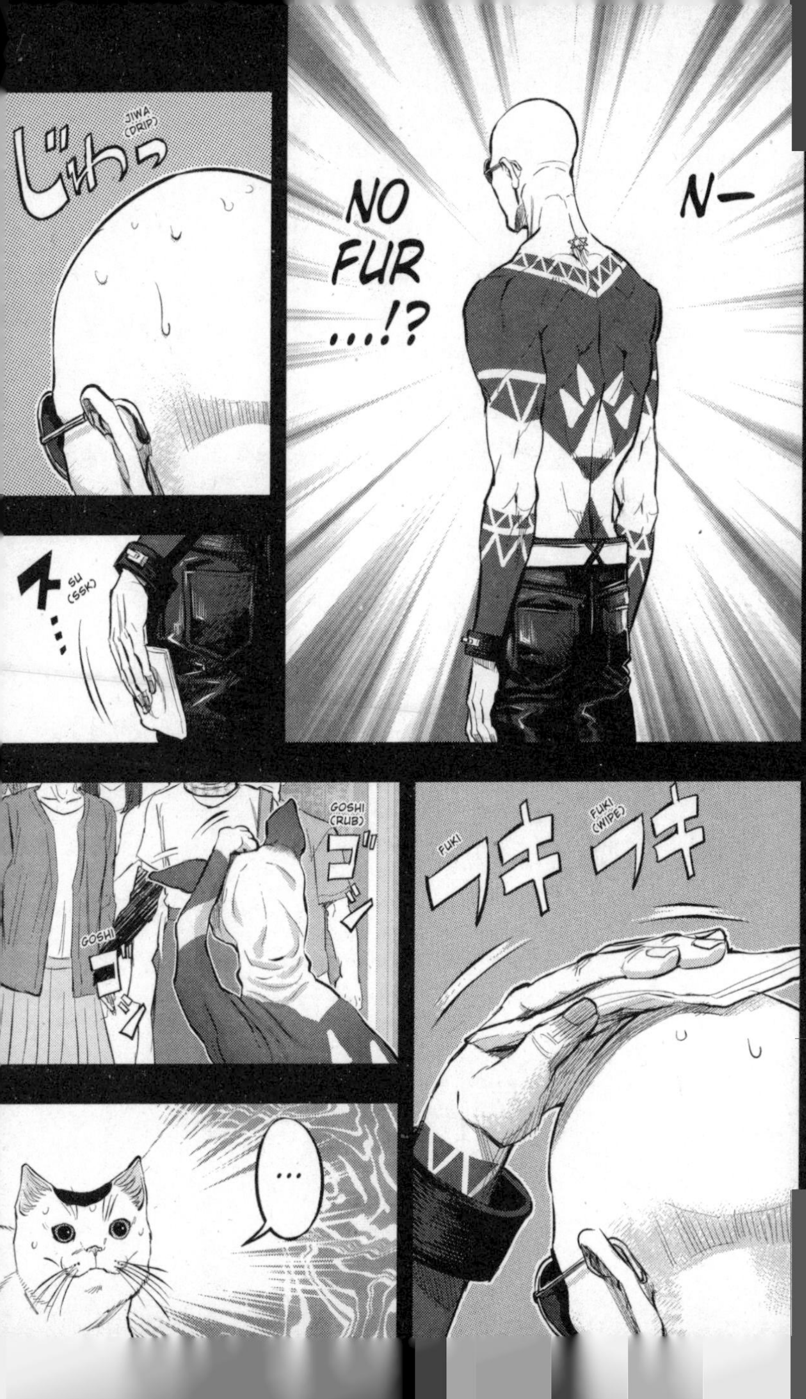
N—
NO FUR ...!?
じわっ
JIWA (DRIP)
ス…
SU (SSK)
フキ フキ
FUKI
FUKI (WIPE)
ゴシ
GOSHI (RUB)
ゴシ
GOSHI
...

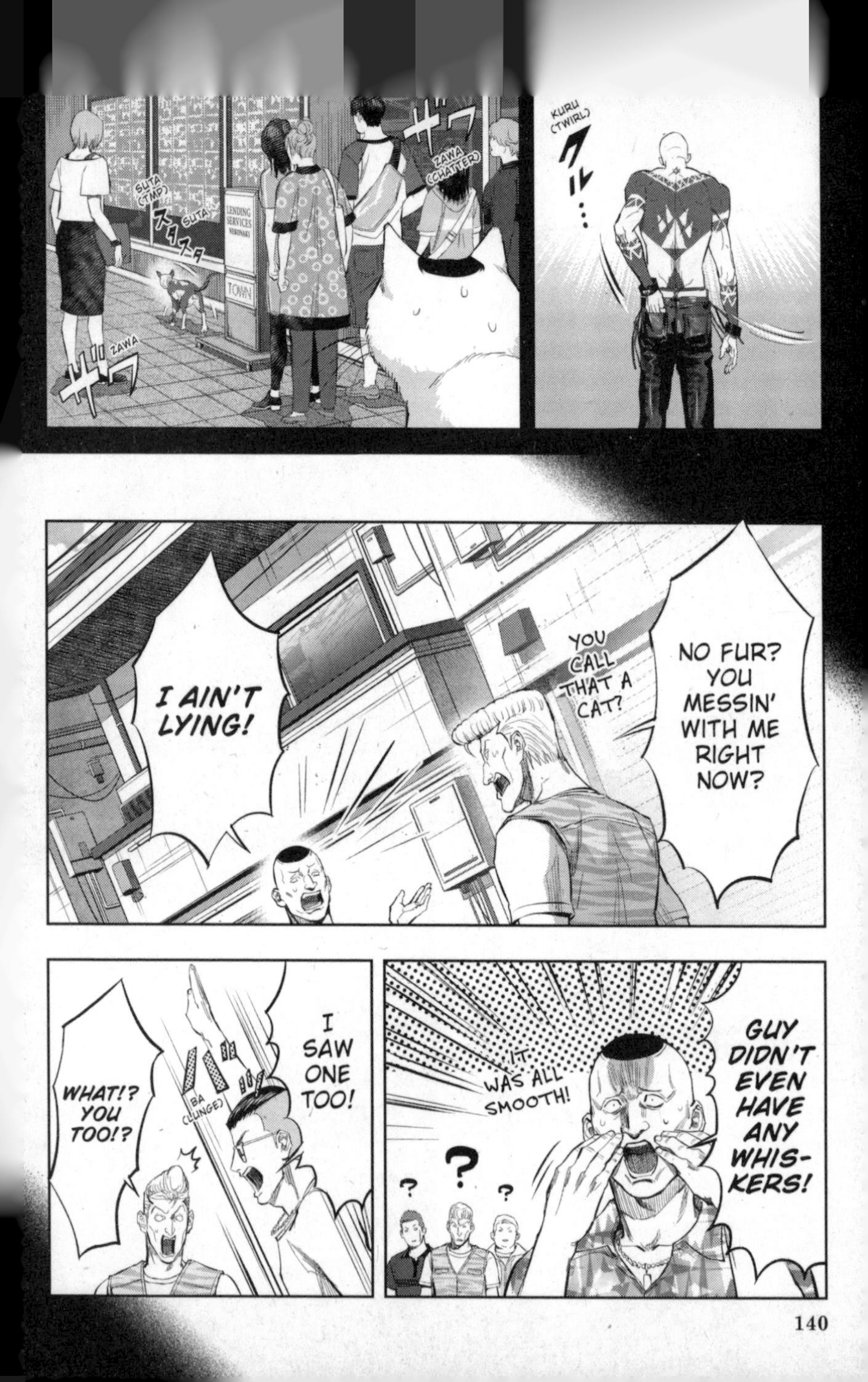
KURU (TWIRL)
ZAWA (CHATTER)
SUTA (TMP) SUTA
LENDING SERVICES
TOWN
ZAWA
NO FUR? YOU MESSIN' WITH ME RIGHT NOW?
YOU CALL THAT A CAT?
I AIN'T LYING!
GUY DIDN'T EVEN HAVE ANY WHIS-KERS!
IT WAS ALL SMOOTH!
I SAW ONE TOO!
BA (LUNGE)
WHAT!? YOU TOO!?

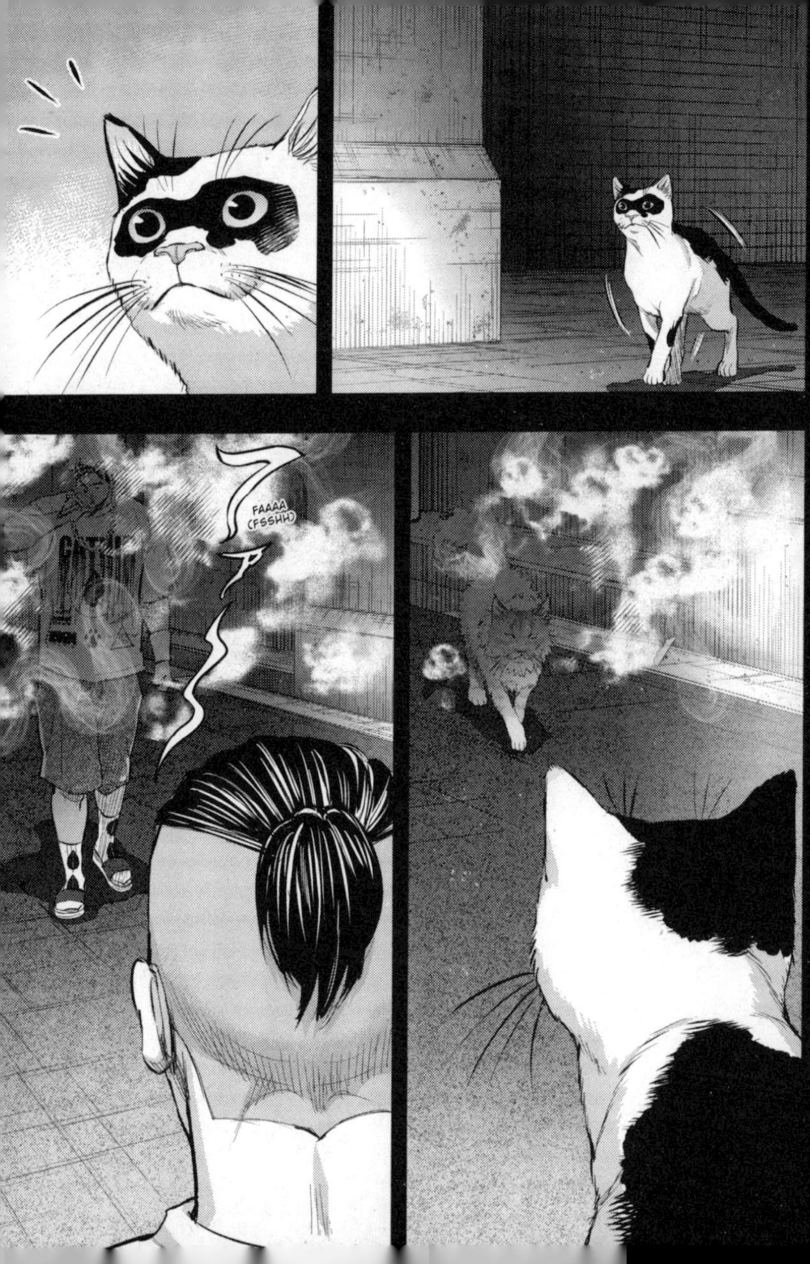
FAAAA
(FSSHH)

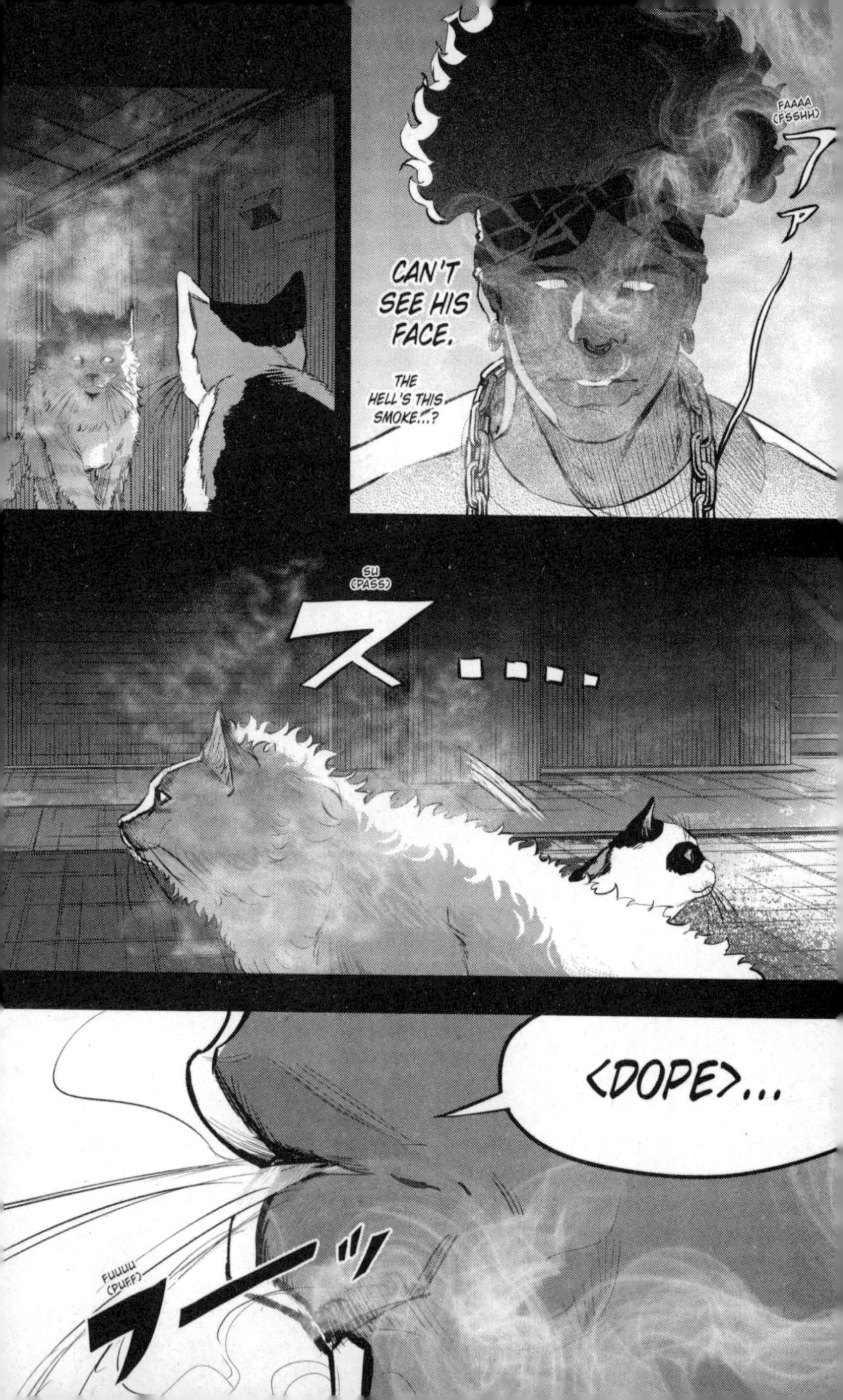
FAAAA (FSSHH)
ファ
CAN'T SEE HIS FACE.
THE HELL'S THIS SMOKE...?
SU (PASS)
ス....
<DOPE>...
FUUUU (PUFF)
フーッ

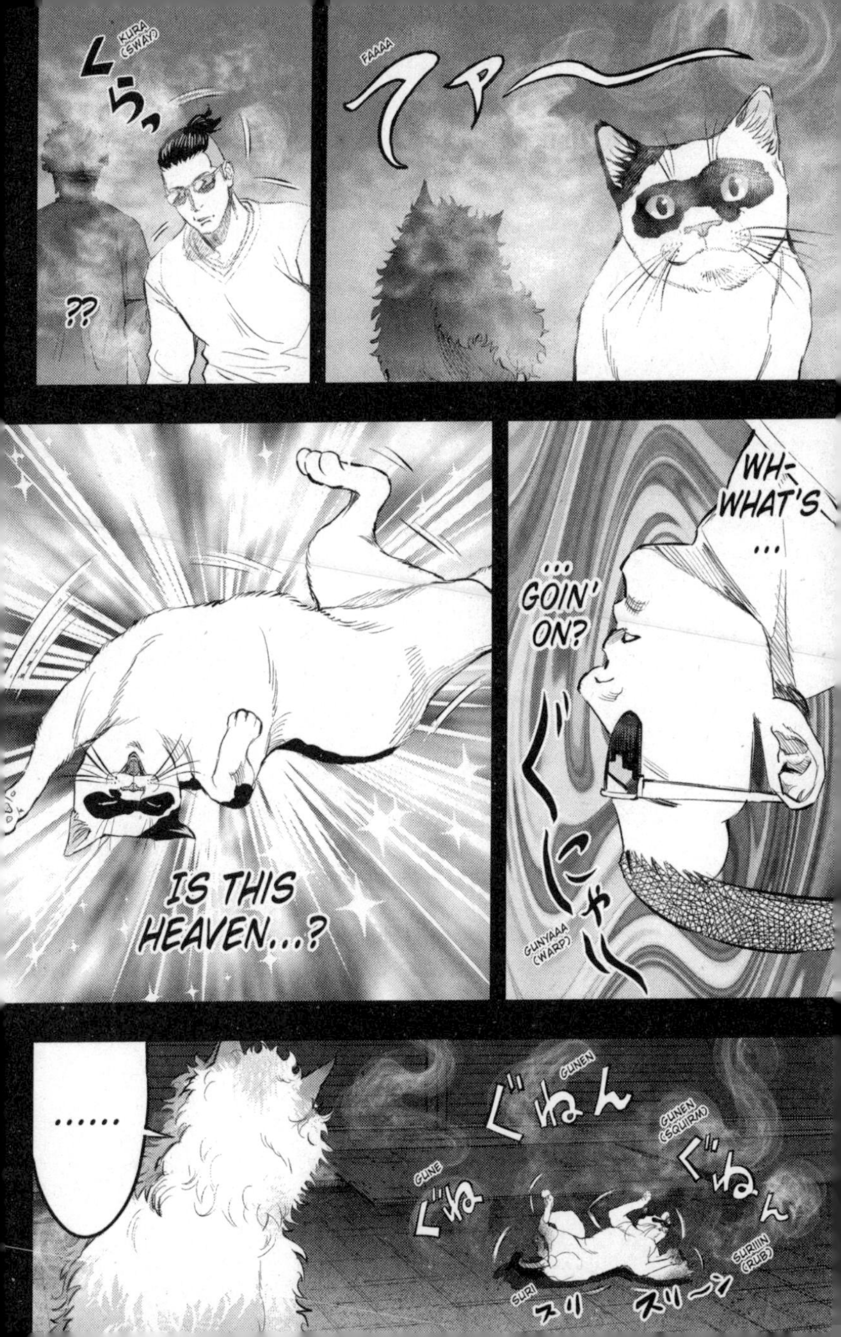
ファ〜
FAAAA
くらっ
KURA (SWAY)
??
WH-WHAT'S...
...GOIN' ON?
ぐにゃ〜
GUNYAAA (WARP)
IS THIS HEAVEN...?
ぐねん
GUNEN
ぐねん
GUNEN (SQUIRM)
......
ぐね
GUNE
スリ〜ン
SURIIIN (RUB)
スリ
SURI

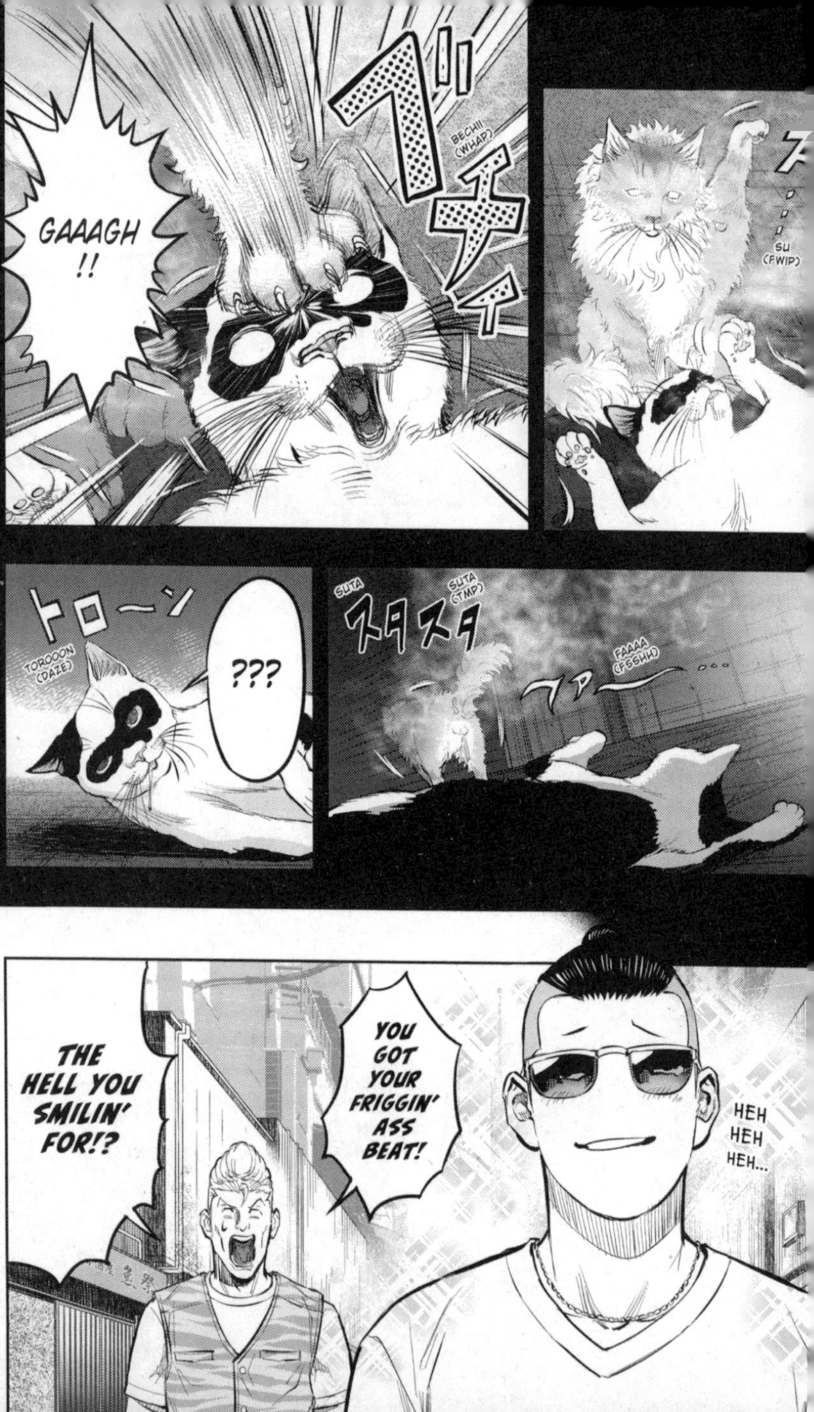

SU (FWIP)
BECHII (WHAP)
GAAAGH !!
SUTA SUTA (TMP)
スタスタ
FAAAA (FSSHH)
ファー
トローン
TOROOON (DAZE)
???
HEH HEH HEH...
YOU GOT YOUR FRIGGIN' ASS BEAT!
THE HELL YOU SMILIN' FOR!?

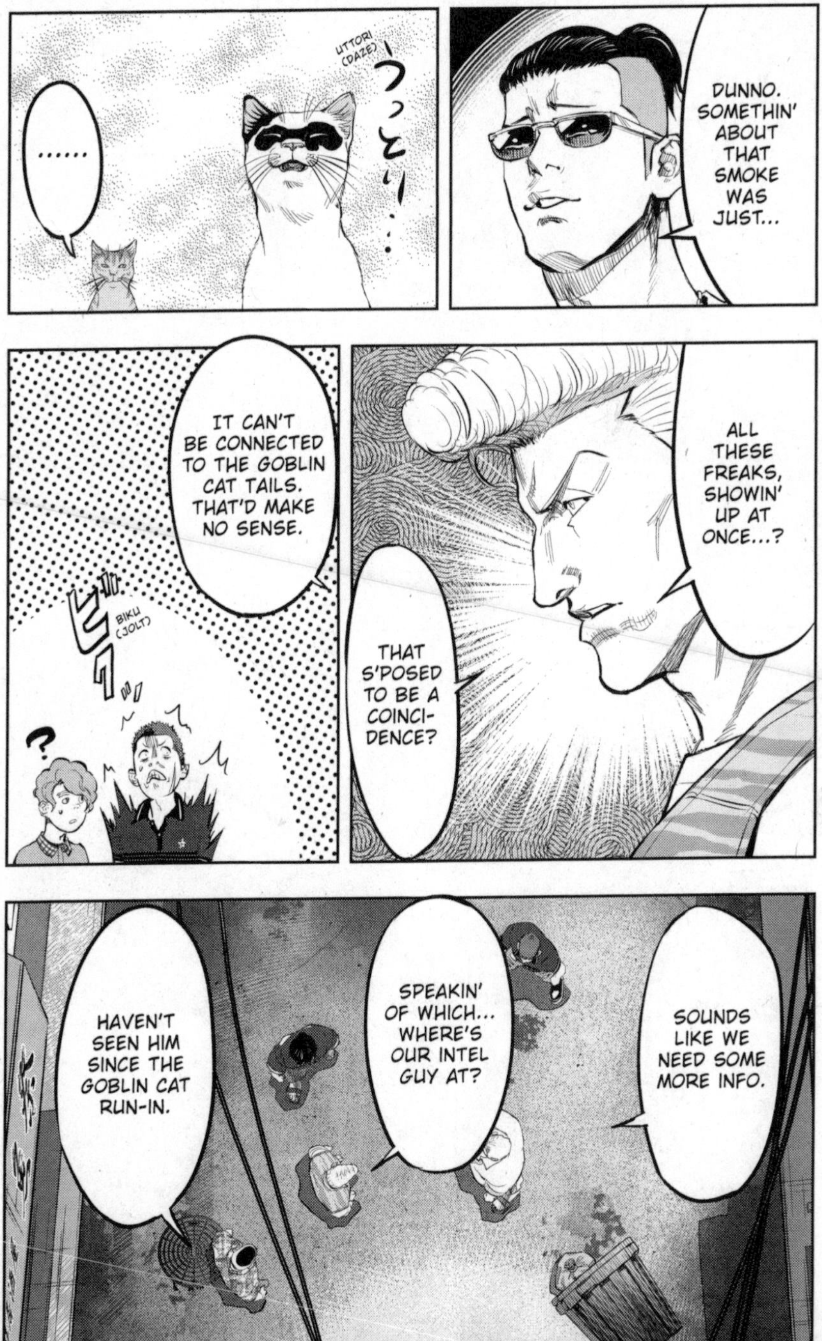
DUNNO. SOMETHIN' ABOUT THAT SMOKE WAS JUST...
UTTORI (DAZE)
......
ALL THESE FREAKS, SHOWIN' UP AT ONCE...?
THAT S'POSED TO BE A COINCIDENCE?
IT CAN'T BE CONNECTED TO THE GOBLIN CAT TAILS. THAT'D MAKE NO SENSE.
BIKU (JOLT)
?
SOUNDS LIKE WE NEED SOME MORE INFO.
SPEAKIN' OF WHICH... WHERE'S OUR INTEL GUY AT?
HAVEN'T SEEN HIM SINCE THE GOBLIN CAT RUN-IN.

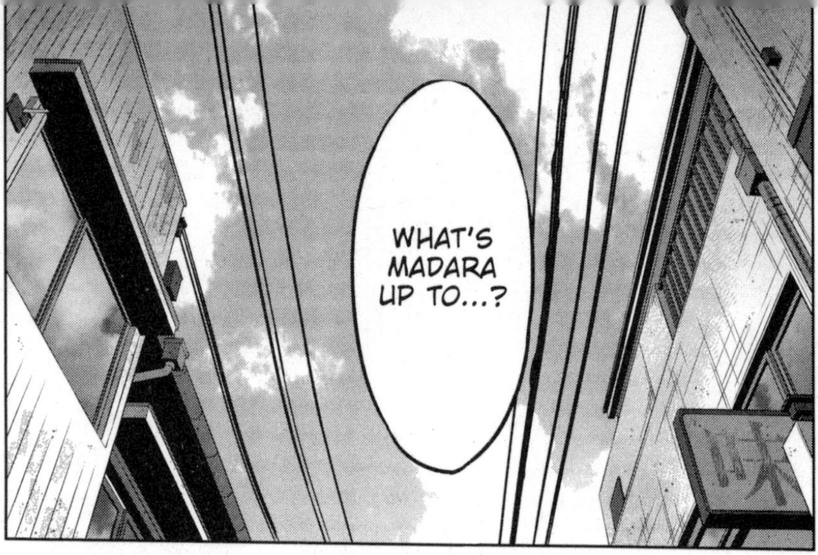
WHAT'S MADARA UP TO...?

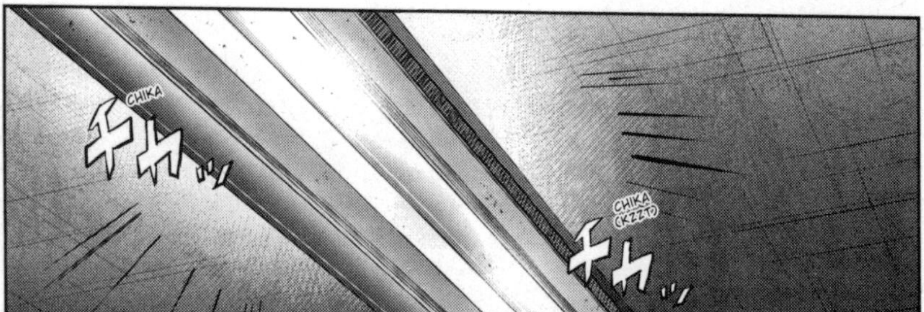
CHIKA
チカッ
CHIKA (KZZT)
チカッ

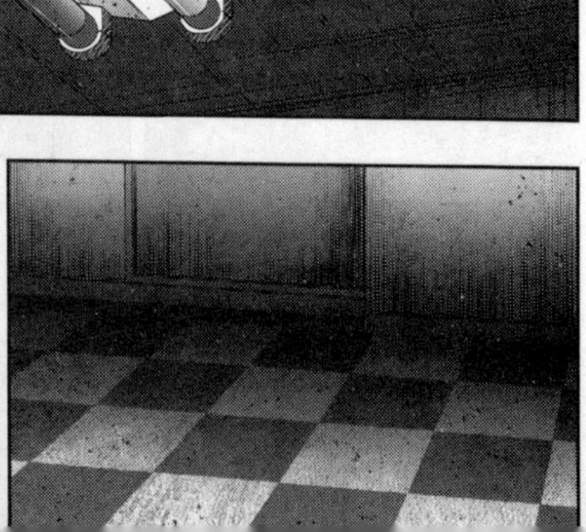

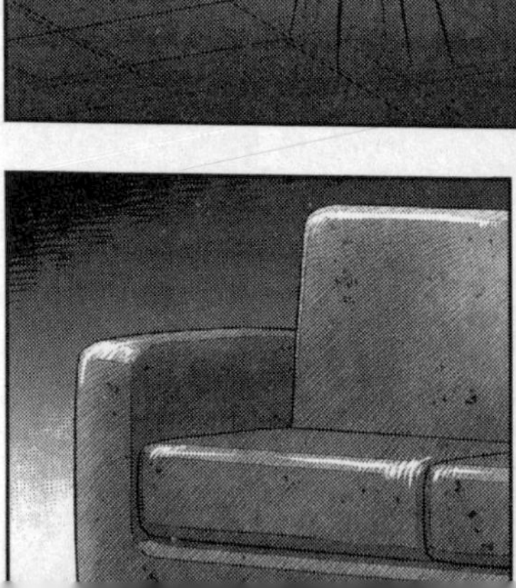

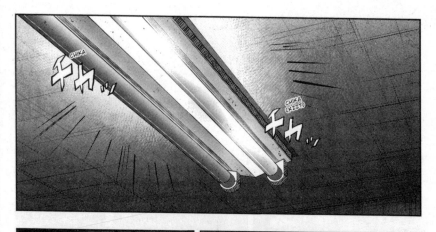

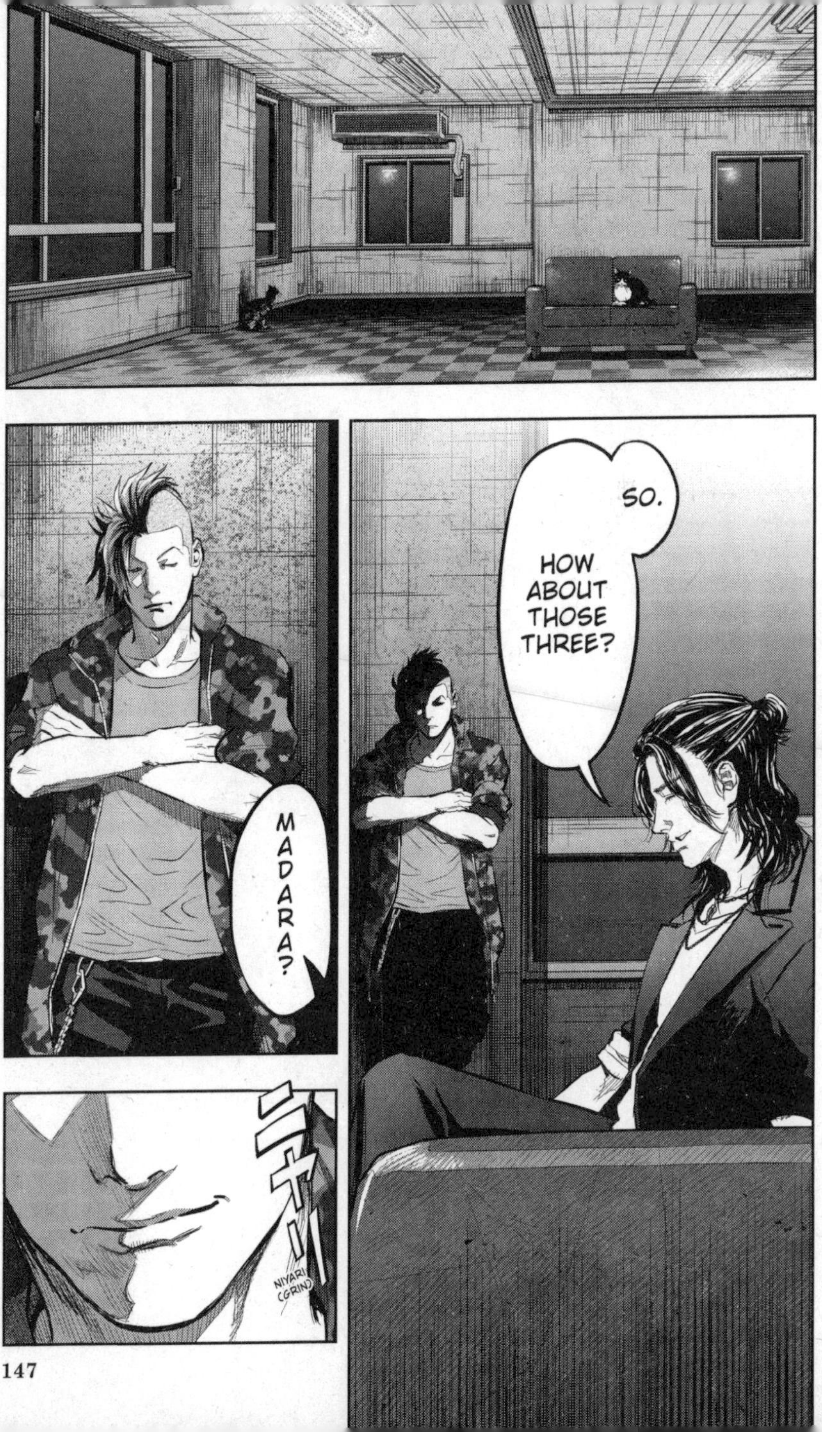
SO.
HOW ABOUT THOSE THREE?
MADARA?
NIYARI (GRIN)

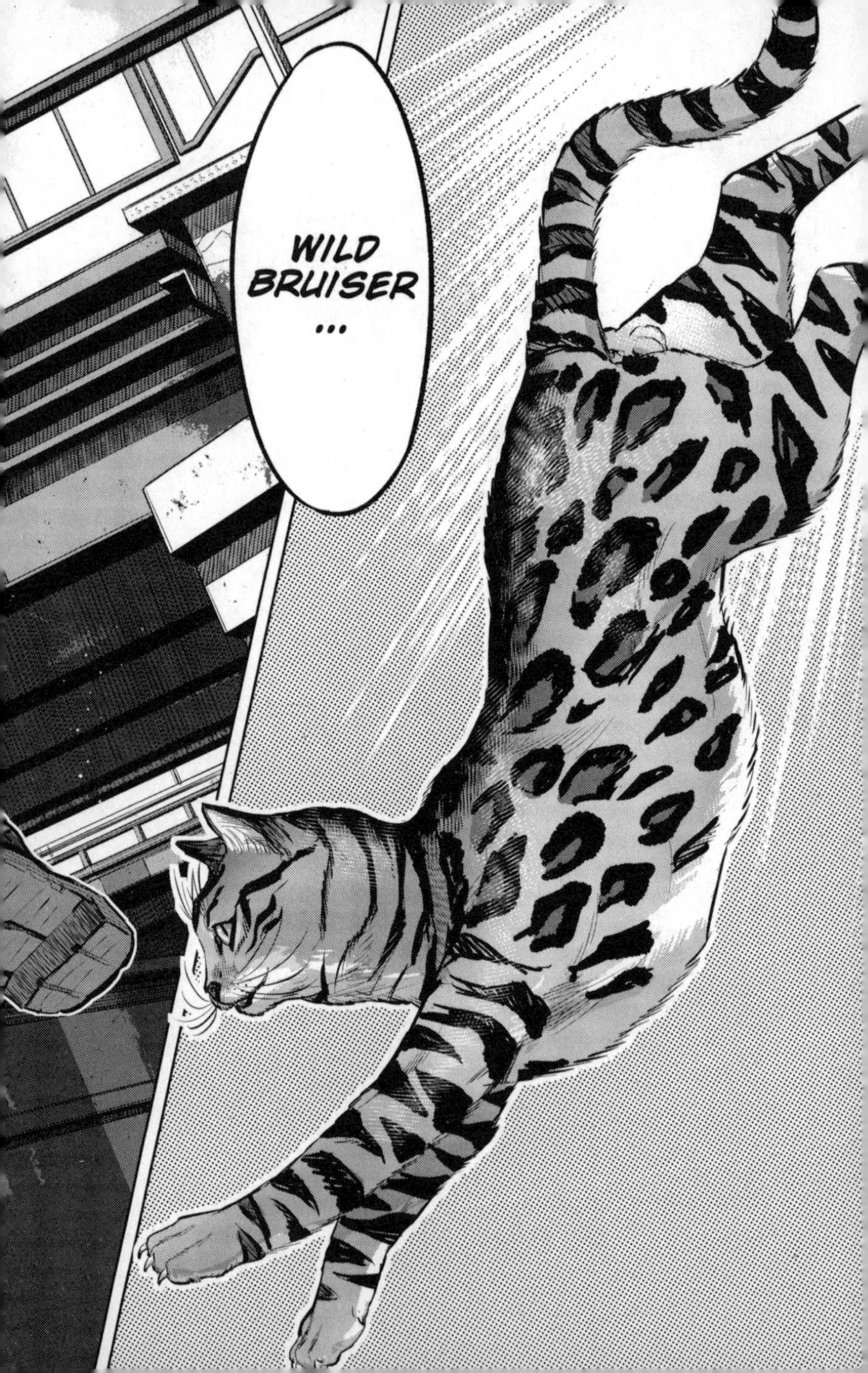
WILD BRUISER ...

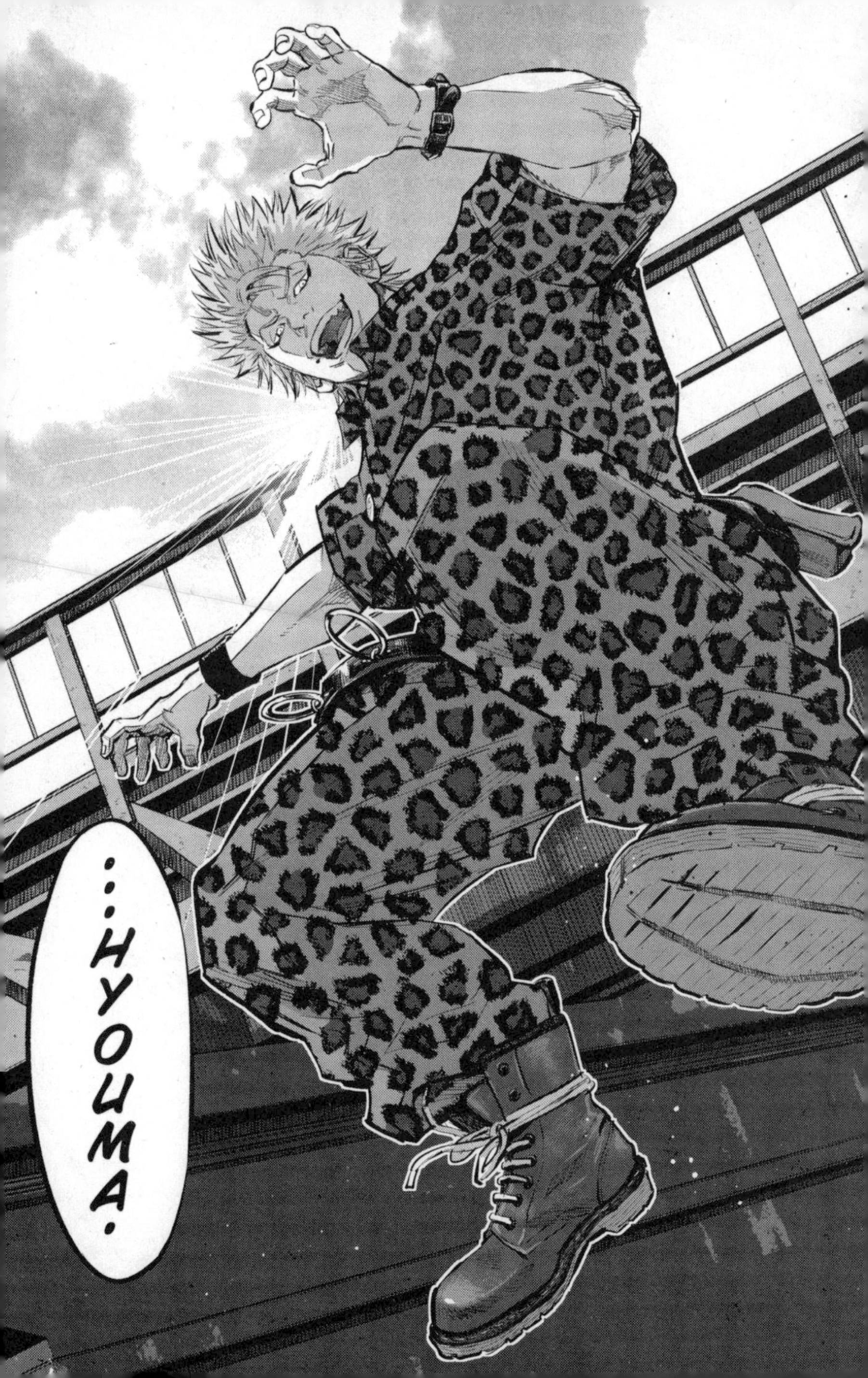
...HYOUMA.

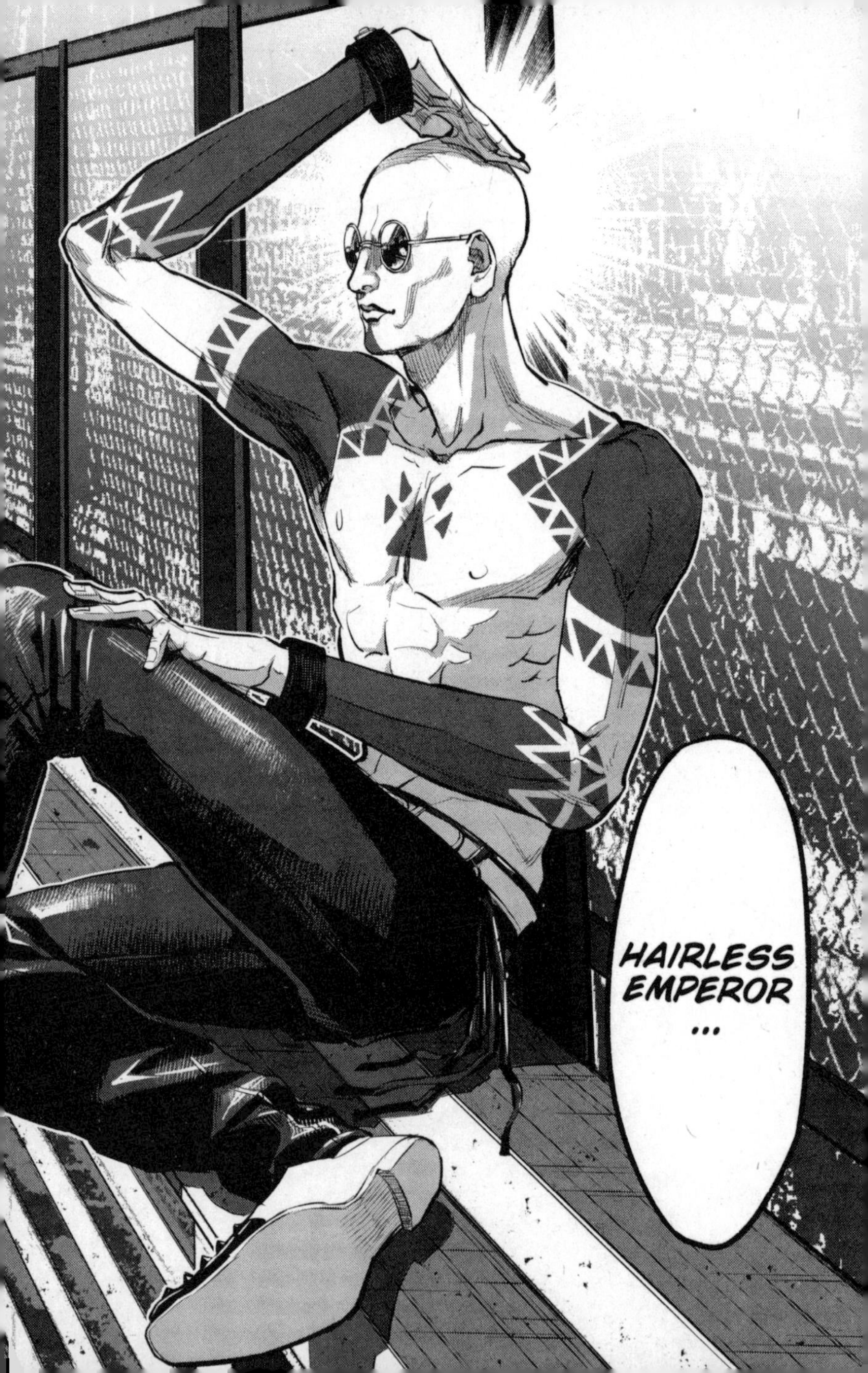
HAIRLESS EMPEROR ...

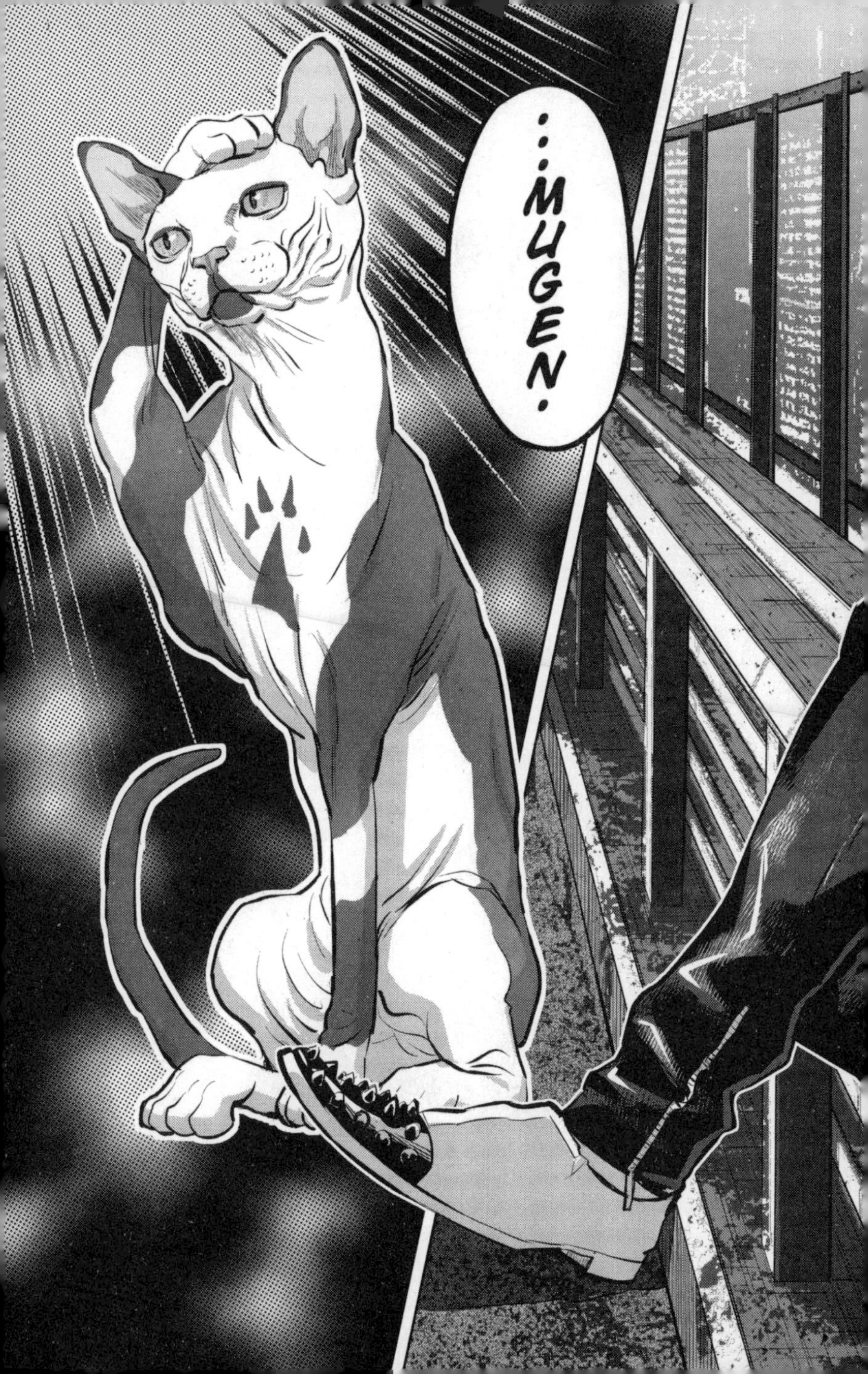
...MUGEN.

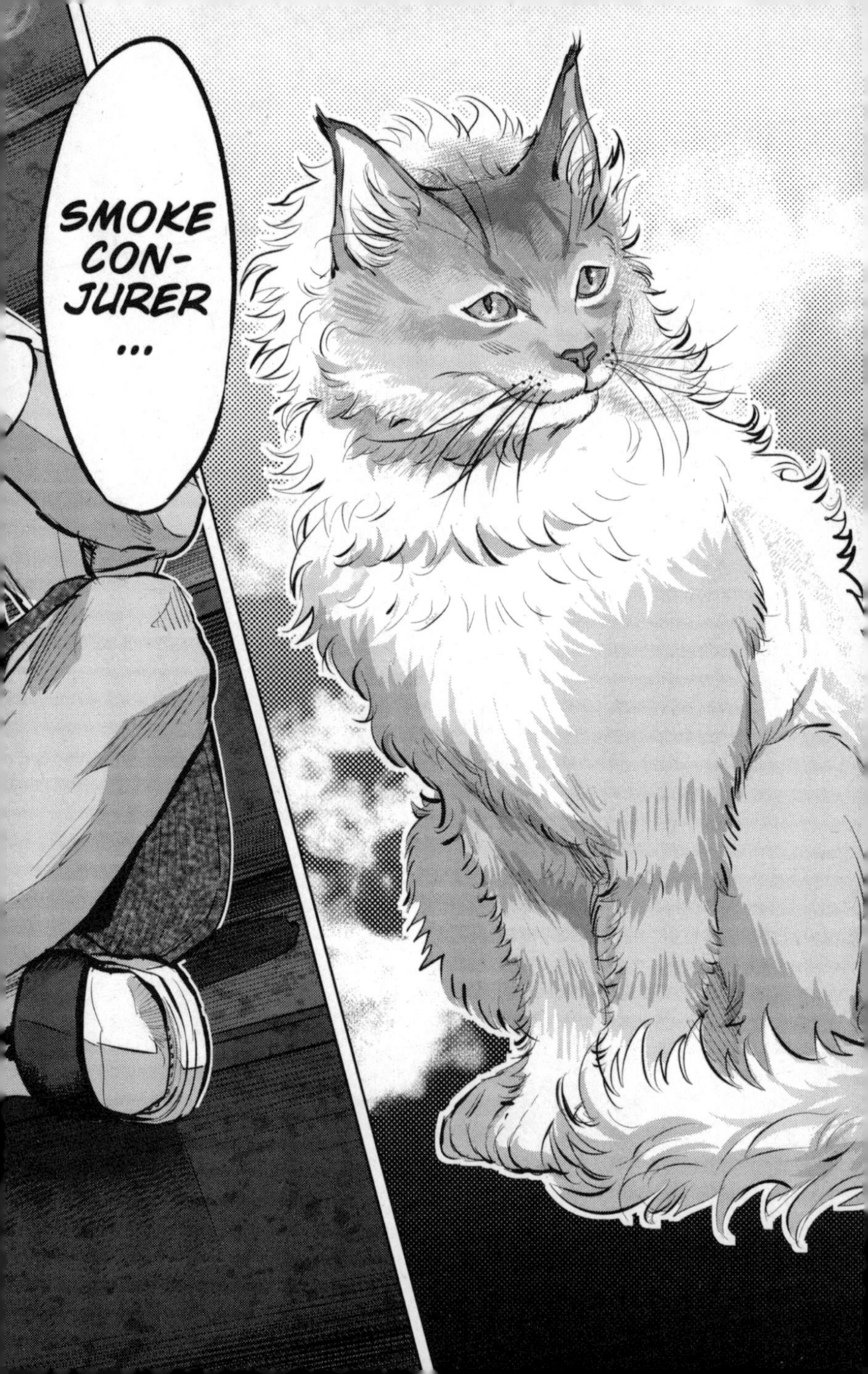
SMOKE CON-JURER ...

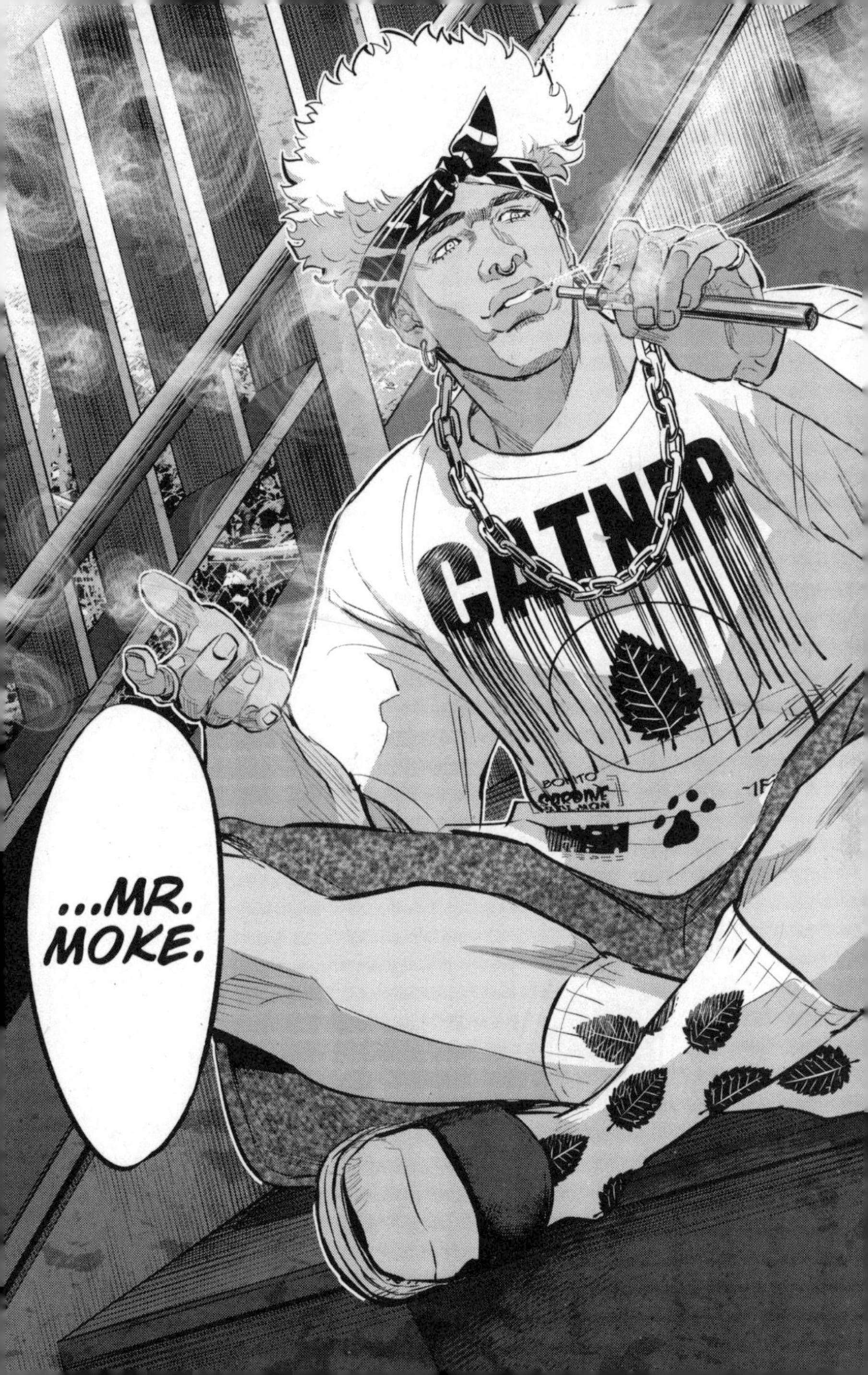
...MR. MOKE.

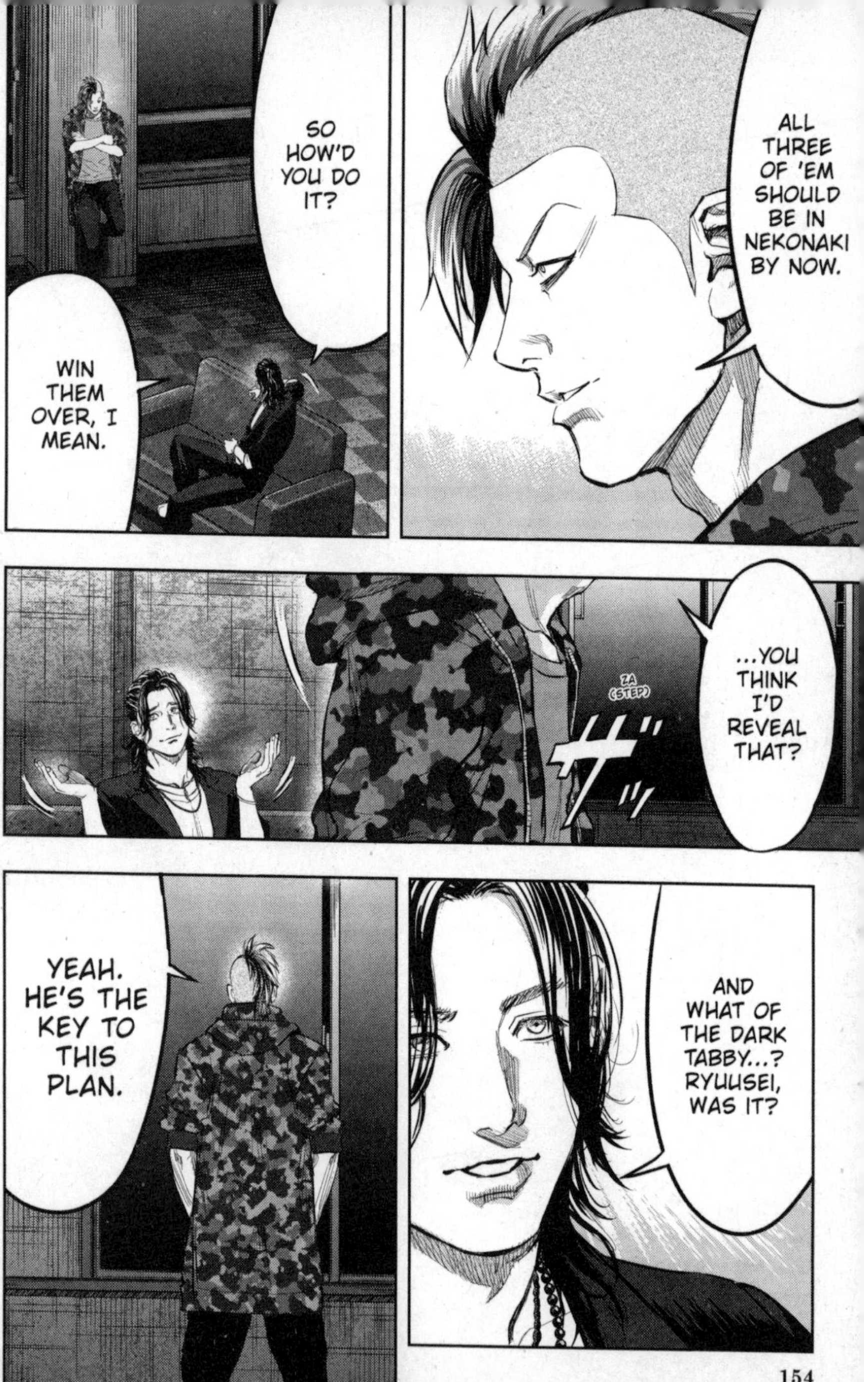
ALL THREE OF 'EM SHOULD BE IN NEKONAKI BY NOW.
SO HOW'D YOU DO IT?
WIN THEM OVER, I MEAN.
...YOU THINK I'D REVEAL THAT?
ZA (STEP)
AND WHAT OF THE DARK TABBY...? RYUUSEI, WAS IT?
YEAH. HE'S THE KEY TO THIS PLAN.

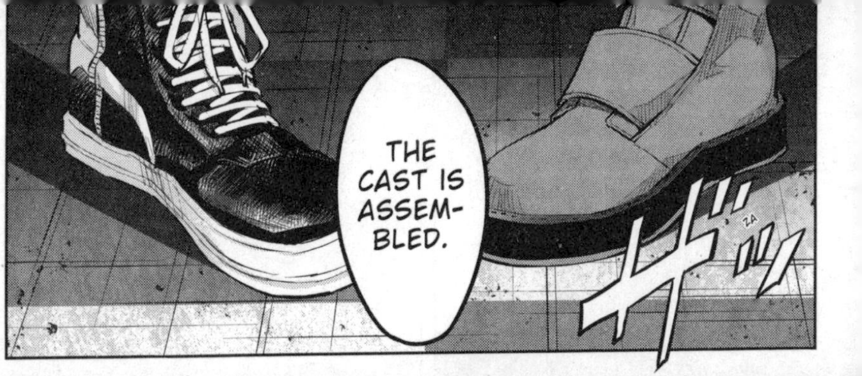
THE CAST IS ASSEMBLED.
ZA
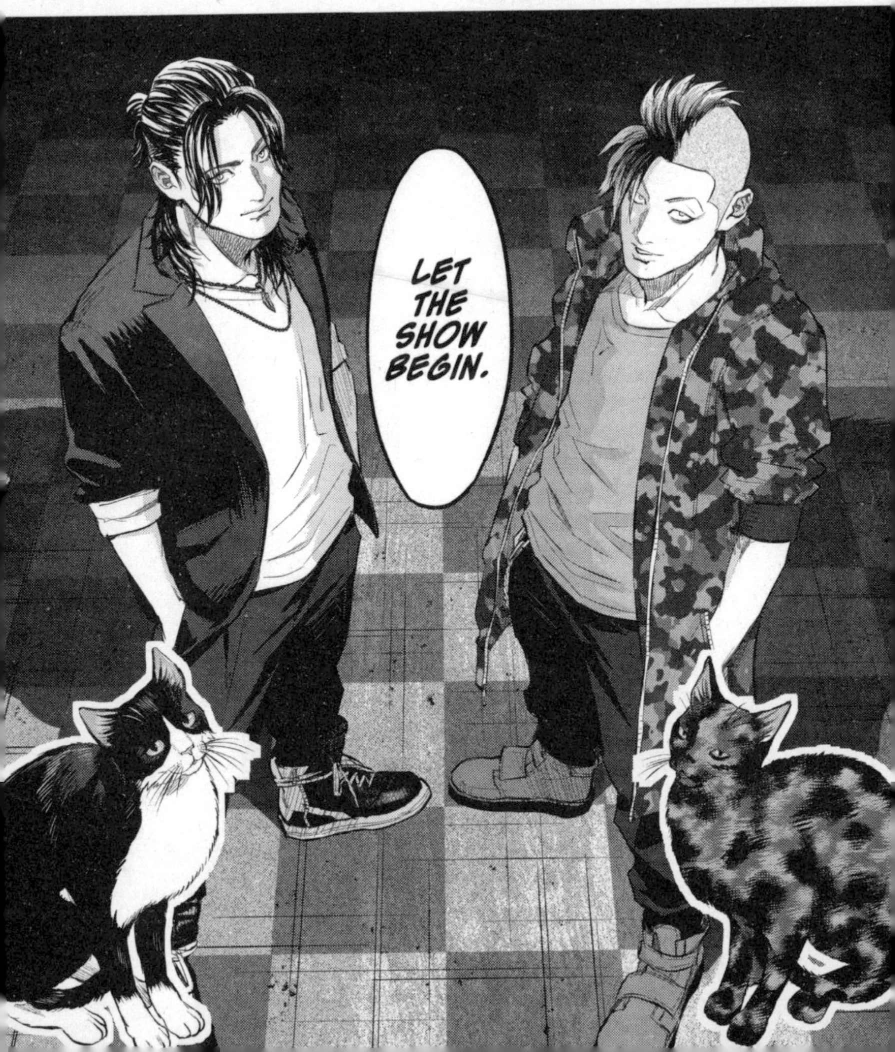
LET THE SHOW BEGIN.

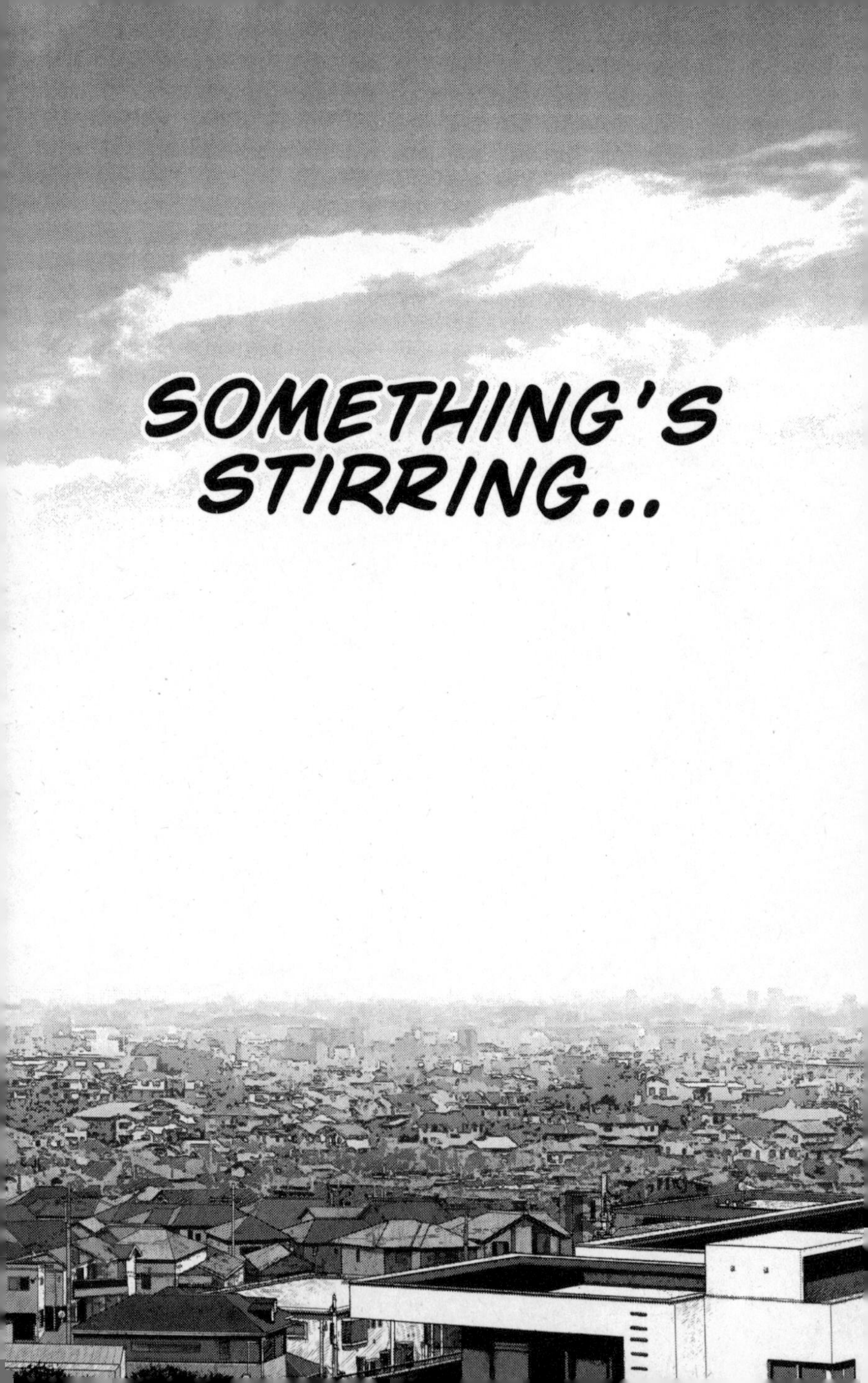
SOMETHING'S STIRRING...

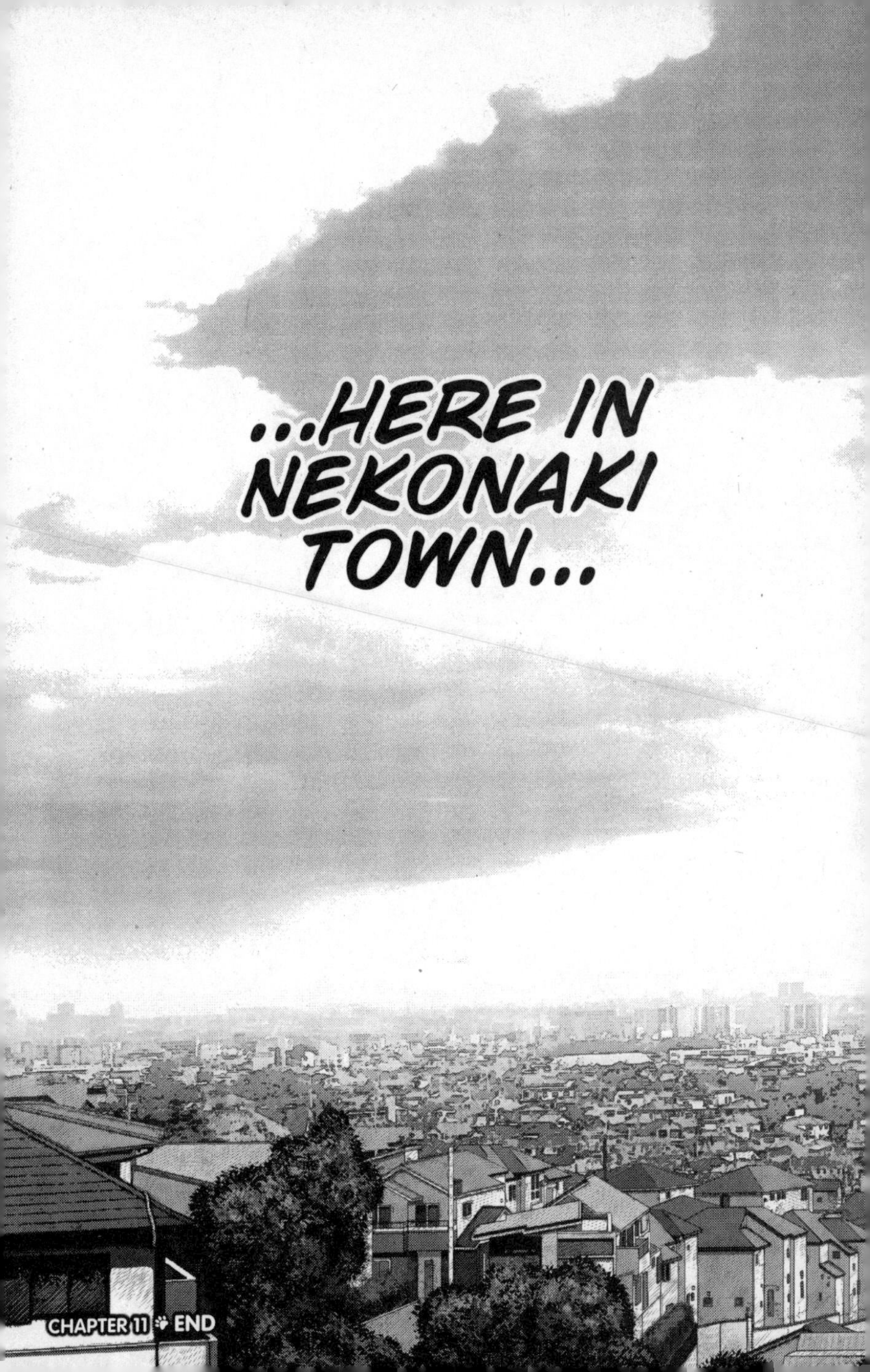
...HERE IN NEKONAKI TOWN...
CHAPTER 11 END

...BEGINS !!!!!!!!!!!!''''''

WHO WILL BE THE NEXT KING?!?!?!?!

NEXT VOLUME...

THE ULTIMATE FIGHT FOR THE THRONE...

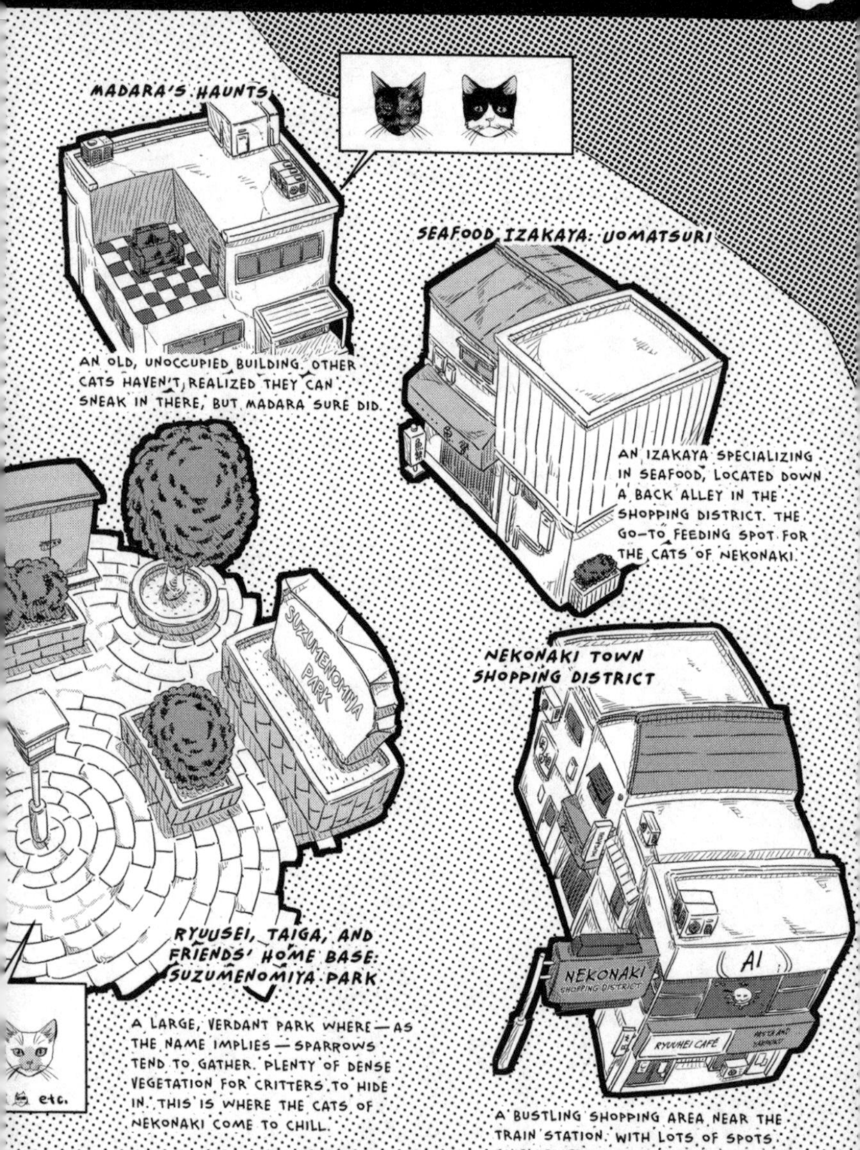

MADARA'S HAUNTS
AN OLD, UNOCCUPIED BUILDING. OTHER CATS HAVEN'T REALIZED THEY CAN SNEAK IN THERE, BUT MADARA SURE DID.
SEAFOOD IZAKAYA: UOMATSURI
AN IZAKAYA SPECIALIZING IN SEAFOOD, LOCATED DOWN A BACK ALLEY IN THE SHOPPING DISTRICT. THE GO-TO FEEDING SPOT FOR THE CATS OF NEKONAKI.
SUZUMENOMIYA PARK
NEKONAKI TOWN SHOPPING DISTRICT
AI
NEKONAKI
SHOPPING DISTRICT
RYUUHEI CAFÉ
RYUUSEI, TAIGA, AND FRIENDS' HOME BASE: SUZUMENOMIYA PARK
etc.
A LARGE, VERDANT PARK WHERE—AS THE NAME IMPLIES—SPARROWS TEND TO GATHER. PLENTY OF DENSE VEGETATION FOR CRITTERS TO HIDE IN. THIS IS WHERE THE CATS OF NEKONAKI COME TO CHILL.
A BUSTLING SHOPPING AREA NEAR THE TRAIN STATION. WITH LOTS OF SPOTS SHIELDED FROM RAIN, THIS IS THE PLACE TO BE WHEN STORMY WEATHER ROLLS AROUND.

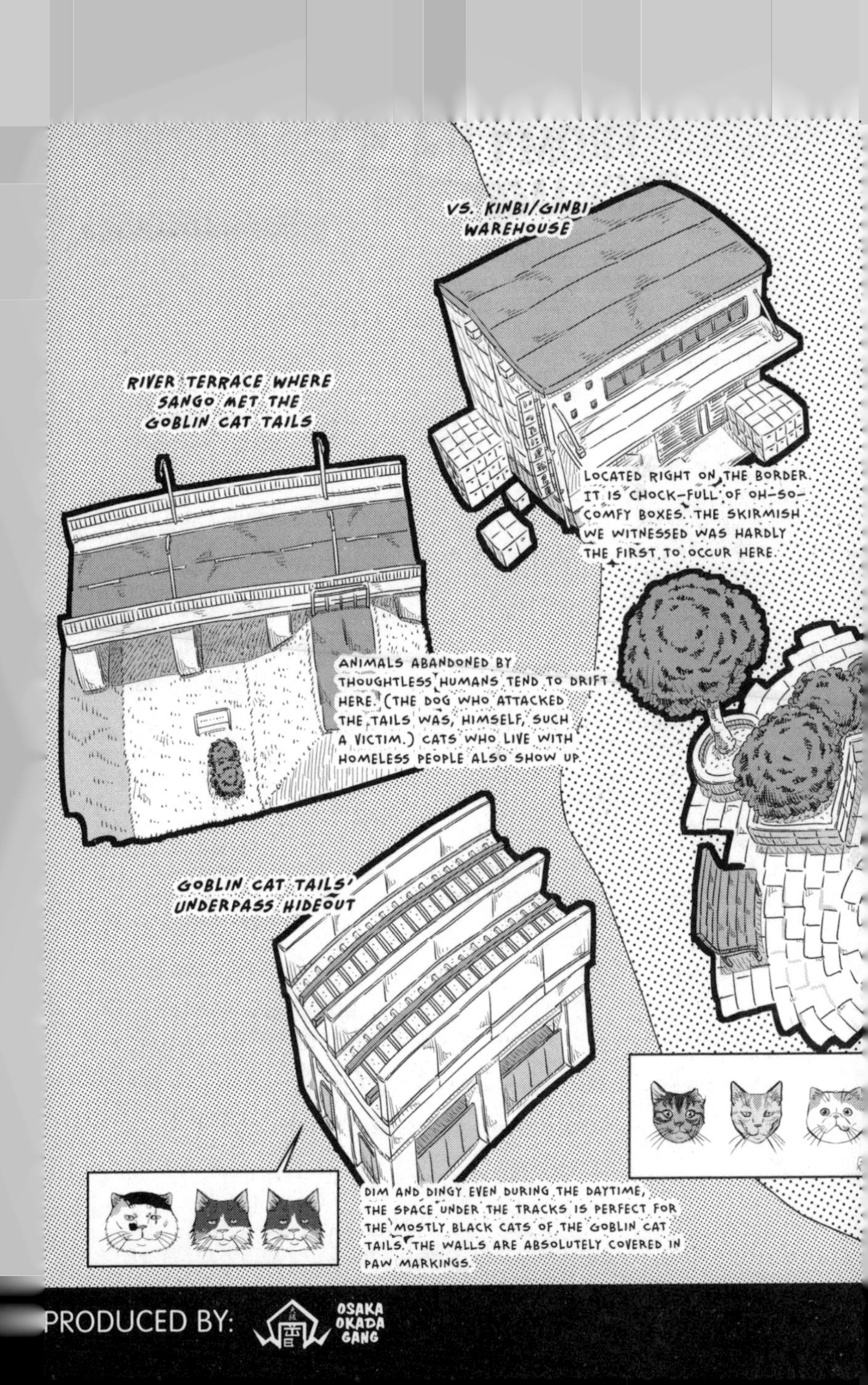
VS. KINBI/GINBI WAREHOUSE
LOCATED RIGHT ON THE BORDER. IT IS CHOCK-FULL OF OH-SO-COMFY BOXES. THE SKIRMISH WE WITNESSED WAS HARDLY THE FIRST TO OCCUR HERE.
RIVER TERRACE WHERE SANGO MET THE GOBLIN CAT TAILS
ANIMALS ABANDONED BY THOUGHTLESS HUMANS TEND TO DRIFT HERE. (THE DOG WHO ATTACKED THE TAILS WAS, HIMSELF, SUCH A VICTIM.) CATS WHO LIVE WITH HOMELESS PEOPLE ALSO SHOW UP.
GOBLIN CAT TAILS' UNDERPASS HIDEOUT
DIM AND DINGY EVEN DURING THE DAYTIME, THE SPACE UNDER THE TRACKS IS PERFECT FOR THE MOSTLY BLACK CATS OF THE GOBLIN CAT TAILS. THE WALLS ARE ABSOLUTELY COVERED IN PAW MARKINGS.

PRODUCED BY: OSAKA OKADA GANG

SACRAMENTO PUBLIC LIBRARY
828 "I" Street
Sacramento, CA 95814
06/19

WITHDRAWN
FROM THE COLLECTION OF
SACRAMENTO PUBLIC LIBRARY

Translation: **Caleb D. Cook**

Lettering: **Rochelle Gancio**

This book is a work of fiction. Names, characters, places, and incidents are the product of the author's imagination or are used fictitiously. Any resemblance to actual events, locales, or persons, living or dead, is coincidental.

NYANKEES Vol.2
©Atsushi OKADA 2017
First published in Japan in 2017 by KADOKAWA CORPORATION, Tokyo. English translation rights arranged with KADOKAWA CORPORATION, Tokyo through TUTTLE-MORI AGENCY, INC., Tokyo.

English translation © 2019 by Yen Press, LLC

Yen Press, LLC supports the right to free expression and the value of copyright. The purpose of copyright is to encourage writers and artists to produce the creative works that enrich our culture.

The scanning, uploading, and distribution of this book without permission is a theft of the author's intellectual property. If you would like permission to use material from the book (other than for review purposes), please contact the publisher. Thank you for your support of the author's rights.

Yen Press
1290 Avenue of the Americas
New York, NY 10104

Visit us at yenpress.com
facebook.com/yenpress
twitter.com/yenpress
yenpress.tumblr.com
instagram.com/yenpress

First Yen Press Edition: April 2019

Yen Press is an imprint of Yen Press, LLC.
The Yen Press name and logo are trademarks of Yen Press, LLC.

The publisher is not responsible for websites (or their content) that are not owned by the publisher.

Library of Congress Control Number: 2018958637

ISBNs: 978-1-9753-8340-4 (paperback)
978-1-9753-8341-1 (ebook)

10 9 8 7 6 5 4 3 2 1

WOR

Printed in the United States of America